The CLEANUP

MILA SIN
MANUELA ROUGET

Copyright © 2022 by Mila Sin & Manuela Rouget

All rights reserved.

No part of this book may be reproduced in any form or by any electronic or mechanical means, including information storage and retrieval systems, without written permission from the author, except for the use of brief quotations in a book review.

Cover by Taylor Dawn at Sweet 15 Designs

Developmental editing by Steph Rawlins

Copy/line editing by Zainab at Heart Full of Reads

Formatting by Mila Sin

Please direct any quality issues to either:

Mila at authormilasin@gmail.com

or

Manuela at manuelarougeauthor@gmail.com

To the women who saw what they wanted and fucking took it.

And to RHRA, because we would never have met without you.

Authors' Note

Please note this book contains British characters, and as such, uses British English for spelling and certain grammatical constructions.

Content includes violent and unlawful situations, grooming, mention of SA, and kinks such as breath play, knife/blade play, and erotic scarification. All sex scenes are consensual.

This book takes place in an alternate 2022, meaning there is no mention of covid, war, or political relevancy to today's headlines.

Chapter One

Olivia
Present Day

"Okay, Via, there you go. Slide it in, just like that. Slowly. Oh yeah, that's good. I think you found that sweet spot. If you stroke it a little harder, it'll—"

"Shut the fuck up, Roark. I'm the one who taught you to pick locks."

The mechanism clicks open as his deep chuckle resonates through the comm in my ear. My hacker friend is my backup on this job, but up until now, he's been a distraction more than anything else. In his defence, he's on the opposite side of the world and will help me hack into the computer on the other side of this door. The mere mental image of his massive frame scrunched over his station does something to me. He was nothing but skin and bones when we met, but fucking hell did he fill out nicely.

We started hacking together when we were teens, but he became a lot better at it when I decided to diversify my skills.

I've just broken into the Yellow Palace, the stronghold of the government of Tesken, a small country in Central Asia. I've spent the past week doing recon in the capital, planning the job I'm currently fucking crushing, if I do say so myself.

The president, Zul Arenon, was elected six years ago, but decided at the end of his term that he liked the power and wouldn't give it back. He framed his biggest opponent for corruption, manipulated the elections, and stayed in power, terrorising the population and selling his country's resources to multinationals and other unsavoury people.

That's where I come in. The resistance movement has had enough of him, so when they heard that there was evidence of electoral fraud, they hired me to find it. They don't know who's doing the job—the beauty of having a middleman handling my contracts. They just know it will be done.

I have a reputation to uphold, after all.

I'm disappointed with the state of the presidential palace's security. I had a craving for jumping through lasers and fighting guards tonight. This is almost boring—I used the front door.

To enter the building, I disguised myself as one of the janitors working for the company I own, who just so happened to get a new contract to clean the Yellow Palace. Who says connections are a bad thing? When I decided to be a full-time international thief, it quickly became obvious I'd need a front. Money wasn't going to launder itself. So, I created The Cleanup, a cleaning company specialising in businesses, and killed two birds with one stone. The other employees are actual cleaners, but I like to use my powers for evil sometimes. Or good. Depending on which side of the line you stand.

Being a CEO explains my opulent lifestyle at thirty. Knowing my business inside and out means that whenever I need access somewhere, I can get it. Plus, nobody ever suspects the cleaning lady.

I extract matte black disposable coveralls from the side of my cart.

The Cleanup

The building is empty, but if I have to run out of the president's office, a dark outfit will help me go unnoticed in the Teskenese night.

"Rory?" I whisper, using Roark's nickname. "How are we doing on looping the security feed?"

"I'm ready when you are." I nod at the camera, knowing Roark can see me. "And, go! You've got fifteen minutes before the guard's next round." I start the timer on my watch, tuning out his chatter, even if the deep rumbling of his voice is hard to ignore. Roark is definitely in my top four of the hottest men on earth.

I slip on the dark material over my uniform and pad through the room on silent feet.

The desk is huge, made of carved exotic wood, and looks expensive as fuck. Since I know not all of Tesken's population gets two, let alone three, meals a day, it annoys me. I almost draw a dick on the dark mahogany in retribution despite the giant portrait of Zul hanging on the wall, watching my every move.

My target—Zul's computer—sits on the desk, all proud and shiny. I fish out the flash drive containing Roark's pirate programme—and an uplink to the web—from my pocket and plug it into the USB port.

Roark doesn't always help me with my jobs. I only call him when I know a computer will try and resist me. Most of the time, I work alone. Aside from Max, my middleman and money guy.

"Okay, I'm in," Roark announces, and I let out a relieved breath. Zul's computer is air-gapped, meaning it doesn't have an internet connection, so we weren't sure what we would find in terms of security.

I look at the clock on the bottom of the screen. "Eleven minutes before the guard is back."

"No problem, I'll have everything downloaded in a few." Mmm, his Irish brogue does things to me.

My heart starts beating faster, adrenaline pumping through my veins. This is what I live for. Danger, breaking the rules, stealing shit, taking down tyrants; it makes me feel alive.

"Five minutes left," I inform Roark. "Hurry up. I'm getting all sweaty and gross." Next time I use one of these outfits, I'm wearing only lingerie under it.

"Almost done," he grunts. "This is the slowest data transfer ever."

I grab one of Zul's pens, a Montblanc that I'm totally stealing, and start twirling it between my fingers. The familiar gesture relaxes me, and I take deep breaths, even with my heart beating hard.

"Two minutes now!" I whisper-shout. "Hurry up."

Roark lets out a long grunt in my ear as I hear footsteps in the corridor. Fuck. I can't get caught in here. *Come on, Roark!*

"Done!" he finally shouts. His voice rings through my ear, and I clamp a hand over it, trying to muffle the sound and remain as quiet as possible.

My janitor cart is in front of the office. I have to get out, or I'll get caught. Ripping my coveralls off like a stripper, I shove the flash drive in my uniform chest pocket, and silent as a ghost, slip out of Zul Arenon's office right when a guard rounds the corner.

With a saccharine smile plastered on my face, I slowly head towards the exit, pushing my cart full of cleaning products in front of me. The guard looks at me a beat too long, and I'm trying to remember every Catholic prayer I've ever heard for salvation but come up empty. *Sorry, Daddy, I've been a bad girl.* No? Shit, I was sure it was something similar. Close enough. If this type of prayer doesn't get the big man upstairs to listen to me, I don't know what will.

"Have a nice night," I tell him in perfect Teskenian, then tilt my head down, keeping my eyes trained on the cart in front of me. Subservient. Unremarkable. The guard doesn't respond, but I keep my pace light and my face hidden by the curtain of my hair.

"That's so freaking unfair," Roark whines through the comm. "I don't get how you can learn languages that easily."

"Trust me, everything's possible with the right motivation," I whisper back as soon as the guard is out of earshot. My language skills have saved my ass more times than I can count. It's not like I know a ton, but I can pick up basics without much hassle.

Making sure the guard is gone, I ask Roark to loop the camera feed again so I can go back and relock the door. From then on, everything's a piece of cake. I store my cart where I initially picked it up and strip off the cleaning uniform. Pulling on my street clothes that I stored in a duffle bag, I complete my all-black ensemble with a big puffy hat. Then, I head out into the night through the service entrance.

"Rory," I say as I sit in my rented BMW, "I'll be fine from here on out if you want to log off and go to sleep. What time is it in Ireland, anyway?"

"One in the morning. But I'm not tired. I'll leave you to it, though. I'm going to shoot some shit and make some guys rue the day they started MMORPGs," he rattles off, citing the online role-playing games he adores so much with his internet friends.

"Night, Roark. Thanks for the help."

"Anytime," he says, his tone turning wistful for a moment, and then disconnects the call.

I'd love to have him as a permanent teammate. But then it'd mean I'd have to give up the others as semi-irregular contacts, and I can't do that, no matter their squabbles with one another.

The opulent five-star hotel I'm staying at is located in the capital and a stone's throw from the Yellow Palace. The glimmering lights are a welcome sight, and as I cross the lobby and make my way to the lift, I'm grateful for the warmth after the few moments I was in the cool night air.

Upon reaching my room, I shuck my coat, kick off my trainers, and toss my cleaning uniform into my suitcase before pulling my laptop out of the bag. Now that the data is in my hands, I have to get it to the right people.

A secure browser pings me around the world through VPNs and multiple proxies so that my location and identity are impossible to pinpoint. I log in to my email server, insert the USB to transfer the data to my computer, and get to work.

Please find the information you're looking for at the following

URL. A password to retrieve the file will be emailed to you as soon as payment is made to our mutual friend. Thank you for your business.

I add the files to the secure server, the link to the payment site, and one for Dropbox. Whoosh, off it goes.

You know what sounds good after a night of thievery? A bubble bath and ice cream. I call for room service and then get everything ready, tossing in more complementary products than is strictly necessary—*what can I say? Ya girl likes bubbles*—answer the door to nab my chocolate chip cookie dough ice cream and then lower myself into the tub.

With my phone to my ear, I prop my feet up on the lip of the tub and relax into the soapy water. Two rings later, Maximillian Arondale IV answers.

"Hello, Liv," he purrs into the phone.

"Why, hello, Max. You sound like you're up to no good."

He laughs, and I tilt my head back against the tile. "How's the job?"

"Oh, fine. Done. I just sent the links, so money should land in the foundation's offshore account in the next couple of days. Just a heads-up to watch out for it." Funnelling money through a fake non-profit might seem like a shit move, but well, it's got to go somewhere.

"One of your fastest jobs yet, Liv. You need an assist? I can send the jet."

Pfft. Too late. I might have borrowed his plane to come here in the first place, but he doesn't need to know that.

"I'm good. Just going to finish my bath, get some sleep, and come home once the money hits."

"You're in the bath now?" He sounds like he's stopped breathing, and I hear the tension in his voice.

"Well, sure. Who doesn't need to get naked after derailing a despot? It's practically a job requirement."

"Liv..."

"Oh! Gotta go, the bath salts are doing this fizzing thing, and I just got an idea. Keep me posted!" I chirp before hanging up the phone and cackling.

Max may be a lot of things. British nobility, equestrian enthusiast, and rich playboy, but he's also one of the best men I know. It's really too bad he can also be a selfish git when he gets something into his head.

I rinse off in the shower and wrap myself in the fluffy bathrobe from the back of the bathroom door. It's during my third episode of *Golden Girls* that my phone pings.

Max: All good, money's in the account. How were the bath salts?

Me: Invigorating.

I check the server, and sure enough, the files have been accessed. Time to get the fuck out of dodge.

I don't want to be here when shit hits the fan. It'll be a coup, and even though I "borrowed"—wink, wink—Max's private jet and likely won't have to deal with airport shutdowns, I'd rather not risk it. Dialling the pilot, I set things in motion and plan to fly out in an hour.

Checking out takes no time at all, and before long, I'm on the road to the airstrip. The rented car can be left at the private airfield—I checked in advance—and the owners will return it for a small fee.

Not going to lie, having money is nice.

My phone pings from my bag, and it isn't until I'm boarding the plane that I finally check what's going on.

Ellie: Hey, where are you? I'm at your place. We need to talk.

Why is Ellie at my place? My best friend doesn't visit me in London more than once a month, and she was just there two weeks ago.

Me: I'm out, but I'll be back in a few hours. Are you okay?

Ellie: Nope. Totally fucked. I need your help.

"Wheels up, Pilot Pete! My bestie needs me!" I call towards the cockpit, and as I get a salute through the open door, we begin taxiing on the runway.

Chapter Two

Olivia
Year Twelve
September

"Welcome to St Stephen's Boarding School, Miss Wraith," the school administrator says after handing me my timetable. It's seven p.m. on the Sunday before term begins, and though the woman is putting on a friendly face, I know she'd rather be at home right now.

My dad thanks her before turning towards the atrium to meet my student guide.

"All right, kiddo, are you sure you've got everything?" Dad asks, his eyes holding pride and only a small measure of weariness. His American accent seems all the more stark in the hallowed halls of St Stephen's. Dad moved here from California for university, met Mum, and they settled down just outside of London before having me. I like to think I got the best of both worlds with parents from other sides of the globe.

Mum walks quietly beside us, her gaze riveted on the old building I'll now be calling home. I'm the last student to arrive for move-in weekend because Dad was working on a presentation for his boss. But hey, at least I'm here now.

I roll my eyes at his question. I'm the one who applied for, got the scholarship, and made all the arrangements to come to St Stephen's.

"Yes, Dad. I'm good. I can take it from here."

A petite, dark-haired Asian girl waits just inside the front doors and watches us approach expectantly. This must be my guide.

"Okay, then we'll leave you to it." He drops a kiss to the top of my bright blonde head, just like he did when I was small. "If you need anything, just call us. Give 'em hell, kiddo."

I innocently smile up at him and deviously laugh inside as I plan to take his words very, very seriously.

"I will, Dad. Thanks."

"Bye darling, be good and study hard," my mum says, wrapping me in a hug and giving the entryway one last glance.

With a squeeze of his hand on my arm, Dad turns towards the exit, dipping his head politely at the girl waiting beside it, and ushers Mum through the large doors. They're happy I'm attending the school, and want me to go for what I want, even if it means living far from home.

As an only child, I felt it was my duty to add some pizazz to the family. My parents, while lovely, are painfully ordinary. I'm sure every teenager thinks that of their mum and dad, but mine? Well, they scream normalcy from the tips of their budget-salon haircuts all the way down to their white New Balance trainers. Don't get me wrong, they love me and have given me a great life, but I've always wanted *more*.

When I was younger, I'd watch films and see exotic locations, expensive wares, and characters living lives I could only dream of. I knew if I wanted my life to be anything but the average existence I was careening toward, I needed to make a change. Travel, luxury, power—I wanted it all. And the first step to that goal? Attending one of the best boarding schools in all of England for my A-levels, which would hopefully lead to an excellent university. And from there? The rest of the world awaits.

The dark-haired girl looks at me curiously, so I shake out of my James Bond villain mindset and cross the marble floor. "Hi, I'm Olivia Wraith. Are you my guide?" I ask, sticking out my hand.

"Hi! Yes, I'm Eleanor Cameron. I'll be showing you around today, and we're also roommates. Where's your stuff?" She shakes my hand and cranes her neck to look around me as if a suitcase will appear behind me like magic.

I pat the clutch I'm holding in one hand. "This is it." Eleanor looks at me like I've lost my mind, and I can't help but laugh at her expression. She seems like someone who follows the rules and regulations to the letter.

She's going to be fun to mess with.

"It's in the main office," I assure her, watching her visibly relax after my joke. "I figured dragging it around would only get in the way, and the administrator said someone would bring it up."

Despite looking forward to the boarding school aspect of St Stephen's, part of me is envious of the American school system. High school seems far less complex with its standard four years as opposed to our secondary school system. In England, it's an entirely different story. I'm starting the first year of sixth form—year twelve—at the ripe old age of seventeen, walking into a new school and preparing to take on the world.

"One of the caretakers will deliver it later." Eleanor turns and starts walking towards the doorway on the right. "Okay, so this is the science and maths wing. St Stephen's is renowned for helping their students receive the highest grades possible on their A-levels, and they don't let you slack off."

She turns to look at me as if I'll be scared off by her words. "That's the reason I'm here," I assure her. "I'm ready to do the work."

Eleanor looks me up and down as if she can assess my determination through the school uniform I was told to wear at drop off, even though classes don't start until tomorrow. At least she's also wearing her uniform. It definitely would've been weird if she were in her street clothes while I looked like every older pervert's fantasy of a Catholic school girl.

She nods at whatever she finds in my posture. We pass a few doors, cross through an archway at the other end of the hall, and turn left. "These are the languages and humanities rooms. Watch out if you get Mr Hall, the literature teacher. He enunciates—like a lot. It leads to spitting on the front rows."

I stifle a chuckle. "Noted. Any other teachers I should know about?" I pry as we continue along, passing a couple of students in the hall.

She taps her finger against her chin as she ponders. "Mrs Lowell is really strict and will confiscate your phone faster than you can blink if she catches you on it. The rest are pretty standard. You'll catch on in no time."

"How long have you been at this school?" I ask as we pass another few classrooms.

"I started here in year seven, so five years ago. The other side of the building is for the younger students, but year ten through A-Level preparation are all over here because the dormitories are on this side." Eleanor points to a door at the base of the stairs we've approached. "That's the dining hall. It opens at six for breakfast; lunch break is from twelve to one; and dinner runs from six until eight every evening." As if to punctuate her point, I hear the sound of cutlery on plates through the lavish doors. I'm thankful Mum and Dad already took me for a bite before we arrived. I'm not really feeling too social at the moment.

"Come on, we're headed this way." She tilts her head towards a staircase and we make our way upstairs.

"The scholarship students are all on this level with some of the fee-paying students, and the others are one floor up."

I nod as I take in the intricately carved bannister, ornate doors, and carpet-lined hallway. I studied the school map before arriving, so I know most of what Eleanor said, but the way she keeps her chin held high and delivers her instructions makes me think she was born for this kind of shit.

"This is us," she says as she extracts a key from her skirt pocket. She stops in front of a door that looks no different from the rest. I count four doors between the landing and this one, noting which one is ours, so I don't walk into the wrong room because I can't tell them apart. Couldn't they have put some kind of marking on each so they're easier to find? "Boys and girls dorms used to be separated, but they're renovating the east wing, so we're all doubled up in the rooms on this side for the time being. But some of the people on the third floor still have their own rooms."

As she fits the key into the lock, the door beside ours swings open, and my head turns. A boy with sandy blonde hair and blue eyes emerges from within. He's wearing a uniform that's slightly too big for his thin frame, and he looks over at us curiously as he pulls the door shut behind him.

He doesn't say a word, but he looks me up and down, his gaze narrowing. "Hi, Roark. This is Olivia. She's new," Eleanor chirps.

Roark nods, some wariness in his gaze peeking through. I step forward and extend my hand. "Nice to meet you."

His warm hand wraps around mine. "You, too. Another scholarship student, huh?" The lilt of his voice gives away his Irish upbringing, but it's off somehow. Like he's adapted to the English accent over time.

At first, I think he's taking a dig at me because my parents couldn't afford to send me here, but then I notice the books under one arm are worn down to their spines, and his shoes are quite scuffed. Everything and everyone else I've seen so far screams wealth and privilege. Roark doesn't give off the same vibe as the others.

"Yep. Are you here on scholarship too?" I ask, not wanting to offend.

He nods in assent and averts his eyes down towards the floor. He's nervous, made all the more evident when he snatches his hand back from mine.

"Great!" I say with enough enthusiasm for the both of us. "Anything I should know on my first day?"

He clears his throat, his Adam's apple bobbing in his thin neck. He's cute—in a scared puppy way—but his eyes scream intelligence and awareness. "Just don't piss off the elite of the school, and you'll be fine."

Eleanor hums, and Roark seems to remember she's standing with us. "I... uh, I gotta go. Welcome to St Stephen's, Olivia." He rushes off towards the staircase we climbed earlier.

"That was abrupt," I murmur to Eleanor.

"Yeah, Roark is smart. Like crazy smart. He's been here since year seven, like me, and has the Arondale Scholarship. It requires insane marks to keep. He's probably headed to the computer lab to study, as usual. Courses haven't even started yet, but he's been in there all weekend."

Good to know. Studying is boring as hell, but I might need to find myself a study buddy to keep to a schedule. Someone as motivated as Roark might be a good option.

The reason I'm arriving years after the other students is simple. It took time to convince my parents it was a good idea. My neighbourhood secondary school wasn't a bad one, and it could have led to a decent career in an average job. I don't want decent. I don't want average. I want to be the best at something, and if being in the best school does not guarantee success, at least it'll help.

So, I worked to save the money to pay for the trips to multiple interviews, studied hard, and got outstanding grades to guarantee I'd get a scholarship. I might have also found someone who made sure my very girl-next-door file would reach the right hands, and ensured I would be interviewed by an attentive and sympathetic school board member with secrets they wanted to keep buried.

I'm not naturally a people person, but I learned from the spy movies that Dad and I watched together, that sometimes you have to apply the right kind of pressure to get what you want. And leaving my admission up to chance was a risk I wasn't willing to take. So, I learned.

Eleanor opens the door and leads us into a small but well-stocked room. There are two single beds and two desks, upon which are two very shiny, brand-new laptops. I poke my head into the little armoire and find four uniforms neatly hanging inside next to a stack of fine linens for the beds. They really do take care of their students here. Everything is done in dark woods and cream-coloured walls. It's an understated luxury for sure, but it'll do.

Despite wanting to dive into the pile of plush bedding, I keep my exuberance in check. For now. As soon as I'm sure Eleanor won't judge me, I'll bounce on the mattress like my life depends on it.

Eleanor and I spend the next few hours getting things situated in the room after one of the school caretakers brings my bag upstairs. I thank him sincerely since I know the kids here won't give him a second glance. He looks surprised, but nods back. She tells me a bit about some of the students and explains where the library is if I need books the school hasn't already provided in the stack on my desk.

Overall, it's a calm evening, and I feel ready for classes to begin tomorrow. We collapse onto our respective beds soon after, and I find myself smiling before I drift off. I could have had anyone as a roommate, but Eleanor—for all her fastidiousness to the rules—seems to be really sweet and could potentially be a great friend.

I'VE ONLY ATTENDED THREE CLASSES AND HAVE ALREADY BEEN gawked at as the new girl more times than I can count. Moving schools between GCSEs and A-levels is quite common, but not at St

Stephen's apparently. Then, to top it all off, I ripped the hem of my uniform shirt. Today is not off to a great start.

It got worse when the mean girl posse decided to pick on me for the damaged clothing. A few well-chosen words got them to shut up and leave me alone. I did my research before coming here, and everyone has a weakness. More importantly, they broadcast that shit online for anyone to find.

Eleanor meets me after my history class and falls in step with me. "So, how did it go?" she asks.

"Fine." I keep twirling a pen between my fingers as we head towards the dining hall. "The syllabus for the year is intense, but nothing I can't handle."

She scoffs, and I glance at her from under my bangs. "The workload St Stephen's likes to foist on its students always intimidates people who transfer in. But you actually seem pretty confident."

I laugh dryly. "The only thing I'm truly scared of is getting bored or becoming boring. Whenever I do something, I do it well. With flair," I add, flicking my hair over my shoulder as Eleanor chuckles.

Our short heels click across the floor as we enter the dining room. It's still set up the same way it was this morning; only instead of the breakfast foods, I smell roasted meat, vegetables, and tomato soup. There's a dull roar of conversation happening around the room as we step in.

We grab trays and load our plates with food before Eleanor leads me over to a table by the window.

"Okay, so fill me in. Who do I need to avoid?"

She chews her lip for a second and puts her cup down before gesturing around the room at the groups she points out. "There's the usual sort here, but instead of dividing by interest, they tend to divide by tax bracket. The politicians' kids are all around that table, divided —of course—by party lines. There are a few oil barons' kids over there. Titans of industry like to send their kids to St Stephen's as well, so you'll find them divided by what business deals and mergers are going down. The international students are sprinkled in various groups based on their parents' businesses, and then there are the scholarship kids like us. We tend to stick to ourselves and avoid the drama that comes with students playing politics in the dining hall."

"Just like every other school in the world. Makes sense." A smirk makes its way across my lips.

Eleanor leans in, dropping her voice to a whisper. "There are a few mean girls, but with the workload this year, I'm really hoping they're too busy to bother. Plus, the worst of the lot, Rachel, has transferred to another school. Rumour has it her grades weren't good enough to maintain her place here."

Well, that's good. At least one former mean girl has moved on. Let's hope no one else has stepped up to fill her shoes. The ones I ran into earlier didn't seem overly awful, and I couldn't discern one clear leader quite yet. I've always found power exchanges fascinating.

Just as I'm lifting a fork to my lips, a guy saunters up to our table and clears his throat. "Eleanor, keeping secrets, I see. Who's this?" he asks, all swagger and drawl.

Raising a brow at Eleanor, who has gone stock-still, I turn towards the voice.

"You'd probably get more answers if you asked me yourself," I quip at him. I don't have many pet peeves, but one of them is when someone talks as if you're not sitting literally right in front of them.

His dark brows raise, and there's the slightest tint of blush on his tan skin. "My apologies," he says smoothly, oozing more danger and sex appeal than someone really ought to. "I'm Viraj. Who are you?"

"Olivia," I say, ignoring his hand extended towards me and stabbing a few more veggies.

"You're new," he states, obviously already knowing the majority of the student body. Duh, I roll my eyes at the observation.

"How many new students does this school really get every year? Your powers of deduction are on point."

Eleanor chokes on her soup before clearing her throat. Viraj ignores her completely. "There are two of you. You and that kid over there," he says as he points across the dining hall at a guy sitting on his own with floppy brown hair and a steak knife twirling between his fingers. He does this little flip thing over his knuckles with the cutlery, and I make a note to try that with my pen.

"Viraj, back off our new classmate. I'm sure she doesn't want you slobbering all over her," comes a posh voice from the other direction.

I roll my eyes... again. Seems like every school is exactly the same. Rivalries here and there, boys flocking to the new girl, and cliques dividing the student body.

A dark-haired boy approaches the table, his uniform pressed to perfection, and he straightens his tie even though it's already immaculate. He looks down his nose at Viraj before turning to me. While Viraj's demeanour screams of dangerous nights and adrenaline, the newcomer exudes a cultured sort of charm that must have our classmates swooning.

"Olivia Wraith. Hello, welcome to St Stephen's. I'm Maximillian Arondale IV, but my friends call me Max." His delivery is smooth, and he extends his hand like a politician. And when mine slips into his, he pumps it up and down exactly the same as our most recent prime minister.

Bloody hell. What are they feeding the guys here?

I look around the dining hall, noticing everyone is quite attractive, sophisticated, and eating like they're at a gala. Even the other girls have their ankles crossed under their chairs and sit delicately, precisely cutting their food into demure, bite-sized pieces.

Just when I think this is an entirely different ball game than the school I transferred from, Viraj snaps, "What do you want, Maxi Pad? Go bother someone else."

Ah, there it is. Name-calling and teasing are alive and well everywhere. And do I want to know why Viraj knows the brand name of sanitary products from the US?

Max just brushes a bit of imaginary lint from Viraj's uniform jacket before saying, "The only person I see bothering anyone is you. Clearly, you've made Olivia uncomfortable. I'm simply here to make sure her introduction to our school is pleasurable." Max winks, and Eleanor scoffs.

"I was doing okay, but thanks," I snark back. I don't plan to be in the middle of their male posturing over lunch, even if the second guy's last name is the same one on the scholarship Roark has been awarded. "Your concern is sweet. However, Eleanor and I were having a chat about our classes. Perhaps we can catch up later?"

They break their stare-off, and both turn their heads in my direction. Viraj lifts his lips in a smirk like he sees me as a challenge he can't wait to dive into, and Max clears his throat. "You heard her," he says. "Let's go. See you later, Olivia."

The two of them split in opposite directions, leaving Eleanor and me to our food. Eleanor aims a look at me that I can't decipher, before reaching across the table and gripping my hand. "That was fucking badass!" she whisper-shouts. "No one dismisses those two."

"What's their deal? I don't want to get on anyone's radar. I just need to do my work and get the hell out of here." Sighing deeply, I take a forkful of food and get back to lunch.

"Max's dad is a lord. There was a rumour last year that his ancestors single-handedly fought off the Vikings. Nothing was confirmed or denied, so the stories spread from there. He's an aristocrat through and through; old money, you know?" I nod my head. "Viraj's family is one of the wealthiest in India. They own the biggest chain store and production factories in the country, and they expanded to a digital audience about fifteen years ago. They've been swimming in cash ever since. The two of them squabble over everything, but it basically boils down to new money versus old."

"That's stupid." I frown. "Who cares where the money comes from? It's not like either of them earned it." Surveying the room, I note that most students wear their privilege in the form of fancy accessories to offset their school uniforms.

After our earlier interruption, lunch continues without a hitch, and before long, the bell rings and most of the students have already cleared out of the dining room. It's time for my anatomy lab. Why I decided to take a pre-med course is beyond me. Apparently, my need for challenges wasn't sated with the whole changing-schools-and-not-knowing-anyone-here thing.

Eleanor leads me to the classroom listed on my timetable and takes off towards art history. The teacher for this lab is Mr Abernathy, and I hope to god he doesn't make me stand up and introduce myself.

I walk into a sterile-looking room with stainless-steel tables and two stools per workspace. The benches are all full, aside from one in the back. I make my way past the other students when I trip on a stool leg sticking out in the aisle. I crumple to the ground in a spectacular heap, and my books go flying. A few students help me up and gather my things as I dust myself off.

My bag is held out by the boy who was spinning his knife in the dining hall earlier. "Hi everyone, and thanks," I say, fighting the heat warming my cheeks. They all murmur their hellos, but the boy holds my eyes.

"Are you okay?" he asks, his voice deeper than I was expecting. It suits his athletic body rather well, in my opinion.

"Fine, just embarrassed," I admit. I walk towards the open seat in the back of the classroom, and he joins me a second later, sliding into the other seat.

"Embarrassment is a useless emotion. The things that embarrass you live in your head far longer than they will in anyone else's."

His tone is dry, and his words are direct. He's right, though. I stick my hand out and decide to just jump in. "Hi, I'm Olivia. I like how you spin knives. Can you teach me that flip you did over the third knuckle?"

He turns his body in my direction and takes me in. He looks me over from head to toe, and for a moment, I'm certain he's going to refuse. After all, he ignored everyone else when I went flying through the air earlier, only checking I wasn't hurt.

The rest of the students seem to give him a wide berth, and maybe it's because he's new here too. Or maybe because he likes playing with sharp objects. But then I see something that looks so out of place on his face, I imagine it's a rarity: his pupils dilate in his amber eyes and his lips tip up in the faintest of smirks.

"Zach. You got a pen?" he asks as he slowly shakes my hand. Might as well try to blend into the expected behaviour of this school with all the weird hand-shaking, right? Politician Olivia Wraith doesn't exactly seem like something I'd be into, but I could learn a thing or two from the other students.

I snort. "Always." Withdrawing a simple pen from behind my ear, I hand it over, explaining myself when he gives me a curious look. "I fidget a lot; it helps me think."

"Whatever works." He doesn't seem to speak too much from what I've seen, but we have some common ground if we're both new here. Plus, I'm kind of curious about the guy who knows how to flip knives through his fingers so easily.

He spins the pen between two of his fingers, and I note the balance on either end. Lifting his thumb, he's ready to catch the long end of the pen as he completes the loop. He does it twice more before I feel confident enough to try it myself.

Just as he hands the pen back, the professor walks in. He's a flurry of tweed and thick-lensed glasses as he drops his bag on the front desk and starts rifling through the files scattered across the surface.

"Good afternoon, students. Last year, we covered intro to zoology and you have all taken biology. If you are in this classroom, you are here to see if medical school is something in your future. Building on last term, we will begin with a dissection. This was part of the assigned reading over the summer, so you should be prepared. However, if you have forgotten what I'm *certain* you read, you can find the instructions in chapter two of your textbooks. Today, and the remainder of the week, we will be dissecting cats. Later this term, we will move on to bipedal creatures. If you are new this year, please refer to the pages as your partner works."

Bipedal... as in humans or monkeys or something? Monkeys make more sense. Is dissecting monkeys even legal? Aren't they mostly endangered species? Also, I'm paired with the only other new student. Thankfully, I did the reading already. I hope he has too.

Mr Abernathy gets down to business, telling us where to gather our supplies as he opens a door on the other side of the room and emerges with deep trays that instantly stink up the space. Zach stands from his stool quickly, telling me to get the book open while he gathers the materials.

Mr Abernathy puts one of the trays down on our table, and while it's kind of eerie, looking at the animal doesn't bother me as much as it does some of the other students. Zach is back moments later and lays out the materials in an orderly manner, keeping a scalpel for himself and starting to twirl it in his left hand.

"That's impressive," I observe. "Are you ambidextrous?"

The corner of Zach's mouth tilts up into a full-blown smile, as if I said something interesting. "Yes," he answers with a bit more warmth.

I've talked to guys before, but now, I want to blush and stammer after that smile. Not knowing what else to do, I change the subject. "Okay, so we're to remove the heart, liver, and stomach," I say, looking up at the board to find the instructions being written out by the professor. Referring to the book in front of me, I pay attention to the details so we know what to do.

"Easy. Let's go. Gloves on," Zach directs. "You want to play nurse, or shall I?" His sarcasm is dry, and I bark out a laugh.

"You can take the lead on this one, Doc."

Zach nods his head, lifting the scalpel in a gloved hand. He begins the dissection, separating the skin from muscle to access the cat's abdomen.

I feel queasy at the smell of the formaldehyde and whatever other fluids the animals have been preserved in, grateful to see I'm not the only one inclined to pinch my nose. Steeling my shoulders, I force myself to focus on the task at hand. Zach has me assisting with quiet words as he finds the organs Mr Abernathy directed the class to remove.

He works methodically, never once referring to the open book before me. Looking around, I see the other students are just finding the nerve to make the first cut, and there are more than a few complaints rising from some students at the assignment. While everyone is still struggling to find the heart, Zach withdraws the last organ with a smile on his face. Odd reaction to cutting open a cat.

"Okay, that's it. Want to take it up to the professor?" I ask.

"Not yet," Zach says.

He pulls a needle and thread from the tray of supplies and begins the tedious work of stitching the cat back together along the belly. His sutures are precise as he ties a small knot every time he passes through the skin.

Should I be worried I'm partnered with a guy who cuts open, removes organs from, and stitches up a creature with no hesitation whatsoever?

Probably.

Am I?

Not at all.

I should probably find out if there's a therapist somewhere in this school. The only things I can focus on are the careful touches Zach uses, the veins and muscles in his forearms, and the confidence he works with.

"So you're new here too, right?" I ask. "Where did you transfer from?"

Zach keeps working on the stitches as he answers. "I got kicked out of Crawford Prep. This is the only place that would take me. Though they charged my parents an additional fifty per cent."

"What did you get kicked out for?" My question comes out unbidden, but I can't stop the curiosity.

He looks over to me and smirks. I see the lack of emotion in his eyes, but I'm helpless to look away. "I got bored."

"You two are done already?" Mr Abernathy effuses from the end of our table. I didn't even notice him approaching.

"Yes, sir," Zach says, appearing to be a model student. I have serious doubts about that.

"Well done. Any issues?" he asks, picking up the tray to grade our work.

"None at all. I'll just go wash and sanitise these," I say, standing from my seat and scooping up the instrument tray.

"Who did these sutures? They're remarkably precise," Abernathy says. Zach just looks at him and lifts his brow. "Ah yes, of course. I've read your file."

With that curious statement, he turns on his heel and walks to the front of the room. I get our stuff cleaned and join Zach, who spends the rest of the class time helping me perfect the pen flip of my dreams, demonstrating on a scalpel. He even manages to nod and dole out praise once I've figured out the knack to the turn. I won't lie and say I didn't get a full-body flush at those words.

I think I might have just made another friend. And I really want his file.

Chapter Three

Olivia
Present Day

"Honey, I'm home!" I call from my foyer. I drop my shit in the entryway and slip off my heels. My voice bounces off the marble tile, echoing through the house.

"Bloody finally!" Ellie—formerly known as Eleanor—sleepily shouts from the living room to the right. I roll my eyes at her dramatics. It's been less than eight hours since she texted me. Her face pops up over the sofa, her black hair a halo of straight-up mess around her head.

"Might I remind you, *you're* the one who showed up unannounced?" She grunts and tries to push me off when I flop down on top of her, but I go dead-weight and refuse to move.

"You smell like aeroplane. Where were you?" she asks with a wrinkled nose.

"I do not! It was a private jet. It smelled like lavender and money. Oh wait, I meant lavender and honey." Laughing, I deliver a playful slap to her shoulder. "And do you really want to know where I was?" Cocking a brow at her, I lift my head from her shoulder.

She mulls it over for a second before decisively shaking her head. After she joined Interpol, we decided on a sort of don't-ask-don't-tell policy on the specifics. Her features are pinched, and it's a look I've only ever seen when she's working on a case... or studying for her art history exams, but I doubt that's what's bothering her.

"Come on. You can explain what the hell's going on as I get my caffeine fix." I drag myself up and haul her off the sofa towards the kitchen. She's still wearing a pantsuit, so she must have waited here for me and dozed off.

Pressing the buttons on my fancy space-age coffee machine with all the bells and whistles, I lean back against the grey countertop and stifle a snicker while she glares at me. Offering the first cup of coffee as a truce, I extend my arm, and her face finally relaxes. She digs a spoon out of the cutlery drawer for sugar as I pull the milk from the fridge.

"So, what's up?" I ask as I prepare my own cup of coffee. Her message from last night has me worried as hell. She was just here two weeks ago, and she's usually stationed in France at Interpol's headquarters. Visits to London are common occurrences, but never twice in such a short period.

"I fucked up, and now I've got a job for you," she states. Despite her sleep-rumpled state, she manages to find the energy to look resigned.

"What kind of job? We're booked out for the next three months. You know how people get when spring cleaning season starts. Although, no one wants to actually put in the work. It's a very lucrative time to own a cleaning company."

"I'm not talking about a legit job for The Cleanup." Her eyes look around my kitchen as if she's afraid she's been overheard.

"You want to hire me... for a *job* job?"

"Yes, well, kind of," she says as she plops down on a stool and rests her elbows on the kitchen island.

"Why all the cloak and dagger? What do you need me to do?" I ask. "You've never been interested in discussing the details of my work before. Is it that asshole ex-boyfriend of yours? Do you need me to take care of him?"

"Fuck, Olivia, no! I haven't heard from Conrad the Connard in months. No, uh..." She pauses as if looking for the right way to phrase it. Her eyebrows are bunched, and she's suddenly abandoned her coffee in favour of concentration. "Interpol needs someone with your... abilities. It's something we can't touch with a ten-foot pole. No one wants to get their hands messy with this one, so we're hiring it out. Covertly, of course."

"Sounds positively scandalous. What's the job?"

"Look, I don't know much about how you do whatever it is you do, but I'm hoping you can help with this one. How much do you know about the Bratva?"

"The Russian mafia?" I ponder the information I've gathered over the years, none of it especially recent, as I tend to avoid organised crime and stick to the assholes who can't rain hellfire down on me if I'm ever caught. But for Ellie? I'm diving in. "Sergei Volkov is essentially the head of it, at least in Europe. The Volkov family are the most powerful, running things in St Petersburg with various factions worldwide, but he's the one they answer to. The other families are always looking for a foothold, but Sergei is the undisputed leader and has been for the last ten years. They handle assassinations, political scandals, putting people into power, and more blackmail dealings than any one group should be capable of. That Bratva?"

"Yep, that's the one." Ellie sighs and sips her coffee with a groan of appreciation. "Well, Sergei is dead as of"—she checks her watch

—"seventy-three hours ago. His wife, Natasha, has taken control of the family, but now comes the real kicker."

"Oh, do tell," I implore her. I love this shit more than soap operas. There's always so much drama with power exchanges. "Was the husband fucking his secretary? Unless all parties agree, sleeping around is just a recipe for disaster."

I should know. Once upon a time, my heart was pulled in four directions by men who didn't see eye to eye on... basically anything. These days, I speak to each of them now and then, but never together. Never all at once.

"Natasha gained confidential data stolen from Interpol, then murdered her husband to take control. With the intel, she's promising the family she'll lead them to greatness, which makes her claim very difficult to challenge."

Ellie sighs as though the weight of the world rests on her shoulders. "Added to that, the police aren't properly investigating Sergei's murder, and we'd like it to stay that way, at least until we recover the data. Obviously, that's where you come in."

I scoff. "Then where does that leave me? On Interpol's watchlist?" I muse aloud. Despite not having all the info quite yet, I know without a doubt I will help her. I can't help it, I like feeling needed. Plus, I'd do anything for my bestie.

Ellie snags her bag from the breakfast nook where she must have stashed it last night and drops a huge file on the countertop. It'll take me hours to go through all of it—even with all the redacting—but it will certainly help to have a starting point.

"We are offering immunity for you, along with a generous bonus when the job is completed. There will be no adding you to any lists. *That* is how important this is. Interpol is willing to work with criminals to get back what we've lost. And just think of the big-ass suitcase full of cash when the job is done. We will cover all expenses if the grab is successful. If it's not"—she looks around my luxe townhouse with all the fixings—"I'm sure you can cover the costs."

"Yeah, if the job doesn't kill me first. Take it out of the estate if it does," I deadpan. "You know this won't be something I can do on my own, right? How many team members can I have, and will they be granted immunity as well?" I ask, already thinking about the scale of the heist and the moving parts I'll have to coordinate.

"As few as possible. The payout for the job is a lump sum of cash to be divided as you see fit, but we have to make sure it stays classified."

"Deal. But I want all of it in writing. When's the deadline?"

"The earlier, the better, obviously, as Natasha is still new to her position, and it's tenuous at best. The boys' club isn't overly fond of a woman leading them, but she's currently holding all the cards."

"What will prevent Mrs Volkov from making copies of the files? I mean, I can probably infiltrate wherever she keeps her stuff and send you a copy of what she has, but I can't retrieve a bunch of copies and destroy them all if they're in multiple secure locations."

"Olivia, this is how big the screw up is. These secrets are so dangerous they were encrypted using cutting-edge technology to make sure no one but us could access them." Ellie rests her hands on the countertop, drawing out the suspense and making me even more impatient for answers.

"What? Where are they?" I ask, like a child eager to hear the ending of a story.

"They're in a diamond."

"As in quantum data storage?"

"Yup."

"Inside a diamond?"

"Yup."

"And we have to steal it back before Natasha Volkov can either build or gain access to a machine capable of reading it all?"

"Yup."

"You know I'm not a jewel thief, right?"

"Yup." I look at her, raising a brow. "Olivia, please, you're the only one I can trust who's got a chance of pulling this off. My ass is on the line if we can't get it back since it was *my* partner who handed it to the Volkovs in the first place. They'll need someone's head to roll—maybe literally—and I think that might be mine. If they can't find the diamond or my old partner, they're going to look for someone to blame."

Genuine concern washes over her face, and I know she wouldn't come to me with this if there was any other way. Our friendship has always taken priority over our work, and the line we've drawn in the sand over what we will and won't discuss has just been obliterated.

I sigh, flicking through the file, knowing there's no way I can let Ellie flounder if I have the ability to help. "Fine. We'll come up with something. How hard can it be to track down an international crime syndicate leader and steal a diamond from right under her nose?" Probably no more challenging than taking down a dictator. Which reminds me, I should check in on how good old Zul's doing.

"That's the spirit," Ellie says, swatting me lightly on the shoulder. "Thank you, O. I'll owe you a million if you can manage this."

I wave a hand in front of me. "You would do the same if the shoe were on the other foot. So that's business done, yeah? Anything else you want to discuss before we move on to breakfast?" I ask, turning towards the fridge and perusing the stock.

"Actually, I need a nap. I stayed up till four waiting for you. What time is it anyway?" she asks, shifting her body to look at the clock on the oven behind me.

"Seven?" I guess, and she nods in confirmation. "Okay, grab one of the guest rooms or the sofa. I'll get to work on these files. Thank god that jet had a quiet bedroom and a high-end bed—no jet lag for me."

Ellie smothers a yawn behind her hand, gives me a glare for being fresh as a daisy, and shakily stands from the stool. "Happy napping!" I call after her as she shuffles away and up to the first floor for her guestroom.

There's no way I can rest now. Not when there's a job to research. Ellie makes her way upstairs, and I follow as soon as I get the dishes in the sink. Shoving the file under my arm, I make my way to the second floor and key in the code to my office door. It swings open on silent hinges, and I drop the mess on my desk.

Flicking on the flat screen as I pass it, I watch the Tesken news channels for word of the takedown. Rumours are flying as the two hosts chat about the news that broke in the morning papers. *Damn, that resistance group works fast.*

Turns out, the people who hired me through Max found a national online media outlet to publish Zul's history of corruption and blackmail, and the revolts have officially started. Max is one of those people with connections everywhere. He rubs elbows with heads of state and government officials on the regular, so most of my international jobs come through him.

I settle into my cushy office chair and kick my feet up, pulling a pack of Skittles from my desk drawer, content to have the news on in the background while I wait for the big dramatic show to take place.

Pulling my attention from the screen, I flip through page after page of information from Ellie. It reminds me a bit of when the guys and I worked together to get our old headmaster fired and replaced in our final year of school. God, that was a good day. I think it was the last time the five of us actually worked as a team. Ellie was also the seed-planter of that little takedown... unknowingly, of course.

The guys are now spread out around the world, each of them consulting on jobs from afar when needed. We may not be as close as we once were, but every now and then, I can tempt them from their humdrum lives for a thrill. Plus, different operations require skills that they have honed since our first smash-and-grab back when we were just teenagers. But this one that Ellie just dropped in my lap? Well, I have a feeling this one will require all of us.

Plus, who's to say they can't work together after all this time? It's been over a decade. Maybe they've matured?

I open the discrete browser on my laptop and begin my search on the new head of the Volkov Bratva before bringing the guys in. Without details, we'll all just be sitting around with our thumbs up our asses.

Natasha, as it turns out, is rather popular with the tabloids. There are photos of her at various events around the world with her "businessman" husband, who looked exactly like you would imagine the head of a Bratva family. Silver hair, a mean glare at the cameras, and meaty hands holding his wife's just this side of too hard. Thank god they never procreated; imagine that face on a baby.

My bet is she killed Sergei for being an asshole. He looks like one.

Scouring the most recent articles about her before her husband's death, I find fashion magazine interviews, homemaking ones, and even a few about a jewellery line she's created. Lord Almighty, this is a basic bitch if I've ever seen one. The files support what the web tells me, but they also have hints that she's been embedded in the Bratva far longer than it might seem.

Natasha is wearing fur in most of her pictures, and while she claims it's faux, PETA still hates her. Everything from her artificial ice-blonde hair, to her spray-tanned skin, to her matchy-matchy outfits makes me want to reach through the screen, shake her by the shoulders, and demand she find some personality under all that Botox.

Or, just maybe, she's an intelligent person who's planning to hide her new priceless diamond in plain sight by looking the part of the trophy wife.

My in-app translator works double-time to turn Russian into English, and my eyes scan the information as I scroll. After an hour of learning more about A-line dresses than I ever wanted to know in my entire life, I finally come across something of value.

NATASHA VOLKOV HAS ACCEPTED THE ESTEEMED HONOUR TO *present the winner of the Monaco Grand Prix with his trophy on 29th May this year. The Circuit de Monaco is widely considered one of the most important and prestigious automobile races in the world. More than any other race, it draws forth celebrities and notable figures who come to experience the glamour and prestige of the event. Nightclubs host parties during the Grand Prix weekend, and Port Hercule plays host to partygoers joining in on the celebrations.*

MONACO. IT'S LESS THAN TWO MONTHS AWAY AND GIVES ME time to come up with a better plan than the one I have at the moment. No one in power will leave valuables at home while travelling. Not even with their most trusted associates.

No, Natasha is bound to have the diamond with her.

It's time to bring the guys in.

Pulling up the tracking app on my phone, I find them more or less where I expected when my app connects to their mobiles. V is the farthest away, so I'll have to call him tonight, just as soon as I narrow down his current plans, then proceed to chuck them all out the window. Zach will be next because, what the fuck is he doing in Lousiana?

Actually, forget I even asked.

Time for a good old-fashioned reunion. Tomorrow night seems like a perfect evening for a dinner party.

The tracker app was Zach's genius idea—he wanted the means to find me in case everything went to shit, and I needed help. I agreed to it on the condition that he let me track him too. The rest of the guys were reluctant, but eventually saw the light after I framed it just right for each of them over the years. And so, they've all got the app on their phones, and I've kept tabs on them; only going so far as to interrupt their plans when absolutely necessary.

They also didn't protest much because they know I'm an expert at what I do. After all, it started all those years ago at St Stephen's Boarding School.

Manipulation.

I'm not just talking about convincing students to hand over their pocket money. Oh, no. I'm talking about using observation and coercion to find out secrets. Those are a lot more valuable than a couple quid.

Eventually, the guys caught on to what I was doing and were brought in. Each for their own reasons—some obvious, some not—but together, we became an unstoppable force. It's too bad they've always hated each other.

I was the one who linked us together—the only thing the guys had in common. I still am, but that's all about to change, if I get my way.

The motion sensors in my house pick up movement a few hours later, and the camera screens flare to life on my office wall. Ellie pokes her head out of the guest bedroom, looking left and right down the hall before staring straight into the camera lens.

"O! Where the fuck are you?" she shouts.

"That's what she said!" I yell, breaking out in laughter over my own orgasm joke. I get up and switch off the flat screen. Maybe it's time Ellie learns exactly what it is I do for work. She knows enough, and that's scary as shit sometimes, but if she's recruiting me for this, I should at least tell her that the best secret thief in the world is on her side.

Like all resolutions, most promises, and the occasional condom... some things are doomed to break. Our don't-ask-don't-tell policy has just become the latest victim.

I zip up the unicorn onesie I slipped into earlier and make my way downstairs. Ellie smirks up at me as I near her. "Let's go, slowpoke."

"I'm coming, I'm coming. Hey, you want ice cream?"

"What? No. It's too fucking early." I roll my eyes at the dramatics. It's three in the afternoon. "Well, maybe. What kind have you got?" Ellie answers.

Ha. What kind *haven't* I got?

"All of them. Pick your poison, but there was a sale on Phish Food," I sing-song as I head towards the freezer.

"Fine, but just one tub." She looks me up and down, noting my incredible loungewear, and smirks. "Seems like you had a good day. Successful research morning?"

"The best," I confirm. "Want to know what I'm planning?"

"Maybe later? I'd like to not think about how fucked I am for a little while. How did I not see any signs?" she mutters to herself. I doubt it's the first time those words have crossed her lips.

"Ellie, I know you," I soothe. "You don't do anything halfway, but sometimes, people one up us. It happens. What I can promise is that they'll regret it very soon when your bestie rides in wearing a unicorn onesie and saves the day."

"Oh, I'm sure your choice of loungewear will definitely terrify the Bratva. Anyway, please be careful out there. Who else would force me into dinosaur jammies and feed me ice cream?" Ellie pouts.

"They're onesies, Ellie. Not jammies. They're entirely different, and you should totally be wearing yours right now." She chuckles and pulls me in for a hug, her arms tense and wooden. She always did wear her stress like a flashing neon sign across her face.

"Come on, let's get you your treat. You look like you might need it," I say as I take Ellie's hand and lead her through the marble entryway and towards the kitchen. Swinging open the door to the hall closet, I grab her dinosaur onesie—the one I keep stashed there for emergencies—and then toss it at her with a wink.

"No, no," she says. "I know that look. I am *not* wearing that and getting drunk on your sofa again," she declares.

We both know she's going to end up in the onesie, eating ice cream and eventually sharing a bottle of wine while listening to gore-filled podcasts as we catch up. Why she puts up this fight every time is beyond me. It's pointless.

"Put it on, Ellie. You don't want to look ridiculous by not dressing for the occasion, do you?" I smirk and continue on my way, listening to her grumble behind me all the while about childish clothing options.

My house, my rules.

"What occasion?"

I laugh, ignoring her question, and the peals of laughter ring through my pristine home. I want to watch the downfall of Zul, and if

Ellie's here, it looks like she'll be participating in the viewing party. It's probably only a matter of minutes now.

My head is buried in the freezer, pulling out the ice cream, when I hear her shuffle in behind me. Looking up, I see she's drawn up the hood of the onesie, the dinosaur spikes trailing from her forehead to her ass, where a stuffed tail drags on the floor behind her.

"Don't. Say. A. Word."

I raise my hands, palms up, in a placating gesture. "Fine, fine. But there's something you should see. Have a seat." I slide a pint of ice cream across the island to her seat, and a spoon clatters along after it.

She plops down where she was perched this morning, and I flick on the small TV in the kitchen. I select the right input, and Ellie gasps as she sees Zul on his knees, his fingers interlaced behind his head, as the Teskenese government police surround him.

You know at the end of films, where the hero has finally prevailed over the villain? That scene where they casually walk away, flicking their hair over their shoulder in the midst of a firestorm and well-timed explosion? I kind of wish real life was that cool.

I mean, why go out all dressed up in some skimpy leather outfit when you can accomplish the same thing while downing a tub of Ben and Jerry's in the most magnificent garment ever created?

It's actually kind of nice sharing this moment with Ellie—usually, I just watch the endings play out alone. Her eyes are riveted to the screen as Zul is arrested; his shouts in Teskenese full of very colourful curses that would make even Zach blush.

I plop down next to Ellie and watch the downfall of Zul's iron-fisted grip on Tesken through my miniature flat-screen TV with a spoon in one hand and a spinning pen in the other.

Some thieves bask in the limelight, coming up with catchy names and leaving calling cards. That's not really my style. In fact, that's how people get caught. I'd rather sit back in the shadows, quietly knowing I'm the best and leave it at that.

I never steal anything people will miss. Sometimes, I'm hired to copy-paste files from a government computer like last night's job.

Another day, someone might need me to make certain business practises public and tilt the stock market in their favour. And now, apparently, I get to add the title of "jewel thief" to my extensive resume, which is fucking scary, because that diamond will definitely be missed.

The Montblanc pen from Zul's office twirls around my fingers and goes flying when I flick it too hard around my thumb. Fucking hell. I send up a silent lament for the one I lost. *Sigh*. It had perfect balance.

"O, what exactly are we watching?" Ellie finally breaks her concentration on the screen when the feed cuts out as Zul is hauled off.

"Evidence," I reply casually.

"Yes, I'm sure that's what the prosecution will say. What the hell was that? And how did you have a view inside the government building?" she asks.

I pick up the pen to start spinning again. "The removal of a corrupt leader. That's what I was working on last night. You don't need to know everything that happened, but you do need to know that I've got this. Consider what you just saw as evidence of my competency."

Ellie's jaw is unhinged as she gapes at me. It looks pretty funny with the dinosaur hood on her head. "You had a hand in a dictator's downfall?"

"Not exactly." A look of relief passes across Ellie's face. "You say it like I was just a small part of a bigger plot. I did all of it."

Well, I finally did it. I broke Ellie. She hasn't blinked in what feels like an eternity. Her body has stopped moving, and I'm not sure if she's still breathing.

"Uh, Ellie? You okay over there?"

She makes this weird noise in her throat before clearing it. "I knew you could hack and get files, but I always assumed it was corporate espionage. This is... Fuck, O. This is insane!"

"We always agreed I'd keep the details to myself because of your career. I'm only showing you this now so you know I've got your back, and I'm capable of doing the job you've brought me on for. But I won't be able to do it alone."

"Olivia Wraith!" Uh-oh, she's using my full name. "You're not thinking of bringing in the guys, are you?" My sheepish smile seems to be answer enough. "All four of them?"

"Maybe? Their skill sets might come in handy on this one." Granted, their professions don't account for their most valuable expertise.

"And how are you going to prevent them from killing each other?"

"Sex, threats, or hypnosis? I've learnt a couple of tricks since we were all together last."

"I just hope you know what you're doing. Those four in the same place have proven to be a volatile combination."

"Zach will help," I assert, naming one of the four volatile assholes.

"Or make it a thousand times worse..."

Ellie's right; it'll be a mess.

"Fuck, I have to get back to HQ and can't stay much longer. You have no idea the shitstorm that's raining down on everyone at the moment with this loss. Even the nap today was pure indulgence. I'm taking my dinosaur onesie with me, by the way. I'm sick of only wearing it when I visit you. It's ridiculously comfortable, and this is definitely my colour."

I pout at her abrupt departure, but am glad she has embraced the onesie lifestyle. My personal life doesn't really lend itself to many social calls, and Ellie is the only person I see consistently. But I do a mental happy dance knowing she'll keep the dinosaur. I doubt she'll leave for her next assignment without it. I win this round. As always. What will I make her wear next?

"Fine," I say, more than put out about her impending departure.

"O, darling, you've got a heist to plan and four dickheads to call—good luck with that, by the way. I'll get the paperwork to you as soon as possible and forward any more intel I can find to help." Ellie stands, dropping the spoon in the sink and puts the remaining ice cream away while I start thinking through plans.

This is how I always knew she wasn't normal. Who doesn't finish their tub of ice cream?

I walk her to the door after she switches back to her normal clothes, and we say goodbye. I can't help but laugh as I watch her walk down the street, that dinosaur tail poking out of the bundle of onesie in her arms.

She's right. There's work to be done and plans to be made. Not to mention, assholes to corral.

Usually, I'd arrange everything remotely, possibly even rope in one of my guys on the job to have some backup, but with Interpol involved, there's a good chance this one won't be as cut and dry as the rest.

Leaning back against the closed front door, I look around my empty townhouse. It's far too big, but it suits me. It doesn't really feel like a home, more like a house I just happen to live in.

Good thing it has guest rooms. I'm about to get a whole host of testosterone up in here. Aw, man. Now I've got DMX in my head.

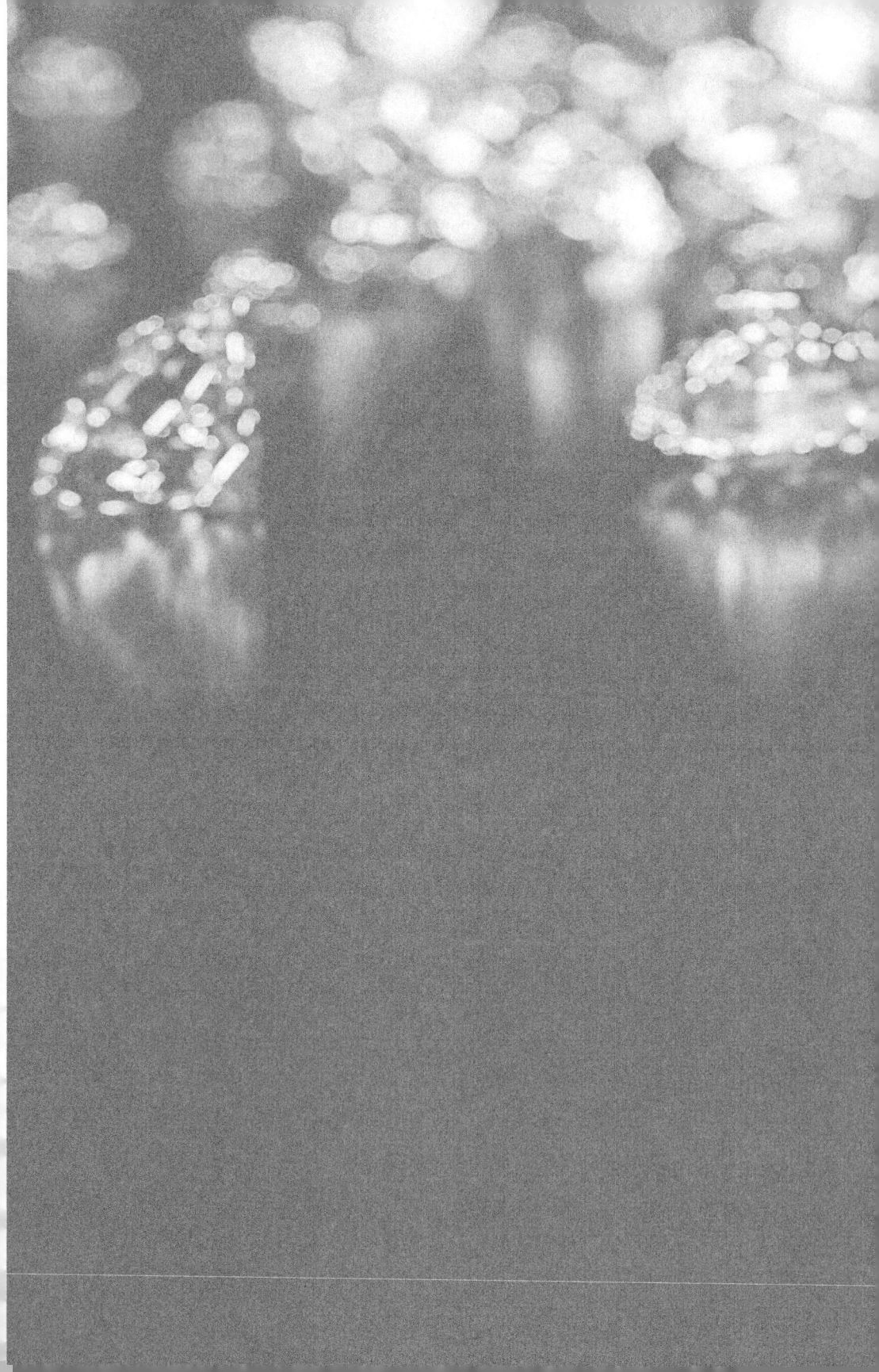

Chapter Four

Viraj
Present Day

I gather all the items on the table and stuff them in my suit jacket. All my clothing has hidden compartments just for them. Some might say going everywhere with a fake passport, ten thousand dollars in cash, and an old memento is a little overkill. And mostly illegal.

Well, I don't give a fuck. I may be a lawyer, but it is not my love for the law that made me pick this career. When I left school, my main goal was to learn how one could do illegal shit without getting caught.

My skills in manipulating rules to my advantage haven't come in handy yet—not since back at St Stephen's, anyway—but I'd rather be safe than sorry. I can legally get someone out of jail if I need to, and that's always a good skill to have.

After hiding my most valuable items, I zip my suitcase closed, make sure it's locked, and head out of the hotel room. My time in Colorado is unfortunately over. I took some time off from work to participate in a rock climbing competition that I've been looking forward to for months. My case win rate is so impressive that when I say I need a month off the firm gives it to me with no questions asked.

Needless to say, I won the hell out of the competition, and even set a new record. I'm just that good.

Magazines have called me the Adrenaline God before. I do not lose at competitions and try to push myself to do anything that gets my heart beating faster. Car racing, snowboarding, rock climbing, scuba diving, base jumping, boxing; you name it. If it makes your blood pump harder in your veins and your head light, I'm incredible at it.

My family's one of the wealthiest in India, and I've taken full advantage of their money to make a dream life for myself. I have a job that I love and more passions than I can count. It helps I have a cousin who actually wanted to inherit the family business and cares about that sort of thing. Swaroop has already settled down with a family and is basically running the company alongside my parents. They all love me, but I'm still the black sheep. I guess it comes from my time in England, but since they were the ones that sent me there, I really can't be blamed.

Pulling my suitcase behind me, I stop at the hotel lobby to give my room key back to the staff and make sure my gear will be shipped to New York. Five years ago, right after I became a partner at the firm I worked for, I bought a loft in Manhattan. It's huge, with an enormous living space, four bathrooms, and four bedrooms. It had two additional rooms, but I knocked down the wall between them, making a dedicated space for all my sports gear, and the medals and trophies I've won along the way.

The Uber I booked to get me to the airport is a huge GMC

Yukon Denali, totally unnecessary for only one person, but I like to have my space. The back seat is wide, the leather smells nice, and the driver is far enough away to not feel like he has to talk to me.

The SUV has barely left the front of the hotel when my phone rings. An irritated huff leaves my lips when I see that the caller ID is unknown. There are two people that might call me from a number I don't have. It's either my mom who finally figured out I'm ignoring her calls, or...

Of its own accord, my thumb presses the green button.

"V-Card!" Her cheerful voice is like time travel.

"Olive branch!"

"Don't call me that," she immediately snaps. The corner of my lip tilts up. She hasn't rung me in a few months now—the last time was when she needed my help with an extraction plan—and I've missed getting under her skin.

"Ollie," I say, ignoring her protest, "what do you need?" I love being an ass, but since she called me from a burner phone, it's not to joke around. The first time she made contact after school, I was in my last year of law school. Since then, she's popped up from time to time, arriving at a sports event, competing, then jetting off again, only to call me a few months later for advice on a plan she was working on.

She lets out an audible sigh. "I need your help. In person. You have to come back to England." My brows bunch into a frown.

"What?"

"It's for a job. I'll need you here, and I've already bought you a plane ticket. I know you're heading to Denver International as we speak and you're already pre-checked in on the flight—first class since I know you're a prima donna. Chop chop, take-off is in three hours." I don't ask how she knows all this. There's no hiding secrets from Olivia. She always knows.

Except for the one thing that I've always managed to keep from her. I smile knowingly and palm the hidden pocket of my jacket.

"What's the job? You've never needed me in person before." And it must irk her to no end that she can't do it on her own this time.

"I'm infiltrating the Monaco Grand Prix. I need someone who can pose as a driver if needed, and also get us out. See you tomorrow, V."

"Wait!" I shout into the phone, making the driver jump in his seat. "Ollie, did you call anyone else?"

Except she's already hung up, and without her number, I can't call her back.

"Shit," I mutter between my teeth. What are the odds that she only called me? Having Olivia owe me one is worth a lot, but not enough to make up for spending time with the three assholes she calls friends. If she's asked for Max's help...

I can't deal with that pompous dick again.

Only one of us will come out of it alive.

Zach

Present Day

"Now, Doctor Vaughn, that's not very nice," I chide as the despicable paediatrician in front of me spews verbal vitriol, thinking her brash words are going to deter the future I have in mind for her.

"Fuck you, who the hell do you think you are? You can't do this!" she shouts with her nasally American accent, pulling on her restraints. The rope creaks against the wooden chair I tied her to in the shed. This really is a nice rental. It's a shame I couldn't enjoy the peace and quiet of the Louisiana Bayou in solitude.

"Really? I don't see anyone here to stop me." In my booted feet, I walk around her in a circle. The scalpels in my hands are ready to do their work, and my soul is singing for retribution.

I first heard about Dr Vaughn on a social media group I frequent. It's usually a place for parents to go when they have questions about their kids or want to share knowledge and resources. But every now and then, we get a post by someone like Cheryl Lloyd.

You see, Cheryl's oldest son was diagnosed with ADHD at an early age, and was started on a regime of pills to temper his symptoms. I asked Cheryl for his symptoms in the comments, to which she promptly answered. Nothing pointed at a concrete diagnosis. But Cheryl lamented about how the medication was supposed to be the best and that their insurance didn't cover it.

And she's right. It is one of the best. *If* the patient is suffering from ADHD.

Well, their younger son is now eight, and at his last visit, Vaughn recommended he begin the medication as well. Cheryl wrote a lengthy post about the state of their looming bankruptcy, all the while wanting the best for her children, and unsure of Dr Vaughn's diagnosis.

"I'm going to report you to the police. Don't you know who I am? I will bury you," she threatens.

"Oh." I pause. "You seem to be mistaken. You won't be leaving. At least, not whole."

Noting the seriousness in my tone, she pauses her tirade. I grip the hair at the base of her skull and tilt her head back in a sharp tug to connect our gazes. Her blue eyes are wide with fear and brimming with the tears this arrogant bitch tried so hard to keep at bay.

"You mistreat the kids whose parents bring them to your practice, dosing them with medication they don't need, all so you can line your already overstuffed pockets with drug manufacturers' kickbacks while pushing the parents into bankruptcy over unnecessary and expensive medication. No one deserves to suffer for your greed, least of all children." My words are delivered flatly, no emotion breaks through my voice. Though, why would it? It's a symptom of my own diagnosis.

"You're insane," she whispers. The tears are coming full-force now, but I have to give her credit for not crumpling into a sobbing heap. Yet.

"The proper term is high-functioning antisocial personality disorder."

I swipe a tear from her cheek and place it on my tongue, savouring the salty indignation. Closing my eyes at the taste, I groan obscenely. There really is nothing better than ridding the world of those who take advantage of the most vulnerable. Sometimes, parents are my target if the child shows signs of abuse. I keep detailed notes of my young patients and make sure to inflict the same injuries the children have been subjected to. It's only fair, after all.

Doctor Vaughn finally breaks and lets out a wail, screaming for help as if someone will come to her rescue. She can scream all she likes; there's no one around for miles.

I'm going to enjoy this one. I've already got a plan for her disposal when the job is done. There's such a lovely stretch of bayou nearby and a canoe ready for a moonlit boat ride for two. By the time anyone starts looking for her, the gators will have had their fill.

My secondary mobile rings on the floor, letting out a piercing cry into the tense atmosphere clouding the shed. A grin breaks out on my face. Only one person has this number, and when she calls, I answer. Simple as that.

I pull the gag back over Doctor Vaughn's mouth, somewhat effectively silencing her, and stride in the direction of the device. I pick it up on the third ring. If Olivia is calling, it's serious.

"Hello, Little Thief," I coo into the phone. The same words I said to her when I found her two years after A-levels when I hunted her down in Morocco during her summer holiday from uni. Since then, well, we've kept in close contact when either of us needs to. Just like the old days.

Doctor Vaughn tries screaming for help, as if Olivia will somehow save her. Idiot.

"Hello, Doc."

"What have you got for me today?" I ask.

"Is someone screaming in the background? I can call back in an hour when you're done." Of course she isn't surprised. Olivia strongly suspects my extracurricular activities. She's been on the receiving end of my own brand of torture more times than I can count, but it always ends in satisfaction when it's just the two of us.

"She can wait." I shrug. "It's just a paediatrician who's been very naughty," I say as I look Doctor Vaughn in the eyes and twirl a scalpel between my fingers. Her whimpers behind the gag begin to sound like a woman who has lost all hope.

"I need you."

"Details, Little Thief. When? Where? And what will you give me in exchange for my help?" I ask.

This game has gone on long enough that my final question is no surprise. If I'm closing my paediatric practice to aid Olivia in whatever job she's conjured up, I'm getting something specific out of it.

"What do you want?"

"No, Little Thief, this is too easy if I tell you. Offer what you think my help is worth." I'd come without payment, just because helping her is fun as hell, but she can't know it.

"I'll let you do that thing we talked about."

"Say it."

"If you help me pull this job off, I'll let you cut me until I bleed and it scars, Doc."

My breath catches at her offer.

"Tomorrow. Be at my place for dinner." She pauses. "Zach?"

"Yes?"

"There's something you should know." I stay silent, waiting for her to continue. "The others are coming, too."

"Viraj as well?"

"Yup." I can picture her saying this. The slight shrug of her shoulders, trying to play it off as though this isn't a big deal. Her slight frown, betraying the fact that she knows it is. And the twirling of a pen in her left hand because she's still thinking through everything that can go wrong.

"You know you'll have to keep them in line, right? I'm not going to be as lenient this time around. If they hurt you—again—they die."

Max

Present Day

"I'm sorry, Sir Robinson," I say, meticulously spreading a spoonful of caviar on a perfectly toasted blini as we sit at the Worthington Club, "but selling John Henry's semen is unfortunately not something I can consider. It's either live cover in my stables or nothing."

"I'll consider it, then. I'm not used to this. Last time, when I dealt with your father, he agreed to artificial insemination."

I purse my lips, looking around the members-only club Sir Robinson wanted to meet in. "Well, people often forget that my father and I do things differently. Providing the sperm was taxing for John Henry and had affected his competition performances. Spending time with mares, on the other hand, seems to motivate him. I'm doing what's best for my stallion, as I am sure you understand."

Satisfied with the way the caviar is spread on my blini, I open my mouth and lay them both on my tongue. My eyes close of their own accord as I savour the salty deliciousness exploding on my palate.

I can't help it; I have a penchant for the finest.

"Your father eats caviar the exact same way." I grunt at Robinson's observation. "You both are so focused, it looks like it's a religious experience." In the meantime, the ageing aristocrat carelessly puts a dollop of the black eggs on an unsalted cracker and swallows it like it's a plain marshmallow.

I shrug. "Well, when you're lucky enough to eat things that cost an average person's monthly salary in a mouthful, you should at least take the time to enjoy them." The criticism is barely veiled in my words. I don't particularly like spending time with other horse owners, but it's the price I pay if I want my John Henry to be the start of a dynasty.

For the umpteenth time, my phone vibrates in my pocket. I put it on silent when this conversation started, because even though Sir Robinson will never be my friend, I'm respectful of my business partners and the rules of the club. Respectability is what got me where I am in life.

That, and knowing how to read a room.

Being born Maximillian Arondale IV probably also helped a little.

"So, Sir Robinson," I start again, "about the insemination—" My phone starts buzzing again, and I switch it off. A waiter approaches as soon as I stash the mobile in my pocket again.

"Sir, there's an urgent call for you." He holds out a small black serving tray with a phone in the centre. I pick it up as both he and Sir Robinson stare at me with concern. Who even knows I'm here? This is an exclusive club with the utmost discretion.

"Answer your bloody phone!" comes barreling down the line, and I yank the phone from my ear. *What the fuck, Liv?*

An unknown ringtone blaring from my previously switched off phone cuts me off. Shit. I excuse myself from the table.

Frowning, I pull the offending device out of my pocket. I don't understand how this happened. On the screen, I see that it's the tracker app making all this noise even though my mobile should only vibrate. That damn app.

I close out of it, and barely a second later, the screen lights up again and an incoming video call makes my phone buzz, revealing the grinning face of my favourite thief. She's also the one who sent me all the messages, making that annoying red notification bubble pop like crazy.

"Hello, Liv," I say as I pick up. Holding a finger to my lips, I slip my AirPods out of my pocket, connecting them to the phone so the few club members milling about outside don't hear every detail of our conversation.

"Go ahead," I tell her.

"Finally!" she scolds, pouting at the camera. "Imagine if it was a life or death situation, I'd be completely toast by now."

"If it was a life or death situation, you wouldn't call me," I observe. "Unless you need a private jet for an extraction, there's not much I could do about it. You're welcome, by the way. Also, I told you to stop hacking my phone. Last week, there was a sudden influx of male enhancement emails."

"I didn't. Okay, I did. But using your horse's name for your Google account password is a stupid idea. I was just trying to remind you to stop picking easy passwords."

"And I changed it after you told me that!"

She rolls her eyes. "Yeah, you added 123+ at the end. Do you know how long that took me to guess?"

I chuckle. Olivia is my friend and not someone I bother to keep out of my private stuff. If she wants to find out something, she will, even if my password was nearly uncrackable.

She's just that good at her job. A year after school ended, we met at a café and had a conversation that changed my life. Since then, she's been working on her own for jobs, but I act as her liaison. I missed her that year we weren't in contact, but I wasn't going to risk it all again. Burnt once, shame on you. Burnt twice, no thank you.

My thief friend turns serious, and I only then notice she's wearing a unicorn onesie. "What are you celebrating?" I inquire. Her blue eyes sparkle in excitement at my question. Their shade is unique, a perfect mix of blue and grey with just a dash of green, like raw denim jeans. But the true uniqueness comes from the golden spot in the bottom of her left eye.

Before meeting her, I didn't know what heterochromia was, but I fell in love with it immediately.

"Oh, General Zul fell yesterday. Apparently, certain secrets were leaked to his opponents, allowing them to overthrow him." I smirk. I met a member of the political resistance in Tesken a few months ago at a soiree for some diplomat. He mentioned wanting a change in leadership, and I happened to casually mention Via, an app Olivia's friend, Roark, created. A week later, a notification came through. I did my homework, checking the funding and ensuring legitimacy before passing the job along to Liv. The app runs through the dark web, leaving Olivia and me protected. When the job is done, I facilitate transfers and continue spreading word ever so subtly. I never imagined I would act as a middleman for an unstoppable thief, but here we are. I've been doing it for over a decade now, protecting her identity. Nobody knows who she is, and nobody ever will.

On the screen, Olivia takes a deep breath.

"How quickly can you get here?" she asks. "I was just offered a job, something big, and I'll need you for this. I'd rather not speak of it over the phone, though. Can you come for dinner tomorrow, maybe?"

"Sure. Do you want me to bring something?" It might be short notice, but I still have my manners.

"Whatever you feel like eating."

"Perfect, I'll think about it."

"Oh, and Max?"

"Yes?"

"Get enough food for five." Without giving me time to ask anything else, she blows a kiss at the camera and hangs up.

For a minute, I wonder who the mysterious other three might be. Quickly, it dawns on me. She's bringing us all in.

What the fuck did she say to get Viraj to agree?

Roark

Present Day

"Die, motherfucker, die!" I shout in precipitous victory. It won't be long now.

My hands are wrapped around the throat of the assassin, choking him out as his fingertips scramble on the dirty concrete below us. He thought he was so slick hiding up on the rooftops and picking off my team one by one as showers of bullets took out my men.

Using a gun would have been the most effective way to make sure he stays down, but no, this shitstain needed to die by my hands.

The light fades from his eyes, and his body disappears as he's respawned somewhere else in the video game. My gaming PC glows with RGB lights like my very own celebratory rave.

Team Roark: 1.

Team Douche Canoes: 0.

The timer runs out, and our body count far exceeds theirs. "Well done, mates!" I congratulate my team over our comms as we all cheer for tonight's win.

Whoops and hollers come through the headphones, including play-by-plays of the takedowns.

"Same time next week?" I ask.

"Yep!" HWakowski4H says down the line.

"Cheers, mate!" echoes RipTide96.

I pull off the headset and lean back in my chair as the screen flashes our victory in bright white letters. We took some hits this time but dropped more bodies than we lost, and our ranking is sure to improve on the global leaderboards.

Shoving my chair across my office with a well-placed kick, I roll across the floor and wiggle the mouse on my work computer, bringing it back to life. I tie my long hair into a bun and crack my tattooed knuckles. Time to get to work.

My screens are littered with code, and I've been working on fixing a bug in my latest program. I'm close, I can feel it. Suddenly, the screen to my left flashes in a myriad of colours and glitches. What the fuck?

Rainbows start appearing all over the screen, along with puffy little clouds and, yep... A unicorn.

Fucking Via. The one that got away. I was never going to be her first choice, but four years after we graduated, she popped up on one of my video games and we've been collaborating on apps for her business ever since. Every now and then, I do hacking jobs for her, like the one a couple of nights ago—or was it yesterday?—but otherwise, we just text from afar.

The mythical creature has a horse's body, Olivia's face, and a horn sprouting from her forehead. A little speech bubble appears from the corner of the Olivicorn's mouth.

Get your ass to my place tomorrow for dinner. Got a job. Be there or get the horn.

I laugh at the audacity of this woman hacking a hacker. Sure, we learned how to do it together, but I never quite had a flair for the dramatic like she did. These days, creating my own apps with microtransactions for those five extra lives you just have to have and hacking a bit of data to make prime picks in the stock market are my bread and butter.

The speech bubble disappears, then a new one pops up with an address and a message.

Bring your gear, and no fighting. We're all on the same team.

Why would there be fighting? Wait, *we*? Who's we?

No.

No, no, no, no.

She didn't. Feck, for the love of Christ, tell me she didn't get those assholes involved.

The screen goes black, and before I can respond, she remotely shuts down my entire workstation.

Fucking hell.

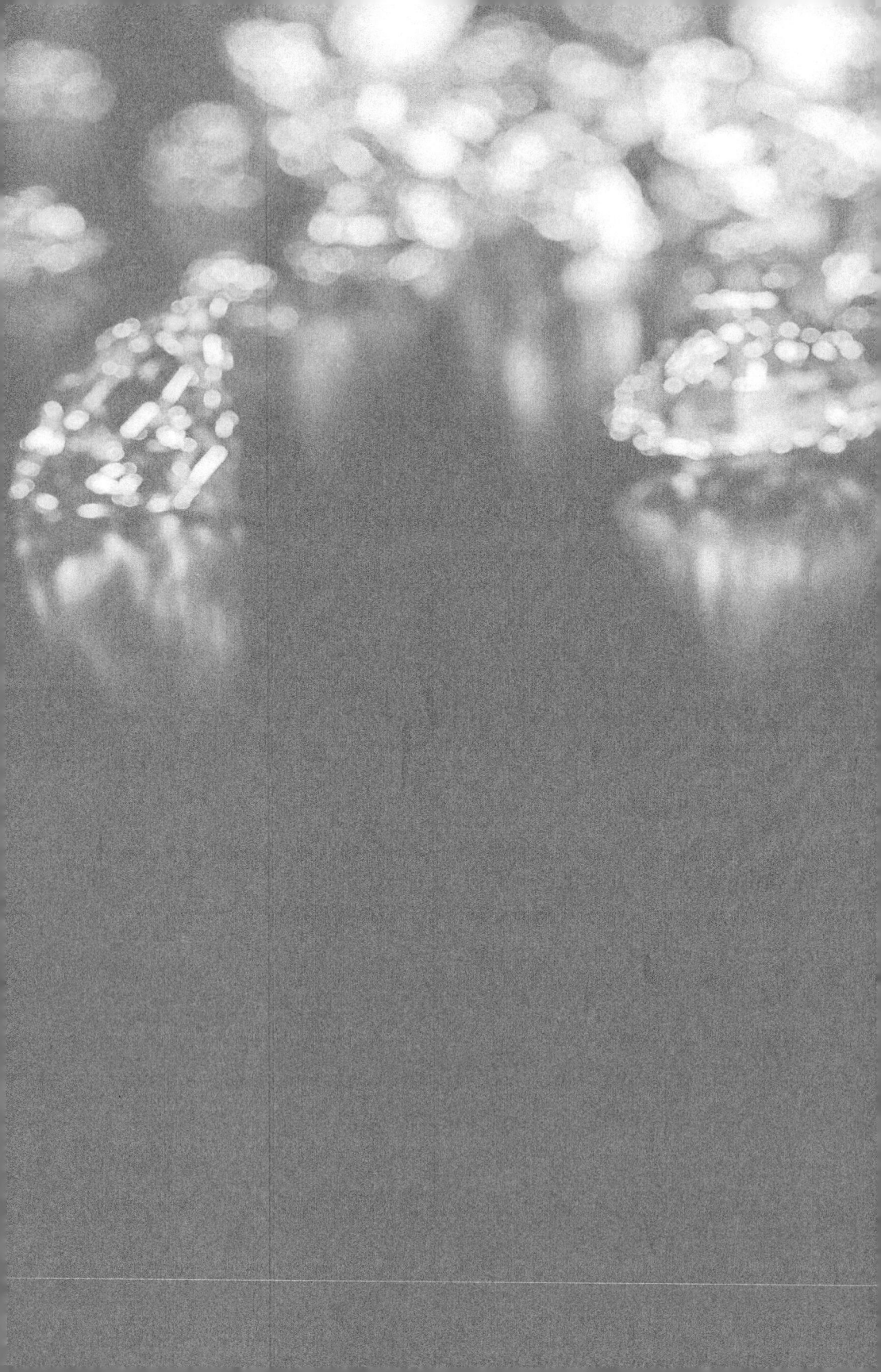

Chapter Five

Olivia
Present Day

Sighing for the millionth time, I go through the options in my walk-in closet yet again. What's a woman supposed to wear when the four people she once loved more than anything come to dinner?

I don't have a particular style. In my line of work, blending in is what matters. Whether that's achieved by looking like a rapper kid, a movie star, or your average girl-next-door, it doesn't matter. My closet has all the options I could ever need.

And it's turning out to be a nightmare.

It doesn't help that the blonde wavy tresses I have on my head decided to have a bad hair day. Why is this happening to me? My hands are clammy and shoulders tight.

I take a deep breath, hoping it'll calm me. Then another one. No one and nothing gets me as nervous as these four.

When in doubt, show off the tattoos. If anything, it will make me feel like the badass bitch I am.

I grab a halter crop top and ripped high-waisted boyfriend jeans, not bothering with shoes since I'm home and nobody wears shoes in my house. It's a simple outfit that I feel comfortable in and shows a considerable amount of skin.

Both my arms are fully tattooed. The left arm is mostly coloured pieces telling stories about where I've travelled. Because I couldn't stop myself and break up the beautiful linework, I was forced to learn how to use waterproof foundation. It pains me to cover them, but for jobs, I need a way to hide what wasn't masked by long sleeves.

My right arm is covered in black and white feminine tattoos because they're cute, and I like them. Then, I have some artwork on my legs, rendered visible through the holes in my jeans.

I pull my hair up in a messy bun, try to get some semblance of order in my thick brows, and decide it's enough. I don't want them to think I've spent hours desperately rifling through my closet deciding on what to wear, even though this is exactly what happened. But they don't need to know that.

I check my phone. Yesterday, Viraj got on his plane like the good boy he is. I made sure I had eyes on the boarding gate of his flight to London and got the confirmation during the night. He should be arriving soon and will probably be in a mood.

Ever the perfect guest, Max will arrive early, since he's bringing the food. Knowing him, it'll be a four-course meal he convinced a Michelin-star restaurant to cook for takeaway. He and I are the only ones really used to fine dining, so he'll use the decorum and endless cutlery items to throw the others off their game. He's the son of a lord, and even if he refuses to be like his father or uncle, he kind of is.

THE CLEANUP

Deciding to thwart his attempts, I head to my dining room and throw a bunch of disposable plates and plastic utensils on the table.

Roark is unpredictable. He might show up early or late, depending on how the work on his app is going. At least, I know his entry will not have hidden purposes. Even though he's a computer genius, he's not calculating. He's smart enough to hack into any system in the world, but his interactions with people are honest, raw.

None of us are truly normal, but Zach is definitely the one furthest from the centre. When he was fifteen, he was diagnosed with a high-functioning antisocial personality disorder. In short, he's a psycho. That's why he left his first school.

He's a paediatrician now. He hates adults—and cats—but Zach thinks that kids are pure and worth saving. If a parent abuses their kid, or is even suspected of doing so, they have a tendency to vanish. Same for the paediatricians who don't do their jobs correctly. I don't know the specifics of what happens to them, and I don't want to either. Plausible deniability and all that.

He's the only one I sometimes take on jobs with me, rather than just ring for assistance. When I'm likely to need him, he closes his practice, reschedules his appointments, and jumps on the first flight that'll take him to my location. The perks of being your own boss, I guess.

Zach also loves getting invited. For someone who's a medical professional with a creed to do no harm, that man does like to inflict pain whenever possible. Who'd have thought a hot doctor with a sadism and blood kink would be on my speed dial? I've lost count of the number of times he's laid me down on his portable examination table and fucked me, despite being hurt and bloody. Only after we both get off will he then fix me up and fuck me again. Cuts are his favourite. He finds the blood pretty, and the stitches even prettier.

I'm not complaining. Since we've started doing this together, I've discovered that orgasms are a great anaesthetic. And an easy one to smuggle through customs, too.

It doesn't hurt—ha, see what I did there—that Zach is gorgeous. And that obsessive vibe is something else.

Contrary to what one might think, he'll probably be the easiest to handle tonight. He thinks in black and white, and doesn't let his mind get clouded by emotions. If neither I nor a kid gets hurt, then he doesn't care. It's been that way since we were teenagers.

The doorbell rings, pulling me out of my daydreaming. It's too early for Max, which means Viraj is here.

It's his first time in my home, and I haven't seen him in person in years. I hack the cameras of his sports award ceremonies all the time. I particularly love the rock climbing ones. The effort needed to climb makes all the veins in his arms pop out and with the tight T-shirts that he wears, it's just about the best forearm porn ever.

Smoothing my hands down my top, I drop them down to my sides and shake out the jitters as I cross my townhouse. Here goes nothing.

I unlock the door and there he is... Viraj is standing at the top of my steps, staring me down with ire in his gaze. It's been a good long while since I've been on the receiving end of that stare. His brows are drawn, and he runs his assessing eyes over my body, taking in my casual attire.

"It's a right shame, Ollie."

I cock a brow at him, barring his entrance to my home with my body. I lean heavily on the door jamb, making it clear I'll not give in until I get an explanation at the cryptic greeting. It's always a game with him—pushing me harder every time, just like he does with his extreme sports. When will he learn I'm not one to be conquered like the mountains he loves so much?

"I imagined you wearing far less in my head." A sly grin creeps across his lips, and I throw my head back in laughter. Do I also make sure to show off the long lines of my neck in the process? Absolutely.

"You wish, V. You've got to earn that."

I push the door open wider and turn on my heel, leading the way into the house. "Leave your shoes at the door."

Viraj enters, kicking them off and pulling his suitcase in behind him. The door shuts, and I spin, dropping onto my circular sofa and waiting for him to join me. I plan to explain the job as soon as they're all here. If they don't kill each other first, that is.

He crosses the soft grey area rug and moves a purple throw pillow from the sofa before sitting down directly opposite me across the round table in the middle.

"So," he starts. Never one to mince words, he dives in. "Where are the other assholes?"

Glancing at my mobile, I zoom out on the map and see three dots steadily moving closer to our location. If anyone other than Zach and I had access to the tracker information, I doubt the rest would have agreed to them so easily. "They'll be here soon. Max is about half an hour away."

"How is Maxi Pad?" he asks derisively, conjuring up the nickname Max hated during our school days.

I shoot a warning glare in his direction. Always one to push boundaries, Viraj and Max never saw eye to eye on anything at all, least of all me. His eyes flash with challenge, but I cut it off at the knees before he gets any more stupid ideas.

"He'll have to tell you himself. You will watch your tongue, Viraj. None of this will work if you can't put your dicks away. And believe me, you're going to want in on this one."

He leans forward and rests his elbows on his denim-clad knees, and I know I've hooked him. I just need to reel him in.

My phone dings in my hand, and I turn it over, smiling at the fortune that just landed in my palm. Viraj opens his mouth and starts to ask what it is when I shush him.

I pulled some major strings this morning, and my offer has just been accepted. "Stay here. I'll be back in a minute."

Telling him not to snoop would be like telling the sun not to shine. Good thing anything of importance is locked up tight in my office. I leave the lounge, take the stairs two at a time, and barrel into my workspace.

I open the email again and read over the details as I sit down in front of my computer. Pulling up the email server, I reply on the keyboard, confirming the job and e-signing the contract.

Natasha Volkov's jewellery chain, Diamond Desires, has shops here in London in the high street. I scoped out their current cleaning company's contract and contacted their business manager in England, underbidding their current contracted cleaner's contract by thirty per cent.

I call Miranda, my general manager for the area, and she answers on the second ring.

"Yes, Ms Wraith? How can I help you?" she asks, despite me asking her to call me Olivia a hundred times.

"Good evening, Miranda. We've just secured a contract for the five Diamond Desires jewellery shops around London. I'm forwarding you their locations and needs. I'll be handling the shops with my own team for the first couple weeks to ensure we're doing a thorough job, so I want a rotating schedule. Pull everyone you can or hire more cleaners if needed. Once I've cleaned all the shops, assign a team."

"Yes, Ms Wraith. Consider it done," she answers quickly. There's a reason she's been my manager for the last five years. She works quickly and efficiently, rarely needing to bring a problem to my inbox.

I hang up and pull up our scheduling spreadsheets after emailing the details to Miranda. I watch as her mouse hovers, scheduling employees and adding us to the rotation as I asked.

An email from her comes in a few minutes later with her suggested schedule and three new potential employees. I check their resumes and confirm my approval.

Things settled, but nerves still on high alert for the impending dinner, I cross the office and open the door when my security system alerts me of an arrival. I step into the hall only to hear yelling coming from downstairs.

Oh goody, they must all be here.

The door auto-locks behind me with a quiet beep, and I turn

towards the stairs, straightening my shoulders as a delectable scent wafts up to me.

Showtime, Olivia. How hard can it be? I slip my phone into my back pocket and descend the stairs into the chaos waiting for me.

Roark is standing stock-still, his shoulders tense as a Henley shirt stretches over the broad expanse. His hair is pulled back into his usual man bun, a few gunmetal grey earrings decorate his lobes, matching the one on his nostril, and his legs are braced in a fighting stance as he stares down Zach.

The good doctor is relaxed, one foot tapping on the marble tile underfoot as he looks passively around the space. He takes notice of me at the bottom of the staircase, and his eyes flash dangerously, all at once filled with promises and threats.

"I like what you've done with the place, Olivia," he says, rubbing it in that he's the only one who's been here since I moved in.

Roark whips his head in my direction, his shoulders relaxing as he drinks me in.

"Play nice, Zach," I chide.

"Oh, Little Thief. You know I always play so nicely." He drags out the last word, eliciting a shiver from me.

My Irish hacker looks around the luxury townhouse and his accent washes over me. "Things sure have changed since we were the scholarship kids at school, haven't they?" Roark is right. We were the outsiders. The ones our schoolmates loved to tease because we didn't have the resources they did. While I worked my ass off to give myself the life I wanted, he internalised it.

He has the means to live as he wishes, but refuses on principle—preferring his small home outside of Dublin. But he has his indulgences like all of us do. He kitted out his bottom floor with all the tech he could possibly want, bought and converted the house next door into his gym, and, apparently, finds joy in throwing axes at targets.

I run my eyes from Roark's bearded jaw to his boots, glad to see he left his weapons at home for this visit. The words exchanged tonight are guaranteed to be sharp enough already.

"Shoes off." I hear rummaging in the kitchen and take off to investigate, leaving the two of them and praying to a deity I don't believe in that Zach doesn't kill Roark for fun.

Max has his back to me as he pulls dishes from the cabinets in my kitchen.

"What are you doing?" Viraj asks. "Ollie already got the plates." He waves a hand to the paper plates and plastic cutlery and catches sight of me on the other side of the island.

"One does not eat this kind of meal on *disposable* plates," Max volleys back as he grabs the stack at the top of the cabinet. "It would be a crime against Chef Michele."

"They do if they refuse to do dishes and clean up after the four of you," I answer back.

Max spins around, almost losing a plate from the top of the pile.

"Watch it, Maxi Pad." Viraj sneers.

"Kindly shut the fuck up, V-Card," Max responds in that posh accent of his as he faces Viraj.

"Gentlemen, you will behave," Zach says from behind me as I feel the warmth of his body at my back. The two of them look over my head, where Doc rests his chin on my crown as his hands wrap around my waist.

Male posturing at its finest, ladies and gentlemen. All we need now is a tape measure, and the night will be complete.

I step out of Zach's embrace, which he makes difficult by tightening his fingers on my hips just enough to bruise before letting me go, and I lean across the counter to lift the covers on the food containers.

The first holds chilled prosciutto and melon, with a smaller container inside filled with what looks like crumbled feta cheese. The second has roast pork, shredded and then shaped into rounds over potatoes au gratin with a boat of truffle cream sauce next to it. The third holds our dessert, which, if the guys don't kill each other, I'm really looking forward to. Maybe I should have dessert first, just to make sure I get to have some. It's sugared figs and candied plums over ice cream, with spun sugar resembling birds' nests on top.

It's a far cry from the simple sandwiches and juice Roark and I used to share during our study sessions in school.

I groan at the sight, and if everyone weren't already looking at me, they certainly would be now. I feel their eyes devouring me, and I can't blame them. That sounded sexual, even to my own ears.

Whatever. Own it, Olivia.

What was it I told Eleanor I would use to get them to work together? Sex, threats, and hypnosis.

Might as well start with the one I'm most excited about.

Chapter Six

Olivia
Year Twelve
October

The first month of classes has flown by. It doesn't seem overly difficult yet, but the required reading list is sure to keep me up all hours. I need a fucking study plan.

Eleanor is sitting on her bed with her headphones on, flicking through one of her books as the music blasts loud enough for me to hear. I love music, but Maroon 5 really isn't my favourite for study time. Dance party? Sure. Learning about calculus? Not so much.

Putting my earbuds in, I try to block out the sound for fifteen minutes, but since they aren't noise-cancelling, I can't help but hear "Won't Go Home Without You" drifting over from Eleanor. Honestly, the lyrics always seemed a bit stalkery to me.

I yank my shitty earbuds out and gather my books. *Focus! Calculus, Olivia.*

Eleanor looks up from her bed at my abrupt flurry of movement. She pulls one speaker away from her ear. "Hey, you heading down to lunch?"

"No, I need a change of scenery. I'm going to get a jump on these assignments. It's Sunday, so I'll grab food and head off somewhere."

"Yeah, they should still have sandwiches and stuff you can take away," she confirms.

"Excellent." I stuff my books in my backpack and sling it over my shoulder. Wearing a pair of jeans and a baggy T-shirt, I don't exactly look like a prestigious boarding school student, but I feel that itchy need to move. Perhaps I'll get a couple sandwiches and head out into the school gardens to do my homework.

Thank god there's no uniform enforcement on the weekends.

I take off and head for the dining hall. There, I grab two sandwiches and two bottles of juice. Who knows how long I'm going to be working? I might need the extra sustenance, and I've never been the best at planning my food intake. I eat when I'm hungry, but when I'm focused, I forget about mealtimes.

Pushing through the doors at the back of the building, I find myself in the fresh early autumn air. The benches and tables are crowded as students enjoy the atmosphere and gossip about whatever hit the rumour mill this week. I'd bet a few are stories about the new kids, but I couldn't be bothered, honestly.

I wind my way through the gardens, finally getting far enough away that the chatter starts to fade. Below my feet is a track that's slightly less used than the others, so when I push through a hedge to follow where it leads, a gasp gets caught in my throat. There, at a lone table surrounded by shrubbery, is my neighbour Roark.

His head whips up at my intrusion, and he slides his glasses farther up his nose. "What are you doing here?" he asks.

"Trying to get away from Maroon 5 and the chatter over there," I say, waving my hand towards the students in the gardens.

"Maroon 5?" he asks, a small smile tilting his lips. "What, are they here at the school?"

"Don't be ridiculous. They're everywhere," I whisper, looking over my shoulder playfully as if the band has followed me. Roark lets out an amused laugh, and I watch as his smile transforms his face. His deep blue eyes fill with mirth, and the cute freckles on his nose make him seem younger than he is.

Every time I've seen him this past week, he's either got his nose in a book, or his eyes are darting around nervously.

"No, but seriously. Eleanor loves them, and I just can't listen to the same lyrics over and over again anymore. I came out here for some quiet. Can I study with you?" I ask. He looks like he's about to say no, so I sweeten the pot. "I won't even talk to you. But, I *do* have an extra sandwich from the dining hall. You won't have to interrupt your study time to go get food."

He looks down at the mess of books before him, then back at me. "I just have one question," he starts. I wave a hand to encourage him to continue. "What kind of sandwich?"

I laugh. Who knew Roark had jokes? "One ham and one chicken salad. Your pick. Oh, and did I mention juice? Apple or orange?" I waggle my brows, like that will swing things in my favour.

"Ugh, fine," he says, shoving some books to one side, so there's space for me. "I'll have the ham sandwich and the apple juice."

Grinning, I pull the food from my bag, hand it over, and open up my books. Roark thanks me and gets back to his work with a single-minded focus. I do the same, and before I know it, the sun is starting to go down, and a chill is sweeping through the gardens.

A black cat jumps up on the table between us, and I almost knock my juice bottle to the ground.

"Woah, who is this?" I ask, staring at the fat beast as he starts pawing at my books.

Roark looks up from his stuff. "Oh, that's Bellatrix. She's been here for about a year now. Most students sneak her food, and she's always wandering around the gardens, looking for her next victim."

I laugh at that. "Why is she called Bellatrix?"

"Someone named her for that Harry Potter character, and it just stuck. She's mellowed out, but she was feisty in the beginning."

The sounds of the other students have completely faded, and with the tall bushes around us, it's getting darker in our little hidden corner. "Roark?" I say, pulling his focus from the books in front of him.

"Hmm?" His eyes land on me for a second before being pulled back towards the text on the page.

"It's getting dark. We should head in before we strain our eyes." I'm not particularly worried about that, but soon we won't be able to see a thing.

He looks around as if coming out of a daze. "Oh, you're right. Hell, I still have a few chapters to go through today." He sighs heavily and rubs a hand along his sharp jaw.

"I do too. Let's pack it up and move to the library. Or the computer lab? Eleanor said you liked to study there," I offer.

"Yeah, that sounds good." Roark stands and stretches his arms over his head. His back cracks at the movement, and I wince at the sound. That didn't seem pleasant. His shirt rides up a bit on his abdomen, and I see a sliver of skin, sending a rush of heat towards my face. I tilt my head back down at the table and start packing up my stuff as Roark does the same.

As we move to leave our little clearing, he pulls the hedge to the side and ushers me through it first. I follow the small path with Roark at my back, and we head towards the glowing windows of St Stephen's. The students have all gone inside, aside from a few stragglers, and I rub my arms to keep them warm as we cross the gardens. Even though it's early autumn, this is England, and I should know to always bring a jacket.

As I reach the steps, Roark leans forward and pulls the door open for me. His shy smile is sweet, and I return one in kind.

"Mr O'Sullivan, what a pleasant surprise," a booming voice says.

Roark freezes for just a second, but it's enough for me to figure

The Cleanup

out he's either scared or intimidated by this guy. I look at the source of the voice and find a middle-aged man with rich brown hair, woven with strands of grey at his temple, a tailored navy suit, and a designer emblazoned pocket square.

"Hello, Lord Arondale," Roark says next to me. He extends his hand, and Lord Arondale clasps it warmly.

"How is the term going for you so far?" he asks.

"Good, sir. Thank you. I was just studying in the gardens," Roark says as he looks back at me. I tilt my head, hinting that I can get the hell out of here as he talks with whoever this is. He shakes his head slightly, so I keep my feet planted.

"Excellent. Excellent," Arondale says. "Do you need anything?"

"Oh, no, sir. I'm okay. The school has everything for assignments," Roark mutters, and I notice his accent is harder to detect when he's speaking to Lord Arondale.

"Dad, come on. The headmaster is waiting," a younger voice says from the other side of the room. Max walks up to us, and it's then that I put it all together. Roark is here on the Arondale scholarship. Max's family is paying for his tuition.

"That old codger can wait for a second while I check up on his star pupil," Lord Arondale says as he beams at Roark. He misses the look that crosses Max's face with those words. I have a few classes with the younger Arondale, and while I don't have time to chat in lectures or even outside of them, I have noticed that he takes his studies seriously. He's a bit of a class clown, but still seems to care about his grades.

Roark blushes at the compliment, his cheeks going ruddy with the praise. "Roark, go shopping at one of the local electronics shops on me. Get whatever you need for your studies. I know you have plans to go into Computer Science. You can't do that without the latest and greatest."

Max seems to have had enough. "Right. He'd probably buy the new Playstation or something. Not very educational."

This is going very badly, very quickly. Lord Arondale turns

towards his son. "You mean the same one you asked for last week? If your grades were as impressive as Roark's, perhaps I'd have offered to buy you one as well." Max's shoulders stiffen at the words, and as his father spins back to face us, both of them straighten their jackets in the same exact way. Creepy.

"Get whatever you want. Whether it's the new Playstation or a new laptop. Send the bill to my secretary. You've earned it."

By this point, Max's cheeks are flaming red, and Lord Arondale bids Roark goodbye as he turns and starts walking towards the administration wing. Max follows him after sending a scathing look at Roark in his wake.

"Bloody hell, that family scares the crap out of me," Roark says on an exhale.

I step forward and rest a hand on his bony shoulder. "Yeah, I can see why. Come on, let's finish these next few chapters. Now that I know you're the best in class, you can bet your ass I'm claiming you as my new study buddy." Roark laughs.

"Get used to this face," I tease. "You're going to be so sick of me by the end of the year."

Chapter Seven

Olivia
Present Day

"Max, stop looking at the paper plate like it's going to bite you and fucking eat," I scold. My strategy worked a little too well, and now Max looks despondent, staring at the food in front of him with a pout on his lips.

His very kissable lips.

He's wearing a white turtleneck that looks like cashmere under a navy blue sport coat and a pair of tan trousers. His hair is artistically tousled, and short, neatly trimmed stubble covers his strong jaw. I bet his whole outfit costs more than my dining table.

Everything about Max screams power and aristocracy. His gestures are measured, and he never speaks out of turn. He knows every unspoken rule of every single high society in the world, and his family has been part of the British nobility for generations. They probably had a hand in creating St Stephen's, and the Arondale scholarship they've created has given dozens of geniuses a chance to thrive.

That's why he's such a great middleman for my jobs. I need the high-paying customers only he's capable of bringing in.

Viraj's family is insanely rich, too, but they're new money, and Max loves to remind the Indian lawyer that he doesn't know the societal norms for the wealthy.

Shaking my head, I turn my eyes away from Max to take in all the others. My team. My heavily dysfunctional, completely deranged mess of a team.

I grab the pen I'd previously laid down on the table and start spinning it between the fingers of my left hand. Getting them all to sit after the mess in the kitchen was a challenge, up until Zach started growling, then they all scurried away like scared little mice.

"So," Roark starts, laying a hand on the twirling pen and giving my fingers a slight squeeze, "I think now's the moment you tell us what was so urgent and secretive you couldn't tell us about it over the phone or via text."

I nod. "To make a long story short, Interpol screwed up. Ellie was here yesterday and—"

"Look how cute," Viraj interrupts, earning a glare from Max. "Ellie and Ollie are still besties."

"Stop it," I snap right as Max tells him to shut up. "And if you cut me off every other sentence, this dinner will last a year, and I'm pretty sure nobody here wants that."

"Of course not," Zach agrees. "Your bed is a much more comfortable place to spend time, Little Thief."

If my looks could kill, he'd be dead right now. It won't take much to send this dinner into a tailspin, and he's not helping.

Question: If you suspect the person annoying you to be a serial killer, is it still unethical to murder him when he's being a smartass? Discuss, you have two hours.

But at least, while Roark, Viraj, and Max are busy glowering at our resident doctor, they shut up, so I take advantage of the silence to continue. "Ellie was here yesterday and told me there's been a change of leadership in the Volkov family Bratva. The new boss murdered the old one, which isn't very surprising. Now, the plot twist is that the new boss used to be the old boss's wife, and her underlings aren't too happy she's in charge. Her name is Natasha Volkov, and she is, in appearance, every bit the fashionista trophy wife. But her actions already tell us she's as smart as she is ruthless. She managed to acquire a bunch of confidential data from Interpol and is using it to make sure her newfound control doesn't slip through her fingers."

"And why is that our problem?" Viraj asks.

"Ellie was part of the team that lost the data. They're all in trouble."

V scrubs his jaw with his hand and starts poking holes. "But you mentioned infiltrating the Monaco Grand Prix. It's in two months. That gives Mrs Volkov a shit tonne of time to make a billion copies that we'll never be able to retrieve."

"It would, if it weren't for the encryption method of the data. Have you guys ever heard of quantum data storage?"

Max

Present Day

Watching Olivia lead Viraj exactly where she wants him reminds me why I find her intellect so hot.

Liv straightens her back, launching herself into an explanation.

"To make sure the data didn't fall into the wrong hands, Interpol encrypted it inside the atomic structure of a diamond. It's not a well-known technique, but it makes the information virtually eternal. Diamonds are the hardest material known to date, so erosion doesn't impact them. They're small enough to be easily transported and hidden. Plus, the specific type of diamond necessary for data storage must have very controlled flaws in its atomic structure, which means they have to be artificial, hence not that valuable, which makes it an asset to go through customs."

A stunned silence follows her words.

This is a bad idea.

"Basically, we're stealing a diamond?" I ask.

"Yes." Her unique eyes meet mine unflinchingly.

"Liv, this will be the first time you've ever stolen something people will miss. Usually, you can copy-paste things out of computers, but this... Are you really qualified for this?" This is not a lack of confidence in her abilities. I've been the one booking her jobs for over a decade, and I know for a fact she doesn't usually accept the ones where stealing a physical object is part of the deal. She recovers secrets and rumours, only immaterial things—which can do just as much damage in the right hands.

"It's not the first time she's done something like this." Of course Roark would have her back. He's always been her obedient little puppy. He and Liv exchange a knowing look, and her lips tilt up.

"School doesn't count, guys!" I throw my hands up in exasperation. "This is the real mafia, and someone could really get hurt."

"That's why I'm here," Zach says. "My little thief likes it when I put her back together. I make her scream in pain and in pleasure."

"First off," Viraj says, "she's not your anything, psycho—"

"That's not what she says when it's just the two of us."

Viraj is breathing hard now, visibly struggling to keep his cool. "As I said, Ollie is her own person, and if she thinks we can pull this off, I trust her."

What are the odds he's saying this just because it's in direct opposition to what I said? "Oh, if we have the 'Adrenaline God' on our side, then, everything will be fine," I snark.

"Why the Grand Prix?" Roark asks, his rumbling voice stopping our bickering.

"It's the one and only confirmed time Natasha will leave Russia in the next two months," Liv explains. "And even though Monaco is locked up tighter than a nun's vagina, it's still better than stealing from a mafia boss on her turf."

"We'll need tickets, then. It's not that easy to get in," Viraj says.

"Well, it is if you know the right people," I say while looking at my perfectly manicured nails.

"Or if *your father* knows the right people," Viraj counters.

Liv is devouring the contents on her aberration of a paper plate and watching us with amused eyes. "I'll tell you what. Whenever we get a solid lead on how to get our hands on that diamond, I'll fuck the person who finds said lead."

Four pairs of eyes immediately focus on her. I'm not sure this will stop the infighting. If anything, it is likely to make it worse. The competition between the four of us for her attention has always been ruthless. So much so that when we asked her to finally pick, she chose the one person she said she'd never regret picking.

Herself.

"Four VIP tickets to the 2022 Monaco Grand Prix, coming right up!" I announce cheerfully. "Surely the Adrenaline God can get his own through his own merit, since apparently he's above using my connections."

"Max," Liv scolds, "I said 'true leads.' As in, they have to solve problems, not create more. I do not fuck people that are pains in my ass."

Zach's lips twist in a devious smile. "But you like a little pain in your ass."

Liv scowls at him. "Shut up, Zach."

"Did you guys know I put in her coil?" the jackass continues anyway, talking about her IUD. "That day was fun. I literally rearranged her organs."

Liv shivers, and by the looks of it, not in pain or disgust.

Viraj's knuckles are turning white under the pressure of gripping his chair. "Is now really the time to dredge things up?" he spits out.

"When would be better for you, Viraj? Let me censure myself for your comfort, please. I insist," Zach says with sarcasm that shocks the hell out of me. He's not really apt at reading the emotions of others, but he must have picked up some tricks in recent years.

"Enough," Roark grumbles out. He always was the best of us. Not that we'd ever fully admit it to ourselves, let alone say it out loud.

And just like the old days, V resorts to name-calling. "Shut it, Lucky Charms."

Roark slams a fist down on the table, and if the cups weren't made of plastic, they would have shattered on their way down. Wine spills across the table, and a fork that snuck under his fist flings a bit of potato up to the ceiling, only for it to fall right back down on Liv's dessert plate, smashing her spun sugar nest and embedding in the sugared plum.

"Oh, for fuck's sake. I knew I should have had dessert first," she grumbles.

"Now look what you assholes have done," Zach snaps upon seeing the frown on Olivia's face. Ah, fuck.

"You've made her sad. Little Thief, do you want me to take care of them?" he asks as he swaps dessert plates with her.

"Take care of us?" Roark asks in challenge. Zach is tall, but Roark is broad and muscled. I'd put money on the Irishman in a fight if I didn't know Zach's willingness to abandon all sense of self-preservation and fight dirty. The outcome is all that matters to him. Well, that, and Olivia.

"No, Doc. But thank you," Olivia says, tucking into her new ice cream.

She looks around the table, careful to make eye contact with each of us before speaking. "There's another reason you're here," she starts.

THE CLEANUP

"We've only got two months to plan and pull this off. We need to work together. Here. And then again in Monaco. You'll all be moving in tonight."

Zach grins maliciously. Roark and V exchange looks of disbelief while I stare at Olivia, my gaze unwavering.

"My room will remain my own. There are guest rooms for you to use, so don't get any ideas about any favouritism. I meant what I said. I will reward leads and not tolerate asshole behaviour. Well"—she scoffs, side-eying Zach and Viraj—"no more than necessary. I know some of you can't help it."

Zach's smile gets wider, and Viraj's frown deepens. Yeah, she was talking about those two for sure. Couldn't be me; I'm a delight.

"Your rooms are on the first floor. You boys are already behind, as this evening, we got confirmation on our first lead, brought to you by yours truly. Therefore, I'll be fucking myself tonight," Olivia states as the rest of us stare at her with varying amounts of incredulity.

I clear my throat to ask if this will be open to spectators when she cuts her eyes to me, effectively knowing my thoughts. "No, you are not welcome to watch.

"Get some rest, gentlemen. Tomorrow, we leave for a cleaning/recon job at four in the morning." With that awful bit of news, Olivia stands, tucks her pen behind her ear as she tilts her head at all of us, and leaves the table. "And someone clean up this mess," she calls over her shoulder and clicks something on her phone. The sound of locks engaging sound out through the townhouse, and I realize she just locked us the fuck inside.

"Not it!" V shouts and puts his finger on his nose.

Roark and I call, "Not it," while Zach does absolutely nothing.

"You idiots. Doing nothing won't get you Olivia's sweet pussy." He shoves his chair back, carefully moves the uneaten desserts to the sideboard, gathers the tablecloth at the corners on his side, and folds them towards the middle. Picking up the whole thing like a sack of presents from Father Christmas, he hauls it over his shoulder and goes into the kitchen, only returning to pick up the desserts so he can hand-deliver them to Olivia. He's the only one who's actually been here before and knows the way. That he's been here when he doesn't even live in the city and I do, grates on my nerves.

Is he right? I realise I might have to change tactics to finally have a shot with Liv.

Looking at Roark and Viraj, I see the two of them having the same epiphany. Olivia has just offered us an opportunity to get what we've each always wanted. Her. Sure, she only offered sex, but it's only a few steps from sex to finally having the girl of my dreams. I have faith that once she crosses that line with me, she'll never want to let me go. The ladies usually love my considerable assets.

Ever since I said those nasty things to her on our last day of school, I've been plagued by regrets. We've been friends and colleagues since our reconciliation a year after we traded barbs, but she never implied she was open to us being more.

Now the question is, do I want to risk eleven years of partnership on the off chance she still feels something for me? I don't see her very often—only when the job strictly requires it—but I still consider her one of my closest friends. My world is eminently superficial, and in the middle of it, Liv is a breath of fresh air. I need her.

Then again, friends can sleep together and stay friends. Winning her favour wouldn't mean anything had to change between us.

Plus, she must be wild in bed. For once, I would love to sleep with a woman who doesn't keep worrying about breaking a nail. My cock twitches as I think about what I'd want to do to her. Could she take me whole? Would she claw at my back as I stretch her? Fuck, I have to think with my upper head or the others will beat me to it.

Decision made, I slap my palms on my thighs. I don't want to sit around with the competition, so I stand, straightening my velvet blue sport coat, and follow Olivia's instructions to find my room. I need to make some calls before disappearing off the map entirely. John Henry will need seeing to, and I want to make sure Sir Robinson doesn't pressure my replacement into artificial insemination.

Climbing the stairs, I can't help but admire the townhouse. Modern luxury, clean lines, but it feels... cold.

I reach the first floor and follow the hallway. There are four doors. Excellent. Privacy is best for my sleep. The slightest sound tends to wake me these days. Irritatingly, my father said the same happened to him when he hit thirty.

Opening the first door on my right, I find a bathroom with a door leading to what is probably a bedroom. Okay, so only three rooms. Two of those suckers are going to have to double up. I turn and open the first door to the left. Another bathroom.

Oh, Liv. You have got to be kidding me.

"Fuck," I mutter.

Sure enough, each of the other rooms has bunk beds. Bloody bunk beds. We're *all* doubling up. At least each room has its own en-suite bathroom, thank the lord.

I spend the next thirty minutes in blessed silence, which I know will be disappearing momentarily as three sets of feet climb up the staircase. I listen as Viraj makes the same discovery I did earlier.

"I am *not* bunking with *him*." V seethes, barely lowering his voice.

Roark responds, keeping the peace, "I'll bunk with Max. You and Zach have fun."

Grumbles of agreement echo in the hallway, and Roark opens the door. He heaves out a sigh and shakes his head. "Look, Max. I've got about five stone on you. You're going to have to take top bunk unless you're cool with the possibility of this thing crashing down. And I doubt Olivia would keep me around long if I killed one of you."

"She does have an unhealthy attachment to Zach. If you're going to hulk-smash someone, make it him," I mutter as I roll off the lower bed. Olivia was considerate as fuck leaving clothes in the closet, an array of phone chargers on the dresser, and even toiletries in little packs in the adjoining bathroom.

Everything is immaculately clean, and if the floor wasn't that gorgeous—and hard as fuck—marble tile, I'd sleep there rather than the bunk bed like a child. I already checked, by the way; she secured the mattresses to the frame, so I can't just toss one down for the night.

Fuck. Leaving at four in the morning sounds like a nightmare. I need my beauty sleep.

I settle onto the mattress of the top bunk and scroll on my Facebook app. I'm reading through someone's sob story that they felt the need to broadcast to their friends list when the internet cuts out. I check my signal and find absolutely nothing.

"Lights out, boys!" I hear Olivia call from the hallway. "No internet and no data until after work tomorrow!"

How the fuck did she do that?

It's a question I've asked myself a million times over the last fifteen years. The lights in the room flick off, and my mobile dies, despite having nearly a full charge.

What. The. Fuck?

"Aw, come on, Liv!" Roark shouts from below me. "First my workstation and now my phone?"

"To bed! Can't have you sleeping on the job tomorrow."

"It's not even ten o'clock," I groan out. Roark agrees, but doesn't initiate conversation. Why would he? It's not like we're particularly close.

I'm counting the ceiling tiles I can barely make out in the dim moonlight, when a buzz filters through the silence.

My mobile!

I scramble through my sheets, looking for where I dropped the fucker. I find it, except it's not on. "Is that your phone?" I ask Roark.

"No, it's still dead. I can't believe she killed them. That's modern-day torture," he complains. "I hope to fuck she turns them back on in the morning."

"What is that?" I ask, listening intently to the vibration.

The sound is getting louder, then there's a thump above my head.

"Ah, yes," Olivia moans.

True to her word, she's fucking herself tonight. And while we may not be spectators, we are certainly her audience.

"Is that...?" Roark trails off.

"Well, it's certainly not internet porn. Now shush."

Olivia's moans get louder, and my cock grows with every sound above me. Within minutes, I'm aching for her, and the sweats I took from the drawer earlier feel like they're two sizes too small.

Roark is breathing loudly below me, and as much as I want to tell him to shut the fuck up, I'm certain my own panting is just as loud as I listen to the woman of my dreams bring herself to orgasm directly above me.

The buzzing intensifies, the vibrator clearly having been switched to a higher setting. A piercing shriek sounds above me along with pounding on the floor. I imagine her spread on the floor, her thighs wide and quivering at the intensity as her head falls back in bliss, her hair spilling onto the pristine white flooring between us.

Two knocks reverberate above me, and the sound fades away. My palm is around my cock, pumping at the visions in my head and the sounds of my Olivia. Just when I think I can't take any more, the buzzing starts again, but this time it's farther away.

She's doing the same above the other room, I'm sure of it.

The sound is so faint, I'm almost certain I'm imagining it, but no, it's there if the sudden door rattling is any indication.

"Little Thief! Unlock the fucking doors so I can fuck you!" Zach shouts as he kicks the door to his room across the hall.

The buzzing stops, and for his bad behaviour, she repositions herself above our room to continue round two.

"No!" Zach roars.

"Yes," Olivia moans. "*Fuck* yes!"

My hips move, thrusting into my waiting fist faster and faster as I listen to the vixen just above me. Roark is doing exactly the same thing if the slight movements of the bed frame below me are to be believed.

Olivia screams the house down with her release, and I follow right after with a groan that shakes me to my very core as I spill onto my stomach. Roark is seconds behind me, and I know it's something the two of us will never speak of.

When the buzzing in my ears dies down, I hear Viraj talking Zach down and encouraging him to go back to bed. "I promise, Zach. You can yell at her tomorrow morning over some waffles or some shit. There'd better be waffles."

Good to see some things have never changed. Viraj and his love of food knows no bounds. His very first "date" with Olivia was over waffles way back then. He made sure I knew it was happening too; the prick.

As I rub the back of my head against the linens, something catches my eye. Oh look, she even left tissues next to the pillows, knowing we'd need a cleanup after her performance. I tuck my cock back in the sweats and climb down, heading to the en-suite bathroom on unsteady feet to clean up. Fuck, if any of us needed motivation, Olivia just gave it to us in spades.

Chapter Eight

Viraj
Year Twelve
November

"Maa, I promise I'm studying," I say for the third time since this phone call started. She insists I call her *Mum*, but whenever I'm annoyed, it slips to the more common *Maa*.

"Fine, fine. But remember, this company isn't going to run itself when we retire. You need a good education before you take over," Mum reminds me. Again.

No matter how often I've said I didn't want to run their company or end up on their board, she doesn't hear me. So I've stopped arguing about it. My parents' company has done very well over the past few years, but it doesn't interest me. My cousin, Swaroop, on the other hand, is already their intern. He's a good choice to take up the reins one day. More importantly, he actually wants to.

"Are you ready for your classes this morning?" she asks.

"Yes, Mum. But I have to get back to studying for this literature mock exam on Friday. Some of these stories are told in some form or another when kids are younger. The others already have a leg up, so I need to learn the material. I gotta go."

"Okay. Study hard, Raj. Call your father later. He has a friend in London he wants you to meet with." Sure, and start hearing about how that man's daughter and I would make a lovely couple. The international marriage market, ladies and gentlemen. "And don't forget to visit Dai Ma this weekend," she chides, talking about the guardian my parents sent with me when I moved here. She lives in the hamlet near the school, but we check in daily. No way would my parents send me here without having some kind of adult supervision.

"I will. Bye, Mum." I hang up after her own farewell and at least two more reminders to eat my vegetables, consume curds before exams as a recipe for success, and head to bed. If she were here, my mother would scold me for foregoing my nightly prayer, but I don't really believe in all that stuff anyway. My parents didn't love that the best school for me was a Catholic one, but the rigorous academic program, their track record for students' grades on the A-levels, and connections I would make, framed St Stephen's as the prime pick of schools for me.

Turning my phone off and stuffing it in my desk drawer, I drop my head into my waiting palms. No phones during school hours is a tempting rule to break, so I never bother to take it with me.

I love my parents. I do. But they've had my life mapped out for me since their company took off. Never, not once, have they asked what I actually want to do. Not that I could answer them; I'm seventeen. My mind cycles through possible future careers faster than I can keep track. But I plan to stay in England. Or go to America. Or, hell, maybe South Africa.

One thing is sure, I don't want to do my job sitting behind a desk and listening to people bring me problems all day long. I need challenges that I have a hand in solving, not just delegating this and that to the next person down the chain of command. Though I can name one good thing about my parents having more money than they know what to do with—I get my own room here at St Stephen's, and can do all the extreme sports I love. I gather up my books, shove them into my bag, and lace up my shoes.

Flicking off the lights, I step through the door, locking it behind me, and head down to breakfast, sending flirty winks and cheeky smiles at a few of the girls I've had my eye on lately.

We have chapel once a month before classes, and today is that day. I don't particularly subscribe to any religious ideology, another thing that sets me apart from my family, but I certainly enjoy making some of the girls in my year shout for the big guy as they come on my fingers or cock.

What? You were expecting a saint? I'm a seventeen-year-old guy in a boarding school where the girls wear little skirts all day. Not even a saint would survive this shit.

I round the bannister at the bottom of the steps and walk into the dining hall. It's still twenty minutes until chapel, and there are students in varying states of exhaustion wandering around the refectory with breakfast foods in hand like mindless zombies. If they really wanted people to pay attention to the service, they should have made it start at noon. Hell, even classes would be better starting then.

A lone waffle sits on the tray, and I make a beeline for it. Just as I'm about to claim my prize, a hand grabs the tongs and reaches for it. It's too late in the morning for them to make more. I didn't even have my heart set on the damned thing when I walked in here, but now that I've seen it, I can't let it go.

The tongs close around my breakfast dream, and I follow the arm to see the new girl, Olivia, staring at it. I step up next to her, startling her when my hand lands on her shoulder, and she lets out a little yelp at the contact. She drops the waffle on the little metal bars running in front of the food display where we slide our trays, and we both watch in horror as it tilts one way, then the other, and then just enough to slip through the bars and onto the floor.

"Ah, motherfucking shit."

Well, I wasn't expecting that to come out of her mouth. With her blonde hair and blue eyes, she looks like goldilocks, and hearing her swear like a sailor is... surprising. To say the least.

She whirls on her heel, her skirt lifting a bit in the breeze she creates with her movement. "How badly do they judge people here for abiding by the five-second rule?"

When I don't answer immediately, she snaps the tongs in my face. "Answer quickly; I only have a few seconds left!"

"There would be judgement," I manage to push past my lips. Has anyone ever snapped at me? I don't think so. Unless you count my mum.

"Dammit," she says. "You will never be forgotten, little waffle." She scoops up the food and tosses it into a bin before coming back for her tray.

I laugh at the genuinely forlorn sound in her voice and find myself watching her intently as she rejoins me at the scene of the waffle murder. "He fought a brave fight but loved skydiving too much to miss that opportunity."

"You owe me breakfast," she says with a raised brow.

"Seems correct. I mean, it's included in tuition, so tomorrow, I'll get you a waffle," I agree. "But that probably means you'll have to sit with me."

She appears to mull over the terms of the deal, and like anyone would, nods her agreement at the promise of waffles. She sticks out her hand, and I shake it with a grin. It's then I notice her blue eyes aren't entirely blue-green. There's a splotch of amber in the left iris, and suddenly, the mix of colours has become my favourite combination.

"A waffle tomorrow does not help me today, but it's better than no waffle, I guess. We've said 'waffle' a lot in the last few minutes. The word has lost all meaning," she muses as she begins sliding her tray down the line to get a croissant as a replacement and calls over her shoulder, "See you tomorrow, V."

"It's a date," I answer loudly.

I just scored a breakfast date with the new girl. A movement across the dining hall catches my eye. Max Arondale—or Maxi Pad as I prefer to call him—is watching the exchange from his usual table. I lick my finger and put an invisible one on the scoreboard above my head. That asshole thinks just because his family has some title, it means he can act like a pompous dick at all times.

Gathering up some fruit, muesli, and tea, I drag my tray to a table and scarf down as much as I can before chapel. The bell rings overhead, and the students around me let out a collective groan. It's not the whole religious thing that upsets them; the problem with chapel at St Stephen's is that they use it as an announcement space that they then follow up with an email that sums everything up. Numbing our asses on the wooden pews for an extra hour is entirely unnecessary.

Chapel starts as it always does, the younger choir singing a few hymns as the rest of us pretend not to notice all the missed notes. I'm sitting in the back, eager to bust out of here as soon as it's over, when I feel someone slide onto the bench next to me.

"You want that date now?"

Turning my head, Olivia's long blonde hair catches my eye, and I choke. Literally. On my own spit. Smooth move, Viraj.

"What do you mean *now*?" I whisper back.

"You get me out of here in the next ten minutes, get me some goddamn waffles, and get a date out of it. What do you say? Unless, of course, you're afraid of getting caught." She shrugs a shoulder. The challenge in her mismatched eyes has my need to prove her wrong rising to the surface as I lean closer.

"Let's go."

I slide out of the bench seat and head towards the small door at the back where Mr Hall is standing guard. Olivia's right behind me, and I hear her steps falter as we get closer to the exit. I reach a hand back and pull her closer, wrapping my arm around her waist and encouraging her head to rest on my shoulder.

Mr Hall is watching the students to his right, so I startle him a bit when I approach him. Seems to be a theme for me today. "Mr Goenka, back to your seat."

"Olivia here isn't feeling well. I'm just going to get her to the infirmary, and I'll be right back. Do you need to escort us?" I ask.

To my surprise, Olivia follows my lead without hesitating. She starts breathing heavily, and I even notice her hands are shaking. Her big blue eyes meet the teacher's, supplicating. Encouraged by her flawless performance, I continue. "Or do you need to stay here to watch the St Pierre twins? I heard they bought stink bombs this past weekend. The last thing we want is them ruining chapel for everyone. I swear, they're worse than those wizard twins from those books."

His eyes dart over to the students I mentioned, and they narrow with laser focus. "You go on. I've got a few things to confiscate. Back as soon as possible, Mr Goenka."

"Yes, sir. Just need to make sure Olivia is taken care of," I say, bending the truth and the intentions just a bit. Olivia lets out a little groggy groan and rests more heavily on my side.

He pushes open the door behind him, and we slip into the silent halls. Olivia keeps up her charade until we reach the front doors, and I push them open, letting the crisp autumn air filter into the stuffy corridor.

As soon as the door is shut behind us, she straightens up and whoops in excitement. "That was amazing! How did you know the twins bought stink bombs?" she asks.

"They were bragging about them all night in our hallway. They live across from me. I doubt they brought them to the chapel, but it was worth a shot. They play their music too loudly for my studying times anyway. Let's call it payback. And you weren't so bad yourself!"

She grins at me as she rubs her hands on her arms. "God, it's chilly today. Okay, so where are the waffles? Is there a diner nearby or something?"

"There's one about fifteen minutes from here on foot. But the best ones are a couple towns over." I pat my pockets, but realise my mobile is upstairs in my desk drawer. Stupid no-phones rule. "Do you have your mobile?" I ask her.

She shakes her head.

"So we can't call for a car. We'll have to walk to the restaurant. It's not far, and it's not too cold, right?"

"Makes sense," she says. "This place is pretty out of the way."

She taps her finger on her chin as she thinks through her options. "There is an alternative," she starts as she looks me up and down. "But no, I don't really think you're up for it."

"Up for what?" I ask, knowing I'm playing right into her slender hands. But I can't help it. My teenage brain—and dick—is yelling at me to do whatever this girl asks of me.

"How much do you know about hotwiring a car?"

"You want to steal someone's car?" I nearly shout.

She hems and haws for a second. "Well, it wouldn't be just anyone's car now, would it? And I planned to do it after classes today, but since you're here, I could use an accomplice." We're isolated out here. The only cars around belong to the teachers and the staff.

"Bloody hell, you're insane." I could get kicked out of school for this. I could get sent back home. Then again, I could get the girl.

She cocks a brow at me and puts her hands on her hips.

"Fuck it, let's go." I grab her hand like I did in the chapel, but instead of leaning against me like a sick person, she lets out a squeal of delight and races after me towards the staff parking lot.

She looks around as we skid to a stop and points to an older sedan. "That one."

"Why that one?" I ask. If anything, I want to take our headmaster's new Porsche. If I get expelled for stealing a car, I'd rather it be a good one. Going out in a blaze of glory, and all that.

"Just trust me. Come on!" Then she stops and throws a quizzical look my way. "Wait, can you drive?"

"Yes, I've done a couple of karting championships back home, I have my scooter licence valid in England, and now my Dai Ma is making me drive every weekend so I can take the test soon for cars."

"So you're not legally allowed to drive."

"Because you're legally allowed to steal a car?"

She raises a brow at me. "Touché, V. Touché." She heads back to the car. Puffing my chest, I follow after Olivia. She starts fiddling with something on her side, and a moment later, the locks disengage, and I can open the driver side door with ease. What the fuck?

We slide into the car, quickly shutting the doors behind us as I lean down, looking at the steering column and trying to figure out how the fuck to hotwire a car. In video games, it seems so simple. In real life? An entirely different story.

A lone pen in the console captures my attention. Deciding to just fucking go for it, I jam it in the ignition and turn. It slips right back out.

"Fuck, V. Stop!" Olivia holds her hand out, and I do the same, palm up. She drops a set of keys into my waiting hand.

"What the hell? Is this your car?" I ask.

"No, it's one of the office staff member's. But I see her arrive every morning from my window, and she dropped her purse this morning when she arrived. I grabbed these."

I close my eyes and let out an exasperated breath. Olivia let me think we were actually going to hotwire a car?

As I level a glare at her, she raises her hands in supplication. "Whoops."

"Whoops is right. But fuck it. We're here. We can get the good waffles now."

I haven't known Olivia for long, but fucking hell, she's a wild card, and I kind of like it.

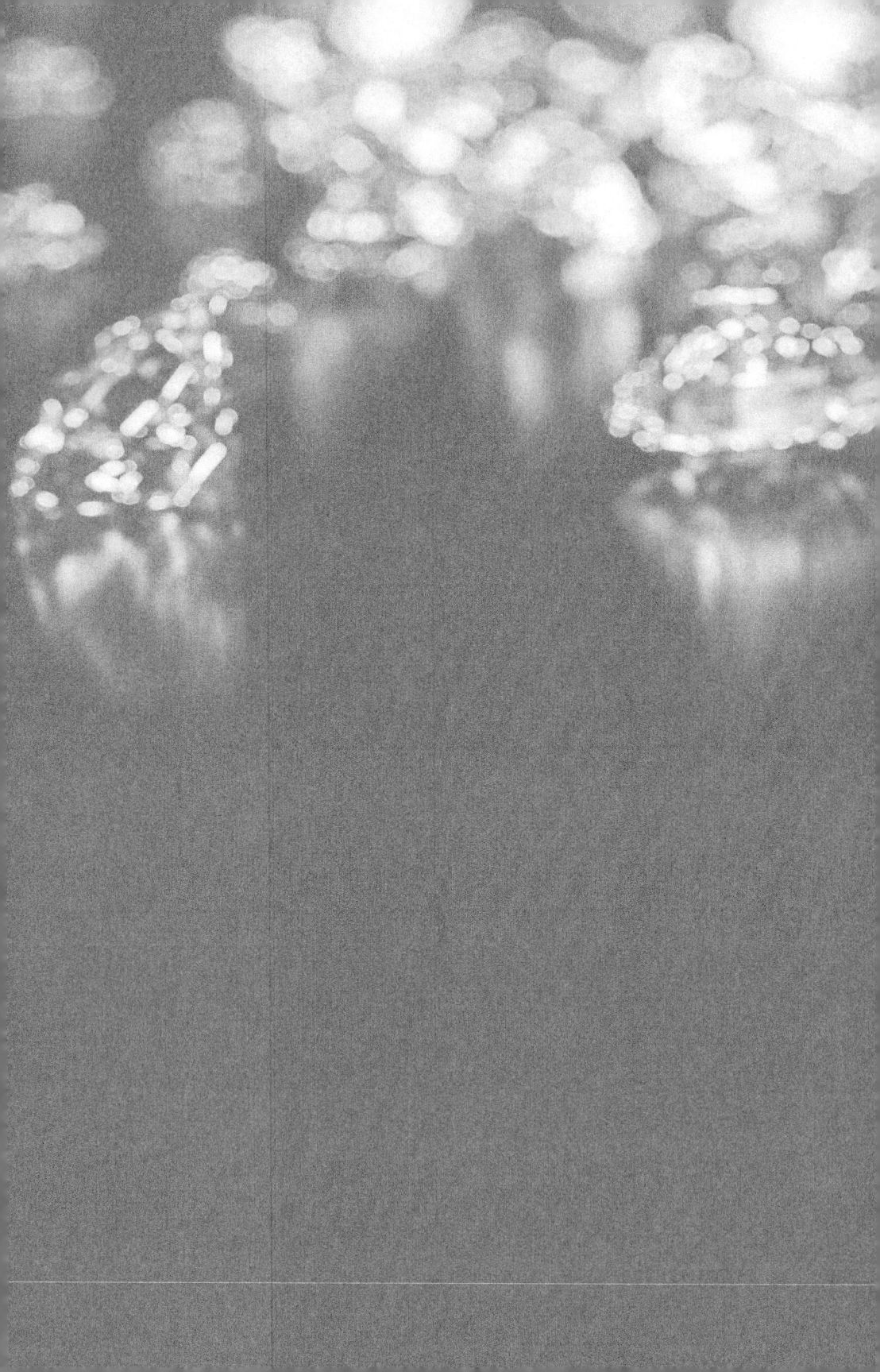

Chapter Nine

Olivia
Present Day

It's three-thirty a.m., and I'm padding on silent feet through the corridors of my quiet house, a wooden spatula in one hand and a frying pan in the other.

I'm being way too childish for a thirty-year-old information thief, but I'm genuinely happy to have them under my roof, and what better way to show it than waking them up thirty minutes before our agreed departure time by making *a lot* of noise?

What? How else do people show affection?

I safely store the spatula between my teeth and use the smart home app on my phone to unlock their bedroom doors and blast music on all the built-in speakers of the house. The song I picked is

"Whenever, Wherever" by Shakira, just because I had to pose as a TikToker several months ago and still know the choreography by heart.

I wonder if that video has gone viral yet.

I start dancing in the corridor while hearing faint groaning sounds coming from inside the rooms. When the part of the routine comes where I have to clap my hands, I start hitting the frying pan with the wooden spatula like a woman possessed.

Why am I torturing them, you might ask? After all, I gave them a lecture last night on the importance of getting along, and I'm creating tension on purpose.

First of all, because I'm having a blast. I spend most of my time alone, and having people to pester makes me feel like a kid on Christmas morning.

But most importantly, I need to know how they'll behave under pressure. I need to know what their absolute limits are, how they react to taunting, if they can overcome exhaustion, boredom, arousal. Sure, I knew them like the back of my hand when we were in boarding school, but graduation was a long time ago, and people change.

Every sword is forged in fire, and I need my team to become the best weapon. Since I only have two months to get reacquainted with these four swords—pun intended—I'm giving them the intensive version of the Olivia Wraith boot camp.

"Wake up! Wakey wakey! It's time to go worky!" I shout, still dancing and hitting my improvised gong.

Epic coordination, right there.

When the guys poke their heads through their respective doors, they don't seem as appreciative of my talent. Hey, they could have set an alarm and woken up on their own. Except I switched off their phones.

Whoopsies.

My ovaries, on the other hand, are very appreciative of the four dishevelled male specimens we gained as roommates. Hot doesn't even begin to describe them, and the half-asleep looks on their faces suit them. I was dead serious when I promised to fuck them if they made decent progress on our mission. I've always cared about these four much more than I liked to admit. Once upon a time, acting on those feelings with all of them might have broken my heart.

But you know what the advantage of turning thirty as a badass bitch with a successful career is? Being liked by boys isn't my priority anymore. I care more about the number of orgasms they can give me than what they think of me.

Or that's how I want to feel. In reality, well, having them back would be nice. Organising Sunday lunches with them and Ellie, cooking together, cleaning up the ensuing food fights, all this would be fun. I can't admit it out loud—it would give them the power to crush me again—but I miss their friendship, even if it was ages ago. My nomadic life doesn't make it easy to create new bonds. Besides, every time I tried, the people didn't compare. That's the problem, when you meet powerful, handsome, smart guys in school and have a crush on them.

They ruin you for everyone else.

What better way to get them back than performing like Shakira before dawn?

"Fuck, Ollie," V grumbles. "It's not even four yet. What the... Are you dancing?"

"Yes, haven't you heard that exercising is the best way to start the day? Come on, get out, I already made breakfast, and we have secrets to uncover!"

I swear, I hear Roark grunt, "Come to bed, and I'll give you some exercises to do." I giggle evilly, improvising a dance to the rhythm of the next song since the first is over. Guys are so slow.

Roark is a night owl, I know. But I expected better from the other three. Even Zach seems to be struggling.

"Let's go, boys! We've got some stealing to do!" I shout, turning around and heading down the stairs to get myself a cup of coffee. I only made four, so whoever is last will have to survive without caffeine. It's just positive reinforcement for the future.

Is it evil? Yes. Do I care? Not one little bit. Playing with fire is fun. Since I'm likely to get burnt, let's call it preemptive payback.

I see an inferno in Zach's eyes as he meets me in the kitchen five minutes later.

"Little Thief, you're inviting trouble," he says as he stalks closer to me. His hand circles my throat, and he pushes me against the refrigerator. His grip is tight on the sides of my throat, always so careful to avoid crushing my windpipe.

I look up into his amber eyes defiantly. "I like trouble," I breathe out, then lick my lower lip to get the last of the coffee off of it. His eyes track my tongue, flaring as I lean forward and flick his chin with it.

"You made a mistake last night," he whispers against my lips.

"And what was that?" My words are hushed as we share the same air, and my body temperature ratchets up.

"Locking us in that room while you took something from me. Your orgasms are mine when we're sharing a roof, Little Thief. Not yours. And certainly, not theirs."

"You're wrong, Doc. My orgasms are *mine*." Challenging him is a treacherous game; one I relish. My pleasure is their pain in this case, and the danger gets me high in a way I can't explain. It always has.

Zach bites down on my lower lip, drawing blood with the snap of his teeth. He licks it away with his devilish tongue and takes a single, measured step away, leaving me a panting mess against the appliance as the blood rushes back to my head.

Roark stomps into the room, giving me a knowing look, and heads straight to the coffee machine. He and Zach prepare their mugs while we wait for the others. I check my watch, noting we have to leave soon and am about to start another obnoxious song to get their asses in gear when Viraj joins us.

Of course, the last person we're waiting for is Max. As much as I

The Cleanup

love his polished, posh facade, it takes time. Time we don't have on the first day of a new contract.

The four of us toss our cups into the dishwasher and are in the foyer putting on shoes when Max comes sauntering down the stairs. "What about coffee?" he asks sleepily when he sees us all readying to leave.

"We're out," I volley back. "My machine only makes four cups." It makes eight, but he doesn't need to know that. "Last one doesn't get coffee. Be faster tomorrow."

Max sputters out nonsensical words while gaping like a fish at the same time. It really is a sight to behold. The others laugh because they saw the big-ass machine in the kitchen. It's not my fault Max didn't pay attention last night when he was dishing up food in there. It will teach him for next time.

"Come on, we've got work to do," I toss over my shoulder as I unlock the door. He moseys down the final steps and slips on his loafers. Those aren't going to last the week with all the harsh chemicals and work we're about to do.

I lead them down the quiet and still-dark street to my private parking space and point to my Union Jack Mini Cooper. Jack's—yes, I named him—lights flash when I press the button on the key fob. "Hop in."

"You have *got* to be kidding me," says Roark.

I press a hand over my lips, feigning a cough that absolutely no one believes. "It's this or walk," I say with a shrug. "It's only about ten miles to our job today."

Viraj rubs a hand over his tired face. "Fucking fine. I'll drive."

Max scoffs at the declaration. "Yeah, no. I'm not getting in a car if you're driving it. I'm not looking to die in an inferno today, thanks very much."

"I'm an excellent driver, dickhead," Viraj snarks back.

"Enough," I cut in. "No one drives Jack but me. So get your asses in the car."

"Shotgun!" calls Roark, startling the birds in the nearby trees.

The others groan, but honestly, it's probably best for everyone if he's in the front seat. He's got bulk to him that the others don't, and squishing in the back seat with his mass would be a bad time for everyone.

It's like watching someone else play Tetris when they can't see the screen. There are asses hanging out of the open doors as they try pushing and shoving each other to fit into their small seats. It's made all the worse by the fact there is no actual middle spot since it's the two-door and four-seater model. It's just the seat belt connectors, which are going to be a bitch to sit on.

Once Max, Zach, and V are smooshed in the back hip to hip and shoulder to shoulder, Roark and I get in. He shoots me a look that tells me he knows exactly what I'm up to, forced proximity and all. I wink at him and watch as the corner of his mouth tips up in a smile.

I start the car, and "Barbie Girl" by Aqua blares through the speakers. It's just loud enough to block out the groans coming from the guys. I start singing along and pull out of the parking spot. By the third repeat, I expect one of them to start singing Ken's lines. After all, I'm nailing Barbie's lyrics.

To Diamond Desires we go!

A COUPLE HOURS LATER, I'VE GOT ZACH, VIRAJ, AND MAX—THE backseat buddies—cleaning the front store room of the jewellery shop while Roark and I are down the hallway in the office. I had uniforms and cleaning masks for all of us stashed in the footwell of the passenger seat, and the matching coveralls make us look like a nineties band. I love it. The security guard stands outside the store, thankful for the smoke break. I admonished him for his dirty boots, and he took the invitation to wait outside, thankful for the takeaway coffee I brought from the gas station. Idiot.

You'd assume a night guard would think twice about leaving a new cleaning crew in a shop he was responsible for. But once again, having breasts and incredible acting skills have paid off.

When we first arrived, the five of us cleaned a little, then Roark used an app he designed to make virtual avatars for me and him who'll keep cleaning while we sneak into the office. You know the filters that make it look like you have cat ears, or there's a dog in your living room, or Shrek is dancing in a leather jumpsuit on the Eiffel Tower? Well, just like that, except the security feeds of Diamond Desires will show five people cleaning the shop instead of three. The only way someone would suspect anything is if the area isn't clean. But it will be. Zach will make sure of that.

Once the cameras are no longer a problem, Roark and I head into the main office and get to work. Roark is seated in front of the computer, click-clacking as lines of code and firewalls stand and crumble on the screen under the might of his hacking abilities. He pops a Skittle into his mouth every few minutes. It's kind of nostalgic watching him snack the same way he used to in school. You could always count on Roark to have sweets in his pocket.

He's got my external hard drive on the desk next to the ancient desktop in case he finds any information we can download and sift through later. It looks like a vibrator because that seemed fun, and it's the best deterrent in case anyone tries to hack my files. Nobody wants to touch someone else's dildo. You never know when it was cleaned last.

The phallus glitters on the ebony desk like a disco ball. While Rory's working on retrieval, I'm doing the actual work of cleaning the manager's office.

I tried to get into Natasha Volkov's servers the other night on my own from the comfort of my very cosy office. Unfortunately—and I hate to admit this—I couldn't. My next thought was to use her businesses to see if there were any internal emails or exchanges that might have slipped in.

The monitors on the wall display the front room as Zach, Viraj, and Max clean the display cases and the showroom. Thankfully, there's sound, so the entertainment has been priceless.

"Max, you cannot use polish on the glass," Zach chides as he goes over the streaks our posh friend has left on the formerly pristine cases housing millions of dollars worth of jewellery.

"But it's polish," he argues. "It polishes the glass!"

"What? Your upbringing didn't lend itself to cleaning?" Viraj snarks at him as he works on hoovering the floor.

"You're one to talk, V-Card," Max says, and if I had a clear view of his face, I'm certain I'd be able to see his eyes roll.

"You two idiots tried to hoover first. Everyone knows you work top to bottom, then front to back if you're leaving from the rear exit. How else are you going to remove footprints?" Zach asks. "It's like neither of you have ever cleaned a crime scene before."

Max and Viraj look at each other, exchanging a worried glance before stepping a little closer to one another. Look at that! They're bonding.

I prop my ass on the edge of the desk, watching the exchange, my dust rag forgotten beside my hip. Steepling my fingers under my chin, I lean closer to listen again.

"Do you think he's serious?" Max asks V.

"He never was one for joking."

"Should we hide the knives when we get home?" Max looks over his shoulder at Zach, probably making sure he wasn't overheard. Aw, so cute he's already thinking of it as home. That didn't take long at all.

"It might be for the best."

If I had a hairless cat right about now, I'd be stroking it as I watch my evil plan for them to get along unfold. I do have one bald pussy, but it's definitely not the kind they show in films. At least, not the films you can find at the local cinema.

I toss my head back in laughter as the three of them bicker back and forth, using the wrong products and creating a mess that Zach is quick to fix before it gets out of hand.

The Cleanup

Max checks his phone for the twelfth time this morning since I turned them back on and types furiously on it.

"I've got it!" Roark announces, pulling my attention back to him.

"Thank Christ," I say. "We have to be out of here in twenty minutes before the manager shows up to start opening up. What did you find?"

Roark plugs in my extra special external hard drive and moves data to the folder on the desktop. "You were right. Her personal assistant sent an email demanding a few pieces of jewellery be made for the event with the due date as May 10th since their flight is on the 24th. They want to be sure the pieces are perfect, and if things need to be 'corrected,' they have time." His use of air quotes tells me he's memorised the email already and finds it haughty and condescending.

"Hey, did Eleanor tell you the size and cut of the diamond? That might narrow down our search if she's hiding it in her newly ordered jewellery," Roark asks. See? Brilliant.

"Yeah, it's one carat, and a round cut."

He scans the monitor before him, focusing back on his work.

"Grab the emails for us to go over. Tomorrow, we're at another one of these shops, so you can keep combing the data on their servers for anything else we might need. Also, please do something about the footage of Zach, Max and V fighting like babies, because if anyone sees this, The Cleanup's reputation as a respectable company is toast."

"Sounds good. I should have it all done in a few minutes." His voice is gravelly from disuse, and we're running out of time, so I wave my hands in a hurry up gesture. I plant a swift kiss on his cheek as he unplugs the external drive. He makes our virtual avatars meet us in the offices and merge with our actual selves. We quickly but thoroughly clean the room, and I follow him out with the hoover, covering up our footsteps on the impressionable rug.

"Guys!" I announce as soon as I see them in the corridor. "Roark wins today! He just found Natasha's travel plans to Monaco."

"At what time?" Max immediately challenges as Zach finishes wringing out the mop and props it against the hallway wall. I don't have any doubt that this place is up to my standards with Zach taking the lead on cleaning.

"About fifteen minutes ago, why?"

"I got the VIP invites to the Grand Prix via email exactly sixteen minutes ago," he answers with a smug smile.

My lips tilt up in an evil smirk. "Well, maybe Rory found his lead seventeen minutes ago. Since we have no way to check, I declare you both winners." With those words, I turn from them and head for the back exit of Diamond Desires, my cleaning gear in hand.

"Liv, wait," Max protests, trotting to my side. "Does that mean we each get a turn?"

"Oh, no. You both won at the same time, and that's exactly how it'll happen."

Max frowns, struggling to understand exactly what I meant by that. "But..."

"Relax, Maxi Pad," I tease. "It'll be okay. After all, you and Rory got some practice last night."

Chapter Ten

Olivia
Present Day

For the drive back to the townhouse, I prepared "Boom, Boom, Boom, Boom!!" by Vengaboys on my phone, and as soon as I turn the ignition, the obnoxious song starts playing at full volume.

It's not my favourite, and I'll have it in my head for three months, but looking at Viraj's face as he listens to the lyrics is worth it. It looks like he's trying to shit a brick. He's stuck between Max and Zach in the back seat, and the former looks positively gleeful as he bobs his head along to the music. Zach has that devious look in his eyes that tells me I'm going to pay for all this later.

I can't wait.

I park in front of my townhouse and exaggeratedly yawn as we pass over the threshold. "Okay, guys, nap time for me. Max, Rory, do you want to join me?"

For a second, I'm afraid they'll refuse. The rejection would sting. They exchange a dubious look, then some silent agreement seems to happen, and they nod in unison.

"Also, take your shoes off!" I add.

Once everybody's in, I lock all the doors and windows with the app on my phone. I wouldn't want Viraj or Zach doing something stupid while we're busy. They can still get up to no good within the house, but the damage will be contained.

My heart is beating faster and faster the closer we get to my room. Everything I say is measured, weighed, and thought out before it leaves my lips. Even when I'm pretending to be a stupid bimbo or a jokester, I'm thinking about the consequences of my actions. I'm always planning, always scheming.

So, the sex as a reward for them, if they behaved, wasn't something I offered lightly. It won't be an issue to have to go through with it. And it's not as if I haven't done my research. I know they're all clean because I keep track of their medical records. Not in a creepy or stalkery way—I think—just to make sure they're okay. Their sexual health just happens to be part of that.

Last night, as I pressed my vibrator against my clit, scenarios where I ended up being with more than one of them were definitely in my mind. I've wanted these four men for a long time, and I do think I'm capable of making it so Rory and Max get along better after we do this. My inner movie villain lets out an evil laugh.

Sex has a way of connecting people. Even though I'm sure they won't be touching each other, I hope it helps Roark and Max work better together towards our common goal.

Yeah, I know, there's a dirty joke hidden there somewhere.

But since I'm me, as soon as the door to my room is closed and locked, I lie down fully dressed on the bed in starfish position and announce, "Okay, guys, I'm ready, you can go ahead and get on with it."

A stunned silence answers me.

I tilt my head up from the mattress so they enter my field of vision. "What?"

"Are. You. Fucking. Serious?!" Max growls. His posh accent is so pronounced when he says the last word that I can't help but giggle.

Still laughing a little, I sit up and cross my legs. "No, I'm not." I smile sweetly at the two of them.

"You know, you don't have to do this," Roark says.

"Rory, you know me better than that. I don't make empty promises—or threats, for that matter. And I don't do anything I don't want to do. Now, if you guys would prefer not to do anything, that's okay with me, too. I'm not going to hold it against you. We can even pretend the wildest orgy is happening so Viraj and Zach can't fuck with you later." I look alternatively at Max and Rory as I say this, holding their gaze without flinching. I'm not going to back down, and I want them to understand how serious I am.

Looking at them so intensely is also starting to make me seriously horny. They're vastly different from each other. Max has a suave look, what with his hair and stubble being dark and his complexion pale. His skin is bare of tattoos—as far as I know. Rory has long blonde hair, deep blue eyes, is covered in tattoos, and his heavy jewellery places him halfway between a Viking and a rock star.

They're equally hot, and I've always been attracted to both their looks and brains, but for very different reasons. That is why I could never choose, and the one time I brought it up, it was shut down spectacularly.

They're still hesitant, so I say as sweetly as I am capable, "I want you. Both of you. And you already know I've wanted you for a long time."

My fantasies have run rampant in my head ever since I announced today's winner, so if they leave now, I'm gonna end up with a blue clitoris and a broken heart, and I want neither. But I've survived the latter once and the former more times than I can count, so it'll be okay.

Max nods almost imperceptibly. Roark was looking at him as he did, and our eyes meet when I ask the same silent question to my Irish hacker.

"Okay. I'm in," Rory finally says, and my vagina does a happy dance. "How do we do this?"

"Do I have to give you the talk?" I tease as I get to my knees. "About the birds and the bees?"

Roark growls and rolls his eyes, but my teasing had the desired effect. Some tension leaves his shoulders.

"Come here," I order, tilting my head towards the bed. It's a King size—obviously—so we should be comfortable.

They sit on the edge, as if they're still not sure we're doing this. I can't have that; the pussyfooting around will kill me if it continues. With just our talk, I can already feel myself getting wet.

"Let's do a test run, okay?" I propose. They both nod. "We're all clothed, nothing weird is happening." *Liar, liar, pants on fire.* "Rory, watch what I'm going to do, really *see* what's happening, and tell me if it looks wrong." Without giving me time to second guess myself, I wrap a hand around Max's neck and kiss him deeply.

His entire body tenses in surprise, and for a fraction of a second, I fear I've monumentally screwed up. Then he relaxes, and I allow myself to do the same. I melt against him, and the position is a little awkward since he's sitting and I'm kneeling, but I don't care.

I've dreamt of doing something like this for years, then completely gave up on that dream, and now the hope that flashes through my chest is all-consuming.

I'm not scared that being physical will screw our friendship. We've come back from worse, after all.

I open my mouth, tangling my tongue with his. Max doesn't miss a beat and kisses me back with everything he has, his arms finally twisting at my back, pressing me harder against his lean chest. He tastes like toothpaste and smells like expensive cologne, something so truly Max that it makes me moan.

Our tongues dance together, and I hear him grunt when I nip at his lips. Fuck, this is a great kiss.

I reluctantly break it and turn towards Roark, expectant. "So? What do you think?"

"It looks weird."

"Bad weird?"

"Not really. You guys look good together, maybe I should leave you alone. You'll be better without me." His eyes avoid mine.

I turn to Max then. "You know what I'm gonna do next, right?" He nods. Smart man.

Before any more self-deprecating bullshit can come out of Rory's mouth, I grab his face between my hands, making him meet my eyes so he understands how serious I am. "I don't want you to leave. Besides, the door is locked." And then I kiss him, just like I did Max.

It's nothing alike. Roark smells like a forest. Like pine, cedar, and oak, all nature and outdoors. His stubble is longer, and I can feel it prickling my sensitive skin. And he tastes like the Skittles he ate as his fingers reduced Diamond Desires' firewalls to smithereens.

Just like Max, he freezes for a fraction of a second before relaxing in my arms.

I've kissed Rory once before, but we were exhausted, and it was clumsy. Max is a first. Kissing them both so sensually, and in such close succession, is making my heart somersault in my chest. The fact that Max seems to be panting in lust only adds to the experience.

My skin craves their touch like nothing before. My panties are embarrassingly wet, and my nipples are so peaked they could cut glass.

I guess that's it. This is happening.

I hear movement at my back, and Max's hand lands on my hip, just below Roark's. His other hand palms my upper thigh, and I can feel the weight shift on the mattress when he gets to his knees behind me.

Roark takes control of our kiss, bending my neck harder to the side. He feels nothing like the teenager I remember. His body is wider, his movements more assured.

Max takes advantage of the freed space and plasters himself to my back, pushing me resolutely against the Irish hacker. A porn-star-worthy moan escapes my lips when I feel Max's soft lips latch onto my neck.

Shit, fuck, shit, someone pinch me because there's no way this isn't a dream. I'm gonna wake up with the worst case of blue ovaries in the galaxy.

Max bites, a bit harder than necessary, as if staking his claim and right to be here, proving for a fact that I am not dreaming. My left hand reaches back, and I grab his neck, pulling him harder against me.

They seemed hesitant at first, but now their dicks are rock hard, and their hips are starting to tilt to get more friction against my front and back. The material of our jeans is in the way. Letting out a frustrated moan, I claw at their T-shirts, and they understand the message, both taking the offending pieces of fabric off at the same time.

My lips are swollen when Roark frees them to get his T-shirt above his head.

Using my hands, I crawl over the bed and lie down on my back. I need to see them. The sight is one to behold. My lust-addled brain counts about twenty abs, and no matter what I tell it, it fixates on them. There are too many sculpted ridges, too many hidden valleys, I want to explore them all.

Since I'm not in the middle of them, Roark and Max face each other for the first time since the groping started.

"I'm not touching you," Roark growls at Max.

"Of course not. Just help me get her clothes off." Max turns towards me. "What do you like?"

"In life? Ice cream, animal onesies, the breeze off the Indian Ocean, and pen spinning."

They both roll their eyes simultaneously, and I swear I'm an evil mastermind. If I continue acting ridiculous enough, they might ally against me. They might even punish me for it. My breath catches at the thought.

"I'll get her T-shirt," Roark decides. "You sweet-talk her into giving us the user's manual."

Without any protests, Max obliges and starts pulling on my jeans. He peels them off my legs, exposing my thigh tattoos as Roark helps me sit up to free my T-shirt. Taking advantage of the position, he also unclasps my bra and immediately sits behind me.

"We have to work together, man," my hacker says. "Zach will never let us live this down if we don't make her scream."

Max looks up from where he's currently lying on his belly between my legs. "You're right."

"Love." Roark's baritone voice in the crook of my neck almost has me coming. "Help us give you the best orgasms of your entire life? It's in all our best interests." His accent grows thicker in the cloud of lust surrounding us, and fucking hell, I could listen to it all damned day.

They both still have their jeans on while I only have my purple lace thong, making it feel deliciously wanton. My head is propped up on Roark's abs while his legs are extended on either side of me, and when he moves to get comfortable, my phone temporarily enters my field of vision. The thought of opening the door and letting the other two in crosses my mind, here and gone, barely even there.

They have to earn it first.

Max pulls down my underwear and bares my bald pussy to their hungry eyes. "Liv? Are you going to help us or should I improvise?"

I aim a challenging look at him. "Impress me."

"Did you hear that, Roark?"

"I got her top half. I guess you'll have to show off that silver tongue of yours."

"And it'll be my pleasure."

Max swiftly dives in. With the focus of a man on a mission, he sucks on my clit and nips at my lips.

He's good at this. So much so that I'm not sure I want the

screaming orgasms I was promised a few moments ago. Because then he'll stop, and I don't want him to.

He pushes two of his fingers inside me and brings his other hand flat against my lower abdomen. Knowing what's coming, I start moaning immediately. Placing his hands and mouth like this theoretically allows him to press on my clit from all sides, both the outside nub and the inner roots.

Zach taught me that.

And the climaxes that usually follow are blackout-worthy. Max has got game.

When he hears the sounds leaving my lips, Roark sits up, tangles his tattooed fingers in my hair, uses his grip to angle my head the way he wants it, and captures my lips in a bruising kiss. His other hand keeps playing with my nipple, leaving me a panting and squirming mess.

Waves of pleasure consume me from everywhere. My abdomen, my lips, my torso, everything starts feeling like it's tingling with electricity. Max suddenly finds a rhythm and pressure that hits just right, and I detonate.

I scream my release in Roark's mouth, clawing at the sheets.

"One," Max counts. I chuckle, lips still kept busy by our kiss. "Get on top of me, Liv; it'll give me a better angle."

I wait to come down from my high to oblige, then I eagerly straddle his face, lowering myself until I hover just over him.

"Perfect," Max says appreciatively.

The new position also places my face exactly in Roark's lap, where his dick is straining against the confines of his jeans. The outline seems... proportional. To the rest of his body, that is. Not overly long, but thick.

A need rises in my body. I want to suck it.

"Open your zipper," I order. "Help me get it in my mouth."

Roark obeys so fast, I'm seriously concerned something is gonna remain stuck somewhere. Since my arms are busy holding myself up, he holds his dick straight up for me. Eagerly, I wrap my lips around it.

I reach his hand, still wrapped around his base, without gagging on the way down, humming and moaning around it; partly because my second orgasm is building between my legs, partly because sucking on Roark like he's my favourite lollipop is getting me off quickly.

He lets out little groans of pleasure, stroking the base of his cock while I suck and lick.

Probably feeling left out, Max crooks his fingers as he sucks on my clit, making me mewl in pleasure and come for the second time.

"Two," Max counts.

I haven't even had a dick in me yet, and my body already feels hypersensitive, overstimulated by everything that's happened.

"Get undressed, guys," I say, momentarily taking Roark's dick from my mouth. "I want you in me next."

"Holy fuck," Roark says when Max removes his clothes. "What the fuck is that? It's fucking huge." Mmmh. Not exactly the reaction I hoped for from a man I'm going down on. "Is that why you like horses so much? You guys have the same dicks? Shit, even your stallion must feel threatened by that thing."

I try to laugh, but since my mouth is currently occupied, I end up snorting and accidentally inhaling saliva. I immediately sit up, coughing and sniffling to try and clear up my lungs.

"Wow," Max exclaims. "Did you blow when you saw my dick and drown her in cum?"

I turn around slowly, expecting an anaconda to jump at my face.

Roark didn't overreact. Max's dick is big. Around ten inches, probably. It stands tall, slightly curved to the left, its head way past Max's belly button.

"It's... curved," I manage to articulate.

Roark sits up at my side. "That's your first thought?!"

"Well, it's got character. I like it." And I lick my lips. Because I can't help it. Imagining the reactions this cock could cause inside me makes me want it in me. Right the fuck now.

Zach will have to step up his game in the organ rearranging department if this is his competition.

"I don't think I've ever felt self-conscious about my cock before," Roark observes in a stunned voice.

I chuckle. "Some people fear the monster under their bed. At least in your case, it's original; you have a monster over yours."

While we're having our cutesy little conversation on our side of the bed, Max stands at its foot, a smug smile perpetually planted on his lips.

Seeing the intensely hungry look in my eyes, he crawls on the bed to lie down beside us.

Both him and Roark lie back on the pillows. The hacker tilts his head in Max's direction and says, "Go ahead, Via. We all know you want to try to hop on that thing."

It's true. I'm not sure I can take it all, not without more foreplay. But I'm not one to back down from a challenge, and I want to try. But I also don't want Roark to believe that I'm forgetting him because the other guy in bed with us has got a huge dick.

Dilemmas, dilemmas. Life, why are you so hard?

"Do it, Via. I'll watch. Make it a show; it'll be hot as fuck."

Well, you don't have to tell me thrice.

Slowly, I straddle Max's hips, looking him straight in the eyes to make sure he's still good with this. In confirmation, he presses a sweet kiss on my lips. "Go as slow as you need," he says afterwards.

I don't want to go slow. I want to ride him like I'm Calamity Jane and scream yeehaw when I'm done.

Better safe than sorry, though, so I angle him up and start lowering myself slowly onto him. The head of his dick is narrower than the rest, and enters easily. Progressively, his girth increases, and I'm about halfway down when things start getting difficult.

"You look gorgeous, Liv," Max encourages, "you feel amazing. Keep going, love, just a little more."

I want to retort that it's a helluva lot more than that, but for once, I don't. I'm officially dick drunk, the sensations coursing through my body silencing me more efficiently than any gag.

So I go down a little more.

"He's right, Via. This is the hottest thing I have ever seen."

My face strains under the effort. It feels great, but it's not easy. Even though he'd sworn he wouldn't touch Max, Roark starts rubbing my clit, dangerously close to the monster dick. His other hand is on his own shaft, and his eyes are fixed on where Max and I are joined.

I take him in a little more.

Then a little more.

Until finally, my inner thighs meet his hips.

I've never felt this full. Not even when there was a massive sale and I ate both tubs of ice cream I'd bought.

Tentatively, I start moving my hips, feeling Max rub *everywhere* inside me. Thank fuck I was so wet from the foreplay, or this wouldn't be fun. I grow increasingly crazier with arousal, and things become easier. I can move around slowly, enjoying how my walls are stretched around him.

Roark's lips latch onto my nipple, and I moan in ecstasy, "Oh, yes."

His hand works more fervently on his own shaft, matching mine and Max's pace. His fingers rub delicious circles over my clit, and as our movements speed up, he takes my nipple between his teeth. The sharp sting of pain has me moving faster, harder. He relieves the hurt with a swift lick of his tongue. My breaths are sawing out of my lungs at the sensations around me.

"Liv, this feels so good. You took my cock like a good girl, and now you're riding it like a bad one. This is incredible." He bucks his hips, like he cannot control himself anymore, and the movement sends me spiralling into orgasm. Everything tightens, pulses, and spasms; it's like my body has a will of its own.

"Fuck yeah," I scream. "Oh, Max, Rory, yes!"

My back arches, and I throw my head back, my hair flying everywhere as I do, even as Roark continues flicking at my nipple with his tongue. He keeps his callused fingers on my clit, the pressure abating, but the torturous touch remains. I'm panting, desperately trying to relearn how to breathe.

Slowly, I come back to reality.

Then I see something. The two men in front of me are as spent as I am, both staring at me with awe and hunger for more in their eyes. My orgasm seems to have triggered both of theirs.

"Shit," I swear, still straddling Max. "Rory, I'm sorry."

"Don't be. This was hot as fuck. I won't mind if you want to call a rain check, though."

"Rain check it is, then—" I'm about to add more to that statement when my phone rings.

I hop off Max's anaconda and grab the device.

Chapter Eleven

Viraj

Present Day

THE THREE OF THEM HAVE BEEN GOING AT IT FOR FIFTY HOURS. Or, that's what it feels like.

Never in a million years would I have predicted hating a luxury townhouse like the one I'm currently sitting in, but the minuscule amount of carpeted floors means everything echoes. *Everything.* It was bad enough last night when the sound of Ollie orgasming came through the ceiling and filtered into the room I was sharing with Zach, but this? *This?*

Fucking hell. I can't fucking think straight. I have to get out of here. I have to go somewhere, *anywhere* the moans won't reach me. Except Ollie engaged the locks, and I've already tried to open four of the downstairs windows, only to find that they, too, have been sealed shut. There has to be a failsafe in case of a fire, right?

Although, on a positive note, all the moaning and screaming got that fucking song out of my head from the drive home.

The Army should use this as a torture method. Right along with wailing babies, blaring rock music, and waterboarding. Too far? Maybe, but I'm not convinced.

"So, Viraj," Zach begins as he sits down opposite me on the rounded couch and crosses an ankle over his knee. He's changed his clothes into faded denim with a simple white T-shirt. Ollie had the drawers stocked in our rooms with clothes that fit us. I don't know why I was surprised she knew our sizes. She seems to know more than she lets on—she always has.

"Yes, Zach?" I answer, desperate for the interaction to distract me from the others. I will latch on to this conversation with everything I have. *Focus, V. Focus.*

"Why are you here?" he asks.

"Ollie changed my flight from Denver to New York. She bumped me from my plane and put me on a flight to London." Which reminds me, I have to double-check that the concierge at my apartment building put my shit in storage. I really hope the hotel in Denver didn't fuck it up.

"That much is clear. But if you didn't want to be involved, you could have left when we got out of the house this morning. Or at the jewellery shop. Or on the way back. But no, here you sit." He takes me in, that detached and slightly unhinged gaze pausing on my throat. I imagine he's thought about cutting it a few times since dinner last night. Even back in school, he was one to keep an eye on. "I know why I'm here. Finally getting what I've always wanted from my little thief is motivation enough. I wonder if it's the same for you."

"I don't know what you're talking about. I'm here because I was promised a joyride"—his brow raises at my words—"in a hot car."

"Keep lying to yourself, Viraj. It's unfortunate, really." He pauses,

THE CLEANUP

tapping a finger against his chin. "Some people are scared of me or pity me for my diagnosis. But you know what? I live a life more truthful than most of them. I know what I want and don't shy away from my proclivities and desires. I can only wish the same for the rest of you. Truthfully, you don't know what freedom you're missing out on."

Zach gets up and starts walking towards the staircase. He's probably going to go listen to the action from the other side of the door. "Oh, by the way, there's an indoor pool through that door there." He points to what I assumed was a closet door. "It's a bit quieter so you can gather your thoughts about your real motivations if you need a reprieve from the symphony upstairs." Another moan makes its way downstairs, and a visible shudder of pleasure rocks through him as he ascends the staircase.

Asshole.

Nevertheless, I find my way to the door and swing it open to find stairs leading downward to a basement. At the bottom, there are glass doors showing off a small pool inside with steam wafting off the top and terracotta-coloured stone tiles lining the sides.

As soon as I open the door, I'm enveloped in humid warmth and sweet, blessed silence. I take a deep breath for the first time since we got back from the cleaning job and make my way to a lounge seat beside the pool. Pulling my phone out and thanking the Wi-Fi gods, I check on my gear, and thankfully find it's all settled and tucked away at home.

Staring at the still water before me, I wonder if Zach is right. Am I lying to myself about why I'm here? Ollie has always been a friend and someone I admire. Someone I once stole a car for just to go get some fucking waffles. Her work is intriguing and challenging, dangerous and exciting.

And the offer she laid before us for helping? Well, it's a challenge all on its own.

Far earlier than I'm expecting, Zach is standing on the opposite side of the entry doors, knocking a fist on them. He motions with his hand to follow him, and I reluctantly get up. I don't want to hear all the fucking again.

"What's going on?" I ask.

"Eleanor called Olivia."

Oh, they must have hated the interruption.

I lead the charge up the steps, ready to find out when we're going and what the plan is. Patience has never been a virtue of mine.

Barrelling into the kitchen, I find the three of them looking far cosier than they were before their fuckfest upstairs. Zach closes the door after himself and strides over to Ollie, knocking my shoulder on the way.

He takes her face in his hands and aggressively kisses her, stealing the breath from her lungs and causing her knees to go weak at the onslaught. He binds a hand around her waist, keeping her up, and I'm close enough to hear him whisper in her ear, "There, now all you'll taste is me."

She clicks her tongue. "Not quite."

Olivia slips from his grasp and stands beside me. "You're not going to maul me too, are you?" she asks, tilting her head up to look at me. I see a beard burn on her neck and the tag of her shirt sticking out of the top. A woman ravaged.

"Fuck no," I blurt and watch a little light dim from her eyes. Again, I wonder if I'm lying to myself as Zach suggested.

"Then let's get to it." Olivia takes off, leading us to the round couch and claiming the seat in the direct middle, leaving the rest of us to fan out around her. She piles three pillows over her body and crosses her feet to sit on the couch like it's storytime at a sleepover.

I end up next to Zach—why am I always partnered up with him in this madhouse?—and finally take in Max and Roark on the opposite side of the table. They look more at ease with each other than they have since this little reunion started.

Roark clears his throat and begins to lay out the facts. "Natasha's personal assistant sent an email requesting jewellery for the event in Monaco. Two bracelets, a set of earrings, one necklace, and three rings. She wants them delivered by May 10th because they leave for the trip on the 24th."

A thought clicks in my brain, and I know just who to call. "And they'll likely be flying private, meaning the airstrip might not be the closest one or the biggest airport in the region. I'll check in with some pilot friends to see if they know of any private strips nearby."

Zach leans closer to me and whispers while Max goes on about how he got the tickets to the event. "Trying to get the next lead, eh?"

I shove him back to his side of the couch just in time to hear Max saying, "—it only took a few well-placed suggestions for the tickets."

"You mean bribes," I counter. He uses his money the same way I do—to get what he wants and enjoy life. The only difference is, I'm not afraid to call it like it is. We're lavish. We use money to do shit most people only dream of.

"Of course, I mean bribes, you dolt. But I find the word rather unsavoury."

Okay, so maybe he's not as blinded by his posh upbringing as I thought. Although, his straight-laced decorum is still infuriating.

I shoot a message to Hannes Arch, a Red Bull Air Racer I haven't seen since his victory in Croatia in 2015.

Me: Hey, I'm looking to go skydiving near Monaco in the summer. Got any suggestions for airstrips in the area?

Wheels in motion, I look back up to find Olivia watching me with a knowing look in her eye and a hunger I knew the two dickheads across the room couldn't satisfy. I toss her a cocky grin and place my arm on the back of the couch, flexing my chest and arms in the process.

"So, how did the prince and the pauper compare, Ollie?" She blinks at me, her cheeks pinking at my tease.

"Fuck you, Viraj," Roark lobs across the coffee table. "At least I don't play with my mortality like a gambling chip in an effort to feel something."

I lean forward, refusing to feel the words as they burrow under my skin. "Isn't that what you assholes are doing here? Hoping to impress Olivia just to have her spread her thighs in reward?"

"Hey!" Max shouts. "Watch it."

Zach clamps a hand around the back of my neck, and with strength I didn't know the doctor possessed, turns my head towards him. "You shut your fucking mouth, or I will carve a frown into it so deep you'll be able to fit Max's giant cock in there without needing to hear the phrase 'open wide.'"

I hear Max gasp at my side. Ew. I didn't need to know Mr Fancy's pants had a python hidden in them. Also, how does Zach know Max has a giant cock? You know what; I'd rather not know the answer to that question.

"Thank you, Zach, but I'll take it from here," Olivia says from my other side. He lets go, and I turn to look at her.

Her pink cheeks have reddened, not in a blush but in anger. Her brows are drawn, and her lips are turned down in a frown.

"That was the stupidest thing you've said in years, Viraj. Who I spread my legs for is my business, and my business alone. Yeah, other people might be involved, but it is *my* decision. My motherfucking right to fuck who I want to, so long as they are willing and enthusiastically consenting." I'm rendered speechless as this woman rips me to shreds, and my palms grow sweaty at my blunder.

She takes a deep breath, and her words land like bullets. "If you don't want to be here, leave. It's as simple as that, V. No one forced you to get on the plane in Denver. You could have taken the next one to New York. No one forced you to get into the Mini Cooper. You could have walked down the street to the nearest tube stop.

"No. You're here because you want to be. And that scares the shit out of you. No one tied a noose around your neck or coerced you into agreeing to the terms. You did that all on your own."

Max and Roark are glaring at me, and I feel Zach breathing down my neck. Feeling daring, because apparently I haven't taken enough risks with my stupid-ass behaviour today, I sneak a glance at the psycho.

He looks fucking livid.

Part of it has to be aimed at me, but the other part? I bet that's because he hasn't had anything to contribute so far. With the rules Olivia set last night and all the teasing she did through the ceiling, he looks to be on edge. He clearly has more recent history with her than the rest of us if his behaviour in the kitchen both this morning and when we came up from the basement are any indication.

His foot starts to shake next to my knee, and he pulls it down to hide the tic. I bet he would deliver on his threat to cut me just to have something to stitch up to get into her good books and a chance at her bed.

I make a mental note to watch for pointy objects in his vicinity. Between what just happened and last night when he realised he couldn't get to her through the locked door... he's going to go on a rampage soon, and I'm partly to blame. Aw fuck, I'm sharing a room with the psychopath. He's going to gut me in my sleep.

I wonder if I can sleep in the shower. Or maybe Max will switch with me?

"Okay, so what's next," Zach asks, looking directly at Olivia as if the rest of us don't exist. Maybe to him, that's the case.

"Thanks to my impeccable detective work and some killer hacking by Rory, we now have a location, an arrival date, and an idea of what the diamond could be hidden in. Now, all we need is a place in Monaco to rent. I want to get there a month in advance to lay the groundwork, get a feel for the city, and V will need to practise a few drives." Olivia turns her head towards me. "Ellie called with our extraction coordinates in France. I did a quick search for the location, and we'll need to get out of Monaco on our own. You'll drive us as far as you can, and we'll hike the rest of the way to the pickup point."

"And then what, Via?" Roark asks. His hands are clasped before him, wringing with tension. "You fall off the map like you did after school?"

"Rory." The concern in her voice is palpable, and I don't blame her. He looks as if he's dreading her answer, but she squares her shoulders and delivers it the way she does everything—unabashedly, unflinchingly. "That is yet to be determined. But I don't plan to disappear."

"Where did you go after school? You never told us. Or, me at least," I ask, despite knowing I'm on her shit list. Hell, maybe that will get her to open up after holding her cards close to the vest all these years.

She exhales and fluffs the pillow on her lap as if looking for a distraction. "I needed to get away from you. All of you," she says as she looks around at us. "You four twisted me up into so many knots I needed not to see you for a while. You were selfish assholes, and so help me god, if you do that again, I *will* vanish into thin air. But I don't want to."

I feel Zach relax next to me. With the way he and Olivia seem close now, I assumed she kept in contact with him after school, unlike me and what appears to be the rest of the guys. She didn't pop back into my life until my last year of uni. Maybe she ghosted him as much as she did us and he only recently got her back, too.

One thing is certain; she brings something out in me. More than any high-speed race, mountain to climb, or black diamond slope to board down. Hell, after the first job she called me for advice on, I swore off any woman who didn't make my heart thump in my chest and turn my blood to ice with fear and anticipation.

The reason we worked well together in school was that we pushed each other enough to go through with whatever plan we concocted, no matter our fears or reservations.

I mean, hell, one time we orchestrated a diversion that should have had us sent to juvenile detention, all in a bid to get something back a teacher had confiscated from Ollie in our final year.

"If we're leaving the country, there's a paediatrician here in London I'd like to see before we go," Zach says.

Olivia grins, but Roark looks confused. "Professional colleague?" he enquires.

"Of course not. One of my patients moved here about two years ago. I just want to make sure their new doctor is taking care of their needs."

"That's actually really good of you, mate," I say, earning a glare.

"Oh, it isn't," Olivia says ominously.

Max picks up the thread of conversation before I can ask. "And what if they aren't minding your patient to your standards?"

"Then they'll need to find a new doctor."

God, he fucking scares me. He has since he showed up at St Stephen's. There were always small whispers about him—nothing confirmed, of course—but he got Ollie in his sights early, and they were inseparable once they became friends. My phone buzzes next to me on the couch, and my eyes turn away from the menace to focus on the screen.

Hannes: Monaco? Not exactly. The closest are Cannes Mandelieu or Nice Cote d'Azur. Nice is closer. Most people get to and from Monaco itself by chopper from those airports.

Me: Great to know. Thanks, man!

"Okay," I say, interrupting a conversation I give zero fucks about. "Hannes just told me there are no airstrips relatively close to Monaco, and the only way is by chopper. That's probably what Natasha will do."

Ollie rolls her eyes, then glowers at me.

"That's exactly what Via was just saying, man," Roark says, still sporting a goofy expression on his face. "There aren't that many ways into Monaco. They'll have to take one of the two roads that connect it to France, a boat, or a chopper. As far as we know, the Volkovs do not own a yacht, so the chopper is the likeliest option."

"But our true problem isn't the entry into Monaco," Ollie adds. "It's how to get out if the alert has been given. The city is sandwiched between the mountains and the sea, has the highest density of law enforcement per inhabitant of the entire world, and prides itself on its reactivity. Apparently, the country can be locked down in fifteen minutes. The principality is also a tax haven, so they want to ensure the rich and famous will be safe there."

Olivia lifts her eyes from her pillows, diving deep into mine, the golden spot in her left eye teasing me amidst all the blue. "That's why I need you, V. We need an extraction plan, and the geography of the region makes it right up your alley. We'll have an escape car, but I don't think it should be inside the city since it is so easy to close the roads. Ideally, we won't even get noticed and the roads will be wide open, but I'm not going in without a backup plan on this one.

"So, Adrenaline God, do you think you can get us out of a locked-down Monaco, or not?"

I slowly nod. It's the first time one of them has used my nickname without making it obvious they're mocking me. There's a shade of respect in Olivia's tone as she used the two words.

I don't know for sure if Zach is right and I'm lying to myself.

But I do know one thing; I want to hear that tone more often.

And it sounds like I have my work cut out for me.

Chapter Twelve

Zach
Year Twelve
January

"And tell me, Mr Bennett, do you have those urges often?" the therapist asks. Dr Linda Forsyth, St Stephen's solution to my... tendencies.

"Not all the time, just when I'm annoyed." I look at her with bored eyes.

She visibly gulps. We've been meeting weekly at various times to not disrupt my class schedule too much, and every time feels exactly like the previous. Her office is stuffy and stale; I sit on the chaise across from her desk as she leans back in her ergonomic chair and tries to figure me out.

"Well, the police report was quite detailed, and your last school's therapist noted that you hadn't shown any signs of needing intervention whilst you were attending Crawford Prep. Did something change that day?" she gently prods.

Yeah, the last therapist only met with me once, so how would she know my inclinations? A visit with her was mandatory upon acceptance to the school, but she asked me the usual questions, and answering like any other teenager would was far too easy. I never set foot in her office again.

"I don't know what you are referring to," I drawl in a bored tone. There was no evidence to indicate I was behind the incident she is talking about. Sure, rumours flew left and right and former classmates were happy to point the finger at me on the local news channels, but there wasn't much the police could do without evidence, means, or motive.

"The..." she trails off. "You know what, that's fine. I've been studying your file, and I think it's safe to say, based on the behaviour you have exhibited in your past and over the last four months, an antisocial personality disorder is a likely candidate for your diagnosis. While psychopathy is not an official diagnosis, you fit a majority of the criteria widely accepted for an informal one." Dr Forsyth looks down at her notes, circling something a few times when I send her a winning smile. "You and I will continue to meet every week during your time with us here at St Stephen's. You will keep me apprised of your school work and any feelings you may be having, and I will help guide you in proper expression of those feelings."

"All right." There are no other options if I wish to pass my A-levels. After the finger-pointing—correct finger-pointing, I might add—no other school would take me, hence my parents paying extra to send me here.

"Is there anything else you wish to discuss? How was your Christmas?" she asks me before tearing a piece of paper from her pad, excusing my tardiness to my next class.

"I didn't even want to discuss what you dragged me in here for, but to expedite this process, Christmas was fine," I reply. She doesn't need to know about how my parents made me go to their physician, and he tried convincing my parents that drugging me was the best course forward. Never again would I allow myself to be suppressed by chemicals. I spent my preteen years being given antipsychotics that were inappropriate for my age, and left me too drugged to voice how ill I felt.

"Well then, that will be all. I'll see you next week. I want you to try to make a friend this week," Dr Forsyth says. Yeah, like it's that easy.

"Fine." I gather my things and give her a little wave as I make my exit.

Make a friend? Yeah, if it hasn't worked for the last sixteen years, I doubt an additional week will make a difference. Now that I've missed the majority of my anatomy class, I have an option. Either I can use the slip to go to class, or I can fuck off for the next twenty minutes.

Looking outside through the windows, I debate my options. It's been storming all week, but there looks to be a reprieve this afternoon. Tempting, very tempting.

Then, a fat cat waddles across the grass, and I immediately shut the idea down. I fucking hate cats, and Bellatrix here is weirdly drawn to me. I'd rather not spend the next twenty minutes being pawed at and covered in hair. Plus, cats see too much.

The therapist's words ring through my head. A friend. Olivia Wraith might be a good option. She doesn't seem put off by my demeanour. In fact, after I showed her that spinning thing I did with my knife, she only asked me if I knew any more tricks. It's been nearly three months since then, and I've taught her a few more things.

That constitutes friendship, doesn't it?

I fling open the door to the classroom, and Mr Abernathy stops speaking abruptly. I unhurriedly walk across the tiled floor, handing him the note, and move to my seat in the back next to Olivia.

She hasn't taken her eyes off me since I walked in, and after sitting on my stool, I lean close. "Want to be friends?" I ask.

Olivia looks at me quizzically, her mismatched eyes searching mine for something. A shiver wracks her body when I smile at her. "I thought we were, but, yeah, okay."

And that's that. Therapy assignment done.

Roark
Year Twelve
May

Two months until this damned term ends. It feels so close and so far all at once.

I really hate going to school here, but what was my alternative? Stay in Belfast with my parents, three sisters, and very loud grandparents while attending the local secondary school? I wouldn't get nearly enough of an education to move on.

Everyone in my family lives within a ten-mile radius. While it's great for holidays, it can be a bit much year-round. I never expected to get the Arondale scholarship, but I worked my ass off to at least be a contender.

Now, I have to maintain impeccable grades, avoid trouble, and in a little over a year, I'll have had one of the best educations money can buy, for free. All it took was some hard work and absolutely no social life.

Well, no social life aside from—"Via!" I chastise. "What are you doing here?" I ask, looking around the dark computer lab. Her head pops up from behind the screen, and she's sporting a guilty face.

"What? Oh, nothing." She smacks her hand against her forehead. "I mean, studying. Yeah."

"Real convincing," I say with a laugh. "'World domination' probably would have sounded truer had you said it."

The guilty look on her face deepens, and she coughs. "It probably would have been truer, too." Her face lights up. "Hey, what do you know about hacking?"

"Some stuff, but definitely not enough to take over the world."

Her laugh rings through the darkened lab. "I don't need to take over the *whole* world, Rory," she says, using the nickname she decided I absolutely *had to have* a few months ago. "Just a small corner of it. Maybe an island somewhere?"

I move to her table and drop down into the chair next to her. I see lines of code across the screen, far more advanced than what they teach us here in our classes. But not too advanced for me.

"You're hacking? How do you know how to do this?" I ask, astonished.

"I watched some YouTube videos, scoured Reddit, and put it all together. I'm stuck, though. So if you know anything about this, now would be an excellent time to chime in."

I study the lines of code as Olivia walks me through what she's already done. Apparently, you really can find everything on the internet because her work so far is flawless. At least, according to my own prior internet research. I figure the school's firewall is the least of our concerns if she's gotten this far already.

An idea occurs to me, and I pull the keyboard towards me, scanning the lines of code and making minor adjustments here and there, hoping a back door exists for whatever it is she's breaking into.

Via watches me with rapt attention as my fingers fly across the keyboard, and I manoeuvre my way through the relatively simple security system. She doesn't tell me what we're breaking into, and I don't ask. A gorgeous girl is asking me for help, and I can't be arsed to care.

She shifts on her seat, crossing her legs and tilting towards me. Her cherry blossom perfume dances in the air, and my dick pops up to say hello. Not the time, man. I've never really thought of girls that way, not that I don't like them, but there's something about Olivia that draws me in. She walked in here as the new girl. More than that, the new *scholarship* girl, and she fit right in, unlike my own experience. No teasing, no exclusion. She just... blended.

After an hour of sweet torture, I find my way in. Olivia whoops and cheers next to me, throwing her arms around my neck and pulling me in for a hug. We've been studying together for months. Casual banter has been built, small touches here and there when we pass each other our traditional sandwiches for our study sessions, but this is the most contact I've ever had with her.

I wrap my arms around her and tug her close, subtly inhaling her scent and counting myself the luckiest bloke alive. She slowly withdraws, and I'm reluctant to let her go, but I force my arms to loosen.

Her blue eyes search mine, that fleck of amber as intriguing as it is strange, and I tilt my head forward, resting my forehead against hers. I've had a crush on her since the first moment I saw her. But I've seen how Max Arondale and Viraj Goenka watch her. Not to mention Zach Bennett. He scares the shit out of me with his intensity. What chance does a guy like me have when compared to those three? They could give her everything.

The colours and shapes on the screen catch my attention, and I sharply inhale when I recognise the crest.

"Olivia?"

"Yeah?"

"Did we just break into the school mainframe?"

"A little bit."

I pull back, taking my hands off of her sides where they had apparently migrated, and run my hands through my cropped hair. Blowing out a hard breath, I slide my glasses higher up my nose and look at the screen.

I am so fucked.

"Why?" I ask. "Do you know what could happen to me if I get caught doing this? I'd lose my scholarship. I'd have to go back to Ireland to my family. I have three younger sisters, Olivia. I already have all the tea parties and Barbie dress-up afternoons I can handle over the summer. If I go back, I'll have to do them daily. *Daily!*"

I'm spiralling. I know it; she knows it. Fucking hell, I hate Barbies. Olivia starts singing "Barbie Girl" by Aqua under her breath and I know I'll have that damn song stuck in my head all night.

"No one will know it was you. If someone ever traces it back to a school computer, we were both studying like the perfect students we are. I would take the blame, I promise. Plus, I told you I covered my tracks going in." She crosses her arms over her chest and harrumphs. "If you need to go, I understand. I wouldn't jeopardise your schooling, Rory."

Her face has fallen from the exuberance of moments ago into one of sadness. She was happy to do this with me. Excited, even.

I rub my hand over the back of my neck and lean forward to see the screen. "In for a penny, in for a pound, Via. What are we looking for?"

She smiles that beaming grin at me, and I mirror it with my own. Her hand rests on my thigh, just above my knee, and I marvel at the touch. I would become the greatest hacker there ever was if it made her happy.

"Eleanor said something that didn't line up with my own research. I kind of need to investigate Headmaster Barkley."

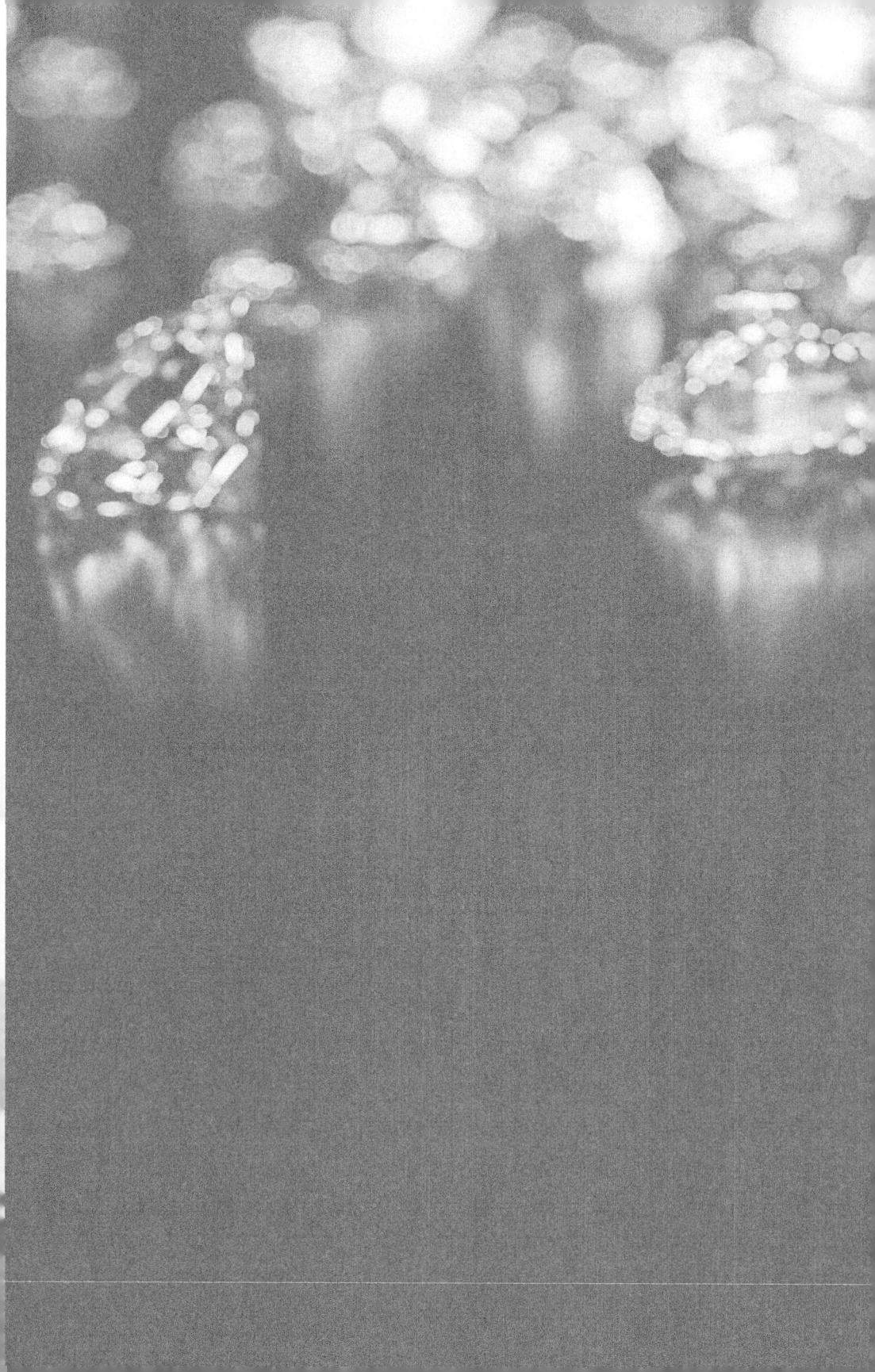

Chapter Thirteen

Roark
Present Day

The following week is much quieter. We keep hitting the different locations of Diamond Desires, hoping some firewalls will be easier to crack into than others, or that someone will have locally saved some information they shouldn't have.

The fifth location is the charm. Olivia finds a notebook in one of the drawers where the manager wrote down all their passwords and the sites they are for. This is the problem with multinational companies. They create so many security systems and passcodes that their employees have no hope of remembering them all. So they write them down, ripe for a thief to nab.

Hacking the accounts is possible, but very time-consuming. Stagnating is boring, even if I like spending time with Via doing my thing in the office while Max, Zach, and Viraj clean the shops. Zach's saving our asses on this one. The Cleanup is selling a team of five people to Diamond Desires. With Via and I hanging back, the three of them have to do the job of an entire team. And since Viraj and Max are essentially useless when it comes to cleaning, Zach is compensating and doing it all.

He deserves Via's favours for this, but there's no way I'm telling her that.

Since our threesome, things have been good between her, Max, and me. I still don't really like him. For so long, I felt like I was beholden to the rules of the scholarship and used as a pawn for Max's dad to compare us and make Max feel like shit. The younger Arondale didn't help things in that regard—he's looked down on me as a charity case way too many times for me to forgive that easily—but now I'm scared of waking up to being slapped by a monster dick, so I'm doing my best to be civil towards him.

He seems to be feeling the same way—monster dick phobia excepted—so we even manage to have decent conversations.

"Yes!" I exclaim when I finally find the computer file I've been looking for. "Via, look. These are the exact designs she ordered."

Via bends her legs, kicks the wall at her right, and uses the momentum to make her chair roll across the room. She was searching for clues in the drawers on the other side of the room after cleaning.

"Are they precise enough to be used to make replicas?" she asks, bending over me to see the screen.

"Let me check." I try to open one of the files and get an error message from the computer. "Okay, these are three-dimensional files. We can definitely use them. Let me copy everything." I grab the ridiculous glitter schlong hard drive and connect it to the computer where I download all the 3D data of the jewellery Natasha Volkov will wear during her appearance at the Grand Prix.

The Cleanup

"Via, if you don't mind me asking, how are you going to get these things off her? She'll have guards and will probably be paying very close attention to the diamond."

"We still have six weeks to plan this. If I were her, I'd hide the diamond containing the data in the middle of a bunch of other stones. Can you check what stone quality they're planning on using from within the system?"

I'm not quite sure where she's going with this, but I oblige anyway. I have to hack my way through because the manager of the London shop does not have access to the inventory data of the Moscow shop. After some manoeuvring, I'm in.

"They're using G for the colours, and VS_2 in terms of inclusions, at the very least. Some are even nicer. The necklace will have sixty-eight diamonds ranging from one carat to a giant of four carats in the middle. Her earrings will be pendants composed of five diamonds each, one of two carats placed on her lobe, three smaller ones going down and the last one pear-shaped and weighing three carats." I scratch my head, having learnt more about women's jewellery in the last five minutes than I ever had in my whole life. "At least we know it's not that one. The shape is wrong. Natasha also ordered two bracelets and three rings, and they're just as luxurious." I look at Via in disbelief. "How the fuck will we know which diamond has the data? There are so many one carat stones on these."

Via leans back in her chair with a smug smile. "We'll need a refractometer."

"A what?" I ask, frowning. I'm good at computers—great, even—but I only vaguely remember my physics class from school. I was too busy coding apps to really pay close attention.

Via grabs a pencil from the desk and starts twirling it between her slender fingers. "It's largely used by jewellers to measure the quantity of impurity a diamond contains. In short, the more inclusions there are, the less shiny the diamond is. We know the data is stored inside the impurities of the Interpol diamond, meaning it's got a lot of them."

"You've never stopped doing that," I remark, nodding at the spinning writing utensil.

"Nope. It helps me think."

She stands and begins pacing the floor in front of the desk, giving a lesson in tech while still twirling the pencil between her fingers. "A refractometer will measure how the diamond refracts the light and tell us which stone is the least shiny, hence the one we're looking for. Now, the only problem is: we need to gain access to the jewels long enough to measure the refractive index of every single diamond that matches the size and cut. We can't steal the whole set. Too risky." She shakes her head with conviction.

Watching her face as the wheels turn, I sit enraptured as she goes on. "If it were me, I'd either hide the data in the necklace and use the pretext of its price for it to be heavily guarded at all times, or in a ring as discreet as possible, and I'd never take it off. We should make replicas of the full set, just in case, but I say we focus on those two possibilities."

"Do you have a plan on how to make the replicas?" We don't have much time.

"Yup." She perfectly executes a launch of the pencil above her thumb, catches it again and starts twirling it around her index. "3D printing. We could do it directly in gold, but since very few companies master this technology and they're mostly using it to make jewellery sets, Natasha will probably have connections working there."

That makes sense.

"So, we'll print them in plastic and plate them. It'll be time consuming, but a lot harder to track, and the colour and cold feel of the metal can be recreated exactly. The weight can come very close. Then we'll add zirconiums, and boom! Untraceable fake jewellery."

I stare at her in astonishment. Since she often acts like a seventeen-year-old with her music, sexual innuendos, and the ridiculous objects she owns—I'm looking at you disco dong—it's easy to forget how smart and thorough she is. The onslaught of information just reminded me that her blonde hair and denim blue eyes are a front for a wicked brain that's downright treacherous.

My thoughts must have transpired on my face because Via says, "You know, I do my homework." And she winks at me, the twirling pencil never faltering in her hand. "Speaking of doing what I say I'll do, I believe this is the second capital piece of information you've got us, and you were barely even rewarded for the first one." Her voice turns sinful when she checks the clock and finds it's only six in the morning. "We have an hour. Want to collect your prize now?" A devious smile stretches her lips.

"Via, we're basically behind enemy lines. Are you sure that's a good idea?" Is DNA evidence a concern we need to be worried about?

"We're alone. I'm the owner of The Cleanup, remember? I have access to the schedule of this place's employees, precisely because nobody wants to see the cleaning lady. We have to remain invisible, in the shadows, and it just happens to be where I work and play best." She saunters over, seductively approaching until her thighs are between my own.

On the screen behind her, Max just threw a wet sponge at Viraj while Zach seems desperate for intervention. I don't tell her the three others are this close to an all-out detergent war, though.

Especially not when she leans forward, that cherry blossom perfume awakening my senses, and opens my zipper to reveal my rock-hard dick.

And even less when she takes off her own jeans and straddles my legs.

Then, I palm her cheeks, bringing her face closer for our lips to meet. I take my time with her. Slowly, I push my tongue between her lips, caressing her own. She meets me stroke for stroke without hesitation, as lost in the kiss as I am. Her panty-clad pussy starts rubbing against my length, and I grunt in pleasure. She's wet; I can feel it seeping through the material.

I know this means nothing besides the fact that we're two

consenting adults attracted to each other. We'll do this job, and she'll go back to living a nomadic life on her own because that's Olivia Wraith for you. She needs no one, especially not her childhood friends who have a pile of issues as tall as the Shard. The startling fact is she seems to want us around, even though she's made it abundantly clear she's not choosing.

As a teenager, I thought I'd rather never have her, than have her and lose her. Now that I already lost her once, I know that was stupid. Watch out, psychopaths, aristocrats, and athletes because I'm gonna enjoy every fleeting second of this job with her.

With this thought in mind, I stand up. Via squeals, but my hands hold her ass, making sure she doesn't fall. I free us of our remaining clothing as fast as I can, savouring the hungry look that flashes through her eyes when she sees my tattooed chest. I knew all that exercise would pay off at some point. I'd always been the scrawny one at school, and part of that was genetics. The other part was that it was impossible to maintain my grades *and* participate in sports. But with uni, came my growth spurt, and my enthusiasm for the gym grew since my education was secured and I couldn't lose anything by getting less than stellar marks.

My dick is standing proud, determined to show Olivia I'm not the same man I was back then.

Grabbing the back of her thighs, I hoist her up so her mouth can meet mine. She starts rubbing against me again, making me groan in desire. I love how reactive she is, both today and during our threesome. She whimpers and moans in my arms, nipping at my lips. Her hands are wrapped around my neck as she loses herself in our kiss.

There's a slight chance that Zach, Viraj, and Max will hear us, but I don't want to let Via go and lock the door. Not when she's melting in my arms and making those sweet sounds against my lips.

So I walk to the door, and slam her back against it instead. The advantage of fucking a girl who also has her eyes on a murderous psychopath and an aristocrat hung like the stallion he owns? You know she can take it rough.

"Rory," she moans before biting my earlobe. Her voice is breathy, already panting with lust.

For me.

She tilts her hips, desperately seeking more friction from my dick and trying to line us up so I can fill her. Barely a second later, I grant all her silent wishes. Holding her ass, I slam into her and start pumping, uncaring whether she's ready for me or not.

She cries out in pleasure and surprise. Her pussy is warm and dripping wet, so it wasn't hard to slide in at all. She's tight, though, her walls pressing against my dick like she never wants to let me go.

I start moving, thrusting in and out of her like my life depends on it. She cries out in my arms, her nails digging into my back as if it's her lifeline. Her heels are firmly hooked above my ass.

To get a better grip on her, I move my hands and start pumping even harder, making music with the door slamming against the frame and Via moaning in my arms. My palms are so big and fingers so long they almost cover her entire ass.

Why have we waited so long to do this? Her pussy feels like heaven, and her bites and kisses are everything. My back must be bloody at this rate, but it doesn't matter. This is fucking amazing.

"Fuck, Roark, yes!"

"I'm going to come," I warn. I swear the vixen clamps around me on purpose, and I can't suppress my climax. I shoot my load inside her, crying out at the exquisite sensation.

Without even giving her a second to breathe, I put her down and drop to my knees. "Via, did you come?" I ask, looking up to see her face.

"No," she says, confirming what I already suspected and looking into my eyes with acceptance.

I dive into her pussy. She tastes like my cum, but all I feel is pride whilst licking my own release. I claimed her. Fucking finally.

With two fingers, I push the wetness that threatens to escape back inside her. "Oh, Roark," she shouts as I lick and suck at her clit.

When her legs threaten to give out from under her, I hold her against the door with my free hand and suck even harder.

I lose track of time, high on our tastes mixed together and the sounds she makes. Her hands tangle in my hair, pressing my face harder against her sweet pussy. I don't resist it. If Olivia says to jump, I ask how high.

She starts to shake, and I pump my fingers in and out of her with a punishing rhythm, determined to make her climax.

"I'm coming," she moans. "Roark, yes, like that!"

She shouts her release so loud, there's no way the others didn't hear us. Too bad for them. Next time, they'll find a lead.

Standing up, I make sure nothing has dripped on the office floor. Fortunately, it's not carpet this time, so wiping the few drops on the tile will only take a moment.

"I'm not sure I can walk," Olivia says.

"Come here." I help her walk to her clothes, and put them on—why does she like skinny jeans so much?—then sit her down on one of the office chairs. Preening like a peacock, I get dressed and retrieve all of our materials, giving both the door and the floor next to it a quick swipe with an antibacterial wipe.

All the while, Via has her eyes on me. She takes my every gesture in, and I intentionally put my T-shirt on last. After what we've done, I'm showing off a little, I'll admit it. I'm convinced she got me a smaller size in the branded Cleanup shirt so that she can look at my muscles.

It's close to seven a.m., and we have to meet the others and get out of here. I throw a glance at the screen, where the shop seems pristine, but Zach is holding both Max and Viraj by the scruff of their necks like troublesome children.

Via follows my eyes. "We should go," she comments.

"Yeah. I never thought I would be sad to finish a cleaning shift."

Pocketing the pencil she was playing with earlier, she smiles sweetly, and we leave the room hand in hand.

THE CLEANUP

"So, what have you fuckers been up to?" she asks as soon as we enter the shop, stopping right in front of Max and Viraj. My heart does a little somersault in my chest when I realise she's not letting go of my hand.

"Little Thief, these two are terrible at this," Zach whines. "Will we have to keep doing these shifts much longer?"

"Actually, I don't think so. I think Rory found everything we needed."

"Oh," Viraj spits. "That's what was up with all the banging and shouting, then."

Via just shrugs. "We had to wait for you to finish cleaning. If you'd done it quicker, we would have gone elsewhere." She gives him a condescending pat on the cheek.

V grunts in frustration, and we all head out.

This time, the car song waiting for us is "Wannabe" by the Spice Girls. I wonder if there's a hidden message here. Is Olivia trying to tell us we have to all get along to become her boyfriends?

And more importantly, that we're forever?

Back at the townhouse, the guys all sit on the massive round couch, ready for Via and me to tell them what we found. She takes the stolen pencil out of her pocket and twirls it between her fingers.

"We learnt about the jewellery set Natasha Volkov ordered to wear at the Grand Prix. It's composed of at least a hundred diamonds, so finding the Interpol one will be like searching for a needle in a haystack. We'll need special gear for this. A refractometer, to be exact. I already texted my contacts, and we're getting one. I also sent the three-dimensional mockups we found to another contact, and they'll start 3D printing the replicas as soon as possible." How the fuck does she do that? I barely even saw her touch her phone since we left Diamond Desires. And I've been watching. "Then we'll need to make plans to check the diamonds before stealing them."

"Won't that take too long?" Max inquires.

"We'll have to check that when we get there and have the layouts of the race and associated parties. Identifying our target before doing anything will be key here."

They nod, all seemingly agreeing with this. At the same time, Via is a true born leader, and she's always one step ahead. This is why I could never have her.

I was never good enough.

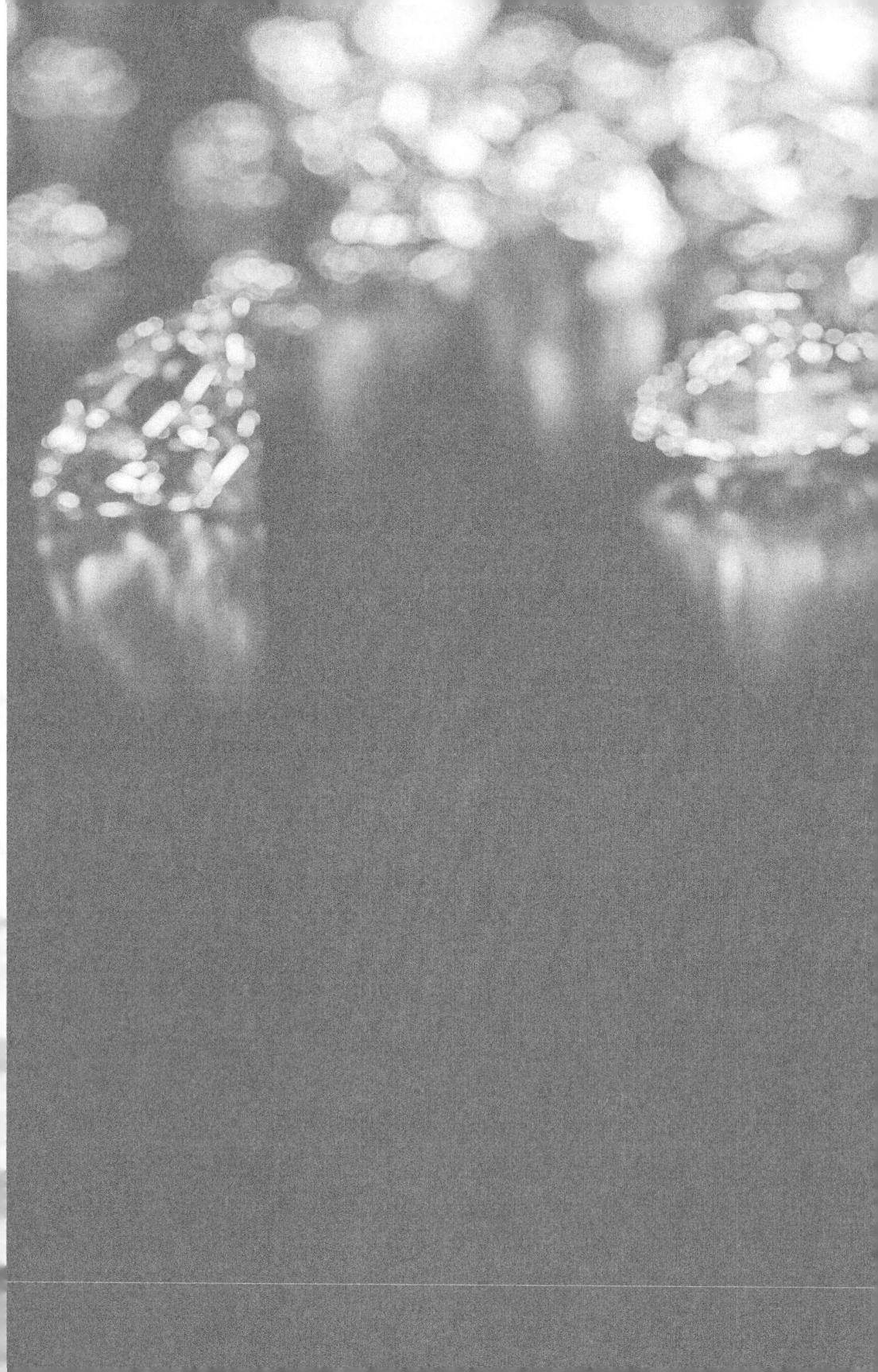

Chapter Fourteen

Zach
Present Day

Looking at the red brick terraced townhouse before me, I consider the best way to announce my arrival.

Most would probably knock on the door or ring the bell. How quaint.

As I twirl Dr Friedman's spare set of keys on my index finger, I contemplate how appropriate it would be to throw the door open and announce, "Honey, I'm home!" I shake my head. That's something my little thief would do, but dramatic entrances are her thing, not mine.

I'm just going to improvise. Yeah, that seems more natural.

I climb the steps, fit the key into the top lock, give it a twist, and shove the red door inward. It swings on the hinges before slamming against the interior wall to my right.

A shout rings from inside the house. Thankfully, Dr Friedman is long divorced from his wife, Amelia, and his kids are grown and moved out. They barely check in, according to the emails and call logs Olivia was kind enough to gather for me the day after our final cleaning of the jewellery shops. This week has been better for my... tendencies. Cleaning up after the shitty job Viraj and Max did irritated the fuck out of me, but I've got to stay in Olivia's good graces until things get bloody.

"What the fuck is happening?" he shouts from further within the house and comes barreling towards the front door just as I get it shut again and turn the deadbolt.

"Who are you? Get out before I call the police," he threatens.

"Now, now. That won't be necessary," I tell the not-so-good doctor. "In fact, why don't we have a seat? I assume you were just sitting down for dinner if the stench is anything to go by."

His face has changed from an irate red to a blustering purple. I decide to make it a game to see what colour he turns when he hears what's in store for him.

"What's the meaning of this?" he bellows as he pulls his phone from his pocket. I pluck it right from his hand and store it in my trouser pocket. Pulling out a scalpel from the other, I hold it up to his neck, stepping into his space and watching him shrink back in fear when he catches the cold look in my eyes.

My little thief never shies away from me.

"Let's sit the fuck down," I growl in his face, watching as sweat breaks out across the bridge of his nose.

I press the tip of the scalpel against his throat, leading him back to his kitchen with a wave of my arm to usher him in the right direction.

"What do you want? I'll give you anything! Anything! Just leave," he begs as his jowls wobble with his tremors. The blade pushes harder against his skin, and when he tries to fight, I restrain his arms behind his back using one of my own. Funny how he thinks his out-of-shape fifty-something physique can dislodge me. I tighten my grip and shove him forward.

"You have nothing I want," I respond succinctly. "Well, nothing material."

I see a microwavable tray full of shepherd's pie and a disgusting amount of gravy drenching the whole thing. Gross.

"Have a seat," I invite him. "Please eat, as this will be your last meal. We have a few things to discuss."

He's visibly shaking as he lowers himself into the seat. The stench of urine permeates the air.

Originally, I had planned to kill him in the bathroom to make it easier for whoever has to clean up this shitstain's remains, but perhaps, suicide over his lonely meal is another way to go. It will explain the stain on the cushion under him.

I'm careful to not touch anything, keeping my gloved hands to myself. I take off my backpack, remove the length of rope I brought with me, and secure Friedman's middle to the wooden dining chair—just tight enough to secure him but not leave any marks if he struggles.

I leave his hands free, so he can eat with his pathetic little plastic fork. I meant what I said. It is his last meal, so he should enjoy it if he can.

"Why are you here? Did Amelia send you? That horrible woman. I can pay you double! Triple!" he counters.

"First things first," I say, taking the frequency finder Olivia lent me out of my bag and waving it around the room.

"What are you doing?" he asks.

"What does it look like? I'm searching for cameras, you idiot. I don't intend to end up on the six o'clock news today. Although, who knows what tomorrow holds," I muse, letting a bit of mania enter my tone. Finding nothing, I settle into the chair across from him and fold my hands in front of me. Friedman is wiggling in his chair, trying to untie the knots behind him. This isn't my first murder, and it won't be my last. Those ropes aren't going to give. I've mastered shibari as well as all sorts of sailor knots. *Will my little thief let me tie her up when I permanently mark her beautiful flesh?*

"So, I bet you're wondering what I'm doing here. Oh, forgive me. Where are my manners? My name is Zach Bennett. I'm Simon Westgate's former paediatrician."

"Si-Simon?" he stutters. "What does Simon have to do with this?"

"Everything. He has everything to do with my visit. You see, I've just come from your office. I received an email from Simon's mother a couple of weeks ago, saying she felt they weren't being heard regarding Simon's therapy.

"She said his progress has stopped completely, having gone off the rails with your change in his diagnosis. Going from severe autism to mild in a matter of months is remarkable, especially considering you've cut off all accessibility to therapies."

I click my tongue at him as he shrinks back in his seat. "Imagine that. Suddenly, he doesn't qualify for an educational aide, speech therapies, sensory rooms, and occupational therapy. Not to mention, he hasn't been in for a neurological evaluation, though he's overdue. But at the same time, I've had a friend check your finances, and see there's a big push in the area to lower government spending in health services so a certain politician gets reelected. And who's shell company did I find dumping money into one of your accounts? Hmmm?" I pause my tirade and take a deep breath. The financials don't matter as much as Simon's care.

"The point of these services, if you need reminding, is to give a child the tools necessary to flourish and grow. In fact, the entire reason they moved to London was for Simon to have better access to the therapies he requires. I know his parents didn't just spend their life savings finding a home here, uprooting everything Simon knew to give him the help he needs, only to be met with *you*. The one person outside of Simon's family, meant to champion his therapy, is suddenly the one person standing in the way of it."

Dr Friedman's bottom lip is now quivering, and his eyes have gone unblinking for far too long, in my opinion. "Now, I know you come highly recommended in certain mum groups on social media sites, but in this case, you have failed. Simon is clearly severely autistic. They put their trust in you since they've chosen to prioritise their child and go with private medical care instead of the NHS, so I am here to remove you, so that they may find a new physician better suited to Simon's needs.

"I feel a bit like an evil genius giving you the whole run down before the show, but it's something I saw in a film recently and have been dying to try it out."

Dr Friedman's eyes are glassy, and tears drip down his cheeks when he realises there will be no way out of this. Taking a deep breath in, I let it out slowly, ready to deal the final blow.

"Because we're—unfortunately—colleagues of a sort, I'm going to give you two options."

Friedman looks hopeful for a moment before I continue speaking. "I can kill you myself, which will probably be messy, scar your adult children for the rest of their lives, and give your ex-wife immense delight, or..."

"Or! I choose 'or,'" he announces, like that option will give a different end result.

"Or you can do it yourself." I smile at him. "You have twenty seconds to decide, then we do it my way."

I spin the scalpel in my hand, watching it refract the light from the sad little lamp above our heads. "This is not a courtesy I extend to everybody, so you should feel pretty special right about now." Ah, damn. I lost the bet with myself. His face has gone white as a sheet; I had guessed green earlier. My eyes are steady, my fingertips drumming out a beat on the tabletop between us.

"You don't have to do this," he says as the timer in my head counts down. Six seconds left.

"I know. I want to. If someone doesn't stand up for the children, people like you will continue to grind them into the ground under your boot on their quest for more money, more prestige, more, more,

more. Have you made your choice? You're out of time," I chide as I point the scalpel at his throat.

"Shall I make a choice for you and give your ex the satisfaction she undoubtedly missed out on while you were married?" I ask conversationally. "Or would you prefer the pills?"

I remove the bottle of ADHD medication I snagged from his office earlier, ensuring it would be noted as missing from their supply closet, and hand it over.

Methylphenidate is a controlled substance, mostly used here in England for ADHD, but in the US as well as rare cases here in the UK, it's also used for narcolepsy. Taken in proper dosage, it would be fine. In excess, well, it leads to seizures, coma, and eventually death. Good thing I brought enough for Dr Friedman.

Tentatively, he reaches his hand out for the container of pills.

"Oh! How could I forget? You'll need something to drink." I get up from my chair and fill a glass with vodka from the freezer, knowing the alcohol will mix with the medication nicely. When I return, I upend the pill bottle in his hand, shove the peach-coloured pills in his mouth, and whisper, "Bottoms up."

Olivia

Present Day

"Open the fucking door, Little Thief. I just left a doctor face down in his sad little dinner for one, and I need you," Zach growls into the phone, not a second after I answer it.

"Gimme a minute," I tell him, fiddling with the app, as I get up from the couch where Rory and I were discussing 3D printing, while Max and Viraj glared daggers at one another. A crash sounds at the

THE CLEANUP

entry, and an irate-looking and impatient Zach comes barreling in as I step into the open hallway.

My bare feet slap on the marble tile as my breath catches in my throat when I catch sight of him. I decided to be extra devious and motivating today, so I'm in spandex shorts and a too-small camisole designed to remind the guys—not subtly—what they stand to gain if they make some headway in our planning.

He charges towards me and dips his shoulder, banding an arm around the back of my knees, and lifts me in a fireman's carry.

"Zach, what the fuck?" I cry as he sets off towards the living room. My hands come down on his back, but he's wearing a backpack, and my tiny, ineffectual fists are having trouble finding a decent landing spot. He smacks a hand down on my spandex-clad ass and keeps walking.

Zach blows past the others in the living room, but they stand as one, and a chorus of shouts from their general direction rain down on us when they see our current positioning.

I wave a hand over my head, trying to curb the incoming argument, but that all gets blown to shit when Zach opens his mouth. "If any of you fuckheads disturb us, I'll cut off your dicks and pull your fingernails from your body before dumping you in the Thames."

Viraj opens his mouth, and for a moment, I hope he's going to rein in his dickish comments. "What the bloody hell are you doing? You can't just come in here and steal her away."

Great job, V-Card.

"And why not? I'm taking what I'm owed," Zach answers.

"Owed?" Max asks, echoing my thoughts. "You got a lead?"

"No," he replies tersely and turns towards the hidden door, leading to our playroom.

Zach pushes the panel open and then slams it shut behind us, locking it from the inside as lights flicker on.

Fists pound on the other side, and they shout about how Zach has thrown the rules out the window, and they're not wrong.

"It's time to pay up, Little Thief."

Pay up? Oh, shit. The bargain. His help in return for my willingness to let him scar me.

A shiver runs through me at the realisation. "Guys," I yell through the door, "I'm fine. Don't break my fucking house!"

The banging subsides, but the shouting continues. Well, at least we know they can take direction well.

Zach crosses the playroom I had built into the house, and an air of electricity surrounds us in anticipation of what's to come. The lights are dim as instruments hang from the walls and various surfaces are pushed out of the way until needed. He lowers me to my feet and runs his gaze over my body, missing nothing. My nipples are peaked and visible through my thin top, and I subtly shift from foot to foot, rubbing my thighs together at the ache that's been building since he threw me over his shoulder and hauled me off like a caveman.

"In need of some relief, Little Thief?" he asks as he removes his backpack and starts on the buttons of his jacket. I nod my head, soaking in Zach's undivided attention. It's a heady thing, being wanted with such single-mindedness, such obsession. "You haven't sought me out. I thought perhaps the others were keeping you sated, but apparently not."

"Oh, they are," I answer, thinking of Roark, as a smile unfurls on my lips. "But I like your brand of fuckery too."

"Is that so?"

I hum, taking a step closer. "Now, are you going to take what I promised you, or is this your new version of foreplay?"

His hand snaps out, raking his fingers against my scalp as he fists my hair at the roots. He pulls me in, taking my mouth with his in a bruising kiss that sends my pulse skyrocketing and my lust pooling low in my belly.

"My brave little thief," he murmurs as he pulls away, leaving me to chase his lips and lean into him. "Take off your clothes," he orders, releasing me from his hold.

My skin itches at the command, my body and mind wanting to rebel. And even as my teeth cut into my inner cheek, I shove the reac-

THE CLEANUP

tion down. I made a promise. One I trust Zach to administer with efficiency and, hopefully, a few orgasms.

I drag my camisole over my head, drawing out the torture as we stand in the cavernous room. Zach follows suit, pulling off his jean jacket and shirt. My sanity goes haywire for a second when I catch a glimpse of the veins on his lower torso and the salacious body he hides under his functional clothing.

Seeing this as a tit-for-tat game, I hook my thumbs into the waistband of my shorts and shimmy them down. Zach slowly, torturously, undoes his button-fly and pushes his trousers down, along with his underwear. His cock bobs between us when he straightens, just begging to be touched.

I reach a hand out to do just that, and he returns the gesture in kind, skimming two fingers along my pussy, dragging them slowly as I close my hand around his length.

"Are you ready to bleed for me, Little Thief?" he whispers against my ear as he takes a step closer.

"Yes, but if you carve a dick on me or fuck up my tattoos, Zach, I swear to fuck I will kill you."

He laughs, tilting my face and fusing our lips in a passionate battle. He presses forward and spins as he drops both of us onto the nearby lounge chair. We land with me sprawled across his tan body, his light smattering of hair tickling my sensitive skin and causing me to mewl at the contact.

"Ride my cock, Little Thief. You have to earn your marks."

Noting the challenge in his eyes, I plant my feet on either side of us and lift my body. Zach does absolutely nothing to help. He just tucks his hands behind his head like some modern-day psychotic Adonis, waiting for me to do all the work.

I grip his dick in my fist, and his lips part at the sensation. He's as hard as stone beneath me. Is that from the murder he just finished, the fact that I'm about to ride him, or the scar he's wanted to brand me with for years?

I'm guessing all of the above.

Zach is unmoving as I slowly rock over him, sliding him in, inch by delicious inch. My hands land on his pecs, giving me leverage as I lift my hips and lower them, working to impale myself. I'm aroused, but not wet enough for the glide down to be smooth. I cry out in frustration as the seconds tick by, and Zach's lips tilt upwards.

"Do you see now how frustrating it is to be denied what you want?" he taunts. "To have it so close, and yet so far?" He punctuates his final question with a thrust upwards—gaining the remaining inches in milliseconds where I struggled for what felt like an eternity.

My head drops back, my hair brushing the tops of his thighs behind me, and he stops moving.

"Your teasing that first night. Your denial of my mark." He clicks his tongue against his teeth. "You play a dangerous game with the others, but I am not *like* the others," he hisses.

Zach hooks a leg around mine and flips us, so he's now hovering above me. How he did that without making us both fall off the chair, I have no clue. His hand reaches for the nearby backpack and he withdraws a new scalpel from the front pocket. He rips off the protective cover with his teeth and drops his arm to the space beside my head.

Pulling out of me, he holds his cock in one hand, the blade in the other, and starts taunting me, slapping his rock-hard shaft on my upper thigh.

"Do you want it, Little Thief? Do you need my dick inside you as much as I've wanted to fuck you raw?"

"Doc, please." He lets go of his cock to push two fingers inside me.

"Stay very still, otherwise you will ruin it all. Did you know that in some African cultures, scars are used to show the bravery of a warrior?"

I moan. Yes, some part of my brain probably knew, but the organ switched off the moment his cock came in contact with my aching pussy.

I twitch when the blade first comes in contact with my upper stomach. "Do. Not. Move," Zach growls.

"Yes, Doc. I promise I'll try to be a good patient."

The Cleanup

Zach starts cutting my right side with his left hand, the first point of contact just below my breast. His face hovers mere inches above my belly, and he's got this intense—surgical, almost—expression of focus on his face. It doesn't hurt that much. Yet. My body is flooded with endorphins, and the blade is sharp enough to part the skin without resistance.

While his left hand cuts, his right one presses and strokes me from the inside. He knows my body like no one else does—maybe not even me—and finds my G-spot in mere moments. I whimper, consumed by pleasure, desperate because I can't move.

The hand with the scalpel reaches the level of my belly button, and he cuts a swirl in my skin next to it. My orgasm is creeping up on me, and climaxing without letting my lower abs move will be an exercise in self-control. Control I'm not sure I have.

"Please," I beg. "Please, Doc, let me come. Stop cutting so I can—"

"No." His tone is final, uncompromising. He presses his thumb on my clit, and my entire body tenses in pleasure. "You will come, but you won't move. If I gut you while we're having sex, the others will murder me." A psychotic smile graces his lips. "But I wouldn't fucking care. Even if my soul is but a forgotten whisper, it will find yours and make it cry out in both pleasure and pain."

A shiver of fear courses through me. Zach has a scalpel right next to my belly button, the blade parting my skin and making blood pool over my stomach. If I'm not careful, I'll impale myself on it. And then we'd both die, like an even more fucked-up version of Romeo and Juliet.

Why doesn't that turn me off?

"You love this, Little Thief, don't you? The danger, the thrill, the adrenaline, playing with a predator—it all makes you wet. I can feel you clamp around my fingers. Now show me how much you like it, and come for me."

I can't. If I come, I'll move, and the blade will do real damage.

"Olivia, obey me," Zach growls. "Come, *now*."

The fear, pleasure, and pain are mixing in my brain, tangling together until I don't even know my name. Zach presses harder on my clit, stroking my G-spot at the same time.

I won't last long.

Goodbye world, it's been nice knowing you.

I come with a shout, abs contracting hard, body shaking under the waves of pleasure. The pain doesn't come, though. When I look up, Zach has an amused expression on his face and holds the scalpel over my stomach, the blade away from my skin.

"What did you expect, Little Thief? I can't hurt you yet; I still have to do the other side."

He switches hands like nobody's business, passing the scalpel to his right hand, still slippery from my juices.

"Little Thief, you got my hand all wet," he scolds.

Still, he gets started on my left side, repeating the exact same ornamental lines on my belly while his left hand buries itself inside me.

"This is going to be the prettiest art," he coos, completely absorbed by the blood pooling on my abdomen. "My designs cut into your skin while you writhe in pleasure. You're so brave, Little Thief."

All trace of humanity has left his features as he inflicts such exquisite pain. This really is art for him, even when it's hurting me. There's no compassion, no understanding on his handsome face, just the empty look of a creator focused on his masterpiece.

"Olivia, are you going to be a good patient and come again for me?"

This is fifty shades of fucked up. Yet, I crave this shade of perversion; I crave the abandon that only he brings.

"Yes, Doc. I will," I pant.

The hand inside me starts stroking again, for real. This feels amazing—the pain on my stomach and the pleasure coming from my clit once again merging until my skin becomes hypersensitive.

I don't care about impaling myself anymore. It would be dumb, but what a way to go.

I come even harder than the first time, all my muscles shaking and contracting like I'm having a seizure. The scalpel slides a little to the side, and I cry out at the sting.

As I pant and try to catch my breath, Zach quickly finishes his design, holding me down with his now free hand. Then the blade leaves my skin, and he leans back to admire his masterpiece. "You moved. You ruined it."

"Or maybe I made it better. Now I have the orgasm you gave me permanently etched on my skin." It's obvious he loves the idea if that devious smile on his face is any indication. Psycho.

He drops the bloody scalpel on a nearby table and grabs his dick violently, pressing on it. "Now I'm going to fuck you while you bleed, and you're going to take my dick and beg for more."

Yes, please. I lick my lips as he surges forward.

"Ahh," I cry at the decadent invasion, unable to hold back the sound. He does it again. And again. Each withdrawal and subsequent roll of his hips as he pushes forward sends me closer towards the precipice. The friction between our bodies is made much more obvious by how it hurts me, rubbing on my wounds and spreading my blood all over us. I unleash myself and claw at his back. I might wear his marks now, but he'll wear mine, too.

His hand moves from his cock to my clit as he presses his thumb against the bundle of nerves, but without giving me the stimulation I need.

My head swims with the heady sensations, my body lighter than air as I spiral higher. Zach lifts onto his knees, and I plant my feet on the chair, lifting my hips and meeting him thrust for thrust. My hands hook onto the edge of the headrest to keep me steady as I work to get what I want. Another motherfucking orgasm.

Zach's breathing is rapid, but his thrusts into me are measured, calculated. He still hasn't lost his unwavering focus, and I want to see him shatter. My walls stutter, desperate for an orgasm to sweep me away into oblivion, dragging him with me.

I look up, watching as his abs flex with every movement. His shoulders tense as he starts strumming on my clit again.

My release builds, stronger than before. Zach's movements get more erratic, and he wraps both hands around my hips, using the angle to drive into me with reckless abandon, throwing me right off the edge again and into eternity.

He pulls out, stroking his cock until cum shoots across my abdomen and breasts, painting me in his release. Lowering himself between my thighs, he runs his tongue over my hip, lapping up the mixture of blood and cum he spilled, as my fingers nestle in his chestnut hair.

"My brave little thief," he repeats, murmuring the words against my belly and wrapping his arms around my waist. We stay like this for a while, catching our breath and coming down from our high.

"Let me clean you up," he announces after a moment.

This is the room we often use together, so he knows where the antiseptic spray is. He uses copious amounts of it on my abdomen and removes the mess with some gauze, making sure I don't need stitches. When he's finally sure I am, in fact, peachy, he leans back to admire his masterpiece. "The scars will be thin."

He bandages the wounds, adding more antiseptic spray and gauze that he affixes with tape. When he finally looks satisfied with his work, he kisses the free skin just below my belly button.

"This is perfect. When this belly carries our baby, they'll have proof of how far I will go if anyone hurts them."

Chapter Fifteen

Olivia
Present Day

This time, for once, our planning session happens in my office. There are tons of things that still need to be ironed out. Namely, accessing the diamonds, identifying the one we're looking for, stealing it, and getting out.

Yeah, I know, that's everything.

We've been poring over maps of Monaco for hours, familiarising ourselves with the streets, avenues, and major landmarks. We can't go into this completely blind. It'll be different with boots on the ground, but for now, we have to start somewhere.

I need a distraction from looking at the same images yet again; I've been studying these nonstop. I look around at the guys to find them all continuing the assignment and following routes with their eyes. Good boys. Though, occasionally, Max's finger wanders over to the Monte Carlo casino.

"Viraj, did you work on a getaway plan, or do you need help?" I ask. He was responsible for it, but we're a team. If he's struggling, I'd rather help now than face problems later. I gave him this assignment days ago and haven't heard a peep about it since. He should have something by now, even if it's just a notion. We can build upon a notion.

A grunt is all I get in return.

"V, are you okay?" Now everybody's looking at him, and it's not helping the situation. His chest puffs at the attention, and the vein in his neck starts pulsing. He's standing against the wall, arms crossed in front of his chest and feet crossed at the ankle.

You don't need to be an expert to read that body language.

"What's wrong? If you haven't found a solution yet, it's okay. We can work on it together."

"Of course, I haven't found a fucking solution." He throws his hands up above his head. "And you guys have been too busy fucking to even notice the extent of the fuckery she got us into! We have no fucking way out, and we'll all end up in a motherfucking Monegasque jail."

That's a lot of fucks.

"V, take a breath, okay?" I suggest, which seems to have been the wrong thing to say. He breathes in, but doesn't exhale. His face reddens profusely and his fists clench at his sides. "We're going to get out of this; everything will be fine. We just need a plan."

"How do you fucking know?" He leans over the desk suddenly, getting all up in my personal space. Roark and Max are split apart with V's sudden need to put his clenched hands all over the map and yell at me face-to-face. "You've never stolen a diamond either; you're just as inexperienced and incompetent as the rest of us!"

I take a deep breath, then another. At my right, Zach is starting to growl, and I put a steadying hand on his denim-clad thigh to calm him. Being a leader is exhausting.

"I know," I say. There's no point in lying; everybody here knows I'm not a jewel thief. "But I've been asked to retrieve data on flash drives before. I've stolen information from governments. Hell, I even took down a dictator just before you guys arrived with nothing but secrets exchanged and the right information dropped at the most opportune time."

I slam my hands down on the desk before me, splaying my fingers wide and rising from my seat to meet Viraj without being looked down upon while he spirals. "Sure, in those cases, I didn't leave with anything physical—apart from a shiny dick hard drive with downloaded data, that is—but I've never failed, and this time won't be any different. We'll just find which piece of the jewellery set contains the Interpol diamond, switch them for the replica, and get the fuck out." I'm conveying more confidence than I feel. There are still a lot of unknowns in our plan that I'm not comfortable with.

"If you're so sure of yourself, why's he here?" Viraj tilts his head in Zach's direction. "Apart from breaking the agreed-upon rules and being menacing, he's done nothing till now."

Rory and Max exchange looks and lean farther away from the sudden team unbonding exercise happening before them. Roark, so often our peacekeeper, doesn't interject this time. Max, on the other hand, looks like he wants a bowl of popcorn to watch the damned show.

Our doctor smirks. "I bet my little thief would disagree with that. I did plenty of things to her the other day."

I glower at him. He's not helping. The guys had plenty to say about the scars Zach left on my torso, but with a few swift words about how it is, in fact, *my* body, they shut the hell up.

I dive back into Viraj's dark eyes. "I said I'd never failed, not that I didn't get hurt. He's here as a precaution. Besides, I think I'll have to hypnotise Natasha at some point, and I need him to practise since he's naturally more resistant to it."

Viraj frowns at my explanation, but listens.

"Psychopath, remember?" Zach adds. "I have superpowers."

"I'm well aware of your superpowers," V hisses, venom dripping from every word. "We all heard her scream the other day."

"Guys, back on track; we're missing the point here," Roark attempts to persuade the others.

"No," Viraj snarks. "This is exactly the point. Why would I work my ass off following the rules, only for this psycho to come in and ruin it all?"

What he just said takes a second to register. "V, are you telling me that the only reason you were working on that escape plan is to *get laid*? Are you serious right now?!"

"It was my turn," he protests like a petulant child whose toy has been stolen.

I see red. Beyond red. Fucking crimson. "Let's get something straight here. I fuck who I want and when I want. Whether that happens to be because they've found a lead, or because my pussy started throwing her pom-poms in the air and said, 'That one, I want that one!' I owe none of you an explanation for it. It was my choice when we were in school, and it still is. Grow up, Viraj!"

"But—"

Deciding an image is worth a thousand words—or a demonstration, in this case—I stand up, an eerie calm rushing through my body. Lifting my chin, I square my shoulders at the man before me. "Come, V, I think we need to discuss some things."

Zach pulls my chair away, giving me space to round the desk. Max and Roark are looking at Viraj with vitriol in their gazes and not one ounce of sympathy.

I lead him downstairs and into the same room Zach and I played in, not so long ago.

The chair in the corner of the room is the only tool I'll need. Dragging it over, I get it situated in the centre of the room, while V stands against the west wall. I need good lighting for this performance. I got this particular piece of furniture custom-made as a present for myself after a successful job, and it has an anchor for a massive dildo in the middle of the seat. In case anyone's wondering, yes, the matching dildo is currently fixed to the chair. It's not bigger than Max's dick, but damn close.

Viraj's black eyes are challenging me through the loose curls falling over his forehead. Does he think I'm not going to do it? This big dick energy contest only has one winner, and—spoiler alert—it's me.

I reach for the back of the chair and turn it around, so I'll have to straddle the silicone dick to sit and face the man currently driving me insane. V is still looking at me like he's waiting for me to stop bluffing.

What he doesn't know—or maybe he does, and that's why he's being such a cunt—is that Roark fucked me again this morning. It was a lovely quickie in the kitchen pantry and has prepared me perfectly for this. He was cautious of my healing scars, but not put out by them in the slightest.

I'm wet as fuck at the verbal sparring from upstairs and the challenge shining in Viraj's gaze. I'm currently sans underwear, and the tightness shouldn't be an issue; not when I'm this determined to prove my motherfucking point.

My jean skirt rides up my thighs as I step forward and straddle the base of the chair. I rest my hands on the back support, crossing them daintily at the wrist. Because I'm a fucking lady. A sinful one, but who's keeping score?

I line myself up and start lowering my hips. Viraj's eyes go wide.

"Liv, come on, you're not gonna do this."

"Why not? This chair is my favourite." I look him dead in the eyes as I say those words. "I'll fuck whoever I want to fuck, remember? Even if it's silicone." I lower myself onto the huge dildo, feeling the blunt head stretch my entrance as my fingers splay on the back of the chair, gripping the edge. I lift just a few centimetres before returning to my descent, using my slick juices to coat the toy and ease its passage.

Our asshole lawyer looks like he's been struck by lightning, and damn if that doesn't do something to me. I moan, focusing my eyes on him and watching as he looks his fill. "You don't have to like it," I purr, "but I'm in charge of this crew, and this is my job." My words catch in my throat as I keep taking more of the silicone toy inside me. It's big. Not bigger than my forearm, but close. I've always loved how it stretched me, pushed me to my limits, then hit me in all the right places inside. "And you agreed to the terms when you arrived. I even gave you an offer to leave, and you didn't take it."

Ever since I started talking, I haven't broken our eye contact, and Viraj looks more mesmerised than anything else now. "You'll speak to me with respect, V, or you can leave. I have done hundreds of jobs without you, and I can take care of this one, too." Okay, that's one hundred per cent a lie. Where on god's green earth would I find another lawyer/climber/driver on such short notice?

"So, stop being a dick. Otherwise, I'll treat you the way I treat all the other dicks; I'll use you to masturbate, then store you someplace convenient where everybody will forget you until I have an itch to scratch again. The rules are simple, Viraj. You understand this is a matriarchy, or you leave."

I rock back and forth on the toy to drive the point home; little moans escaping my mouth when it hits my cervix. Fuck, this feels good.

"I won't promise I'll stop challenging you," he says, licking his lips. His eyes are fixated on where the toy disappears inside my body, and he runs a hand over the bulge in his trousers, giving his cock a squeeze through the material.

"I can live with that," I answer, flexing my leg muscles faster, fucking myself on the toy.

"But I can agree that your decisions are final."

"Good. That's all I'm asking for." My hands drag my top higher on my torso, and his eyes narrow in on the bandages wrapped there. The look of satisfaction on Zach's face flashes through my mind, along with the words he uttered about "our baby." I don't even know if I want kids, but fuck, maybe I should start figuring that out at some point. Not today, though. Viraj wisely doesn't say anything about my gauzed torso when my eyes flash in warning. I let my fingers rise to my breasts, and I pinch my nipples, whimpering in pleasure. "Now, get out."

It takes a second for the words to register in his lust-addled brain, but when they do, he shouts, "What?!"

"I'm not in the habit of rewarding bad behaviour. So take your blue balls, the jaw you dropped on the floor, and get out. Go sulk in your room. I'm not leaving here without multiple orgasms, and you're killing my vibe." Another lie. Fighting with Viraj always gets me hot and bothered. And him watching me come with this angry look in his eyes would be sexy as sin, but it'll have to be another day. "Leave, V."

Reluctantly, he heads towards the door, his hard dick tenting the front of his trousers. When he passes me, he leans in to whisper against the sensitive skin of my neck, "One day, I'll fuck these sassy words right out of your mouth, Ollie. You'll turn to putty in my arms and forget all the men that came before me, no matter if they were Vikings, psychopaths, or lords. You'll be mine."

"Bring it, asshole." Then he bites my earlobe so hard it triggers an earth-shattering orgasm, making me cry out in pleasure. My muscles clench, and I ride the toy while waves upon waves of ecstasy flow through my veins.

Spent, I collapse against the back of the chair, pussy still pulsing around the silicone. "Fuck," I mumble.

Once my post-orgasmic haze fades, I look around to find I'm alone in the room.

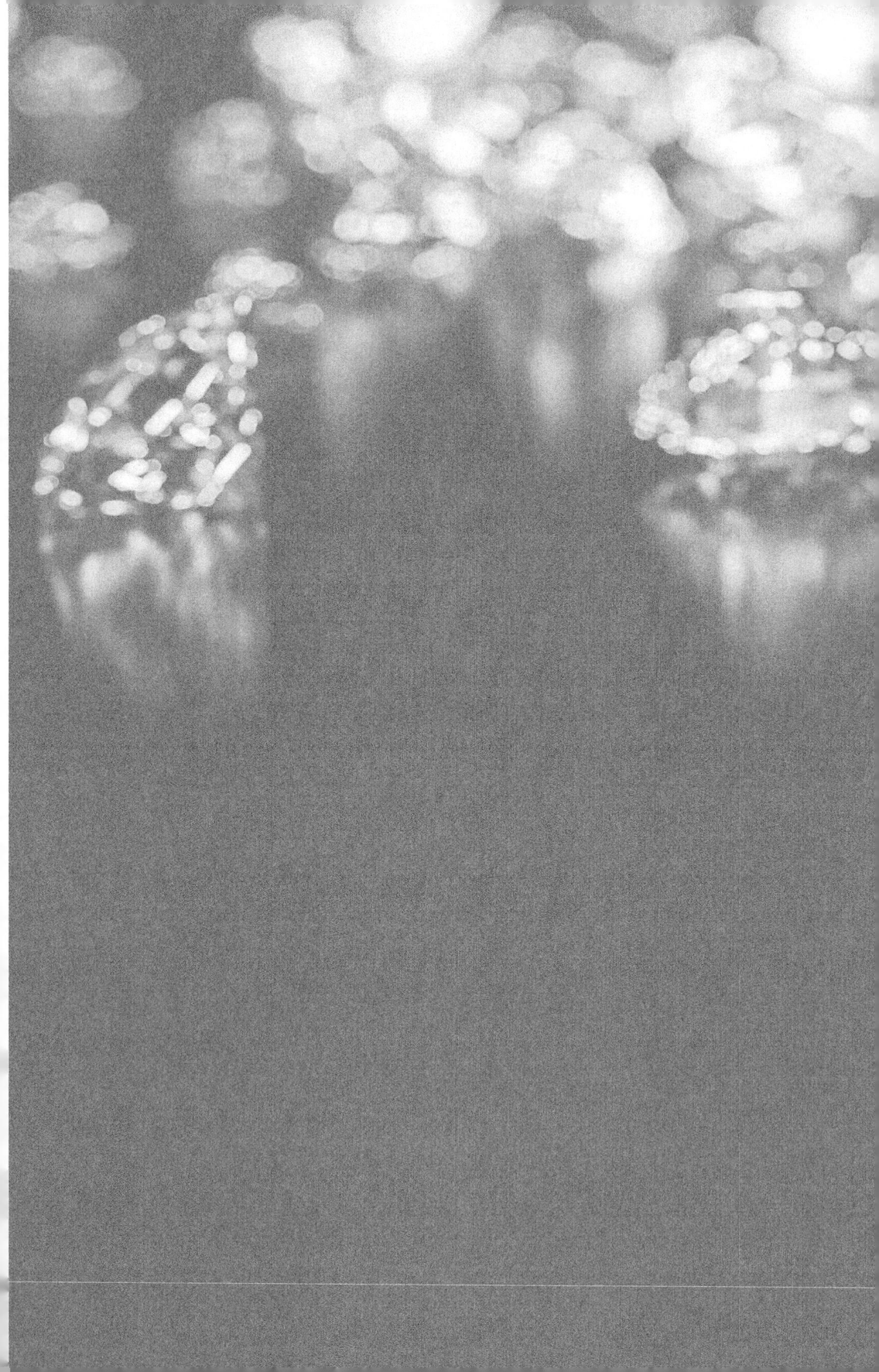

Chapter Sixteen

Max
Year Twelve
June

"Maximillian, darling, your father is just doing what's best for you, you know that," Mother says down the line.

"I disagree," I counter. Dad's looking for a way to rub elbows with royalty. He has just signed me up to intern at a law firm that I have absolutely no interest in joining. The reason? Some distant relative of the Queen will also be there.

Mother sighs stoically and clicks her tongue. "You are free to disagree, but you are not free to refuse. A lot of work went into securing you this position. Your father held a similar one at your age, and you are expected to do the same." I inwardly groan. The last thing I want is to be a carbon copy of my father. "Term ends in a week. The driver will be there to pick you up on Saturday afternoon. Your things will be stored in your room over the holiday, so just bring what is essential."

With that, Mum clicks off, and the line goes dead.

Splendid.

I shove the mobile into my pocket and look up at the sound of measured footsteps, walking as if they're trying to be quiet. It's Saturday, and the administration offices are empty aside from the custodial staff today and the two admin assistants I've seen making copies. It's why I chose this hallway.

Standing from the bench, I poke my head around the corner and find Olivia Wraith reaching for a closed door.

"Miss Wraith, not trying to break in now, are we?" I ask, sauntering over to her with my hands in my pockets and a grin on my face.

Her hand flinches, and she withdraws it, wringing them together. "No, I wanted to ask about moving out and timing."

"On a Saturday?"

"Yes."

"When no one is working?"

"Apparently."

"And you still have this question after all the information about move-out day has already been emailed to all of us?"

"Yes."

"Well," I drawl, cocking a brow. "Maybe I can help. I've been here for an eternity. What's your question?"

She looks me up and down, her blonde hair falling over her shoulder with the movement. "I, uh..."

"I knew it," I say with a smile. She's going to be a half-decent liar one day, but she has to work on her acting skills a bit more. Unless this was all a ploy to get me to help the pretty new girl with the blush on her cheeks. Fuck it. I'm in. "What are you looking for? You know the things they confiscate eventually end up in the headmaster's office, right?" I hook a thumb over my shoulder, pointing at the door across the hall.

"Nothing." She sighs. "Nothing. I just..."

"Just? Come on, Liv," I coax, using the nickname I randomly started calling her a few months ago when we had a history project together. "Like I said, I've been here for ages. I can probably help you."

"Fuck it. Fine." She takes a deep breath. "Have you ever needed to know something so badly you couldn't stop thinking about it? But you can't get the answer because it's locked away somewhere? Does that make sense? Probably not. Okay, let me try again. I need to see a file. But I can't find it online, and this room has the records I need. I'm not going to steal anything. I just need to read something. And maybe make a copy of it." She winces.

"Fine." Olivia's face lights up with a smile at my agreement. "But it will cost you."

Her lips tilt up in a small grin. "Oh, yeah?" she says as she steps closer, running her hands down my jacket lapels and stepping into my space. Every thought I've ever had has just vacated my mind.

I've been interested in Olivia since the start of the school year, but she seems to keep to herself. Finding myself looking for her in the halls and ignoring the very willing and available girls around me has had me questioning my sanity. I mean, she's gorgeous, but I don't really know her.

I know she's clever—she wouldn't be here if she weren't. She's kind to the other students but never overly engaged with anyone aside from Eleanor, her roommate. Her grades are perfect, and the teachers like her. She blends in, making herself easy to overlook if you aren't paying attention. I have been paying a lot of attention, though.

Swallowing my nerves, I go for it. "A date."

Her big eyes blink up at me, and she smiles wider. "A date?" She brings her finger to her chin as she mulls it over. After the longest seven seconds of my life, she says, "And a promise that this stays between us." She motions her hand between us and the door she wants to get through.

"Agreed."

After talking with Mum, all I want to do is something my father hasn't done before. Breaking into a records office might be on that list. The date is an added bonus, and there's something about this girl that I need to figure out.

Olivia steps back and looks up at me. "So? How are we getting in?" she asks.

I peer down the hall, finding it empty and test the knob. Which is, in fact, locked. "Easily," I reply. Raising my arm, I feel along the top of the doorframe. On the right, my fingers strike gold. I slide the little key over the lip of the frame and hold it out in my palm.

"Fucking hell," she mutters.

I slide the key into the lock, turn the knob, and swing the door open. "After you."

"Nope. You stay out here and guard the door. I'll be five minutes, tops."

But I want to know what she's looking for. She turns those big mismatched eyes to me, and there's a challenge in them. More than I was expecting, honestly. She's never given me a look like that before, and I know one day, this girl will be the queen in her own story.

"Fine, fine," I say.

She slips inside, and true to her word, an uneventful five minutes later, she's back. "All done, lock it up. I'm ready for that date," she says as she shoves a thick pile of copier paper under her arm.

"Now?" I sputter. I've only been out here a few minutes. I haven't planned a date yet! Bloody hell, I can't keep up. "How about tomorrow?" I ask.

"Can't. I've got study plans. But we can go to the dining hall after I drop these off in my room," she says as she pats the pages under her arms. I put the key back where I found it, and then we make our way through the hall.

"But I wanted to take you on a real date."

"Will that date have food?" she asks. I nod. "And conversation?" Again, I nod.

"Then, aside from spending a bunch of money, how is it different?"

My feet stop moving. Olivia walks a few steps before realising I'm no longer with her. "How—? How is it different?" I repeat, and she shrugs. "The food is a hundred times better, the atmosphere is impeccable, and while I do appreciate the cleanliness of the dining hall, I'd rather not be interrupted every five minutes by our classmates."

"Okay, that's fair." She encourages me to keep walking and then turns to me. "I really can only do lunch today, though. I need to keep my grades up, so studying comes first."

Not wanting to miss the opportunity, I concede. But I can make this work. "Okay, you drop that off, do whatever you have to do, and I'll meet you back here in thirty minutes."

"Really?" she asks, checking the time on her phone.

"Really. I have a plan."

She heads up the stairs, and I pull out my phone, dialling one of the local restaurants to help me out. I hit up the dining hall, and after bribing a few of the other students to help me, I have set up the perfect date here in the dining hall.

The timer on my phone sounds, and with one last look, I rush back to meet Olivia at the foot of the stairs. She's already there, and when I skid to a stop in front of her, I extend an elbow. "This way, please."

She laughs at my chivalry, but it's not every day you get to take a girl on a first date. We enter the dining hall, still milling with students, and I guide her to the right and away from the food cases.

The art students helped me hang drop cloths from the ceiling, carving out a small area towards the back of the hall just for us. One of them hastily painted an Eiffel Tower on one of the sheets, and while it's a little drippy since it's vertical, it's memorable. She gasps, then laughs as she looks at what I've been putting together.

I prepared a basket of bread and rolls from the dining hall to tide us over until the food from the restaurant gets here, and I stuck an LED candle in the middle of the table. There are juice bottles in a serving tray full of ice and sparkling water from my own fridge upstairs, already uncapped.

Olivia lets out a squeal of joy and spins around, taking in our date locale. "How did you do this in thirty minutes?" she asks.

Money. The answer is always money.

We sit at the table, and I offer her a choice of drinks and tell her food is on the way.

"You didn't bribe someone to act as a waiter, did you? I doubt the kitchen staff would enjoy that, Max."

"Of course not!" I say, smacking a hand against my chest in mock indignation. "I ordered us takeout."

A minute later, someone ruffles the drop cloth, and a head pokes in. "Mr Arondale, I have your order." I wave him in, and three bags of to-go boxes weigh down his arms.

He places the bags on the nearby table and starts unpacking the food. "Max, what the hell is all this, and oh my god, that smells so freaking good."

I laugh at her abrupt change in conversation. "It's from this Italian place a few miles away. I ordered every pasta dish on the menu. I figured I couldn't go wrong with carbs before you have plans to study."

She beams at me, and we thank the delivery guy before selecting our food. We both take spoonfuls of every kind, and we sit in our seats. The hour rushes by, and Olivia fawns over the carbonara.

Far too quickly, she's patting her stomach and looks like she's about to slip into a food coma. We might have overdone it. "Max, that was amazing. Thank you. I don't think I've ever been so spoilt for choice."

"You're welcome. It was really fun. How about I take you out Friday for a proper date before we all go home for the summer?" I ask, thinking again about that wretched position I'll be forced to endure for the next six weeks.

She bites her lip and looks down at her lap, blonde hair shielding her face. "I, uhm, I don't want a boyfriend, Max. Or to date, really. I can't afford the distractions. Plus, I'm one of the unlucky ones who has a final exam Saturday morning."

I feel my cheeks go red and clear my throat. "That makes sense," I say, hoping my voice doesn't betray my disappointment.

Maybe next year, when we're all back after the summer...

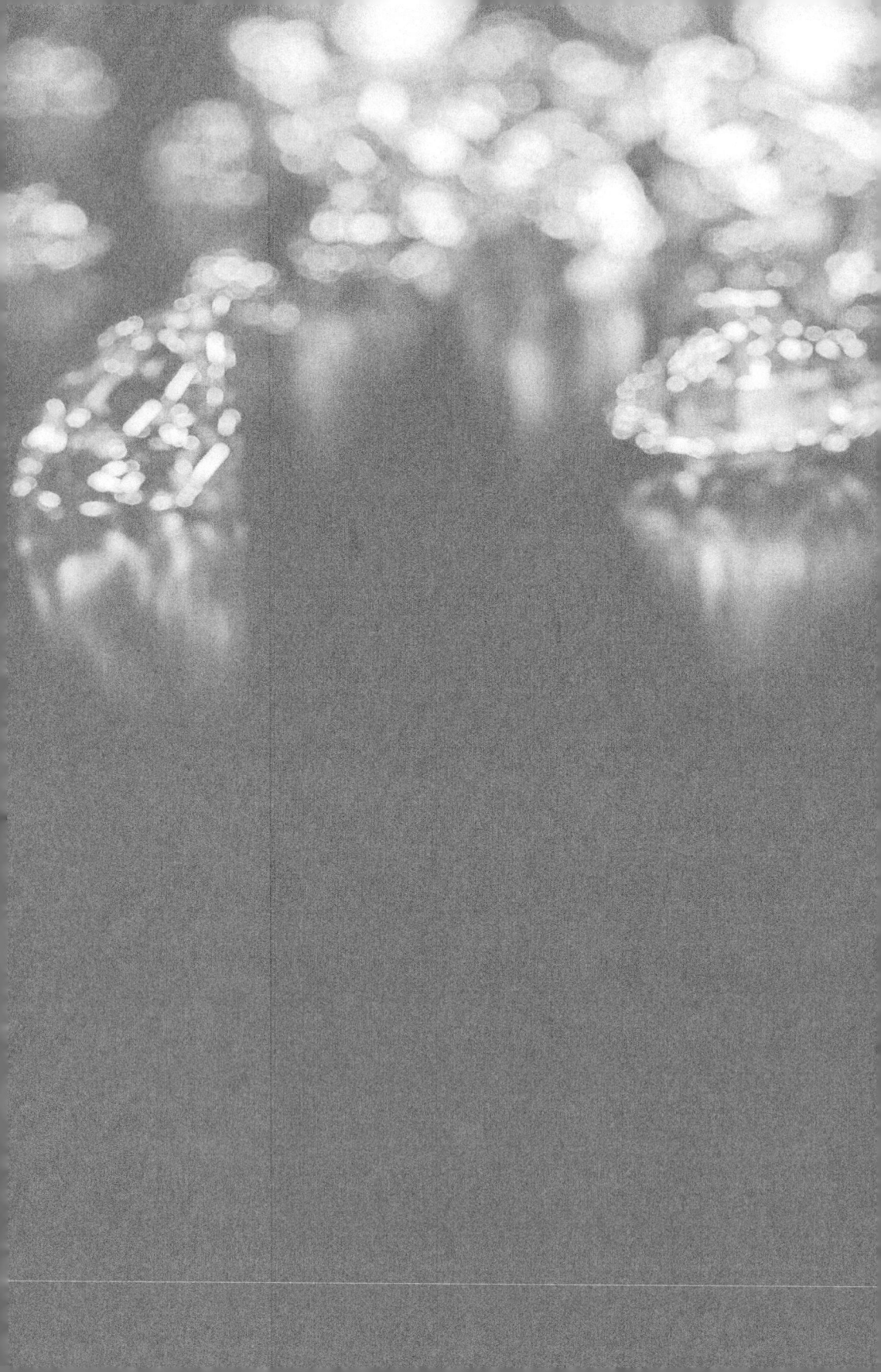

Chapter Seventeen

Olivia
Present Day

Rory and I got the replica pieces of Natasha's jewellery made. I've had more deliveries of men's clothing than I ever thought possible—I may have peeked at their credit card statements to find out where they like to shop and ended up buying too much—and we've talked through our plan to get the diamond. It will require some on-the-ground work in Monaco, but that's why we're going a month ahead of the Grand Prix to get the lay of the land and take copious notes on security and possible pitfalls. We leave in four days, and we have no concrete escape plan.

Time to change that.

In all the research I've managed to sneak in at odd hours, I've only found a few instances of someone successfully getting out of the principality. And I only found those by doing a deep dive online. They were buried in the web so exhaustively, it took ages to dig up.

Their security is top of the line, overinvested in, and rigorously tested by not only law enforcement but fellow thieves.

They've employed the age-old tactic of hiring black-market agents to poke holes in their system to shore up against possible invasions and paid exorbitant fees to ensure it doesn't happen again. As shrewd as that is, it poses a problem for us. I can respect my fellow thieves and admire their work, but fuck if they aren't throwing wrenches into my plans left and right.

Our preparations will all be for nought if we can't get the fuck out of the principality, and more importantly, Ellie will be fucked.

It might be stupid to risk so much for someone else, but not when that person is your found family and the only person to be in my corner since we were teenagers. She has kept my head above water more times than I can count.

Ours is an unlikely story. One that could have ended a million times but hasn't because our bond runs deep despite what we do for work. The thief and the Interpol agent. If we both swung differently, it'd make for an incredible romance novel. Unfortunately, that just isn't the case.

I put my slice of pizza down and look at my team as they inhale their food. Max, of course, uses a knife and fork. Why did I expect anything different? I keep forgetting to feed them. Who knew four grown men could be so needy?

Viraj's comments about the lack of sustenance in this house have driven me mad. Still, it's fun to watch him open the pantry every few hours, only to shut it again when he realises the only things in there are rice crackers and a few packets of instant noodles.

They demolished my snack stash in record time, and I have to admit, it was kind of impressive. Two of the guys like to leave their shit all over the house, and after the first time I threw it into the fireplace, lighting it all ablaze, that has thankfully improved.

The Cleanup

A hand slides up my thigh through the rips in my baggy jeans I've been living in to avoid too much pressure on my healing scars. The fingers tease my skin and send a pleasant warmth shooting through my system. Max isn't looking at me as he strokes the soft skin but argues with Rory and Viraj across the table about the best pizza in the city.

His fingers find the more significant rip and dive in as he carefully eats his pizza with the other hand. Rory watches as his own hand disappears under the table and does the same. Suddenly, two of them are touching me on opposite sides and I end up focusing all my attention on the contact.

Rory's hand squeezes my thigh and slides higher on the outside of my jeans as Max's fingers delve deeper under the denim, closer to my drenched core. The slide of his fingers is painfully slow towards my dripping and naked pussy, and my lips curl in a grin when their fingers find the other's. A set on either side of my pussy, divided by denim but united by their single-minded focus on my pleasure, has me imagining stroking that hairless cat again as I enact my evil laugh in my head. A girl could get used to this.

Zach notices me looking at them and finishes his slice of pineapple-topped pizza. If there were any doubts in my head that he was genuinely psychotic, the fruit and ham combination would have given him away.

"What's on your mind, Little Thief?"

Max, Rory, and Viraj stop their argument to look at me. All the while, Max dips his fingers into my dripping pussy, and Rory pushes on the denim over my clit. The movement causes a ripple of pleasure to course through my body.

Focus, Olivia. Focus.

They have not earned more sexy time yet.

But I have, retorts the devil on my shoulder.

"We need a way out of the city," I say with a rough swallow. "It might take time for Natasha to notice we've made the switch, but it might not. She can raise the alarm in, let's say, three minutes give or take thirty seconds. If that's the case, we'll have twelve minutes to get out before they lock everything down. I have an idea, but timing will be everything."

"What are you thinking, Via?" Rory asks as he presses harder against my seam, drawing a gasp from my lips as Max pumps his hand and uses his forearm to widen my legs, giving him better access as the other one handles his fork with ridiculous ease. "Is there a way for me to scramble their comms?"

How is he so fucking calm and collected? He trails his blue-grey eyes up my neck, probably seeing the blush rising as I distract myself by wiping my mouth with a napkin.

"No, that would alert them even more quickly. There is twenty-four-hour surveillance on all streets, roads, ports, and access points. We need a way to bypass that. If their tech goes down, good old walkie-talkies are always an option, and I'm certain there are more channels in case of a cyber attack. I'm thinking something a bit more 'Bond villain'."

"I thought I was driving us out," Viraj comments, flinging the rest of his pizza slice onto the plate and getting defensive.

"You are, but we need to get to the car. What if there is traffic on the way to the borders? Plus, there are only two roads to get out of Monaco, and they're very easy to close, with law enforcement on either side. No, we'll get to your part. But it will have to happen outside the city."

"Okay," Max plays along, curling his fingers in my channel, and a low moan escapes my mouth. I cover it with a cough, but he smirks at my attempt. Zach is staring at me, and I'm certain he knows exactly what's going on under this table. "So, how do we get out of the city?"

"I'm so glad you asked, Max," I praise as more wetness seeps out of me, covering his fingers and probably his whole damned hand. "Have you got a boat?"

His brows raise. "Of course. Two superyachts, two exploration vessels, and a catamaran. But you just said they have eyes on the harbours." He pauses his hand as he considers, and I shift my hips, demanding more.

Rory picks up on the cue and strums faster along my clit, working my body into a frenzy. My hips shift on the chair, and my legs go slack, my feet sliding on the floor below me as my head drops back against the chair.

"They do. Eagle-eye views. CCTV that spans the city and is stored on a secure server that I can't access, no matter how amazing I am at it," I admit a bit begrudgingly. I roll my head to the side and look at Rory. "I doubt you could do it without triggering a failsafe. We can attempt it when we're in Monaco, but I'd rather not tip anyone off until then. We can even use it as a training exercise if we do cause a lockdown."

Rory nods, not offended at my lack of faith but understanding of the risks it poses. His fingers pick up speed, Max withdraws a finger, and with my cheeks hanging off the edge of the seat, he slides it to my ass and nudges at the entrance.

"Max, are any of your boats docked in the Mediterranean?" I ask despite already knowing the answer and getting back to my point while I still have somewhat of a grip on my sanity.

"Yeah, I have one of them in a dock close to Rome and another in the Adriatic," he answers as he breaches my ass and begins teasing me.

Italy. Hmm. Hmmm, Rory is working with unfailing focus, and the edge is right there. So fucking close.

"Does that one have a submersible?" I ask, again already knowing the answer. There isn't much I don't already know regarding these four, but sometimes it's nice to lead them to the answer and make them feel important.

"It does..." he trails off. "Oh, Liv, that's brilliant. That's fucking brilliant!" With his shout, he passes the tight ring of muscle, Rory's work on my clit comes to a culmination, and I see fucking stars; shouting right along with Max before he slides his hand out of the rip

—no doubt leaving a gaping hole in the denim on my thigh, and returns it to his lap and his properly laid napkin.

Viraj is looking at me with barely concealed rage when I open my eyes, obviously having figured out what just happened, and Zach is drumming his fingertips on the tabletop. He mouths the word, *Mine,* but a small smile plays on his delectable lips.

Rory continues stroking me down from my high, but it's softer now—calming rather than invigorating.

The others are slower to catch on to the conversation. "You want us to take a submarine out of Monaco?" Viraj asks. "What about radars?"

"You think their first thought is going to be checking underwater? And I think the term you're looking for is sonar. Radars search above or close to the surface," I toss back before taking a swig of my beer to clear the dryness in my throat. Considering all options is part of my job as the coordinator; I'm a little offended that he thinks I haven't done my homework.

"The submersible has a layer of Anechoic tiles," Max says. Rory cocks his head, and Max explains further. "It's basically a layer of rubber attached to the outer shell that absorbs sonar waves. The vehicle is small as it is and dives deep. It could work, but we'd have to haul ass to get as far as possible to ensure it doesn't pick us up."

"Why is your submarine undetectable, Maxi Pad? Been doing some snooping you shouldn't?" V sneers.

"That's none of your business," he snaps back.

"Gentlemen," Zach cuts in, looking delish in the white button-down I picked out for him. "I'd like to hear the rest of this plan if you don't mind."

I give him a grateful nod and continue with the plan. "So the only thing we need to do is get to the harbour and onto the boat. From there, we get into the submarine, steering it away from the docks. Once we're far enough out, we dive deep and hit the gas."

"It's not gas," Max counters.

I level him with a look.

"What? It's a jet that runs on a mixed flow pump which is a combination of both centrifugal and axial designs."

"Interesting. Mechanical or electrical?" V interjects.

Makes sense for the Adrenaline God to be obsessed with motors and engines of all kinds.

"That doesn't matter right now. You two can bond over it when we board." I wave a hand to bring the focus back to the task at hand.

"Then it's settled. We fly into Rome and take the boat to Monaco. I've already booked our accommodation, so that's settled."

"Why wouldn't we stay on the yacht?" Max asks.

"Because we need to scope out the city better—live there to get a feel for the rhythm, find hidden side streets, and note camera locations. The harbour will have its own security, which we will detail, but we need a broader picture to have more information. Don't worry, you'll love the flat."

He won't love the flat. None of them will. But hey, I'll take the silent treatment from them if it unites them enough to pull this job off. Unlikely allies with a common enemy would do wonders for our team dynamic. I'll play that role gladly if it helps Ellie.

"What happens when we get far enough with the submarine?" Rory asks.

"That's where I need some opinions. How do you all feel about scuba diving?"

"Love it," V chimes in, looking smug as all hell. Of course, he does.

"I've never done it," Rory says a little timidly.

Max lifts his glass, takes a sip of his wine, and reassures him, "It's easy. We'll teach you."

Look at the two of them getting along over orgasms and threesomes. I knew this would work.

"Doesn't it require a course and training, and I don't know, like a hundred hours to go solo?" Rory argues.

Max shocks the hell out of me with the next words out of his mouth. "Roark, you've always outsmarted us all. Learning this will be a piece of cake. We should do a bunch of dives together so you know what to expect."

"That's true," I agree. "We can even do a beginner's course in Monaco if that would make you feel better." Rory nods at my suggestion, and I make a mental note to look up instructors in the area. We have a month there, and we'll need something to do other than constantly prowl the streets as we map the city.

"We need a distraction," Viraj says, rubbing a hand through his dark curly hair. "If we get to the boat and into the submersible, we need them focused on something big."

"What would you suggest?" Zach asks.

"We need to blow up the boat."

Max stands up, shoving the chair out from behind him. "The fuck?! You can't just blow up my boat!" He throws his napkin on the table in indignation, making a far bigger show of it than it needs to be.

"V's right," I say.

Max whirls on me. I put my hands up in a placating gesture. "What if we can't dive deeply quick enough? What if there's a snag somewhere, and we cut the timing too close? I will buy you a new one if that's what it takes, but V is right. This is the best course of action for a getaway."

He considers it, twisting his hands into fists at his sides. "Fine, but if we do blow it up, I want a bigger one."

Petulant child.

"Deal," I agree with a half-smile. I give a pointed look at his chair, and he sits back down. "How far can the submersible travel?"

"Considering the energy we'll expend by diving deep? Perhaps one hundred fifty miles. The boat has a remote to it and a tracker we can disable for the escape, and flip it back on once we're clear. The crew can come pick it up when we're done."

I nod my head. "That's plenty of distance for what I'm thinking. Rory, can you set something up for the return of the submersible?" He agrees easily to my request. "We'll have a car waiting for us when we come up for air and take that to the coordinates. V, *that* is where you come in. They'll start shutting down roads closest to Monaco first, spiralling outwards. As soon as we're over the border, they'll have to ask the French law enforcement to move their asses. It should give us enough time to get on the road. I have to call Ellie with an update. Max, thank you for the use of your boat. I was a little afraid you'd try hiding your treasure hunting pleasure yacht from us."

"How did you—" he starts as I stand and make my way from the room with my phone in hand.

Three...

Two...

One...

"Treasure hunting?" Rory asks with a bemused tone.

"Don't judge me! When the famed Carl Allen approaches you to join him for a dive, you don't say no. There was rumour of a sunken ship near Porto Vecchio."

"You bought a boat to join him? Doesn't he have a fleet?" V asks incredulously.

"It was in the spur of the moment!" Max argues.

"You're all wrong," Zach cuts in, raising his voice over the arguing to pick up the argument from the start of dinner. "The best pizza is from Homeslice Neal's Yard."

I laugh and dial Ellie as I step into the living room. Hopefully, the pizza argument ends soon. The best is obviously Oivita Pizzeria.

"Hey," I say when she answers.

"You got something?" she asks.

"We have a plan and a way out. I'll need cars in a few locations in case one is compromised and all the intel you have on how Monaco closes itself down. We'll get to the pickup point, but you should know my plan currently involves a submarine, scuba diving, and popping up in Cagnes-sur-Mer with their daily scuba expedition from one of the local tourist agencies."

"I'll get cars set up where you want. Keys will be in the rear right wheel wells. I can get you some for Monaco's lockdown, but they keep it close to the vest, even from us. And you have a plan to get the diamond?" she asks. "I don't doubt that you can do it, but they're breathing down my neck."

"Yeah, we've got it. And hey, chin up. At least if I die along the way, you'll know where to look for me and recover the diamond, thus saving your job." I laugh, but she doesn't join in. "I'm kidding, Ellie. I'll send you more details on the plan and our route tonight."

"You'd better not die. But if you do, please tell me you left your townhouse to me."

"Of course I did. But I've dictated my dildo collection be sent to our prime minister. He looks like he needs a good dicking."

She laughs in agreement, and we say our goodbyes before hanging up along with promises of exchanging information and plans tonight over a secure server.

It's time to get packed. I've got a flight to book and a lead to reward.

I wonder if I can torture them through the ceiling again.

Chapter Eighteen

Max
Present Day

"How do people fly commercial all the time? That was a nightmare." Groaning, I stretch to my full height and throw my arms over my head. My back cracks an excessive amount, and I sigh in relief when the pressure eases.

"We flew business class," Liv deadpans.

"I know; it was dreadful." I wrinkle my nose.

"You still have a silver spoon up your ass, I see," Zach says. "What does it matter? It got us here." He strolls by, wheeling his carry-on, and joins Viraj as they move through the airport.

"Flying a budget airline with fake passports is far less conspicuous than chartering a jet," Liv reminds me for the fourth time. I know she's right, but that doesn't mean I have to like it.

I roll my eyes, and we follow after the others to baggage claim.

Thirty minutes later, we've got checked luggage in hand, fake passports stamped, and are piled into a van headed towards the harbour to finally get our asses in the lap of luxury. I haven't been on this particular yacht in over two years. I only spent a summer on it, but I sure as shit decked it out to my taste before my voyage.

No one said treasure hunting had to be done in decrepit conditions.

Porto di Fiumicino in Rome is an excellent port because of its location. The waters are calm, and storms are rare. And in today's case, it's close to our destination. The harbourmaster escorts us along the dock, and I see my baby at one of the end spots amidst the other yachts, catamarans, and pleasure boats.

I can't believe they want to blow up my beauty. I'll be arguing that at every possible opportunity.

She doesn't deserve it. She's done nothing wrong.

"Wow," Roark says. "Whoever said people buy big toys to compensate for small cocks hasn't met you." He lets out a long, low whistle as we climb the gangplank to board the vessel.

"*L'equipaggio è a bordo e pronto per la partenza, signore. Buon viaggio a tutti,*" the harbourmaster says as he gestures to the crew standing in neat lines along one side of the ship.

"*Grazie. Buona giornata,*" I return, bidding him farewell before he turns and heads back to the offices.

Liv didn't want a crew, but none of us knows these waters, nor do we have the experience to pilot this ship. We settled on a skeleton crew instead of the usual ten staff members. Viraj was adamant that we keep the galley chef.

I can't say I disagree. Food has been remarkably tough to come by at Liv's house.

"*Unsinkable II?*" Roark asks with a brow cocked, noting the name of the ship. "What happened to *Unsinkable I?*"

"I don't want to talk about it!" I snap. That was a sad day.

"Good evening, Mr Arondale," the captain says, directing our attention where needed.

"Good evening."

"The chef has prepared an early dinner for you in the lounge, and we'll be departing immediately if that suits you," he offers.

I take Liv's arm in mine, escorting her through the glass doors to the main living space and into the cabin.

"Right. Tour?" I offer to our team. I hate to admit it, but Liv's methods are working. We're starting to work seamlessly as a unit.

Zach is looking around the spacious room, while Viraj and Roark have flopped onto the bolted-down seating in the lounge. Apparently, I'm not the only one feeling the effects of the cramped seating on the aeroplane.

The table is laden with Caprese salad, bruschetta, three domed platters, and five place settings. The engines kick on, and I show everyone to their rooms for our overnight trip. The ship has six bedrooms, each tastefully appointed, and most importantly, there are no fucking bunk beds—meaning we'll all be able to sleep separately for the first time in nearly a month. Ah, sweet luxury.

Royal blue runners, pristine white walls, and gold accents on the sconces line the hallway and take this exploration craft from just a working ship to a luxury pleasure craft. Thankfully, the helicopter pad on the upper deck is empty for the time being. If we do end up blowing up the damned ship, I'd rather not lose all my toys in the process.

A picture of John Henry hangs at the end of the hallway, and I press my fingertips to his nose as I pass it to enter the master suite to deposit my things and change for lunch. With the stench of aeroplane firmly lodged in my nose and saturating my clothes, I need a fucking shower.

Dinner was a casual affair. Liv appears to be having the time of her life. I noticed when Roark and I were speaking across the table, she was watching with rapt attention and smiling the whole time.

Now we're all spread out around the lounge; Liv repeatedly checks her watch while Zach sits stoically beside her. Viraj is busy looking out the windows at the stars dancing over the water, and Roark and I are playing cards at the table.

Maybe this is the key to finally making her mine—showing her I've matured since my unruly and pompous school days. I mean, we've all changed along the way. Roark is no longer the scrawny know-it-all he was back in school. He might still actually know it all, but at least now, he's got a personality to go with it.

Back then, it used to drive me mad. Not all of us were as adept in school as Roark was. My father using Roark for comparison as incentive for me to do better in school certainly didn't help things.

Viraj and I are still not on speaking terms as such. It's more that we snipe at each other back and forth until one of us gets pissed off. He's always been that way. Maybe *we* have always been that way.

It started as a little tease when he sauntered into school thinking he was hot shit because his family was one of the wealthiest in India. My father had droned on and on prior to the start of term about old money and our responsibilities, primarily how I represented the family while at school. He was the one to escalate it, but maybe it's time we move on?

Electronic screeching comes blaring through the overhead speakers, and Liv squeals. She hops up out of her seat, knocking Zach's arm away in the process, and stands on the bench seat below her.

"*Grazie,* Nina!" she shouts, and there's a thump from behind the doors leading to the galley. She got the staff involved. Lovely. "Dance party!"

She starts shaking her hips and swaying to the beat. She throws her arms over her head and starts singing along to "'Toxic" by Britney Spears.

While I adore that woman and hold her abilities and intellect in high regard, her music preferences leave something to be desired. Desperately.

Roark has abandoned his cards, leaving them face up on the table and ruining our game of Gin Rummy, with his hands clamped over his ears. I agree. It is obnoxiously loud.

Liv pulls Zach up by his arms and lifts one over his head. She drops down to the floor and starts using him as a prop for dancing. He smiles down at her, watching as her shirt rides up on her stomach. His hands reach out for her, reverently tracing the scars he carved into her. Pain isn't really my thing, but as long as she's okay with it, I am too. His hands wrap around her waist and he slides his thigh between hers.

Roark is watching the two of them—correction, Roark is watching her as she grinds on Zach—and I do the unthinkable. I look at Viraj, who's searching the cabin for a means of escape, and tilt my head towards the exit. *Submarine?* I mouth. He nods his head enthusiastically, and the two of us escape the clamour and meet at the door.

I push it open, hustling into the hallway beyond, and Viraj slams it shut behind us.

"Holy fucking shit, that has got to be the most annoying song to ever exist," he gripes.

"Worse than 'Boom, Boom, Boom, Boom!!'?" I ask.

He points a finger in my face. "Don't get that fucking song stuck in my head again. It took weeks—*weeks*—to get it out!"

I laugh because I hummed the rhythm quite often over the last month, making sure it was firmly lodged in his brain while we were living at the townhouse.

"Come on, let's check out the sub while they have a dance party."

He doesn't thank me for the exit, but he follows behind me down the halls and stairways until we reach the lowest part of the boat.

The submersible is stored within the hull and can be put into and taken out of the water via a mini crane. Viraj circles the watercraft, careful to avoid the equipment surrounding it while he checks it out from all angles. He lets out an appreciative hum when he finds the propulsion mechanism.

"This thing seats four," he muses as he looks inside the bubble dome at the four premium leather seats inside.

"Yes, but combined, we're below the weight limit. It won't impact propulsion," I tell him when I see the question forming in his mind. "And for such a short distance, our air supply isn't at risk."

He hums as he crouches down, getting a better view inside the watercraft. It's not every day someone sees a personal submarine, let alone one readily equipped with plates to dampen sonar detection.

He lobs question after question at me, and I answer them easily at first before my tone starts to grow bored. I shield my mouth when yet another yawn escapes me.

Viraj resecures the latch to the propulsion mechanism, leading the way over the threshold, and I close the door after us.

"We should get to bed. It's getting late, and we have to move into the flat tomorrow," I say as Viraj and I reach the level with our rooms.

"You go on. I want to grab a snack before I crash," he tells me, continuing upwards.

His funeral. I still hear early 2000s pop filtering down from the upper level. I head towards the portrait of John Henry and enter my room. I cannot wait to get a good night's sleep on my own, no Roark beneath me shifting the bed with every toss and turn through the night. Instead, I'll have the roll of the sea as we cross the Mediterranean to Monaco.

Although, the strangest thing happens. It's too fucking quiet. They just turned off the music, and now the noise of the waves feels oppressive.

I distract myself by getting ready for the night and flop into bed. The eight hundred count sheets are a dream, and I sigh as my head hits the soft pillow. I'm still shocked that Viraj and I had a decent conversation without killing each other.

Sure, the focus was on the submersible, but it was progress. We both share the same enthusiasm for the machinery downstairs, and I let myself smile a little. If only Liv had seen me.

All the thoughts in the world are not enough to distract me from the fact that it is absolutely silent—aside from the quiet thrum of the engines and the gentle sea under us. Somehow, over the last month, I had become used to sharing a room. Conditioning at its finest.

I throw the window open and lie back, hoping for sleep to find me. At least now, there's the whistle of the wind as it filters into the room. I settle into the bed and am just drifting off when I hear voices.

"What's going on?" Liv says.

Despite not seeing her, I know there's a look of concern on her face.

"I wanted to apologise." Viraj's voice is louder, so I can surmise he's facing the railing.

I should give them some privacy. I should, but I don't want to.

Awful? Yes, absolutely. Do I feel bad? That's yet to be determined. Depends on how the conversation goes.

"So apologise," Liv says.

Viraj pauses, probably exhaling and forming the sentences in his head before he speaks. It's not something he often does, but right about now, he's going to need some tact with him trying to get back into Liv's good graces.

There's a soft knock on my door, and desperate not to miss the show I'm listening to, I ignore it. The door opens anyway, and Roark comes in.

"Shh," I tell him, waving my arms for emphasis.

"Are you wearing matching silk pyjamas?" he asks, looking at my ensemble. It's not like Liv had a set for me in the townhouse. I will revel in these and take them with me when we disembark.

"Yes, now shut the fuck up and shut the door."

He swings the door closed. But he's still on this side of it. "What? No. With you out there." I gesture to the hallway beyond my door.

"I want to hear. It's too quiet from my room." He crosses the bedroom and hops up on the bed with me. We're sitting knee to knee just in time for Viraj to find his balls. We crane our heads towards the window to listen.

"I'm sorry."

Duuude, you've got to do better than that, I mentally chastise him as Roark just sighs in defeat.

"I could give you a million reasons and excuses about why I've been a dick, but I don't want to reason them away." He pauses. "You hurt me a long time ago, Olivia. And I know I hurt you too. Being here, with you, with everyone, is something I never thought would happen. It's brought up a lot of old rivalries and tensions."

Roark's mouth is hanging open as we listen. Mine is, too, if I'm being honest.

Viraj finishes with soft words Roark and I strain to hear, leaning as close to the window as possible without pushing our heads through it. "But that's no excuse to continue acting like an asshole."

"You're right. And I'm sorry that me choosing myself all those years ago hurt you, but I won't apologise for the decision itself, only for how it affected you. If I could go back, I would do it all the same. It was a no-win situation. I did what was best for me."

"You made the right call," Viraj says, shocking me. "Whoever you had chosen would have been a lucky bastard, but the rest of us would have lost you forever. At least this way, you reached out to each of us eventually."

My thoughts stall. I had replayed that moment Liv told us to fuck off many times over the years and only ever envisioned the scenario of her picking me. I hadn't let my imagination wander enough to what would have happened if she had chosen Roark, Zach, or Viraj.

V was right. I certainly wouldn't be here right now. None of us would.

"It's been a month of us all working together. There are bound to be some growing pains," Liv says. "Do you regret getting on that plane in Denver?"

"No," he answers quickly. "Not at all. I just..."

Roark leans further out the window, trying to hear what's happening, but I yank him by the boxers, pulling him back in. The last thing we need is Viraj or Liv seeing him and halting this breakthrough. My reward for my efforts is an eyeful of ass cheek, but it's not like I haven't seen it before.

"Just what, Viraj?" Liv asks, her voice cracking in frustration. "You are here because I want you here. Because I think you want to be here. Is that not enough? Or are we about to have the same issue we had over a decade ago? I said it when you arrived, and I'll repeat it. I am not choosing. We are all working on making this go as smoothly as possible, but your snide comments have created tension we don't need. I *have* to help Ellie with this. If I don't, she'll lose her dream job. Bringing you all in is the only way to pull this off." Because if Ellie is no longer an Interpol employee, who knows who will come for her? She put some pretty scary motherfuckers behind bars.

"Dammit, Olivia. I want to be here—I *need* to be here. But it's hard! After everything, the past and the present..." he trails off. "There was a good chunk of my life I never thought I'd see you—any of you—again. And part of me was glad for it. I get what you're doing. Making us work together and showing us we could be friends if we only got our heads out of our asses, but there's a lot of history to unpack before that happens, Ollie."

"So what are you saying?"

He forcefully blows out an exhale I can hear clearly from my room below them. "I will watch my words with you and the others. I'll admit that some of the things I said were out of line, but there are some things that won't lay to rest so easily, Ollie. There are years of history and hurt between the five of us."

"I understand," Liv says. "But, I hope we can all find a way to at least work together without ripping each other to pieces along the way."

"I won't change who I am to fit into this team."

"No one is asking you to, V. In fact, I'd be pretty heartbroken if you did. I'm just asking you to start treating everyone with some fucking respect. Do you think I would bring someone on who didn't deserve to be here? Someone who was dead weight? You each bring something to the table that the others lack. And that's not a failure on anyone's part. It's just the way life is. So when I look to Roark for his computer abilities, it's not a slight against you or Zach or Max. It's his area that he fucking excels in. Yes, I just made an Excel joke; you can laugh now." Liv pauses as Roark giggles to himself beside me. Idiot.

"We need each other to pull this off. *I* need each of you to pull this off. So, I'm going to bed now. I accept your apology, and in the morning, we start fresh. No sniping at the others or me, and we try to get along. Deal?"

"Deal," Viraj agrees.

"Come on, let's get to bed, or we'll be dead on our feet tomorrow. Gimme a second to fart in peace out here," Liv says. A second passes, and I hear the door open and shut above. "Night, Max. Night, Roark!" Liv whispers over the side of the boat, just for us.

"Night," we mumble in unison, knowing we've been caught, but grateful to hear V is on board—heh, get it—and we will all be working to make things right.

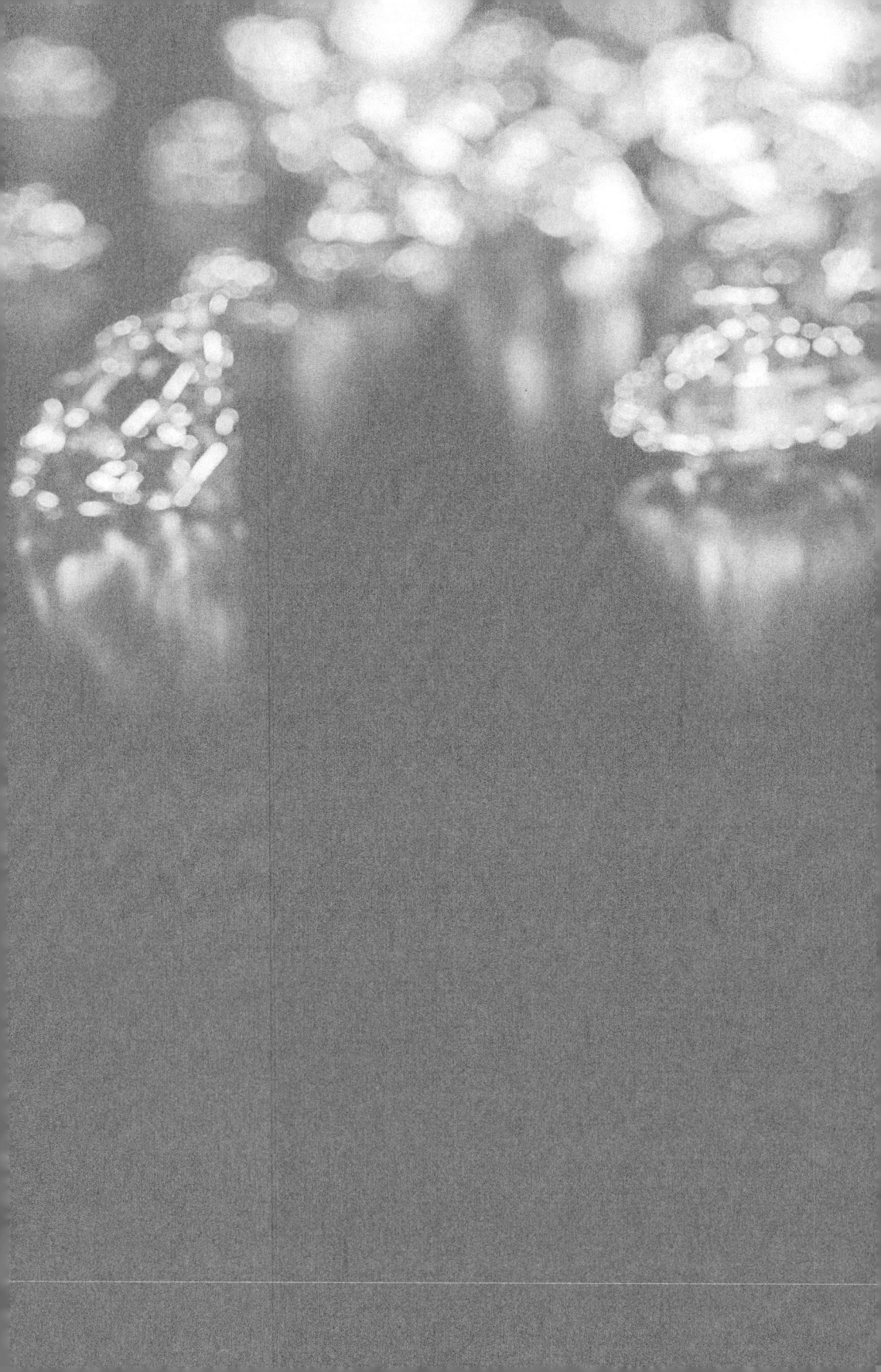

Chapter Nineteen

Olivia
Year Thirteen
September

I turned eighteen just before the start of term. My parents organised a luncheon with their neighbourhood friends. There was food and a cake, and I blew my candles out wearing a pretty sundress and my hair up. My parents hired entertainment in the form of a hypnotist and the man even got my dad to give up smoking for a day or two. It was fascinating, and definitely something I plan to look into.

The day was beautiful; the sun shone, the little birds sang, and everything went exactly as planned.

Listening carefully revealed that two of our neighbours were sleeping together and had plans to meet up later that evening. It amazes me how quiet people think they are when they trade secrets. All it takes is a well-placed ear to catch the tail end of a rendezvous conversation. Knowing this ensures I'm only ever overheard if I want to be. For fun, I almost stole my dad's friend's wallet and dumped it in his neighbour's handbag to observe the ensuing chaos and trump the boredom.

But I didn't do it. My parents are good people, and I love them. Causing problems for them would only serve to hurt them—and me, if I took my remorse into consideration. I never ever want to live like them, but it's not a reason to make their lives hell. They're happy and never hurt anybody. If the entire population lived like my parents, nothing bad—or good, for that matter—would happen.

All chaos would disappear.

It'd be boring as fuck.

Today's the first day of school, meaning I get to see my friends from last year. Eleanor and I will be roommates again, and we caught up this weekend. Of course, we texted during the break and never really lost contact, but it felt good to hug her again.

Roark and I talked every single day, and he told me all about his adventure in Arondaleland. As the recipient of the Arondale scholarship, he was invited to some family events where Maximillian Senior paraded him in front of his rich friends, whereas his own son barely got a glance.

Apparently, Rory successfully completed his mission of avoiding Max Junior while being in his house because Max was interning at a famous law firm with all the other super rich kids.

I don't really have news of the other two. Zach's silence was to be expected; he doesn't strike me as the type to keep in touch despite us exchanging numbers when he asked me to be his friend.

And Viraj, to be honest, I'm not even sure we can be called friends. After that day we stole the car, not much happened aside from small conversations here and there. I still thought about him, though. A wild, dangerous part of me is attracted to him like a magnet to steel. And if the glint I saw in his eyes that day is any indication, he feels it too.

As I turn the corner to head to the chapel where the introductory speech will be given, I am stopped dead in my tracks by a hand wrapping over my mouth as an arm secures around my waist. I'm hauled to the side and tugged inside a cleaning closet. My mysterious abductor flips me around and wraps his hand around my throat, pushing me against the door with a bang. The movement freed my mouth, so I could yell or call for help. But it wouldn't be smart.

I don't resist. The person is a lot stronger than me, and struggling would only make my situation worse.

Plus, I recognised his particular scent as soon as his hand was on my mouth.

Copper and peppermint. Zach.

I meet his amber eyes unflinchingly.

"Hello, Zach," I say with a nonplussed voice. "How was your summer?" His hand tightens around my throat.

"My summer?" he growls, his face close enough for me to lick his lips. "You want to know about my summer? How about we talk about the fact that I just found my file in your room."

I can play this one of two ways. I can tell him the truth, or I can deny it, but that's not really who I am.

"I was curious." My shoulders lift as high as possible in my current position and drop back down. "Why were you in my room?"

"Isn't that how this 'friend' thing works? I let myself in and saw it in your desk drawer." Okay, so he broke into my room and rifled through my desk, somehow thinking the invasion of privacy on his end was okay, but mine wasn't. Surprisingly, I'm not really upset about that. Mostly, I'm excited he decided to seek me out.

"Do you know what I do to little thieves?" His voice is low and menacing, but I'm definitely not experiencing the fear he's hoping for.

"No, but I can't wait to find out." He leans back, and his eyes run all over my face.

"You're not scared of me," he observes.

"No."

"Why?" He narrows his eyes at me. Am I the first person to have this reaction when faced with his wrath? A shiver runs down my spine at the thought.

"Apart from boredom and routine, not much scares me."

He tightens his grip on my throat again, and I still don't struggle. If I behave like prey, he will act as the predator he is. But he needs to understand something. We're the same, him and I; two deadly creatures, one thriving in bloodshed and carnage, while the other lurks in the shadows.

His lips part and his pupils dilate as my lungs start crying for oxygen. My arms and legs are free, but I still don't move. We're trapped in a potentially fatal battle of wills, and I bow to no one.

My control over my body starts slipping, and I gasp for air. Zach's still cutting off my airway, intently watching every emotion on my face while he deprives my brain of oxygen. His breathing is loud, and his eyes narrow in on my lips.

His muscled, lean body crowds my space, so I angle my hips and legs to bring us in contact. His dick is hard in his trousers. He's a killer that gets off on control and has a hand wrapped around my throat.

Great.

Gathering enough strength to speak, I croak, pushing my pelvis against his, "Have you done it before?"

His brows shoot up, and surprise makes his grip falter. I gulp down air. "Done what?" he questions.

"Sex," I ask in-between pants. "Have you ever had sex before?" There's no way I imagined his rock-hard cock pressing against me. He was aroused as he was strangling me.

The problem? So was I. I'm playing a dangerous game, and I love it.

He scrunches his nose. "Of course not."

I've been thinking about it over the summer, going as far as getting an appointment with my GP so I could go on the pill. I'm not overjoyed by the idea of going to university as a virgin. I have no issues with people who make that choice; I would just like to be done with it before I leave school.

And every time I imagined having sex for the first time, alone in my room, the faces of Viraj, Max, Roark, and Zach appeared in my mind next. I don't own a vibrator—waking up my parents with the noise would be way too embarrassing—but I experienced enough with my fingers to know what I like.

Zach still wears his repulsed expression on his face, his hand slack around my throat, and I want to push him.

People say your first time should be memorable, unique, special.

Now what could be more special than having sex with an unleashed Zachary Bennett? I bet he'd make me scream, and I want to find out how.

But I have to push him first.

"I read your file, and you want to break me for it," I say, my lips tilting up in a half smile. "But I don't think it's a good idea."

He bares his teeth at me, his face inches away from mine. His hand hasn't tightened around my neck again, though, so I take it as the good sign it is.

"Why?" he snarls.

"You hate being bored. I hate being bored. I bet we could... entertain each other. In a way that wouldn't get us unwanted attention from the staff, our parents, or the police. And we'll have more fun together if I'm alive and kicking than you'll have breaking me."

His hand drops, and I instantly miss its warmth around my throat. It was like the most fucked-up scarf. I want it back.

"How?" he asks, and my back straightens now that I have his attention. I brush imaginary dust off my skirt.

I grab his tie and use it for balance as I stand on my tippy toes. "I want us to have sex."

Zach's brows furrow. "And why would we do that?"

I truly love how he thinks. It's unique and different. Cold and calculating, too, but unlike anything else I know. I want to crawl inside his mind and figure out everything that hides within. "I'm a virgin. I'll probably bleed."

His amber eyes come alive like wildfire. I can almost see his jugular pulsing in his neck as he bares his teeth again.

"Little Thief," he growls in a way that has my panties damp. He pushes me against the wall, hips digging into mine again. "You're playing with fire. I am not like your other boyfriends. Once we start playing, I won't stop."

He wanted to break me. Now, he wants to play with me. It's already a massive improvement, if you ask me.

My free hand wraps around his neck, and I move until our lips are within kissing distance. His lips part, but instead of closing the gap, I whisper, "Game on."

Then I push him away and open the door to leave. As I turn my back to him, he reacts as quick as lightning and grabs a handful of my hair. Veins in his forearm bulging with the effort, he forcefully twirls me back to face him and kicks the door closed.

His left hand wraps around my throat again, and he kisses the shit out of me, trapping my head in his unfaltering grip. The kiss is clumsy, aggressive, inexperienced. I've had one kiss in my life, but I doubt that peck from year seven counts. Our teeth clash, our tongues tangle, and the taste of copper invades our mouths when he bites my lower lip. A grunt rolls from his throat, equal parts animal and man.

Then he rips himself away, leaving me panting with my lips swollen. "Tonight. Meet me in the psychologist's office at ten. Don't be late."

Without another word, he leaves the room.

What the fuck did I just get myself into?

My hands are shaking as I head towards Dr Forsyth's office. I search my memories as I walk and don't remember ever feeling so rattled. Apparently, losing my virginity to someone I suspect of being a murderer is my limit. I can't act cool and collected when this is what I'm heading towards.

It's not that I don't want to. As disturbed as that may be, I want to have sex with Zach. The alternative would be much easier to deal with; I'd hide somewhere, convinced I need to get away and start plotting his demise.

Wanting it makes me a quivering mess. I'm afraid of so many different things; that I won't be good at it, that he won't be good at it, that he'll hurt me. I'm scared I won't like it, and I'll like it too much. I'm nervous, excited, and aroused. I feel like this is wrong; I should play hard to get, make him court and woo me. I feel like this is right; when I want something, I take it, fuck the consequences—pun intended.

Running away screaming that this isn't a good idea would be much simpler.

Because it is a good idea. And it isn't.

I push open the door to the room where Zach should be waiting for me. I'm exactly five minutes late. I didn't want to wait for him. Walking around the empty buildings with all the tumultuous thoughts twirling in my head was already bad enough; imagine if I had to spend some time alone with my thoughts and without the possibility to pace.

It would have been torture.

"You're late," Zach growls from beside the door as soon as I enter the room. "I told you not to be late, Little Thief."

"And what are you going to do about it?"

I'd rather provoke him into taking the initiative than spend another minute thinking about what I'm doing. Danger is where I thrive, not this weird, anticipatory, jittery mood.

The knife he sometimes plays with appears in his hand, and he holds it to my throat. His other hand snakes under my uniform skirt and cups my pussy. "I read that some women like pain with their pleasure. Would I be able to make you come and cut you at the same time?"

"No," I say, meeting his eyes unflinchingly.

"You're awfully sure of yourself for an eighteen-year-old virgin."

I clear my throat, trying to move as little as possible to avoid the sharp blade of the knife. "I meant, no, you can't make me bleed." A dangerous spark lights up his eyes. He's taking it as a challenge, and this isn't good. "If I show up with wounds or scars, it'll attract scrutiny. And that's something neither of us wants."

The spark in his eyes dies down. I almost hate that I did that to him, but it's the truth. I can't afford to show up anywhere covered in cuts.

To my surprise, he puts the knife away. "So that's a one-time thing, then. I want to fuck you as you bleed, Little Thief. So I'll take your virginity, then we're done."

His apparent detachment almost hurts. If I didn't have an answer to break him, it definitely would. "You know I get periods, too, right?"

His pupils dilate so quickly, his eyes almost turn black. He parts his lips, and I can see a hint of teeth right before he captures my mouth with his.

Zach kisses me like he's starving and I'm food. He's aggressive, rough. He doesn't care about gentle touches or caresses. This is pure possession, and I want to melt into him.

He pushes my panties aside and ruthlessly shoves two of his fingers inside me. I'm wet; Zach seems to get me going with just a look. Still, I've only had my fingers in there, and never that quick, so it hurts a little.

And yet, I moan.

Zach leans back and observes my face, his own completely devoid of emotion. "Did you know that if a woman is ready enough, she won't bleed during her first time? The hymen can be stretched so it doesn't break."

He starts pumping his fingers in and out of me. My breaths turn shallow. "But you're not interested in that."

"Of course not. I want you to bleed all over my dick and make me yours, Little Thief." A shiver runs down my spine. "You said we could

The Cleanup

entertain each other. You know what that means? If I get bored, I'm going to come to you, and you'll either keep me busy or be responsible for the consequences." This should horrify me, but it doesn't. The only thing I can think of is that I just gained an ally who cares as little about the rules as I do.

This time, I'm the one who initiates the kiss. I push his hand out of me and make him lie down on a leather chaise that occupies a corner of the office. In one swift gesture, I peel both his trousers and underwear from his legs as he takes off his T-shirt.

To make it more convenient, I take off my panties, leaving the rest of my clothes on. He's naked, I'm still mostly dressed. It's the ultimate power move, and I love it.

I straddle his thighs, slowly lowering myself onto his length. I didn't even take the time to look at it, too scared I'd get intimidated and back off. This is a fuck-or-die situation, not something I can easily get out of.

I wince in pain; I needed more foreplay. I'm too tight, and the friction is very close to becoming unpleasant. Zach's only answer is to grab me by the hair, forcing me to look at him straight in the eyes. His other hand grips like a vice around my hip. Suddenly, he bucks his hips, burrowing balls-deep inside me without any buildup or warning.

My eyes close, and I cry out. This hurts, but I want it, and now my insides feel full and warm. Zach uses his grip on my hair to bring my forehead to his chest and whispers in my ear, "Shush, Little Thief. I'm inside now. I'm all the way inside you, and I'll never get out. I'm inside your body, your skin, your gut, Olivia. You're never getting rid of me." Fuck, he's intense. Everything about this situation is.

Then again, my body seems to like intense. I'm growing wetter by the second. Soon, he can move without hurting me. After that, I start undulating my body, chasing my own pleasure.

Quickly, it's his turn to close his eyes. He does it reluctantly, as if he's been fighting the pleasure but can't take it anymore. Zach's dick starts pulsing inside me, but before he spills, he pulls out and flips us so I'm flat on my back. He kneels over me, smears of my blood dotting his cock and thighs. From his vantage point, Zach looks at us, his eyes darting between my pussy that must be apparent between the folds of my skirt, his cock, and my face.

I expect him to wank himself off and come all over me. Or get out of the room and leave me like this.

What he does instead is utterly unexpected.

He lifts my skirt higher up on my stomach and buries his face between my legs. Obviously, this is the first time anyone has gone down on me. I'm sure this is also the first time he's gone down on anyone. "You don't have to do that," I breathe.

He lifts up his face, and his lips are smeared with red. "Oh, but I do. I'm not missing a single drop of this." And he dives back in, his hard cock bobbing between his legs.

Zach licks me everywhere. He laps me from ass to clit, then sucks my nether lips into his mouth. He plays with my folds and nibbles at my nub, as if this is all he needs to be happy forever.

I come harder than I ever did during my solo sessions. My back arches, and he holds me down, pushing his tongue inside me as I feel my walls clamping and expelling wet heat.

My head drops against the leather, and when I open my eyes again, Zach is already half-dressed. "What are you doing?" I ask. "You didn't even finish."

He licks his lips. "I got everything I needed. You were right, Little Thief. I think we can entertain each other for the foreseeable future."

I lift up on my elbows, smirking at him. Fuck, for a first time, I don't think I could have imagined anything better. The danger, the thrill. It fogs my head and has me looking forward to our next encounter.

"Agreed," I say, straightening my skirt and tucking in my shirt.

"This was delicious. I'm already looking forward to our next time." Then he pulls his T-shirt over his chiselled abs and heads towards the door. Before opening it, he faces me again. "And remember—I'm yours. Which means you're responsible for my actions from now on."

And with that promise and threat, he leaves, disappearing into the dark hallway. I flop back onto the sofa, recounting the touches and sensations he elicited from my body as I stroke between my folds, reliving the pleasure for as long as possible. This is going to be a very good year.

Chapter Twenty

Olivia
Present Day

No matter how many times I've been to the French Riviera, the landscape never ceases to amaze me. The cities here line up one after the other, condensed on a thin strip of land between the infinite blue of the Mediterranean Sea and the steep slopes of the Alps.

Monaco is no different. It's a little more than a half-mile wide at its largest, but almost two miles long, the luxury buildings and houses pressing along the coast.

I'm alone on the upper deck of *Unsinkable II*, soaking up the last quiet moments before the planning and scheming starts again. I didn't unpack anything, so it was just a matter of closing my bags and hauling them up onto the main deck to be ready to disembark.

The temperatures here are a lot warmer than in London. I'm wearing my favourite jeans and a crop top, savouring every ray of sunshine I can get on my skin.

It's late afternoon, but we're in the middle of spring, and the sun is already sinking down over the horizon. There is still plenty of light to make our docking at the port easy. There are no waves, and the dimming rays reflecting on the sea turn it into a mirror. The water is so calm and quiet that the superyachts around us are reflected in it, a reproduction so perfect it would be impossible to say which is the boat and which is the mirrored image.

We enter the three hundred metres limit, so the skipper reduces the speed of *Unsinkable II* to five knots. The noise of the engine dies down, allowing me to hear the heavy steps of the guys as they come looking for me. We're making progress together, so much so that something very dangerous has already started blooming in my chest.

Hope.

Zach finds me first, making me jump when he props his forearms on the rail beside me. He's the only one of the four who can walk as silently as me. I grunt. Although I love sneaking up on people, I hate being snuck up on.

"It's pretty out here," he says. I turn towards him, eyes blown wide in surprise. Zach isn't usually sensitive to beautiful landscapes.

When I take him in, it's not the view he's looking at. His eyes are giving me a slow once-over, pausing on the thin strip of skin between my jeans and top where the scars he gave me are visible. As if understanding my train of thoughts, he presses a soft kiss on my cheek. Smooth motherfucker.

"I called Julie Pastor; the flat will be waiting for us as planned," he adds.

We only got the mission a month ago, and all the holiday rentals were already full. I asked around for help, and Interpol found us a villa outside the city limits, but it's too far away from the action for my taste. Going through the border between Monaco and France every day to explore the city is way too risky.

So Zach saved the day, silent and in his corner, as usual. It turns out, a few years ago, a very influential Monegasque paediatrician was abusing not only his patients but his own kid as well. Since he was well-connected, none of the witnesses or victims knew what to do about it. One day, Dr Pastor went to a conference in England and never returned. His rental car was found on the right side of the road, apparently having had a head-on collision with an unknown obstacle. Quite the mystery. Since then, his widow feels like she owes Zach for a reason I'm very intent on never learning.

She helped me rent both the docking spot at the port and the flat in central Monaco during the busiest month of the year. With her late husband's connections, it was a piece of cake.

Max, V, and Rory join us, taking in the view of the city we're going to try to escape.

"How big is the flat?" the former asks. "I need to know what to bring from the boat."

"You'll see. We can always come back to the boat or go shopping if you need anything, so pack light."

Unsurprisingly, Max's wardrobe on the boat is filled with clothes, and I swear his sigh of relief as he put on his silk pyjamas yesterday was audible even from the top deck.

Roark and Max come to stand at my side while Viraj leans against the rail next to Zach.

I'm glad—and also a little surprised—he apologised yesterday. It felt genuine, but I'm waiting to see if he backs it up with actions. Talk is cheap.

And I'm not mad that Roark and Max overheard us. Secrets and lies won't help us fix everything that's broken between the four of us. I say four because Zach is the least involved and affected by the baggage we all drag around. Everybody needs to be on the same page for this thing to work. At least, *I* need everybody to be on the same page.

I'm not sure whether Zach knows what happened. He always seems to have all the information, even when he's not present for conversations that occur.

The *Unsinkable II* successfully docks; we say our goodbyes to the crew and head to the flat we rented. A shiver of excitement shoots up my spine. I can't wait to see the guys' reactions when they discover where we'll be spending the next month.

The building is old, with high decorated ceilings and a fancy reception desk. It looks like a hotel, to be honest, but I know for a fact that people live here. We take the lift—even the buttons look like they're made of ivory or another equally precious material—and make our ascent.

I type the code on the app on my phone—yes, I got this place properly equipped, too—and the door opens. "Take off your shoes," I yell.

They oblige as I throw my trainers in a corner of the entryway.

We all rush inside like excited teenagers on our first sleepaway trip without guardians. The place is gorgeous, colourful, and offers a great view over the pier and the city. We can see *Unsinkable II* from here and even bits of the tribunes for the race being built. This is a fantastic location, an incredible vantage point, and a perfect operations base. The guys dart outside, where the rooftop terrace will be great for tanning. It must be around two hundred square feet, about the size of my kitchen at home.

The guys look around outside, but quickly, Max comes back inside. "Wait, Liv, where are the rooms?"

"Here," I answer with a devious smile. "It's a studio flat, but it had such a great outdoor area that I couldn't resist using Zach's contact for this place. If you look, there's a double bed in the alcove." I point out in the corresponding direction. "Then, folded against the wall are bunk beds, and this is a sofa bed. There's no real living room to speak of unless we ignore the beds, but the kitchenette over there should have a few supplies, and the bathroom is through that door."

I just made a huge mistake. My camera isn't ready during my

explanation, and I snap the picture of Max's face a millisecond too late. I missed his vacant eyes, the lost expression on his handsome features, and his jaw nearly touching the ground.

Shit, I should have been more prepared.

Zach is, though. "Dibs!" he yells from outside.

He, V, and Rory come back inside. "Dibs for what?" Max asks. "We're not discussing anything yet."

"No, but soon you'll move on to the sleeping arrangement, and I call dibs to sleep with Olivia in the big bed. And if anyone wants to challenge my claim, well, go ahead, I dare you," Zach says with the coldest tone I've ever heard.

If I listen really hard, I can hear three barely audible gulps.

Is it bad that even if I want them to get along, I love when one of them tries to stake a claim over me? It gets my heart pumping harder and my pussy wet. More than that, I'm waiting for them to get it through their heads that I am *all* of theirs.

"Okay," I announce, "that seems a little lopsided on the fairness, Zach." He looks at me and his eyes narrow in annoyance. "You did secure us the flat, so you can have one spot in the big bed if that's okay with everyone." The others agree easily because, well, it was a solid lead for accommodation. "Who sleeps in the big bed with Zach is entirely dependent on who brings in a lead. That seems fair. I'm glad you all agree."

Fish. They all look like fish with their mouths moving like that. Zach gets over it the quickest, shrugs his shoulders, and makes his way over to the bed. He flops down on it, groaning obscenely and making snow angel motions in the bedding.

Roark follows Zach's lead and sits on the sofa, rearranging the cushions and giving the spot beside him a thump with his fist. He'll be fine there and deserves to escape the monster hovering over his bunk bed at my place every night.

Speaking of Max and his giant cock, he and Viraj are wearing the exact same grimace on their faces. It would be cute if they got along. But instead, they catch sight of each other and wipe the looks away simultaneously when they notice they mirror the other. One day, gentlemen. One day, you will be friends, even if it kills me.

They both look at Zach lounging on the bed, and V turns to me. "You take the big bed tonight. Max and I will be fine on the bunk beds." Would you look at that?

Nodding my head, I move towards the front door, and slip my feet into a pair of flats from my bag. "I'm going to go for a walk around the city. I need to get the lay of the land and call my parents. It's been a while. Have fun, gentlemen!"

Roark

Present Day

Via went on a walk, so I decide to more thoroughly explore our newest prison—ahem, flat.

"There are beers," I announce after opening the fridge. "Anyone want one?"

Viraj, Max, and Zach nod in unison.

"Let's go outside," Max proposes. "This multipurpose room is making me feel claustrophobic. Why do people accept living like this? And on holiday?! Aren't these supposed to be pleasant?" I chuckle, Viraj rolls his eyes, and Zach keeps his usual poker face.

We all get sweaters and sit around the table on the rooftop terrace, admiring the view. The temperature gets much colder when night starts falling, but not cold enough to rival London. All of us are used to less forgiving climates, and sitting outside feels a lot better than the cramped bedroom doubling as a living room and a kitchen. Thank Christ the bathroom isn't shoved in the same space too.

The sun sets as we sip our beers and watch the city in silence.

The Cleanup

"Do you really think we can do this?" Viraj asks. "It's happening in less than a month."

"When was the last time one of Olivia's plans failed?" Max asks.

"Her pen did get stolen at the end of school, and she never managed to steal it back," I chime in.

"It was a dumb pen, and I'm still sure she lost it."

Max shrugs. "Anyway, that tells you what her success rate is. In thirteen years of scheming, she arguably failed one job. There's a reason people pay exorbitant fees for her services."

Viraj takes a sip of his beer.

"What are you going to do when this is over?" I ask. The night is dark, and I can't really see their faces. There's probably an outside light, but nobody switched it on, and I can't be arsed to stand up now.

"Go back to New York, I guess," Viraj says. "Ollie cleared my schedule until two weeks after the Grand Prix, but then I have to get back to work. I have clients who count on me and a life to get back to." Max raises a brow at his words but otherwise keeps silent.

"What about you, Max?" I inquire.

He scratches the back of his neck. "Same. After not seeing me for months, John Henry will be all out of sorts, and I'll also have to get back to the property management of the estate. What about you, Rory?"

"Hm, I have this app I was working on, then I'll keep helping Olivia on her jobs. There's also a gaming tournament I'm looking forward to." Does our conversation sound as pathetic from the outside as I feel on the inside?

Zach snorts, making all of us jump since he's behaved like a statue for the past ten minutes.

"What's so funny?" Viraj asks, always ready to go on the offensive.

"Nothing, it's just cute, is all," the doctor answers.

"What?" V snaps.

"How you're all still sure you're in control."

Trying to diffuse the situation, I ask softly, "What will you do when this is over?"

233

"Same as ever, same as now, and probably same as you. Whatever she wants me to."

I finish my beer, tipping my head back to get the last drops. "And what do you reckon that is?"

Zach is looking intently at me when I look back from my drink. "Olivia has virtually everything she might ever want. She's rich, has a successful career, a business that runs itself, and friends who would do anything for her. Now, if I had to guess, I'd say she wants her family back." His eyes navigate between the three of us, making it clear who he thinks she considers family.

Viraj abruptly finishes his beer and stands up. "This place obviously lacks a chef, so I'm going to cook. I hope you guys like Indian food." He doesn't give us time to answer before he heads inside and starts rummaging in the cupboards, no doubt looking for ingredients. He must find what he's looking for since we hear him start cutting and frying shortly after.

"Obviously, emotional maturity is still Viraj's best quality," Max observes. I snort. The more time I spend with Max, the more tolerable I find him. I'm almost ready to call him a friend—at least in my head. The threesome started it all, but since then, we have grown closer, and I'm discovering that having friends that aren't virtual isn't unpleasant.

I'm just about to speak, but at the same time, music blares from a speaker hidden only god-knows-where. The song is "Jenny" by Studio Killers, and at that moment, I'm dead certain Via bugged the place. The music very explicitly speaks of ruining friendships and becoming lovers instead.

"She always was the subtle kind, wasn't she?" I tease, looking at Max.

Zach's poker face melts away, replaced by an expression I've only ever seen when he's thinking about Via. "Little Thief does enjoy making an entrance."

Indeed, shortly after the chorus starts, she dramatically opens the door to the flat and starts twerking in the short hallway. I shake my head.

"Bitches, I'm back," she exclaims, shaking her ass. Then she stops dead in her tracks. "Wow. I was expecting weird shit to have happened when I came back, but Viraj cooking and you three calmly drinking a beer is too much. Let's go to the hospital; we need to evacuate whatever drug you've taken."

"Ollie." She turns to Viraj, who just called her. The flat is so small they're within touching distance.

He cradles her face in his hands as if he's going to kiss her, and everybody freezes. Is he finally going to give in to what everyone knows he wants?

Then he licks half her face as she struggles to get free. "Shush if you want food." Stunned into silence, she stumbles in our direction, and V uses the opportunity to slap her ass—hard. She yelps and runs into Max's lap, curling into a ball in his arms, rubbing her face to get the saliva off. "He licked me," she whines.

"We saw, love," Max coos. "Do you want me to kiss you to get back at him?"

"I heard that!" V yells from the kitchen. She still nods, and Max doesn't miss a beat. He kisses her softly, snaking his tongue between her parted lips. A pang of jealousy streaks through my chest. The problem isn't that she just kissed Max outside of sex, without hesitation and as easily as if they'd been together for years. It's that she's never done the same with me.

When I glance around, Zach is watching me with a knowing look.

"Food's ready!" V shouts. "Stop eating each other's faces and come eat what I made. For once, someone's thought of feeding this team."

This does feel like family.

A weird, dysfunctional, broken family, but a family nonetheless.

The question is, can we fix it?

We eat, chatting comfortably, none of us touching the delicate subjects of our shared history, the heist, or what will happen after.

Via spreads sauce on V's face as revenge for his licking. Max drones on and on about his stallion, and the dick jokes are out of control. Zach talks about how much he loves his job and the patients he helps—and I finally start understanding what Via sees in him. It surprises me to witness that level of care from him, but every word out of his mouth is one of utter devotion to being an advocate for his young patients. It gives me reassurance because I know that's how devoted he is to Olivia; I've seen the reverence for her in his eyes daily. Viraj explains all the unique gadgets of the escape car he chose and how excited he is to do test runs. Since arriving in Monaco, he's been much more personable, even going so far as to incite conversation rather than just reluctantly participate.

And I watch it all, unsure if I belong—if they really need me when everybody gets along.

We play "not it" when the dishes' time comes. For once, Via loses, and I offer to dry the plates as she washes.

"You know," she says as she hands me a soaked glass, "you belong here as much as they do." She doesn't elaborate on what "here" is. I know what she means. Here with her, here on this team, here on this job.

I give her a weak smile. "I guess I never really stopped doubting myself."

"I know." She finishes up, takes a plate and the towel from my hand, and rises on her tippy toes. Her lips brush over my own as she draws me in for a sweet kiss. I lose myself in the tangle of lips and tongues, my hands snaking around her waist to draw her closer and deepen our connection. With a stuttering breath, she pulls back just a hair's breadth and whispers, "You're amazing, Rory. Never doubt that."

We finish our chore with playful hip bumps and small smiles and then turn towards the living room/bedroom to get ready for bed. I guess Via missed seeing Max in his silk pyjamas last night because she looks like an anime character who just fell in love as her eyes narrow in on the outline of his soft cock.

"Ollie, control yourself!" V scolds with a smile.

"In my defence, it's huge, it's there, and I can't help it. Look at it! It's even wrapped up in silk, like a pretty present! All we're missing is a bow! Although"—she pauses as she pretends to ponder something—"the bow might hide too much. I take it back. No bow."

Max chuckles and starts hopping where he stands, making his considerable package jump with him. "Stop it, asshole," Viraj orders. "She's going to drool all over the carpet." Olivia opens her mouth and sticks out her tongue, emulating a dog and panting on the spot.

I shake my head at their antics and go brush my teeth.

"Are you ready for bed, Little Thief?" Zach asks behind me. She probably nodded because she yelps before something heavy lands on their bed. "Time to sleep, then. You can play with Max's monster cock tomorrow."

"Promise?"

Shaking my head, I leave the bathroom and start my fight with the sofa bed to unfold it. I'm losing 3-0 when Viraj intervenes. "I know this system. I've slept on a friend's sofa for a competition, and it worked like this."

He pulls on a strap I couldn't have found if my life depended on it, and the evil thing finally surrenders.

I make my bed with blankets and sheets from the closets. In the meantime, I hear Viraj and Max bicker in the bunk beds, and Zach and Via are definitely kissing.

It's the first night in a long time that we've spent together without animosity. Nobody fought, nobody yelled, and it feels like this could work.

Chapter Twenty-One

Olivia
Year Thirteen
February

I wonder how long it would take to walk to town. Maybe there's a bus? I could always talk Viraj into helping me liberate a car from the teacher's lot. He's so wound up these days, if his tense shoulders and shaking knee three desks down from me are any indication.

"Miss Wraith, your attention please," Mr Hall says from the front.

"You have it, Mr Hall," I say, turning my head from the window and spinning the pen in my hand. It's the same one Viraj jammed into the ignition of that car we borrowed on Waffle Day—as it is now known in my head.

Mr Hall scoffs and fires a question at me. "Wonderful. Could you please inform the class of the symbolism present in *The Bell Jar*?"

I move my pen in a slow circle around my thumb and smile at Max, who has turned in his seat to watch me. Rory is seated to my left and Zach to my right. Viraj is in Max's row but clear across the other side of the room as if there aren't enough desks in the world to create a big enough divide between those two. From what I can see, I bet they'd actually be decent friends if they could see past their bullshit.

Despite how many students are currently looking at me, their faces are the only four I see. Probably because I've kept to myself aside from them and Ellie. She's not a fan of her new nickname, but we're working on it.

"Certainly, Mr Hall!" I say cheerfully. The pen swirls around my index finger, and I pinch it between my middle and ring finger to rotate. "*The Bell Jar* is a moving and deeply personal novel to many people. Simply because the bell jar in the story is a metaphor for depression, something which, at last count, nearly twenty per cent of UK citizens suffer from. Not only that, the author herself suffered from depression and succumbed to her despair a mere month after publication."

The classroom is silent as Mr Hall takes the last two steps to my table. If I hadn't been looking directly at Max's grinning face, I might have noticed Mr Hall plucking my pen out of my hand. "Very good, but you're distracted. I'll be keeping this."

He walks back towards the front, and my fingers fidget around absolutely nothing.

"How will I take notes?" I ask loudly. That is *my* pen. The one from *our* car stealing expedition with Viraj last year. It has the perfect fucking balance for spinning.

"The rest of the hour, you will be reading from these supplemental materials," Mr Hall says, waving a stack of thin books in his hand. He gives them to another student to pass out, and I glare daggers at him.

The next twenty minutes are torture, but I make it through by bouncing my knee under my desk and twirling a lock of hair in my left hand to keep from going insane. Fidgeting has always been a

The Cleanup

problem of mine. It's like if my hands aren't busy, my mind loses all focus. There has to be a dick joke in there somewhere. Sure, I may stare out the windows, but I'm listening and paying attention as well.

Finishing the material, I look at the clock and see there are only two minutes left of class. A knock sounds at the door, and Headmaster Barkley pokes his head in. "Mr Hall, a word, please. Students, you are free to go."

The scrape of chairs on the floor is deafening after the silence of reading time, and everyone begins packing up. I shove everything into my bag as quickly as possible, but it's not enough. Headmaster Barkley is already speaking with Mr Hall in the corner of the room near the desk, and the last thing I want is that man's attention on me. But I want my bloody pen back.

Ellie mentioned something last year that set my curiosity ablaze and got me digging. The simple sentence was: "I can't believe they pay the headmaster enough to afford a beach house in the Bahamas." Nothing outwardly accusatory, but I know everything possible about the school, and one of the things I discovered from my research before coming here was the headmaster's annual salary. No way is he making enough for a beach house.

It took some research, and with Roark teaching me about hacking in the computer labs, I've been keeping tabs and looking backwards in time. Not only does the man have the beach house, but one of the school's benefactors had been paying him handsomely up until a couple of years ago when a girl dropped out, citing "personal reasons" for her departure.

I saw files in the records room of the girl's transcripts. Perfect student until her last term at St Stephen's, involved in clubs, everything a university would look for in a candidate. But suddenly, she was attending therapy twice a week for her "demeanour." She is no longer at the school, but the rest of us are—and without the facts, without knowing how and if the two events are connected, are any of us safe?

I found the girl last week after a lot of digging and plan to find out her story.

Zach slips his hand around my wrist, tearing me out of my musings, and tugs me towards the door. "Come on, Little Thief." We've been "entertaining" each other since our first time in the psychologist's room, and it's always at random hours in locations we're definitely not supposed to be in. It's a thrill to have my very own secret. Not that it needs to be, but it's easier if we fly under the radar to not draw attention to ourselves during our final year. People are assholes, and even if I know there's nothing shameful in the kinky stuff Zach and I do together, my classmates could still use it against us. Against *me*, more likely, since the woman is the one who always takes the most shit in these situations. Then the bullies would probably disappear, only for eensy weensy pieces of their bodies to be found several months from now.

Really, it's safer for everyone if we keep things quiet.

Viraj and Max are in the middle of a stare off just outside the classroom door, and we walk between them, Zach knocking into Viraj on his way.

"Watch it," he spits.

"Watch what? You're standing in the doorway. If you don't want to be bumped, fucking move." Zach scares me more than just a bit, but he also gives me a thrill unlike anything else.

Viraj looks at Zach, then at me. "Hey, are you okay?" he asks when he sees my crumpled face.

"No, she's not okay," Roark answers from behind us. I turn and find him holding his books, and with all of our attention on him, he shoves his glasses higher up his nose. "Mr Hall took her favourite pen."

"You're upset over a pen?" Max asks, jumping into the conversation.

"It's not just any pen," I answer. "It has the perfect fucking balance, and it's gone. I need to get it back."

"I'll go," Zach says.

The Cleanup

Now that the students have left the classroom, the headmaster's voice has risen, and with Zach's past circumstances, he has to be cautious. One of the conditions of his acceptance here was that he be respectful to the teachers and staff. Interrupting Headmaster Barkley while he's clearly reaming out Mr Hall would violate that.

I shake my head at him, and his body tenses, torn between charging in there and respecting my wishes. "It's just a pen. I'll get it back eventually."

"But you like that one," Max states.

"It'll be fine." I don't really want to admit it's the one I got with V from the car, and there's nothing to do right now. But most of all, I don't like feeling vulnerable. "If you guys want to help, we can come up with a diversion so I can steal it."

Three of them look a little shocked while Zach beams down at me.

"What? Are you guys experienced enough in thieving to pull it off? Let's go, gentlemen. We've got a pen to recover."

We spend the lunch hour sitting huddled at a table, working out how we'll create a significant enough distraction for me to get back what's mine.

Roark sits quietly, absorbing information as Max and Viraj try to one-up each other with more elaborate schemes than is strictly necessary. Zach holds my hand under the table, digging his nails into my palm any time one of them suggests something even slightly risky, and the rest of the student body stare at us with slack-jawed faces from afar. I guess they never thought they'd see two scholarship kids, one unhinged guy, and the two rich assholes sit down and have a meal together.

It's like the Breakfast Club with edge.

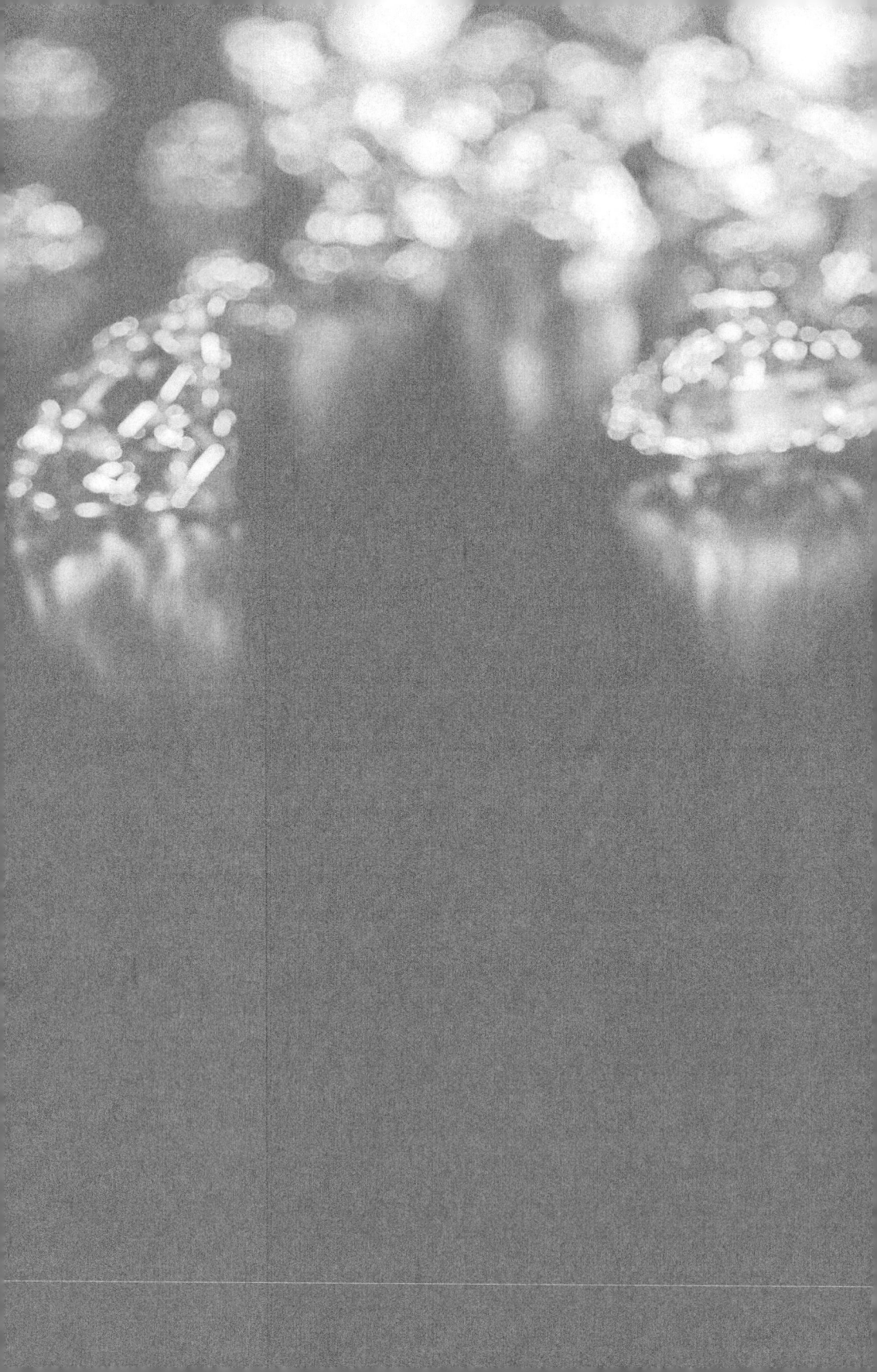

Chapter Twenty-Two

Olivia
Present Day

Part of our plan for getting the jewellery from Natasha requires a bit of hypnosis. Yeah, I know, it's one of those things that seems impossible in movies, but it is actually a thing. In fact, I found out I was good at it a long time ago and kept training, using it on jobs when I could to hone my skill and sometimes Zach when we got together. The first few times, he just rolled his eyes, indulging me because I was so determined. But eventually, I got better and he was curious to see how far I could lull him into a non-waking state.

Zach is naturally the most resistant to it out of the guys. Research shows it's because of the way his brain is wired. He's just not that impressionable. Zach sees something, knows his own internal reaction, and bases his outward expression and actions on a combination of those internal thoughts and social constructs if he's out and about.

If he's not amongst society to dictate or steer his reactions... Well, I don't ask too much about his extracurriculars.

Max, V, and Rory are taking a stroll through Monaco, noting side streets and alleyways we may need to know. They're dressed in touristy clothing with random country names splashed across the front of T-shirts and hats obscuring their faces. The last thing we need is a photographer getting a shot of them on holiday here. Zach also pulled me aside this morning when we were discussing hypnosis and asked for it to just be the two of us for this practice. I get it. There needs to be trust when you're a willing participant, and they're not quite there yet.

The hypnosis backup plan is solid, but Natasha is a bit of a question mark at the moment. For all intents and purposes, she seems like a housewife who loves Instagram just a bit too much and spends money faster than some countries can rake it in. But I have a deep feeling that she's far more than meets the eye.

She managed to get hold of an Interpol diamond that Ellie is being super tight-lipped about. And if all accounts are correct, she also killed her husband and now sits at the head of one of the most powerful criminal organisations in the world.

"Empty your mind, Zach," I say in a calm voice, drawing his attention from my scars to my face as we sit across from each other in the studio flat.

"It's empty."

"It is not. I see that fire in your eyes. I'm not fucking you until this is done." He's tried this trick before. Afterwards, he told me he was listing the digits of pi in his head to focus on anything other than my voice coaxing him into compliance. I've failed with Zach plenty of times in the past, but we continue practising.

One of the methods of hypnosis is what we're doing today—the relaxing one that empties the mind and lulls it into supplication.

The other is called rapid hypnosis. This is the type you find street performers doing with a snap or wiggle of their fingers. I've only managed this twice with Zach in all our years of experimentation, but it's an ace up our sleeve if we need it. Hell, yesterday, I managed to get it to work on our scuba instructor as a little test. The element of surprise is crucial and who's going to suspect a scuba student?

Zach closes his eyes, and when he opens them, where the spark was before, now sits absolutely nothing.

"Good. Listen to me carefully." My words are slow, measured. The goal here is to make him feel comfortable enough to follow my cadence and, eventually, to soften his defences enough for him to do something I want. He knows this is happening, and has been trying to build his own defences against it as well, so his mental awareness is intentionally high. Natasha's won't be.

"Where are we?" I ask him.

"Monaco."

"Good," I reassure him in my calmest tone. I sound like one of the massage therapists at my day spa when they check if the pressure is okay. All liquid vowels and trailing syllables. "We're in Monaco. Specifically in the flat we rented. There is a plant in the corner there, do you see it?" I ask gently.

"Yes," he answers, his eyes drifting towards the ficus tree.

"Keep your eyes on me," I encourage softly. "Use your peripherals." He refocuses, so I continue. "The breeze is warm as it drifts through the open window, the sea air fresh and inviting. There is the distant call of gulls and the faint thrum of traffic through the streets. Do you hear it?"

"Yes," Zach answers, still wholly fixed on me, but his shoulders begin to droop in relaxation.

"Excellent. I see you're shifting your weight. Plant your feet on the floor, root yourself in the present." He settles his feet down and places his palms on his thighs.

"When I count to three, you'll close your eyes and wait for my instructions. Keep focusing on my voice," I coax, and Zach stays steady. "One, two, three."

His eyes fall closed, and his breathing remains steady. Holy shit. Of all the practice we've had over the years, it's never gone this quickly.

"Don't speak," I tell him. "Lift your index finger if you can hear me."

After a moment, he does.

"Good. Your wake-up word will be 'Barbie.' Raise your finger if you understand."

His finger lifts again.

"Excellent. You will not remember this when you wake up, and you are to answer me truthfully. Do you agree?"

"Yes." The word slips from between his lush lips, and he remains calm in his seat.

"Beautiful, Zach. You're doing wonderfully." Okay. Time to test this thing and see how far I can push him. He's given verbal responses and physical responses with his finger. Time to elicit something.

"Tell me about the scars you gave me. What were you thinking at the time?"

His voice is low, his words spoken as if he's sleeping and mumbling in his dreams. "I've always wanted to mark you. You are mine, Little Thief. But you're theirs too, somehow."

I hum. "Does that bother you?"

"No," he replies. His face scrunches for a moment as he thinks but smooths out again quickly. "No, it doesn't. They all give you something I can't. And I give you what they can't. It makes sense."

That throws me for a loop. Zach has always been the most open-minded about me. Sure, he has his possessive and obsessive side, but he's only ever put me first when it came to our encounters. I don't know why I imagined his response to this would be any different.

"I see. Zach, stand up, please." He braces his hands on his knees and unfolds from the chair, towering before me. "I want you to slowly reach into your pocket and take out the underwear you stole from my suitcase earlier." Like I wouldn't see that. Please.

His hand hesitates for only a moment, but he follows directions. Unfurling the lacy thong in his hand, he holds it steady. He's not giving it to me or putting it down, simply following my directions to the letter.

Holy fucking shit.

"Good job, Zach. I think you deserve a reward. Take off your clothes and leave them on the floor." He undoes his shirt buttons, and to test my limits, I flick on the music in the flat. "Naughty Girl" by Beyoncé blares through the speakers, but Zach doesn't even flinch.

He begins undoing his belt, and I rush to pull my thin kaftan off. He stands, naked and proud, in the centre of the room with his eyes shut. I jump up on the bed, lie back on the pillows, and tilt my knees apart.

"Barbie," I say when there's a break in the music.

Zach's eyes flutter open, and he looks surprised to be standing. A stunned expression appears on his face as he takes in his current state.

"Ahem," I fake cough horribly from the bed.

His eyes whip in my direction, and a grin overtakes his face.

"I remember nothing," Zach says reverently. "Oh, Little Thief, how dangerous you are." Then, he pounces.

Zach and I are in a taxi, going through tunnel after tunnel as the road snakes under hotels and apartment buildings. The sea glimmers to our right as we traverse the streets towards the others.

I contacted a tourist agency while on Max's yacht and found scuba classes for us. We've done the theoretical portion and have, thankfully, moved on to the practical. A few of our team members rolled their eyes the entire time, but Roark and Zach were studious in their approach, careful to pay attention despite the audible boredom pouring from the other two. This will be our fourth expedition for the practical certification since our arrival, and each time, Roark gains more confidence.

Roark, Max, and Viraj are already at an exclusive beach, having been encouraged to leave earlier by Zach when Viraj complained—again—about the lack of food. Like I'm supposed to be the one to get groceries. Instead, I told him to shove his misogyny up his ass and go to the supermarket. He has two legs and the doors are no longer locked. Zach was—weirdly—kinder about it.

We sent them out for lunch at the ritzy hotel for some air and privacy while the two of us spent time practising hypnosis... and rolling around on the double bed as Zach worshipped my body and traced my new scars with benediction. It's been a good day, but I'm excited to see the others even though it's only been a couple hours.

The cab slows abruptly, and Zach flings an arm in front of my torso, keeping me in my seat. We've reached a hairpin turn, and instead of following the road to the left, the cabbie turns right down a cobblestone drive and leads us to a hotel front.

Ah. The five-star hotel I'd be staying in if not for the subterfuge nature of our visit. Zach pays the driver as the valet opens the door for me. I step out in my white sundress and turquoise sandals that lace up my calves, all designed to have me fade into the background with the other tourists who flash their cash in a display of designer dresses and accessories.

The grandeur of the hotel is not subtle, and with its prime location, the Hotel de Paris has the appeal to charge such exorbitant fees. Zach steps up behind me, wrapping his arm around my waist as we cross through the lobby, fading in with the other couples wandering around.

We breach the doors on the other side of the cavernous space and find our way around the massive pool towards the private beach, where Max texted that they'd be waiting for us.

At first, I'm convinced I'm seeing a mirage. That's the only explanation. The imported white sand and transplanted palm trees dotting the shoreline make this the picture of luxury. But the three men playing volleyball with their abs, defined chests, and low-slung swim trunks are my own version of heaven on earth.

"Close your mouth, Little Thief. You're drooling," Zach whispers in my ear, causing a shiver to run through me, even with the warm late spring sun shining down on me.

"Can you blame me?" I ask, refusing to tear my eyes away from my men. He chooses not to answer but instead bites my neck, unbuttons his white linen shirt, and tosses it at me. It lands over my head, and when I finally rip it away, he's joined the others and is digging his toes into the sand, ready to play.

Deciding I don't want to unbalance the teams, I take off my dress, revealing my white bikini underneath, and drop down into a lounge chair to watch their antics. Max is surprisingly adept, and Viraj naturally so. Roark and Zach are the deadweights for their partners, but it doesn't stop me from ogling each of them.

Look at this teamwork!

I fucking knew it. They just needed something to bring them together, and while I wish it were the job—or dare I dream, me—I'm glad it's happening regardless.

Viraj and Roark are in the lead, their camaraderie solidifying with every high-five and shouted word of encouragement. Max and Zach glance at each other and nod resolutely. Oh shit, they're going to play dirty, if that look is any indication.

Max stands at the back of the court, the ball in one hand, ready to pop it in the air and serve. A wicked smile grows on my lips. I can level the playing field without actually participating in the game.

I untie the back of my bikini, letting the material go slack and pulling the small triangles over my head, leaving my breasts bare. Max catches me from the corner of his eye just as he tosses the ball up in the air.

I run my finger down the valley between my breasts, drawing attention from all four of them. Max's mouth drops open, and the ball lands in front of him in the sand with a dull thud.

"*Bonjour!*" a voice calls from behind us. "Are we ready today, team?" Maurice calls from behind me. He's been an excellent instructor so far, and despite his no-nonsense demeanour, I got him to smile twice already. I'm calling it a victory.

"*Oui*, Maurice! Let's get wet," I say with a wink. No smile. Dammit.

His gaze runs over the guys, and we both sigh at the sweat dripping down their torsos, my eyes snagging on Roark's tattooed chest and following the ink all the way to his broad shoulders. I turn back to Maurice and cock a brow at him in question. He just shrugs.

"Can you blame me?" he asks as the guys pick up their stuff, and we start making our way to the boat docked a few metres away as I retie my bikini top.

"Not one bit," I reply, thinking that answer would have been nice earlier when I asked Zach the same question.

Within an hour, the boat is floating in the sea, our wetsuits are on, and we're strapping the equipment to our bodies. Roark fills out the suit like a fucking wet dream, and I watch as he ties his long hair back and pulls the headpiece over the mess.

He saunters over, somehow still looking hot as fuck even though he's wrapped up in what is essentially a giant body condom, and helps me tuck my own mane back into the hood of the suit.

"Ready?" I ask.

"Yeah, this isn't as difficult as I thought. Today, I want to get the hang of breathing. I'm tired of always floating up whenever I inhale."

"You can do it." I lean forward and kiss his lips gently. He's branched out of his comfort zone so much these last six weeks. Between joining our team, being the most receptive to the others, and making a genuine effort, I'm really fucking impressed. Roark was always one for online interactions over personal ones.

His lips caress mine, and his hand wraps around my waist, hauling me closer and palming my ass. It feels as natural as breathing to relax into the kiss and give myself over to him.

He hums against my lips when we ease out of the kiss. "You are..."

The Cleanup

"What?" I ask, blinking my eyes open and finding his still closed. His freckles dance across his nose and cheekbones as he smiles.

"Edible," he whispers, finally looking me in the eyes as his accent washes over me.

"*Bon*," Maurice calls from the other side of the boat as he claps his hands together. "*C'est parti*. Tanks on, and let's dive!"

After putting on my weight belt, I slide my arms inside the buoyancy compensators—also called BCD—slide the regulator inside my mouth, and I inhale once to make sure I haven't forgotten to open my air tank. Then, I add my mask, my snorkel for surface-level breathing, and finally my fins. Even if we're all diving with Maurice, he made us pair up since, very soon, we're going to dive just the five of us. I'm with Roark, and Viraj is with Max and Zach since their skill levels balance each other. We all check the pressure of our tanks, inflate our jackets so we float to the surface when we jump, and when everyone gives the OK sign—thumb and index together with the three other fingers pointing upwards—we start walking like stupid penguins to the edge of the boat from where we'll jump off. It's one of the bigger ships—just like *Unsinkable II*—so we aren't training the backward drop like in movies. We take a giant stride into the sea one by one, and form a floating circle once immersed. Maurice makes eye contact with each and every one of us, asking with his right hand if we're ready, the OK sign again. We each answer with the same gesture, then he closes his fist and points his thumb in the direction of the deep.

We're going down.

Sinking is harder than it looks. You have to kick your feet a little, then release all the air from your jacket and empty your lungs at the same time. If you're not deep enough when you take your next inhalation, you'll float back up. But you also can't completely stop breathing because it's dangerous. And you're not supposed to swim either. At least not until you're already a little deep.

For this alone, I'm glad we all took the lessons. Imagine if one of us floated back to the surface when the police are chasing us.

The worst thing is that it tends to be me. Body fat is lighter than water, and I have boobs, which act like natural flotation devices. It's very inconvenient when your goal is to sink.

The sunshine shimmers on the surface and makes the rest of the water around us look green, despite the darker seafloor. Today's dive site is the Cap Ferrat. It's one of the more accessible dives, and its abundant sea life makes for a good time with spectacular views of the underwater biome.

Fish of all colours swim by as I lazily make my way to the bottom. Upon reaching it, I turn around and see Roark has followed me. He's still tense, and his movements are jerky and too quick, not entirely trusting the tank strapped to his back.

I kneel on the seabed and look up at the glittering water above us. Roark watches me as he approaches, and I start singing "Under the Sea" from The Little Mermaid. As the air bubbles escape, he looks at me in panic, but I give him the OK signal and keep singing. Now would be a good time for those air bubbles to turn into speech bubbles. He'll never know that he's missing out on the performance of a lifetime.

He points to his ears and shrugs when he lands next to me on the sand below. Ah, so he *can* hear me, he just can't understand me. I sing louder around the mouthpiece and add an interpretive dance. He shrugs more exaggeratedly.

Fucking hell.

Maurice leads the way as we go explore the site. The rocks are porous, offering shelter to the wildlife. I see an octopus and try to stick my hands into the hole where she's hiding.

Maurice's already scolded me several times this week, but I can't help it. I'm a thief, I want to take stuff and bring it back home as a souvenir. An octopus called Octopussy would look awesome in my living room. She's a female, I can feel it.

Roark really has come a long way in a few short lessons. If he keeps this up, there will be no reason for him to worry during our escape—apart from the possible gunshots, law enforcement chasing

The Cleanup

us, the Bratva at our backs, and the fact that we'll have an invaluable diamond with data vital to the world's safety in our hands.

My Viking hacker gets his bearings, and we take off, following our instructor. Roark goes slowly and methodically, practising signals with me the whole time, including a few he seems to have made up on the spot if his index finger pushing through the circle he makes with the other hand is any indication. We can't fuck underwater. Or can we?

No. Unfortunately, training has to come first.

Six more lessons until he's certified, but the confidence he's beginning to show is astonishing to see. When we were teens, anything new used to throw him off his game. As I watch him glide through the water, his movements slow and measured, I'm glad to see he's matured in more ways than one. When we were younger, he was quick to take words to heart and internalise more than he let on. I'm sure he still does it, but now, it seems to be far less, and he hasn't let the opinions of the other three sway him since we've been together.

Finding Max, Zach, and Viraj circling above like sharks, I put my hand to my mouth and blow them a kiss.

Our escape plan will not require us to swim for long. We'll time things so a scuba diving school is nearby and will join their group as tourists, hiding in plain sight. It means that fortunately, we do not need to be experts. Viraj has all the certifications in underwater cartography—because of course he does—so he'll guide us.

Watching his frustration as he goes through the beginner training all over again is hilarious.

Maurice signals to stop, but too busy saying hello to another new friend, Dick, the Moray eel, I miss the hand signal and almost face-plant in Max's butt.

Our instructor explained when we were on the boat that today's exercise is to put our equipment back in place if it gets ripped away. Watching the others go through it is very funny, but I'm not excited for my turn.

Viraj goes first and obviously makes it look easy. Max is less comfortable, but still, he manages.

Roark, now, looks like a fish out of water.

The main thing to remember is not to panic. Okay, you're dozens of feet deep, you lost your regulator and can't breathe, but you have to keep your wits about you.

The idea is simple. If your air isn't going all over the place, it means that the tubes connecting your tank and the regulator are still attached. So you just have to grab the top of your tank behind your back and follow the tube until the mouthpiece is in your hand. Then you put it back where it belongs, exhale sharply once to push the water out, and breathe more or less normally.

Roark forgets about the tube trick, tries to find the mouthpiece by making arm gestures all around him and starts floating up when Maurice finally helps him and brings the air outlet to his mouth. Our hacker then forgets to exhale first and inhales a nice mouthful of water, which makes him cough hard.

My throat hurts for him. Breathing in saltwater isn't fun.

They repeat the manoeuvre until Roark gets it perfectly, and I spend time cooing at Dick whose head starts peeking out of his hole under my praise. Then it's Zach's turn to practice the recovery of his mouthpiece, and I go to pet my eel friend, hoping it'll show me even more of its length if I stroke him a little. Viraj sees my extended hand and swiftly grabs my wrist to pull it back, glowering at me.

Either touching Dick is dangerous, or Viraj is jealous because I'm not petting his eel.

Knowing the man, it's probably the second option.

Finally, Maurice signals for me to come closer and makes me learn the manoeuvre just like the others. As soon as the mouthpiece leaves my teeth, I let a continuous stream of bubbles leave my lips to protect my lungs. I grab the tube, get my mouthpiece back, and boom, I'm the best student in the class.

Take that, guys.

We go for one last swim before Roark signals he only has fifty bars of air left, and it's time to go back up. We pause three minutes at thirty feet deep for safety, then finally resurface, one arm raised to let the boat crew know where we are.

I inflate my BCD because I'm lazy and want to float, then start paddling to the boat.

We get on it, rinse our gear, and put everything back in its place while the boat takes us towards the coast. As soon as the wetsuit is off, I start shivering. It's only May, after all, and even if the water isn't that cold, the air is brisk. Viraj must be in a particularly good mood because he wraps me in the fluffy towel he brought and sits me in his lap, surrounding me with his big, warm body.

As we reach the dock of the hotel again, my phone dings from my bag with an incoming text. The only people who have this number are here on this boat or Ellie.

I wake the screen and find some good news.

Ellie: Natasha has confirmed her attendance to the Monte Carlo kick-off party on Friday the 27th.

Me: What's the attire?

Ellie: It's the fucking Monte Carlo Casino, Olivia Wraith! What do you think the attire is?

Me: We'll be there. Can you get us on the list, or do we need to handle that?

Ellie: Use that English nobility you have stashed away with you. Security is tighter than a motherfucker and invite-only. Surely, he can pull some strings.

I look over at Max as he throws on a pair of Ray-Bans, looking like a fucking model, and wave him over.

"Hey, what's going on?" he asks when he sees the phone in my hand.

"How good are your connections here in Monaco?" I ask.

He considers for a moment, not giving me the answer I so desperately crave right now. My foot taps the boat deck below me in impatience.

"What do you need specifically?" he asks.

"Oh, you know, an invite to the kick-off party at the Monte Carlo Casino." I just shrug my shoulders.

"The—" he sputters. "You want invites to the most exclusive party aside from the winner's dinner? The one that they send invites for months—years—in advance? That party?"

"Yep!" I pat his chest. "Hop to it, Maxi! Wouldn't want someone else to claim the reward for those invitations now, would you?" I bat my lashes and slip past him, Maurice already waiting with his hand at the ready.

I hop down onto the dock and work on the phone in my hands. A few clicks later, I've found a shop that sells both dresses and tuxedos just over the border in Nice, France. Monaco is bound to be full up on appointments this close to race weekend, and anyway, it's better to spend big money out of the city to avoid unwanted attention.

"We're going on an adventure today!" I shout over my shoulder at the others, who just look at me with confusion on their faces. "I know, I know, every day is an adventure with me, but now we've got an assignment."

"Oh, is the car ready?" Viraj asks, his excitement evident in his broad smile.

"Not yet. But speaking of, we do need a ride out of here."

"On it!" Roark is fiddling on his phone and brings it to his ear. He covers the mouthpiece after he connects and whispers to me, "Where are we going?"

Zach slaps him on the back as he passes us and declares, "This isn't a lead, Little Thief."

It's a lead if I say it's a lead and shall be rewarded as such. Fucking Roark in the taxi probably isn't the best choice, but it sure would be fun.

"Nice."

Roark relays the information and nods his head.

Then, I do the unthinkable. I make them go shopping.

The Cleanup

"For the love of Christ, Olivia! Anything will do. Anything! Just fucking buy something!" Viraj hollers from the other side of the curtained dressing room.

Ugh, men.

Thankfully, someone else gets it. "Relax, man. She'll be done when she's done. Our tuxes are easy compared to what she has to find. Standing out, but not too much. Sexy, yet subtle. Eye-catching and yet demure. Being a woman is hard work," Max says, and I want to hug him. It *is* hard work.

"I'm done, I'm done. Relax!" I shout back. The saleswoman next to me flinches at my volume, and I turn to her. "*Je suis vraiment désolée. Il a les intestins sensibles et un urgent besoin d'aller aux toilettes.*" Then I giggle, because imagining Viraj struggling with sensitive bowels is too funny.

Her face blanches, and she hustles from the room with the garment bag in tow. I rip the curtain open and stare down Viraj as he sits on the cushy wingback chair. Max is seated beside him with a flute of champagne in hand.

"Where are the others?" I ask since Roark and Zach are notably missing.

"They stepped out," Max answers, then takes a sip of bubbly.

"Can you track them down? I'm all done. Did you guys get fitted for your tuxes?"

"Yes, and I have to say, I'm quite impressed. Monsieur Lavigne was very thorough, and everything will be delivered to the flat on the twenty-third." Max puts his flute on the side table and saunters towards the door after bidding the shop owner adieu.

"Oh," Max says, pausing with his hand on the door. "I got us the invitations."

My panties dampen. Ah fuck, now every time they do something I ask or get a lead on something, I've conditioned my body to be ready for sex. Pavlov's pussy.

259

Max's gaze heats, but he steps through the door to find the others... as I had asked. Ah, shit. It happened again.

V and I approach the counter to pay for everything and double-check the delivery address. All the while, I'm shifting around, trying not to think of Max's magnificent cock. *Focus on the job, Olivia.* Job? Scuba diving. Moray eels. Dick. Fuck!

"Avez-vous trouvé tout ce que vous vouliez?" Madame Lavigne asks.

I assure her we are very satisfied with our purchases, and when the point of sale machine flashes a total, I pay using the prepaid card bearing one of my fake names.

"J'espère que votre ami va mieux," she says, looking at Viraj warily as if he's going to ask for her bathroom at any moment.

"Il a l'habitude, ne vous inquiétez pas," I say, squeezing his arm in reassurance as he watches the exchange, not knowing a word of French other than champagne because he chose to take Spanish in school. I just assured her his bowel betraying him is a common occurrence, and she shouldn't worry. Max has returned and is standing just inside the door. He snorts, understanding what I said. Madame Lavigne looks V over, pausing at his belly before giving him a smile and wishing him luck.

I leave the shop, cackling like a deranged witch.

Diarrhoea jokes are always fun.

Or maybe I have the humour of a twelve-year-old.

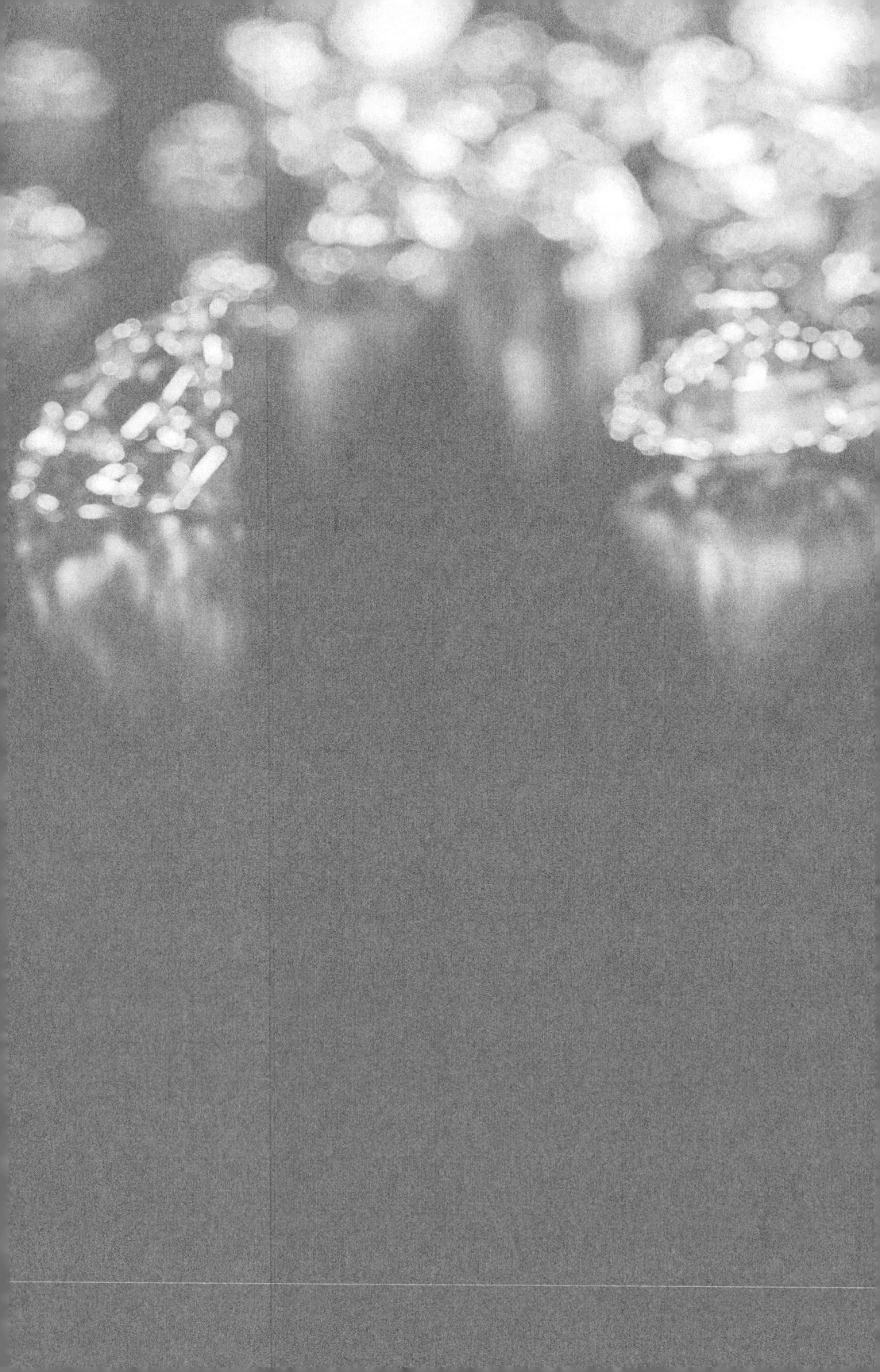

Chapter Twenty-Three

Viraj
Present Day

It's been a long week. Between scuba diving, hypnotising, climbing—because yes, that's one of our escape plans as well—and planning, I'm starting to feel the strain, even if my body is used to it.

But the most exhausting thing this past week has been my suddenly fucked-up sleep schedule. I don't require much. Especially after all the long nights at law school that conditioned me to exist on caffeine alone. But here, it's like some special kind of torture.

We spend the days preparing for the big day, then Ollie corrals us all together for dinner around the tiny table in the lounge. Most of the time we're going over details of the job and any recon we found during the day. But other times, our conversation slips into more present day activities. What do we do? Do we like where we're living?

Every now and then, I see a glimmer of sadness in Ollie's eyes when one of us talks about our lives outside of this bubble we've been existing in. She hasn't been quick to share things about her life, but slowly, she's started opening up. A vulnerability I've never seen in her face flashes over her features when she talks about her life.

She clearly has everything she wants, but she seems lonely. Hell, we all do, if I'm being honest.

I spend my nights thinking over our dinner conversations and willing myself to keep the damned walls up. But there, in the dead of night, while the others are all asleep, I feel the tiniest cracks forming.

All this overthinking and rehashing conversations and details means that sleep's embrace usually finds me around three or four in the morning. Since planning a job like this requires waking hours, we're up at eight and, well, I'm tired.

Coffee is my very best friend at this stage. At least Olivia isn't rationing it here like she was back in London.

However, the great part of this week is that I've started doing intense recon on our possible escape routes. I get to spend days out of the flat and away from the other assholes, driving into the mountains until I get as close as possible to the pickup location. There aren't many ways to get there, but I have to know them all in case we're followed and I have to lose a potential tail.

Today, I'm starting to work on my high-speed driving. Then I'll do the same thing at night without headlamps because there's a chance I might drive under the cover of darkness.

"V," Ollie calls as I leave the flat, "Max and I are coming with you today. The car is finally here, and since Max had to pull some strings for us to have it, it seems fair."

Shit, there goes my quiet drive.

"Don't you have some events to attend and caviar to eat?" I taunt. I really wanted to be alone and the caffeine hasn't kicked in yet. As civil as I've been to Max lately, sometimes these things just slip out.

Max rolls his eyes, ignoring my jab, and follows Olivia as we leave the flat.

We have several cars stashed all around Monaco and Cagnes-sur-Mer in case things go south, but ideally, we'll be able to use the one I will drive today. It's a prototype, a jewel of technology that has my cock hard just thinking of it.

As if it needed more reasons to be. Watching Olivia Wraith act all bossy and confident has always been a major turn-on for me. And I'm the only one she has done nothing sexual with so far.

Dildo-chair fucking excepted, of course.

We arrive at the villa Interpol secured for us if we require a hideout, and sure as a Swiss clock, the supercar is parked in the driveway. It's absolutely gorgeous, black with gold accents and an aggressive look to it. I wish we were staying in this house for the duration of the job, but it's so remote, we wouldn't be in the heart of the city and able to monitor our surroundings as well.

We opted for an electric car, since the noise of a V8 engine would give us away in the echoing mountains. Roark will hack into the car's system and make it as silent as possible. Most of the noise made by electric cars comes from a speaker added under the hood to protect pedestrians, anyway.

"What is it?" Olivia asks.

"This beauty is a Porsche Taycan Turbo S," Max brags. "A prototype of the next version of the car, to be precise. The serial version is already one of the fastest electric cars in the world, and the only four-seater of that category, but obviously increasing performances is always an objective of the brands." Max sees me nearly drooling and adds, "The keys should be hidden above the rear wheel."

I check it, and as planned, I find my newest favourite object ever.

"Shotgun," Olivia yells.

Max grunts, but doesn't protest. I slide in behind the wheel, Olivia at my right, and the aristocrat goes right behind her. As usual.

"Do you have a plan for the last seat?" she asks.

I see Max nod in the rearview mirror. "I'm getting a harness made, so it's safe to sit where the armrest unfolds. It won't be comfortable, but we should be safe in case of a crash."

"There will be no accident," I confidently say as I turn on the car. The engine doesn't roar to life, but the controls light up with LEDs and fancy displays, compensating for the underwhelming absence of noise.

Just like most electric cars, it's an automatic, so I put the beauty in drive, and we leave the villa.

I rigorously follow the speed limit while we're on the coast. We have fake magnetic license plates, but still, it'd be dumb to get caught. Ollie and Max chat at my side while I pay attention to our destination. They're saying stuff about the opening party, and how to approach Natasha there. Whatever.

I'll focus on driving. This is what I'm good at, after all.

As soon as we're in the mountains, I gun it. The other cars I used for practice runs on these roads weren't even close to being as responsive as the Taycan, and the acceleration plasters us all against our seats.

The roads get narrower and narrower, but still, my speed stays the same. I already know them by heart. I've learned every curve, every delicate passage, every bump in the concrete.

The landscapes around us take my breath away. The road is encased in the mountains, bordered by a wall of rock on one side and a river down below on the other. The mountainsides are a bright light green this early in the year, covered in young grass and burgeoning flowers. Only the highest peaks are bare of vegetation, too exposed to withstand the snow in winter, but with small plateaus for picnics.

And perfect for a helicopter to land.

I figured out during my first recon that the coordinates Interpol gave us for our pickup point are on the second highest one.

That's where we're headed right now.

This part of the way is less busy, so I accelerate again. Max yelps and Ollie hollers. They can say whatever they want, she's as much of an adrenaline junkie as I am. How many other women would show up at a snowboarding competition like she did five years ago, do the runs, then peace out after getting her medal?

I brake—only a little abruptly. "You know the roof opens, right?"

Olivia beams at me, her lithe body bouncing in the seat next to me. "Really?"

I press the button that makes the sunroof slide open. Immediately, Ollie unbuckles her seatbelt to stand on her seat and starts whooping and hollering in the air, her upper body exposed to the wind.

"Liv, are you sure this is a good idea?" Max yells.

"Relax, Maxi Pad. She knows what she's doing, and so do I." I'm not going nearly as fast as I was before.

He keeps protesting and being reasonable, so to shut him up, I turn on the stereo. "Pump it" from Black Eyed Peas comes blaring out the speakers. A smile stirs on my lips. It was a popular song choice when we were all still in school, and I remember seeing Ollie and Ellie dancing around to it in one of the common rooms.

I turn up the volume to the maximum, and Olivia starts singing as loud as she can, treating me to a repeat performance.

Glancing to the side, trying to see her face, I finally notice something I should never have missed. She's wearing a skirt. A pleated one that flies around her thighs because of the wind in the car.

And her pussy is almost level with my face. Is she even wearing underwear?

My cock instantly becomes rock hard.

If I extended my arm, I could—No! Better not to think about it.

A siren pulls me out of my fantasies, and Ollie sits back down as fast as she can. "Shit! Cops. Pull over, V. I'll talk us out of this."

I glance in the rearview mirror. They're still far, and their car is bulky, an SUV made for off-road more than speed. The expression on my face becomes devious.

"V, whatever you're thinking, don't do it."

"What?" I raise a brow at her. "Why? I'm supposed to be training for a high-speed chase, aren't I? I bet you I can lose them."

We exchange a look. I see Ollie struggling with the heathen inside her. She wants me to lose them. She wants the speed, the danger, the adrenaline, she wants it all.

And she knows I can give it to her.

"You know what?" I add. "I bet I can lose them and make you come at the same time." My skirt-inspired fantasies never truly left my mind.

From the corner of my eyes, I see her throwing me a dubious look. "Okay. But if you fail to do one of those things, you're going to that party with a butt plug. And if you get me arrested with blue ovaries, I swear to fuck I'll buy you the biggest butt plug ever commercialised."

"Deal. Same stakes apply if I pull it off. You'll be wearing the plug." The two of us share a quick handshake to seal the deal.

"Mm, guys?" Max says tentatively. "You know I'm still here, right? And the cops are getting closer."

Ollie blows him a kiss in the rearview mirror, and I press the pedal to the floor. Quickly, the distance between the Taycan and the police car increases. I can't have that. If I lose them before I make Olivia climax, she'll say I lost the bet.

So I brake, staying within distance of the other car.

Max protests, "What the...? We were getting away, V!"

I ignore him. My cock is straining against the front of my jeans, and now that I know the Taycan has what it takes to lose our tail, I can have fun.

"Ollie," I order, my voice an octave lower than usual. "Hand me your underwear." She doesn't question, doesn't protest, doesn't even fucking hesitate, which sure doesn't improve the state of my dick. Her red lacy thong slides along her slender legs before she deposits it in my extended palm, and I almost slam us into the cliff as my eyes stray from the road for a second.

I'm driving way past the speed limit with one hand and holding sexy-as-fuck panties, already wet from her arousal in the other. The situation would be ridiculous if it weren't so hot.

I can't miss this occasion to screw with him, so I throw the panties in Max's face. "So you can wank on them while I take her pussy." If looks could kill, the one he's aiming at the rearview mirror now would stop my heart.

Chuckling, I focus my eyes back on the road as my right hand snakes towards Olivia's thigh.

It'll require some coordination, but I can do this.

Ollie's thighs spread apart, and she pulls her skirt up higher. Her skin is soft under my fingers, and the only thought in my head is how pretty it'd be with a red hand mark on it. I slap her leg appreciatively, giving it a hard squeeze that makes her squeal. Too bad I can't see how her skin reacted since we're going too fast, and the cops are closing in.

Still, I take a quick look at her. She tilted her head back against the headrest and spread her legs apart, going as far as propping a foot up on the dashboard. She's as exposed as she can be. Max is trying to keep an even face, but I can tell he's not unaffected by what's going on. His lips are parted, and he quickly readjusts the bulge in his trousers.

The road makes a sharp left, and as my left hand steers us away from the precipice at our right, my right plunges inside Ollie's tight pussy. I don't have much time, so I angle my wrist to press my thumb against her clit.

"V," she moans. The sound goes straight to my dick. It's breathless and pleading, just like her.

She's already clamping around my fingers, and she barely offered any resistance as they went in. Ollie's cunt is wet as hell, and if my hands weren't busy, I'd propose right now. I need a woman like her, someone who gets off on high-speed chases and adrenaline.

And she's made it known she wants me too. Why can't she just forget about the others?

I start pumping my fingers inside her, fast and hard, pressing on her clit on each thrust. My foot slams on the accelerator. I can't lose focus and get us arrested.

Olivia grabs my wrist and starts fucking herself, using my hand as a sex toy. Moans slip past her lips. "Fuck, V. Yeah, faster." Both the car and my hand accelerate as she pleads.

Fuck, I need to be inside her.

I crook my fingers against her inner wall and rub furiously on her clit, triggering her orgasm. She cries out, and her back arches against the seat as she pulls on my hand and pushes my fingers inside her as deep as they will go, chasing her pleasure.

"Ollie, the cops are closing in," I say. "I need my second hand."

She's coming hard, her walls tightening around my fingers even as I pull out of her. Before putting them back on the wheel, I slip them in my mouth, one by one, exaggeratedly slowly, savouring the taste of her wet pussy. It's worth the few extra seconds of single-handed driving.

I accelerate as I take the next curve right. The cop car gradually starts to fade, but we're not fully out of reach, even if my cock throbs in my jeans and begs me just to stop the car and fuck Ollie.

The next curve on the left side places the mountain between us and our pursuers. We're out of sight now, and in a few minutes, we'll get to safety.

In my earlier drives, I found this remote road that leads to a small and out-of-the-way trail. It's not the most direct route to our rendezvous with Interpol, but it's a possible alternative, so I know it's a great hiding place.

I take a sharp left, then immediately kill the engine.

The three of us are panting as we listen to the siren coming our way and continuing on the main road.

I lost the cops.

A devious smile stretches on my lips. "Do I get to pick the size of your butt plug, Ollie?" Her answering smirk matches mine. She'd deny it in front of the others, but she wanted to lose the bet.

"Can we go home now?" Max whines. "I think that's enough driving for today, isn't it?" He looks a little green in the rearview mirror, and with the performance Ollie and I just delivered, there's a blush high on his cheeks as well. His chest is heaving with adrenaline or lust; could be both.

"Sure, Maxi Pad. Let me drive us back."

The engine quietly vibrates to life under my fingers, but instead of heading down and back to the coast, I take the road up to the mountaintop. Max turns in his seat to look back the way we came, but doesn't say a word.

The way she's looking at me is telling enough; Ollie wants me just as much as I want her.

And I'm not waiting.

Max watching us will just be a bonus. He'll see me claiming her and know she belongs to me when my cum drips down her thighs.

For a few minutes, I drive in silence. Soon, the road branches out again, and we're hidden amongst the trees. Upon parking, Ollie takes off her seatbelt and pounces, straddling my thighs and rubbing her cunt against my jeans-clad dick.

"Are you really going to do this now?!" Max asks, incredulous and sounding slightly scandalised at the idea. Ha. Fuck him. Or even better, don't fuck him.

"Max?" Olivia pouts, and it takes all my restraint not to bite her full lips. "Can we do this, please?"

I free her breast from her bra and wrap my mouth around her nipple. Max will never refuse her if she's pleading like this.

"Come here," she tells him again. From the way she moves, I can tell they're kissing now.

My hands venture down south. This skirt of hers is indecent. The access is so easy, it shouldn't even be considered clothing. Since I already know how ready she is, I don't delve into her pussy. Rather, I get my hands on my zipper instead.

She whimpers in protest against Max's mouth.

"Max, hold her steady for me. I'm going to make her scream." His hands wrap around the back of her head, pressing her to him as I free my cock.

She moans—in agreement or protest, I can't be sure, since Max's tongue is in her mouth. Either way, she's still rubbing against me like a cat in heat, so it just takes one smooth move to bury myself inside her.

Fuck, it's been so long. I have the reputation of a womaniser, but it couldn't be further from the truth. Ollie is the only girl—woman—that ever got my blood pumping. I dread what it means for our future apart.

Her wet heat wraps around me, and I grunt in ecstasy. She's everything I dreamt of. Tight, warm, and her sweetness still dances on my tongue.

The hand I used to angle my cock wraps around her neck, and I wrestle her mouth away from Max. I'm the one fucking her now, and I don't want to share.

For the first time in our lives, our lips come in contact, and fireworks explode in my brain. She opens her mouth wide for me as our teeth clash and our tongues battle for control.

I can't take it anymore. The past weeks have been atrocious. Watching her fuck everyone but me has been a test for my body and harder than any competition I've ever done before.

So I take what I want. I grab her hips and bring mine up, topping from the bottom. I go all in, fucking her as hard as I can as she struggles to maintain her balance. I pull her down on me as I push up, adding a roll of my hips to hit her clit when we fuse together. She's holding on to the headrest, and her breasts bounce as I pound into her.

As if racing to the finish line, I accelerate my thrusts, making the slapping of skin on skin sound like applause in the enclosed space of the car. "V," she breathes. "Yes, V!"

"Max, fuck off and go for a walk, will you?" I growl.

"Shut the fuck up and kiss her, asshole. If you don't keep her mouth busy, I will."

"Go ahead, fuck her throat then. We'll see who makes her come first." Ollie moans in need and opens her mouth in Max's direction, waiting for him to feed her his cock. Seems that even in the midst of a sex-fuelled haze, the two of us are wired to snipe at each other, throwing all progress out the window in the process.

I continue my punishing rhythm between her legs. I should feel jealous, but I don't. The best word for it is competitive. I want to show them both that her body answers to me as well as the car I drove here. I want her to writhe in ecstasy on top of me and for my dick to make her forget Max's.

So I fuck her harder, her moans turning into little hiccups as her mouth becomes filled with Max's cock.

I refuse to look to the side. I've never seen Max's dick, and after all the innuendos to its size, I don't want to see it this close to my face. I know my limits.

Instead, I focus on Ollie's sweet body and how I'm going to make her climax again. My bruising grip on her hips hasn't let up, and she might be black and blue tomorrow, which gives me the best feeling of satisfaction. I'm marking her hard and fast; I can see why the psycho wanted his marks on her skin. I want more. So, I bite her breast, tongue playing with her nipple while my teeth press against her soft flesh.

Not enough to break the skin.

But enough to make her cry out around Max's dick.

He pushes inside her as hard as he can, tangling a hand in her hair to prevent her from leaning back. She gags while she struggles with his length.

She's focused on him, which is unacceptable. I pinch her clit in retaliation, making her walls clamp around me. Ollie comes, shrieking and clawing at Max's hips as her pussy shudders and gushes on my cock.

The sounds my hips make when they meet hers become wanton as wetness pools between us. The applause turns into splashes, and my jeans must be a mess. I don't care. Three more thrusts up, and I unravel. I come inside her so hard, I see stars. This is a moment to treasure. After all, we know when things will end.

Max comes shortly after, and she swallows his cum before

collapsing on my shoulder. Still sheathed inside her, I relearn how to breathe, my hands running across her soft skin.

"I'm never giving this car back," she announces.

Max and I chuckle as she parks her ass back in the passenger seat. She doesn't even bother asking for her panties. Ollie just grabs a tissue from god-knows-where, cleans herself up quickly, and stuffs it into the pocket of her skirt.

Her hair is dishevelled, her makeup has run across her cheeks, and the look in her eyes tells me it's not the last time we're doing this.

Not if she has anything to say about it.

She has never looked more beautiful, though.

I grab the back of her head, and leaning over the armrest, kiss her with everything I've got, pouring a decade worth of want and longing into one singular kiss. Our tongues tangle together until a begging sound escapes her chest, then I bite her lower lip. She moans in protest, leaning back abruptly, her eyes accusatory. I love it. Then it dawns on me, and my lips part in astonishment.

Shit.

I just kissed her mouth full of another man's cum.

Do I even care?

Chapter Twenty-Four

Olivia
Year Thirteen
March

"And then he said I needed to follow instructions or I'd be punished," Rachel says over the phone, the crack in her voice evident as she recounts her story. She takes in a sobbing breath, and it's soon muffled as if she's trying to smother it with her hand.

"I understand," I say calmly, trying to ease some of the nerves she has at spilling her secrets to a virtual stranger. "I promise I won't say anything to anyone. I need to put a few things in place this week, but I promise you, he will get what he deserves."

Rachel's shaky breaths come over the line, but she inhales deeply before she steels her voice and replies, "Good."

With a plan forming in my mind and a quick overview of what

I'm thinking, we say our goodbyes, and I hang up the phone. Eleanor is on her bed with her headphones blaring as she studies trigonometry and gives me some privacy. I pick up one of my pillows and chuck it at her.

"Oomph." She pauses the music and rips the headphones off. "What was that for? Was it too loud again?" she asks.

"No, you're good. I just have a quick question."

"What's up?"

"Who were Rachel Bernham's friends when she was here?" I ask.

"Rachel Bernham? Why do you want to know about her? She left ages ago."

"Just humour me."

"Uhm, okay. She was one of the popular girls for a long time. She even dated Viraj for a bit, but then again, a lot of girls have dated Viraj," she says, tapping a finger to her chin as if she's running through a tally.

"I don't need to know who he's dating."

"Well, that's easy. He hasn't dated anyone in ages. But in years ten and eleven, he was all over the place." She pauses. "I don't think he's dated anyone since you showed up, really."

"What a coincidence," I reply, turning my head so she can't see the slight smile and blush on my cheeks. I have no claim over V, but even I can admit I'd be pretty heartbroken if he started dating someone.

Somehow, since the pen theft by Mr Hall, the five of us have spent most lunches together coming up with ridiculous ways to get it back. I may or may not be adding more insane scenarios to keep us sitting together every day. It's been a week of our conspiring lunches, and indeed a lot of fun.

Ellie has been stuck eating her lunch in the chem lab as she waits for some kind of fungus growth and tracks the progress, so despite me inviting her to join in on our machinations, she's been too busy.

"Mmm, coincidence. Sure."

"Anyway, what do you remember from her last year here?" I ask, pushing all thoughts of crushes from my mind.

"She seemed fine at the start of the year, then after Christmas break, she was a little off. I saw her going into Dr Forsyth's office more than once since I had a class near the administration wing. It must have been her standing meeting time. She withdrew at the end of term, and I think she's up in Scotland with an aunt or something now. It was all pretty sudden, and her grades had started slipping." I raise a brow, and she correctly interprets my *how did you know that?* look. "Fine," she says with a sigh and an eye roll. "She sat next to me in a class, and her grades were plummeting. I might have looked at a paper or two. I was curious."

It lines up. The connection with the school benefactor was unknown, but all the pieces have fallen into place after my conversation with former mean girl, Rachel.

I need more proof, and I need sway. If one benefactor uses the principal, another might do the same. It would take more than just a student's word to cut out the insidiousness creeping in this school. After all, if it happened with one girl, what's to stop it from happening to another?

Ellie looks at me curiously. "What are you planning?" she asks.

I debate telling her everything. Not because I don't think she can't handle it, but more that if this doesn't work, I don't want her catching any of the blowback. She's going places, for sure. She's been the best roommate and friend I ever could have asked for. I couldn't let anything happen to her if we were caught.

"What? Nothing," I say. She just cocks a brow at me and hums as she goes back to her music. This won't be the last time she asks me that question, but for now, I'll shield her as best as I can.

I need an in with the school benefactors. Who better to ask than the son and the beneficiary of one in particular?

Gathering up my mobile and key, I wave at Ellie on my way out the door. Making my way to Roark's, I straighten my shirt and plaster a smile on my face. I text the other three, telling them to meet me in the computer lab as soon as possible.

Roark opens the door, and his hair is mussed and his glasses are askew on his face. "Oh, Via. What's up? Did we have a plan to study?" he asks, his accent and voice deeper than usual and thick with sleep.

"No, no study date. Something more important." His cheeks pink at the date comment, but then a puzzled look takes over his face.

"What could be more important than studying before our A-Levels?"

I groan in exasperation. I really like Roark. He's been a great friend, and yeah, a crush for a while now. But sometimes, he forgets to live outside the computer lab and misses the world around him. Keeping his nose in his books has ensured he stays here, but I wonder how much of the outside world escaped his attention.

"Come on," I say, yanking his hand until he's in the corridor with me. I check my phone, find responses from the other three, and start making my way to the computer lab. "Keep up, Rory! We've got lives to destroy!" I call down the hall.

He rushes after me, and we pass by students studying in nooks and crannies and a few making out in the alcoves of the halls, until we find ourselves in front of the computer lab door. I push through, dragging Roark with me. Max is on one side of the room and Viraj on the other. I swear, the two of them put as much distance between them as possible whenever they're in the same space. Unless, of course, it's lunchtime theft planning. Then they're happy to sit at the same table discussing distraction ideas.

"Everyone sit, please. I've got some news."

Viraj perks up. "Did you find a distraction?"

"V, we've had a distraction since day one. I was just enjoying everyone's enlightening company," I reply. I'm not being ironic, I just really like spending time with them, despite all the snapping at each other.

Zach pushes through the door, looks at the rest of us gathered, and flips the lock.

The Cleanup

"Little Thief, I had something else in mind," he drawls as he looks at the others. Rory shivers next to me at the calm, detached tone Zach uses.

"This is going to be better," I say with surety.

Zach's brow quirks as he looks at the others gathered. "No, not that." I sigh. Ever since we slept together, Zach has acted completely pussy whipped. He's like a psychotic, aggressive, constantly horny puppy dog. And I fucking love it.

"It wouldn't be possible anyway," Max says as he drops into a chair at the table I've selected. "Viraj here hasn't fucked in so long he seems to have regained his V-Card. Wouldn't want to ruin his newfound virginity."

V's shoulders inch up to his ears, and I know we're going to spend the next twenty minutes arguing instead of tackling this new development.

"Max," I snap. "Now is not the time for that. By the way, when was the last time you had sex?" I ask. His fists clench on the tabletop, and I know I've hit a nerve. Zach looks over at me, and I call him off with a shake of my head. There's no need to rain chaos down when we have work to do.

"We have a problem," I start. "The headmaster had been grooming a student before she dropped out." My words drop like a stone in still waters, causing all four boys to rear back in shock. "The worst part, he was being paid to do so."

I look over at Max. "How well connected to the other school benefactors is your dad?"

He sputters. "If you're insinuating it was my father, I have to tell you you're wrong, Liv." I hold my hand up to calm his indignation.

"No, not your dad. Lord Canton is the one who had been paying the headmaster up until the student dropped out. She was then out of his reach, and the payments stopped. But what if they start again? Can we risk another student being put at risk like that?" I ask.

Zach's body has been thrumming since I started explaining. Based on his file, he's been mistreated and misdiagnosed by doctors for far longer than anyone should be. If anyone would have a problem with an authority figure abusing his power over adolescents, it's him.

"Holy shit," Roark breathes. "How did you find out about this?" he asks me.

I place my palms down on the table and answer honestly, "I've been hacking the school system to find out his salary, breaking into the records room for information on the student, and I swiped an administrator's phone to check for office gossip."

Each one of them has played a role in my information collection. The secretary was the same one V and I stole the car from. The records room key hasn't moved since the first time Max helped me get in. And Roark has taught me more about hacking than I'd ever thought I might need. Zach hasn't had a direct hand in my planning, but his file gave me the idea for the connection between the student and the payments. After all, he assumes his doctor was getting kickbacks from a pharmaceutical company for turning to risky medication before therapy for his patients.

"Lord Canton. He's a creepy fuck," Max says. "I met him before I started school here. There was a student mixer at orientation, and a few of the benefactors were there, my dad amongst them. Oh god, do you think he knows?"

I reach a hand across the table and put it on Max's arm. "I'm sure he doesn't. It seems isolated, and the money is handled as a donation to the principal's Kickstarter campaign. Believe it or not, this is being done as a tax write-off. Because, of course, while paying money for underage girls, he's still looking for a tax break." I roll my eyes.

This whole situation is fucked up.

"So, forget about the pen for a second. How do you guys feel about joining me on this little mission?"

BEFORE WE CAN TAKE DOWN THE HEADMASTER, WE NEED A plan. And obviously, a location to watch it all go down as we bring

The Cleanup

Headmaster Barkley to justice. I rather like watching my machinations unfold.

But today, we have a test. How are we supposed to work together on something so grand when we haven't even got my pen back from Mr Hall? He's had it for nearly two weeks now, and it's driving me batty.

The worst part of it is that he has the pen with him. Every single day in that class, I have to see it gleaming from atop his desk, taunting me. Then, he puts it into his briefcase to take it with him when class ends, not giving me the opportunity to swipe it back.

I've never dealt with actual, physical theft. I just gather secrets, place them in the right hands or hint at them enough to get what I want—or more often—need. Sure, the car thing was technically a theft. But I gave it back, didn't I? She never even knew her vehicle left the parking lot.

But today, I'm getting my fucking pen back. Besides, it's not theft if the object was mine in the first place. It's a rescue mission.

Mr Hall discusses the importance of other cultures in mandatory literature studies for us students, and I can't say I disagree. But he's been droning on for thirty minutes without pause.

I cough twice, then pretend to sneeze. Our signal. Today is the motherfucking day.

Viraj's hand shoots into the air, way over eagerly.

"Save all questions for the end, Mr Goenka," he chides.

"It's not a question, sir." Smooth bastard. "I need to use the facilities, please."

Mr Hall gives him a bored look, then waves his hand at the door. "Make it quick. I'll take a couple of questions, so you don't miss too much."

Max is next. "Sir, may I go as well? I have no questions at present, but if we're pausing, I'd like to take advantage too."

Mr Hall is not pleased. "Fine, fine." He looks around the room. "Does anyone else need a break?" His tone is annoyed, and no one else jumps at the opportunity. "Very well. Go, gentlemen. Hurry back."

He squares his shoulders, and begins the Q-and-A segment of this lecture. "Does anyone have any questions?"

The two of them hustle through the door, and Roark grabs my attention with a subtle wave next to me. I nod to him.

"Sir, in the past, there has been a demand for moving to lesser-known authors and literature published by indie presses. Some say traditional publishing is dried out and no longer reflects the general populace because of its high-brow nature and focus on the past rather than the present. I notice you keep a wide variety of traditionally published literature in the back, but I have rarely seen an indie publication in your library. Do you have an opinion on that?"

Well done, Rory.

Mr Hall moves towards the back of the room, where his gargantuan bookcases stand. They're filled to the brim with everything traditional. He begins droning on about the merits of traditional publishing houses, and I snap my pencil in my hand.

I feign frustration at the break. Rising from my seat, I wave my broken pencil at Mr Hall and indicate the sharpener attached to the wall near the door. He nods his head at me and continues his impassioned speech about the holier than thou presses.

Passing by his desk, I snake a hand out and grab my pen when Mr Hall turns to remove a book from the shelf. I slip the pen into my top and sharpen my pencil.

There are ten minutes left in class, and so long as he doesn't notice the pen before the class ends, I should be fine. I'm moving back to my seat and giving Zach and Roark a subtle thumbs up when a scuffle breaks out on the other side of the classroom door.

Max and Viraj are shouting at each other in the hallway, and there's a thump on the classroom door. It rattles the wood, and the entire class abandons Mr Hall's lecture to stare in their direction.

He races to open the door, and Max and V spill onto the floor in a flurry of fists and shouting.

"Break it up! Break it up, gentlemen. This is no way to behave!" Mr Hall shouts. They ignore him entirely and continue their assault, rolling along the floor and banging into another student's desk before going the opposite way and bumping Mr Hall's workspace. Things go flying when Viraj hauls Max up by his collar and slams him down on the desktop, sending everything crashing to the floor.

"That is enough!" Mr Hall bellows, spittle flying everywhere. The two brawlers pause to breathe, chests heaving and silent. "You two, step apart. I need to report this to the headmaster. The rest of you, go."

There's a flurry of movement, and Mr Hall is dialling the headmaster on his mobile and watching Max and V, keeping a hand between them as if that would stop them from going at it again.

As I pass by, they both shoot me winks and cock-sure smiles, causing an eruption of butterflies to take flight in my stomach.

THAT EVENING, I'M IN THE COMPUTER LAB WITH RORY AND Zach, pretending to study for our classes when the door swings inwards. Max and V saunter in and actually look like they're getting along. Who knew conspiring to steal things would bring them together?

Oh, wait. I did.

They catch a look at my face, and they both rush over. "Ollie, what's wrong?" V asks.

I hold the pen out in my palm, showing them the monstrosity and letting the vulnerability show on my face, an uncharacteristically open move on my part.

"You got the pen. Why are you sad?" Max looks from the pen to my face, trying to figure it out.

Zach leans his body closer to mine. "The cap is gone. It's thrown off the balance."

"It was perfect," I gripe for the millionth time.

Rory has been trying to come up with another distraction so we can search for the cap, but with the destruction of Mr Hall's desk, there's a good chance it's lost forever.

V must have the same thought as me because his face morphs into something determined, and he holds his hand out. "I have an idea. Give me the pen, Ollie."

I reluctantly hand it over, and he walks it to the teacher's desk, pulling out duct tape, and a handful of odds and ends before saying, "We can fix this."

Chapter Twenty-Five

Max
Present Day

Olivia sits astride a chair, her hands draped over the backrest as Zach paints the tattoos on her back. He covers the markings with opposite colours, red with green, yellow with purple, and so on, that way the cover-up concealer better hides the ink on her skin. She wants them all disguised for the party, since they're so recognisable. Olivia explained it, saying it's the same way we use green concealer over red spots on our face before putting on foundation. We are all more lost than ever.

Viraj stares, lust shining in his eyes, and I raise my beer bottle to my lips, enjoying the show and ridiculous tension. I wonder what that's about. I tried to ask him about it, but he only said it reminded him of something that happened at Olivia's house with a special chair, and Liv just smirked at his answer.

Is it about the butt plug she said she'd wear because she lost the bet? Does she have it in yet? Do I want to know and risk walking around the party with my dick tenting the trousers of my tux? Nope. The person who said ignorance was bliss probably had a cock as big as mine.

Roark, on the other hand, is typing away on his laptop, ensuring our comm devices are synced up and recording at all times. Olivia brought everything we needed for this operation. Every time she pulls something out of her suitcase for the job like Mary Poppins with her carpet bag—but like a million times hotter and less reminiscent of my nan—Roark gets giddy.

The most epic moment being when she pulled out a glitter dildo and he made *gimme hands* at it like it contained all the secrets of the world.

And as it turned out, it did. Whenever I think I'm done being surprised by Olivia Wraith, she proves me wrong in the most spectacular way.

I'll be honest; the refractometer on the coffee table still confuses the fuck out of me. But thankfully, I'm not the one who has to deal with that. Zach is handling that in his medical bag and walking it right into the party for his "sick" companion. Our doctor added a false note to Viraj's file that he was diabetic, and we disguised the refractometer as a rather large glucometer. Indeed, it is about four times the size of your average diabetic device. We also checked that the security guards scheduled to be at the entrance have no reason to know what a glucometer looks like—researching through their friends and relatives —to make our plan airtight.

"Done!" Roark cheers from the sofa. "I increased the range, so we can put the transmitter in Via's purse, and it'll keep the recordings. We don't have to sneak a laptop into the party."

"Hallelujah. I was nervous about that," Olivia says as she drops her head forward in relief.

The Cleanup

"Okay, so let's go over the plan again," Viraj says.

Zach finishes the colour correction and picks up the film-production-grade concealer from the table at his side. He puts a dollop on a makeup sponge and goes over all of Olivia's back tattoos, matching everything to the bare skin. I resist the urge to ask him how he knew about this stuff, but it was an easy argument with myself. Whenever I question Zach about something, the answers scare me far more than not knowing.

"I will be with Viraj, keeping eyes on the room and looking for Natasha and her bodyguards," he says as he dabs over the mess on her back.

"Right," Olivia says. "I'll be with Rory, circulating the room and watching as well, while noting the casino security and ready to go at a moment's notice. Max?"

I clear my throat. "I'm the bait. Natasha is recently single, surrounded by men who want to take her spot or think less of her as a leader because she's a woman. I'm to be the knight in shining armour who feigns disinterest, then is beguiled by her wit and charm."

I don't like the idea of being a honey trap, but we need an in, and this seems like the most direct route.

"How do we know Max is the best to seduce her again?" Viraj asks. "What if she's a lesbian?"

"We hacked into her computer and found out the people she follows, and how much time she spends watching each post. Trust me," Roark says assuredly. "Max is her type. Plus, he's got the monster dick trump card." Viraj nods, only looking a little jealous about the whole dick thing.

"Hey!" Olivia protests. "Nobody is petting that anaconda but me."

A smug smile grows on my lips. "Via, are you jealous?"

"No." Liv pouts, and it's cute as fuck. "I'm just worried she won't know how to handle such a big... device. She could hurt you, then you'd be a liability." Nobody buys her bullshit, and we all—except Zach, who's still working on concealing her tattoos—tilt our heads back in laughter.

"Oh, fuck off, all of you," she swears, even as she fights a shy grin.

"All done," Zach says as he dusts some powder over the cover-up and leans back to inspect his work.

"Looks good from here," Roark says. "But I miss the tattoos already."

"It'll be worth it for the dress," she promises. "Okay, I'm going to get ready. You guys should get your tuxes on. Max, when is the car coming?"

"In an hour. And it's a limousine," I correct. Roark raises a brow. "It would look weird if we showed up in an Uber."

"True," he concedes. "Well, this will be my first time in one."

"Aw, a virgin," V teases.

He earns a punch to the shoulder for his joke, and Olivia drops a sweet kiss on Roark's head as she moves towards the bathroom to get ready.

The four of us look at each other. We have an hour before we have to leave. "Beer?" I ask. Everyone nods, and Zach grabs four bottles from the fridge before we head up to the terrace on the roof. Since my hair is already done, I've shaved, and put on moisturiser, it will take us approximately twelve minutes to get our suits on and be ready to go. Might as well relax before I'm dangled in front of a crime boss like a tasty snack.

Once settled, Viraj looks around at the vista before us. "You really think we can pull this off?" he asks, voicing a concern that has undoubtedly crossed all of our minds.

The good doctor is quick to answer. "I do." Correction. *Most* of our minds. Zach has been unwavering in his faith in Olivia. I wish I could say the same, but so many things could go wrong; the niggle of doubt in my mind has been getting louder, no matter how often we go over the plans.

Roark takes a sip from his bottle and sighs. "It's going to be difficult, and our timing has to be precise, but Max and Zach have an opportunity to find the diamond tonight."

We go over our roles repeatedly before Zach tells us it's time to get going. I drain the last of my beer, knowing there will be nothing but champagne and top-shelf whiskey at the party. Somehow, over the past few weeks, I've developed a taste for the cheap beer Roark prefers. Not that I tell him that, but I do make sure it's on the grocery list every time one of us heads to the store.

We're all standing around the room, straightening our jackets, affixing cufflinks, and adjusting each other's bow ties like a goddamned rom-com, but Roark's was all askew, and I couldn't look at it any longer. The door to the bathroom opens, and Olivia steps out, causing all of us to freeze in our spots.

Her hair—a wig she bought in Nice—is short, darker honey blonde at the roots, fading to bright blonde as the curls dip to her shoulders. She's wearing a black lace dress over what looks like absolutely nothing, but must be lined or something, right? The long sleeves reach her wrists, and the waterfall of material kisses the floor with every step she takes forward.

I am acutely aware of my mouth agape as I watch her, but I don't fucking care.

"Olivia, you look..." The words don't come. I can't think of one single adjective.

"Thank fucking Christ," she says with a smile at my lack of vocabulary. "This thing was a bitch to get on, the wig is itchy, and I can barely breathe, let alone wear underwear, but I think it'll do."

Zach recovers from that statement first—because of course he does, the psychopath—and steps forward with his hand raised. Olivia tucks hers into his grip, and he holds her steady as she slips her feet into one of the sky-high black heels beside the door.

Viraj drops to his knees and holds the second out for her. She eases her foot in, and he runs his hands up her calf, eliciting a shiver from our usually unaffected and sarcastic leader. Right about now, she'd usually be making a joke about being a dirty version of Cinderella, and she wouldn't be wrong, but the way she's looking at the four of us, I'm confident she's as affected as we are.

"You guys look really fucking good." She clears her throat of the husky tone and thanks Viraj for the shoe assist. There's a glassy quality to her eyes, and I start putting two and two together. We once attended an event together during our school days that didn't pan out well, and we didn't get to enjoy it as we should have. Now, it looks like we're getting a do-over.

"We should get downstairs. Our ride is here." My phone dings with the notification. I check my breast pocket and find the invitations tucked inside safely. "Roark, you got the earpieces?" He nods in response. "Good. Olivia, your clutch please?"

She hands it over, the small purse just big enough for a few feminine supplies, a credit card, some cash, and lipstick.

Roark grabs the imitation credit card—our receiver—and adds it to the contents. "We're good to go," he says. He distributes the earpieces, and we fit them in. Then, Roark has us each say something, and we confirm we can all hear each other.

This is our first real job together since school. We've been over plans A through H repeatedly, and our confidence is high. Liv is a consummate professional when it comes to the work, as evidenced by her serious face and lack of joking when it's crunch time. The rest of us borrow some of her confidence where we're lacking. We have to find the diamond today. We may not be able to steal it just yet, but identifying it will be paramount.

This is our first real test. Can we get close enough to Natasha to even get a read on the diamonds? Can we get an accurate count of her bodyguards? Will she have others at the finale of the Grand Prix? If we can get close to her, can we possibly find out which piece of jewellery holds the diamond we need? There are a lot of unknowns, but hopefully, tonight gets us one step closer to figuring those out.

The drive is tense, each of us riding the wave of adrenaline and focus. Additionally, the traffic due to the construction of seating and grandstands around the race track creates tourist photo opportunities, thus clogging the already too-small city streets.

The first two practice runs occurred today, and the sound of the engines could be heard from our flat. The actual race is on Sunday, but plenty is going on around the city, and the tickets for the practice runs today and qualifying race tomorrow sold out almost as quickly as the ones for the big day.

"The key here will be blending in. You belong here at this swanky, exclusive party on a Friday night. You can act like you're above it all, but be careful to mask your surprise and appreciation of the grandeur. Those are the people that others take note of, as it airs your inexperience," I remind them for the hundredth time. They nod; not even Viraj snarks back at me for my repetitive reminder.

There are a host of vintage and luxury cars parked in front of the Monte Carlo Casino, each more expensive than the last. I keep my drool contained when I see a vintage Aston Martin, but only just. I'm embodying James Bond tonight, and the car has just endorsed it. It's a sign; 007 would approve.

We follow the line of limousines up the drive, and I hand out the invitations to everyone as I slip into my element. I was raised in events like this. I learned how to do backroom deals and read the other occupants by being dragged to party after party by my father. Olivia schools her face, keeping her chin in the air and scratching one last itch under her wig.

"Let's do this, boys," she says just before the valet pulls the door open. Roark steps out first, reaching back a hand to take Oliva's. Cameras aren't permitted at the entrance, but plenty will be inside.

They walk off, not sparing a glance at the rest of us in the car. Zach steps out next and reaches a hand back for Viraj, mimicking Roark.

"I don't need an escort," Viraj growls from within the limo.

"Don't be ridiculous, darling. You already won't sleep in my bed with me." Zach winks as he tugs Viraj out by the arm and dusts off his jacket as he stands. "A couple will draw far less attention than two men out on the town as friends. So come on, let's go." Zach's fingers lace through V's, and I raise my arm to hide the laugh escaping my lips. They would be kind of adorable together. You know, what with the whole psychopath killer and adrenaline-junkie-with-a-death-wish thing. A match made in heaven, really.

Olivia and Roark are already inside, and Zach and his date are handing over their invitations at the front door. I emerge from the limo, invite in hand, and make my way up the steps with confidence. I can fucking do this. For Olivia, I can do anything. Just as I know she would do anything for me. Hell, for any one of us.

Going through the usual security, I follow the others towards the main room of the casino. There are bodies at all of the tables, poker, craps, roulette, all of the sounds add to the cacophony, and I'm assaulted by a photographer not three steps into the cavernous room.

"Lord Arondale? Just here, please. Yes, against the backdrop," the photographer instructs as he situates me where he wants, while I internally cringe at the Lord moniker. I haven't inherited the title yet, but respond to it all the same. We knew as soon as I got the tickets, I'd have to be photographed because my dad likely knows people here and it will already be gossip I'm in the city anyway. But it works for us. Keeping eyes off the others, I'm the only one with cameras pointed at me for the moment. I smile my cocksure grin at the lens, and after the flash blinds me, I thank him and see my target across the room. I turn away before any actual eye contact can happen. It's a game of cat and mouse, and from what I know of Natasha Volkov, she's bound to be the cat in that scenario.

"Ooh," Olivia teases in my earpiece. "You're so popular, Lord Arondale."

I pluck a glass of champagne from a passing waiter's tray and reply back, covering my lips with the flute. "You would be too if you used your father to get the invitations. He made me promise to behave, and I see three of his peers here taking note of my arrival and actions. How sorely disappointed he's about to be."

"Atta boy, Maxi Pad," Viraj says, and I smile.

We all circulate around the rooms, Olivia and Roark playing a few hands of poker. Viraj and Zach—still uncomfortably hand in hand—are making small talk with one of the local billionaires, and I catch a glimpse of the moment when Zach leans down and kisses V's neck. I stifle my snicker and focus. I've got my eye on Natasha as she moves through the room. The bar has a mirrored back, and I'm using that bastard to my full advantage.

Natasha drifts around the party, chatting with dignitaries, high-rollers, and some of the wives are positively gushing over her. I've been doing my research. I know she is an influencer of sorts between her fashion brands, jewellery lines, and lifestyle blog.

She saunters through the room, wearing a revealing red dress that screams power and seduction while flanked by three bodyguards. They each have earpieces in and are most certainly equipped with more than one weapon if the bulges on their hips and their chest straps are any indication.

I look around the room and feign indifference, turning back towards the bar when Natasha lifts her eyes and looks at me. If there's anything someone looking for attention hates more than being ignored or brushed off, I don't know it.

Our eyes connect for the briefest second, but it's enough for me to see the surprise when I turn back to Pierre, the bartender who I've been chatting with for the last few minutes.

"Oh, *Monsieur*, incoming," he says as he pours a double of scotch for me behind the counter.

"Thank you, Pierre," I say in English—for both the alcohol and the heads up.

A flash of red appears to my left, and pale, slender arms rest on the bartop. "Well, well. I had heard rumours a certain British aristocrat would be here, but I thought they were just that. No one has seen you on the party circuit in a few months." Her Russian accent is thick, and she rolls her "r" like a purring cat.

I turn my head to find a pair of ice-blue eyes taking stock of my features. They'd be gorgeous if they were a shade darker and had a gold spot in the left one. Then again, they'd belong to someone else, wouldn't they?

"I started to find London a bit boring, I suppose. Monaco seems to have exactly what I'm looking for," I flirt as I run my eyes over her features. "And who might you be?"

A look of shock crosses her features that I don't know who she is, but she recovers quickly, tucking a lock of platinum blonde hair behind her ear. I follow the movement with my eyes, thinking of Olivia the whole time.

"Indeed. We've not been properly introduced." She extends a hand delicately, and I take it in my own. "I am Natasha Volkov."

"A pleasure to meet you, Natasha," I say, running my thumb over her knuckles before turning her hand and placing a kiss on the back. I lift my head and continue, "Are you here for the entire race weekend or just the party?"

"The weekend. The royal family invited me to assist in presenting the winner with their trophy on Sunday."

"That's quite the honour," I commend. "Let me get you a drink." I turn towards the bar, and Pierre, the consummate professional, is wiping down glasses and pretending not to listen to every word. "Pierre, a drink for the lovely Ms Volkov if you will." I turn back towards Natasha. "No ring. Can I assume you're unattached?"

"A glass of champagne," she informs Pierre before turning back to me. "And yes, currently unattached."

"Oh?" I say with a raised brow like I didn't already know she offed her husband.

"Widowed a few months ago."

"I'm sorry to hear that. And I'm surprised you didn't order vodka. Most Russians I know stick to that when out of the country."

"Ah, if only. I have a mild sensitivity to potatoes." She clicks her tongue at the admission, the sound distorted in the loud casino, and I feel a pang of sympathy. To never have proper fish and chips is a shame. "Plus, I find champagne suits me better."

I express my condolences over the fish and chips situation, and she flips her hair over her shoulder in laughter. "It's not life-threatening, just mildly annoying. I've tried the combination. It was quite tasty."

We chat about the race, who we're hoping to see win on the gruelling track, and the beauty of Monaco. Her hand drifts to mine, and I listen with rapt attention as she tells me all about her successes in the fashion world. I don't care much, but she looks genuinely happy when she mentions her new line of jewellery—which I, of course, praise as I look at the earrings, the bracelet, and the necklace she has chosen to wear tonight.

After an hour of flirty conversation, our touches are becoming frequent, more daring. Natasha drags her finger along the sleeve of my tuxedo, and I play my role. My voice becomes huskier, my wandering fingers bolder.

"If she tries to fuck you, I'll sic Zach on her," Olivia growls in my ear.

"Ollie, that is literally the plan. It was *your* plan," Viraj reminds her.

"A woman has the right to change her mind, V," she hisses.

She makes promises of retribution over the comms and whispers about what a stupid plan it was. It's an exercise in willpower to keep my cock from standing at attention when I note the possessive tone in her voice. I am hers. But to pull this off, we have to make sacrifices, and she knows that. She just doesn't like it. Neither do I, to be honest.

I lean into Natasha as if I have a secret to share. My breath and words whisper close to her ear. "Have you seen the hidden rooms here at the Monte Carlo?" I ask before biting down on the lobe, right next to the diamond we need to check.

A shiver runs through her body, and her hand tightens its grip on my arm. "Mmm, no, I haven't. Will you show me?" she asks.

"It would be my absolute pleasure. Well, hopefully, *our* pleasure."

I hear Olivia whisper that it's time and watch as they move through the casino while I run the tip of my nose along Natasha's ear.

I reach into my pocket, pull out my money clip, and leave Pierre a hundred euro tip. He thanks me profusely, and I extend a hand to Natasha as I stand.

"Third door down the hallway to your right," I hear Zach say in my ear.

They've been watching the Monte Carlo security, and while there are guards, the cameras are the more fickle beasts. There was no way to turn them off or run a loop without alerting security, so we're using the late hour and lustful nature of the party to downplay the fact we're sneaking off to a cupboard to fool around.

Natasha threads her fingers through mine, and I lead her away. She waves off her security, but they stay five steps behind us anyway. Well trained, even amidst their boss's lust-filled orders.

I make a show of looking left and right before cracking open the door and pulling Natasha inside after me. As soon as the door shuts, she pushes me against it and kisses me. Her tongue licks at the seam of my lips before I open them.

Her hand trails down my tuxedo and finds my cock as her tongue snakes into my mouth. This feels so wrong, and I slow our kisses to sensual ones instead of the all-out assault she started. *Think of Olivia. Think of Olivia. Think of Olivia,* I chant in my head. It works, and Natasha's gasp of surprise as she feels my dick hardening is a confidence booster.

I pull away, and her tongue piercing clicks my teeth at my withdrawal.

Wrapping my arms around her, I turn us and spin her forward so her chest is pressed against the door. "Mmm, Natasha," I hiss her name and grind my hips against her ass as she mewls at the deprivation. "You want my cock?"

"*Da,*" she breathes out.

"Close your eyes," I command.

"What are you doing?"

"Blindfolding you. I love a little spice." *Do not puke, Max, do not puke.*

"Can't we do it without? I want to see you." And boom, just like that, she walked right into our trap.

The Cleanup

"Why, Natasha? Are you scared? Did you feel my massive cock and now fear it will split you open? Are you... fragile?"

We have three reasons to believe she will let me blindfold her. One, she knows who I am. I'm well-known at these parties, and nobody suspects how close I am to Olivia, nor who she is. Two, because I didn't know Natasha before tonight—or so I claimed.

And three, because she's never been fragile and will want to prove me wrong.

"Let me tell you what will happen, Ms Volkov," I growl in her ear. "I will blindfold you, and like a good girl, you will let me do it." Olivia almost shatters my focus into a thousand pieces when she starts singing "Like a Virgin" by Madonna. Roark bumps her—or so it sounds like—because there's an oomph and the comms go quiet again. "Then you'll let me and my monster cock have our way with you. When was the last time someone fucked you so good you screamed? I'm going to make you scream, Natasha, and you'll never forget me. I'll be the best you ever had."

I pull my custom-made pocket square out, unravel the extended length, and slip it over her eyes before securing it behind her head.

Zach is standing next to me, silent as a wraith—Olivia Wraith's wraith, the irony is not lost on me—as I unzip her dress and begin to work it off her body. I surreptitiously unlatch her bracelet as I drag the straps down her arms and hand it over to Zach.

He has the refractometer set up on a small shelf and is quick to examine the diamond as I trail kisses up and down Natasha's arm, then her back.

Zach returns it with a shake of his head. Okay, not the bracelet, then.

He secures it around her wrist as I pin her hand to the door frame with mine. I put too much pressure, and she almost begins to protest, but Zach finishes with the clasp, and I relent. She turns her head quickly, her dangling earrings catching me in the chin with the movement.

"You're going to end up bruising my face, and I can't have that in the photos." I pluck the earrings from her ears without protest, and that tells me it's improbable the diamond is included in the set, but we have to test to be sure.

I hand them off to Zach, and he begins his work as Natasha wiggles the dress from her hips, so it pools at her feet. Letting out a groan—albeit fake—at the sight of her in just her thong, I run my hands over her hips. She tilts her head back so it rests on my shoulder as a shiver wracks her body. I have to fucking do it, don't I? Keeping up this ruse is not helping me maintain my boner, but fuck, Olivia will kill me if we don't get the answers we need.

Olivia. Oh hey, the boner is back.

Zach places the earrings on the shelving next to us and motions to his neck.

It has to be the necklace, then. It's the last piece of jewellery on Natasha unless she's had some kind of custom-made buttplug created to hide the diamond. Which would actually be pretty genius.

I rake my fingers through her hair, fisting it at the root, and tilt her head back. I plunder her mouth and give her the bruising kiss she tried to give me earlier, but I seem to be far more effective.

She leans into the kiss, and Zach's careful hands flip the lock on the necklace.

Pulling away, she gasps, "My necklace fell off."

"I'll get it." I bend down, acting my ass off, and slide my fingers down her torso as I go. Zach is already at the refractometer and checking the stones. There are more of the one carat diamonds on this particular piece, and it will take him longer. "I got it. It's on the shelf next to us with the earrings," I say because she's still blindfolded.

I stick out my tongue and reluctantly run it from her belly button, up her sternum, and dive for her neck, kissing and sucking as I go.

"Oh, Max," she cries.

Olivia whispers a string of curse words that would make the devil blush. Or so I imagine, because it's all in Russian. She's been brushing up on her skills for this particular language all month, but she certainly wasn't practising those words aloud.

Zach puts the necklace on the shelf and shakes his head.

What the fuck? Could the stone be in her safe wherever she's staying?

Viraj whispers in my ear, "Security coming in ten seconds."

Zach stands beside the door, ready to slip out when they knock.

Sure enough, a couple seconds later, someone bangs on the door.

Natasha gasps and says she'll be out in a minute. I hear the casino security reprimanding her personal security, and I pull Natasha away from the door. Olivia's in my ear, and is telling Zach to get the fuck out while the guards are occupied. The doctor doesn't hesitate. He takes the refractometer under his arm, peeks through the door to check what's happening, then bolts. All this without making a noise.

Creepy.

I untie the blindfold from Natasha's eyes and tuck the pocket square back into my jacket. Even though it's dark in here, there's enough light from the small emergency lamp that she blinks rapidly. "Here," I offer, picking up her dress from the floor and helping her into it.

Trailing my hands up her back, I do the zipper as she leans into me. She refastens her earrings and necklace and turns to face me. I need to keep the ruse up because we haven't found the blasted diamond, so I kiss her passionately again, and she melts into my embrace.

"Until later, Natasha. Perhaps I'll see you at the race."

"*Do svidaniya*, Maximillian. I certainly hope so."

I usher her out of the room, and we find her guards standing there, being berated by Monte Carlo security, but you wouldn't guess it by their unmoving faces. The one on the right visibly relaxes when Natasha is in his sights again.

"We could go to my room," Natasha says on a breath, too low for the guards to hear.

I nod my head at the big one on the right. "I think your guards might kill me for trying. It's not in the cards tonight, Natasha. Perhaps Sunday will be our day."

Security is raising a fuss, but I lift her hand, kiss her knuckles gently and whisper, "It has been a pleasure."

She giggles, and her bodyguards swoop in to take her away. I stand in the hallway, watching as they disappear back into the party when Olivia's constant stream of consciousness continues in my ear. "Max, let's get out of here. I need to get the taste of that woman out of your mouth. It is *mine*."

Chapter Twenty-Six

Olivia
Present Day

"Motherfucker!" I exclaim as soon as I'm in our flat, ripping my wig off and throwing it to the side. "Where the hell is that fucking stone?!"

I'm fuming. With the timeline of Natasha's order, the diamond had to be in one of those jewels. There's no way a mafia queen would be trusting enough to leave it unattended, even in a safe in her hotel suite. Unless she has people she trusts enough to watch it. Is that it? Was I overconfident and just went with what I'd do when she chose another option? Hell, for all we know, the diamond could even be in Russia.

Fuck. Triple fuckity fuck fuck with a cherry on top.

I start pacing across the room as the guys watch me with wary eyes, like they would a rabid dog.

What do we do now? We'll have to replan our entire operation, and it'll impact Ellie. I have to call her; she has to know we fucked up.

"She had a tongue piercing," Max says softly, almost to himself.

Jealousy bursts through my chest. Until now, I managed to keep it under wraps... okay, as much as possible. It might not have been as under wraps as I'd aimed for. But I'm not happy he kissed her. I've had a thing for Max for *years*, and to lose him would be devastating. Hearing the wet noises and muffled moans through the comms was torture. Knowing she was probably pawing at his massive cock about killed me.

"What did you just say?" I retort, miffed he would recount his makeout session in that great of detail.

"When I kissed her, I felt the metal," he explains carefully, as if he's scared I'll explode. He's not wrong. "She has a piercing there, and I remember feeling something sharp under her tongue, which I thought was weird. It could be the diamond."

I have very mixed feelings about this.

Aside from the jealousy previously mentioned, I feel a sliver of admiration crawling through my chest at Natasha's wits. The tongue piercing would make it super easy for her to watch over the sensitive data. No wonder she was so relaxed when the guys searched her jewellery! She knew that unless Max had awe-inspiring tongue moves—and he does, but not to the point of unscrewing a piercing—the diamond was safe in her mouth.

It's not often that I'm so blatantly outsmarted. She's a challenge, and I like it. If her actions hadn't threatened my best friend, I'd get Natasha to hang out with me.

I'm also crazy fucking aroused because I spent the entirety of the party with a butt plug in my ass. Viraj definitely didn't forget about me losing the bet and bought one at a sex shop as soon as we arrived home after our drive. I put it in before the party, and now it's been rubbing me in all sorts of delicious ways.

"We don't have a replica for a tongue piercing," Roark observes.

"We'll figure out the details tomorrow," I say, biting my lower lip. "I need to blow off some steam right now."

"Want to go for a walk on the pier?" Roark asks, ever the sweet one.

I definitely don't. But I'm not sure how to let him down gently, so I just do what I've been dying to do ever since I saw Max kiss our target.

I take three quick steps in Max's direction and weld my lips to his. He doesn't immediately return my kiss, stunned that I made this bold first move in front of all the others.

It's like he doesn't know me at all; I've never kept it a secret that I wanted each of them. From our days as teens, they each give me life in a different way, but when we're working together, making plans and causing chaos, the beauty in our synchronicity brings me to my fucking knees.

I slip my tongue inside his mouth, wanting to thoroughly erase Natasha's taste from his lips. Rising on my tippy toes, I press my body to his.

Finally, he wraps his arms around me and starts kissing me back the way I want. His mouth moves against mine, and he cradles my face in his big hands, even as his lightly stubbled jaw rasps over my chin. I melt, anger and possessiveness completely replaced by arousal.

I feel a body at my back, not close enough to touch, yet Zach still whispers in my ear, "Are you jealous, Little Thief? Did it make your blood boil and cold sweat run along your spine when he kissed her?"

I groan against Max's mouth just as he breaks our kiss. "I only did it because it was the plan; I never wanted to." His eyes turn soft. "I was thinking about you the entire time, Liv, I promise." Some of the tension leaves my shoulders.

"I think," Zach says, nuzzling my neck, very much behaving like the devil on my shoulder. "Max should eat your pussy out to earn your forgiveness. Let you come all over his face and replace Natasha's taste with your sweet cum."

Max kissing our target and whipping her into a lust-filled frenzy was my idea in the first place; there's nothing to forgive because he didn't do anything wrong. I tell him this, admitting my faults and irrational reaction for the men in the room to see. Max keeps my face tilted towards his, and his soft eyes reassure me in ways words never could.

Still, a shiver courses through me as my clit starts throbbing with need when his eyes fill with heat as he watches Zach's hand start to lower the zipper of my dress. I'm naked underneath, and they all know it, but V is the only one aware of the butt plug. Max knew I was going to do it, but he didn't see me put it in, so he has no way to be sure I'm wearing it.

Zach sits me on the edge of our bed. "Be good, Little Thief; I'll go grab some makeup remover so we can set your tattoos free."

Max doesn't waste a second and drops to his knees in front of me, pushing my thighs apart to bury his face in my centre. Moving my eyes from Max's blissed-out face, I see Roark and Viraj across the room.

They're standing, arms crossed over their chests. But even if their postures are similar, their eyes tell very different stories. V is devouring me with his gaze, watching everything that's happening on the bed. Rory's eyes are darting everywhere, only briefly landing on Max and me as if he's trying to give us privacy but can't help glancing over. He keeps shifting from foot to foot, and I have a feeling he's going to bolt.

Right when Roark is about to take a step, Zach comes back, holding makeup remover wipes. He takes in the fleeing man, and immediately a knife appears in his hand. I don't know where it came from; I swear it wasn't there a second ago. "Nobody leaves this room," the doctor growls, his voice and demeanour full of a barely veiled threat. "Unless Olivia says so."

Max goes to town on me, and I moan. The buildup has been

The Cleanup

excruciating. He licks me from my clit to the warm silicon of the plug in my ass. "Liv, what is that?" he teases. He knows full well what *that* is.

"Fr-from the bet," I pant.

"Did you go to the party like this?" I nod. "Fuck, that's hot, naughty girl. I can't believe I'm saying this, but we should do the car thing again sometime." I hear Viraj grunt in agreement from across the room. I angle my hips, making sure Max's tongue hits me in all the right spots. Then I crook my fingers in Roark's direction, beckoning him closer.

"I always want you with us, Rory. Always." He takes a step in the direction of the bed, hesitates, then seems to make up his mind and walks all the way to my side. "You're overdressed," I say, looking at him from head to toe. Let me tell you, ladies and gentlemen, Roark O'Sullivan in a suit is a work of art. His long hair is gathered atop his head in a bun, and the jacket frames his square shoulders and muscled chest to perfection.

Maybe I drool just a little.

Max picks this exact moment to push two fingers inside me and suck harder on my clit. As Roark removes his clothes, Zach starts running the wipes along my skin to remove the foundation from my tattoos. He takes his time, doing it slowly, with medical precision.

The contrast of the sensations and temperatures drives me higher and higher by the second. The wipes are wet and cold, making my nipples peak when he cleans up the soft skin in the crook of my elbow. Max's rhythm is picking up, his hot, strong fingers deliberately bringing me closer to the edge. And to my right, Roark taking off his suit is a show I'd trade for nothing in the world.

Max starts playing with the plug in my ass, slowly pulling it in and out. I whimper in pleasure, the need to come intensifying and making my eyes roll back in my skull. Watching the other man's hands, Zach starts peppering soft kisses on the smooth curve of my neck. He's almost done removing the makeup.

"Shh, Little Thief, relax. Let Max prepare you for when I fuck your tight ass later."

I open my eyes and see Viraj looking at me, his hand stroking his dick in his suit trousers. "Is this everything you hoped for when you won that bet?" I taunt.

He tilts his head to the side. "Not quite. But it will be soon." He then winks, and I come. Hard. Max's fingers don't let up and fuck me right through my orgasm, prolonging my seemingly unending high.

"Fuck," I cry out as my ass and pussy clamp around his fingers and the plug.

Zach moves towards the bathroom to put the wipes away after finishing the cover-up removal. "Lie down, Rory," I croak, voice hoarse from screaming.

He throws a questioning look Max's way, still kneeling between my legs. "Go ahead, man. If I fuck her first, she won't even feel you guys."

Roark, Zach, and Viraj groan in unison.

I don't waste time. Grabbing his hand, I pull my sweet Rory down on the bed and move to straddle him. He's already completely naked and automatically props his back up against the pillows.

I succumb to the need that bursts in me whenever Rory doesn't have a shirt on and lick his abs. They're so hard; they feel as if they're made of stone, like Michelangelo took a block of marble and carved Roark out of it, then Raphael arrived and painted the gorgeous tattoos on the blank canvas. My hacker's body is that perfect.

My ass is in the air as I map his lower abs with my tongue, and I can feel the eyes of my other three men on it. The butt plug is still in, and I wiggle a little for their benefit. Three groans echo right after, and I chuckle, loving the effect I have on them and vice versa.

I follow the lines of his tattoos and reach his face, where our gazes meet. Looking into his eyes is like looking in the mirror since they're the exact same shade of blue as mine. He's just missing the golden spot I have in my left iris.

Slowly, without breaking eye contact, I lower myself on him, giving my hips an experimental swivel. When I see his eyes close in bliss, I start moving faster and fuse our lips together.

My pussy is still clamping with the aftermath of my orgasm, and my nipples are painfully peaked. I raise both my hands to play with them, almost performing for Rory's hungry eyes.

I fuck him slow and sweet, wanting to convey with my body how much it means to me that he stayed in this room. I didn't want him to leave, and he decided to participate instead. Okay, Zach strongly encouraged him, but still.

The bed dips behind me, and a cold hand presses on my lower back. I yelp in surprise at the contact, completely absorbed by the intensity of Roark's ocean eyes. Zach pushes me down against Roark's chest, keeping me flat against the tattoos I was tracing with my eyes earlier. He removes the plug in my ass with his other and asks, "All good, Roark?"

"Peachy."

Zach doesn't even ask for my opinion. He just slips a condom on, covers his dick in lube and slams inside my ass. His hand tangles in my hair and pulls my head backwards, dominating my every movement.

"Fuck," I mutter again. This is too fucking full. The plug has been in my ass all night and helped stretch me, and it's also not my first time with double penetration—we all know by now Zach loves pushing me to my limits, and he's experimented on me with pretty big toys—but nothing could have truly prepared me for this.

The fullness is comparable to what I felt when Zach stuffed me full of dildos. But the heat and sensation of being sandwiched between these two men feels entirely different. My abdomen is trapped between hard abs, my breasts pressed against Roark's hard chest. Our legs are tangled together as we struggle to find our rhythm.

If it were my first time, it'd hurt. But it isn't, and my second orgasm builds as their dicks push inside me and their hands run over every available inch of skin.

Roark opens his eyes wide below me. "This is so fucking tight."

Zach just starts pumping in and out of me, not giving me time to adapt and making me feel the stretch.

I love it.

Rory looks like he's ready to explode but starts moving his hips again anyway. I kiss him softly once more until I feel Zach's hand wrap around my neck, and I gasp. He's not cutting my air off completely—his grip isn't tight enough—yet I can feel the strain. "Yes, Doc, harder," I moan, breaking the kiss for a moment.

Zach obeys, pulling me back against him and fucking me in earnest. He's not going as hard as he would have gone if we were alone, but since I have another cock in my pussy, the sensations are intense. His hand tightens around my neck, and when Roark's lips wrap around my nipple, I shatter. Rory follows me over the edge seconds later with a moan that stirs something low in my belly.

The hand around my neck lets up, and I take a deep breath in, my head light from the lack of oxygen as the endorphins rush in with that first free breath. Zach pulls out to free Roark and me, and I collapse to the side.

I'm promptly stolen away by Viraj. "My turn, now," he declares, walking to the sofa, carrying me bridal-style in his arms.

He sits down, making me straddle his lap and effortlessly sliding inside me. My legs are Jell-O at this stage, so I can't help much, but he doesn't need me to. He takes complete control of my body, moving my hips up and down the way he wants it; just like he did in the car. "You know, you're fucking hot when you let me have my way with you," he praises. Then V bites my neck, fiercely enough to leave a mark. "This... this is everything I had hoped for."

I cry out, the contact of his teeth awakening my numb body. He feels so good and my eyes lock with his, a thousand words passing between us in silence except for our moans of pleasure and harsh breaths.

Suddenly, out of nowhere, metal flashes in my vision. I lift my eyes to see Zach, fully naked, dick standing proud right next to V's head.

The Cleanup

And he's holding a knife to the throat of the man inside me.

"I wasn't done with her." Zach's caramel eyes are like smouldering embers.

With a flick of his wrist, he leaves a long cut on Viraj's neck. It's not deep. A cat scratching him would have done more damage. Still, it'll probably scar, and it's bleeding a little. Zach marked him.

Just like me.

I get embarrassingly wet, right where V can feel it. He stares into my eyes as if trying to understand what just happened. "Fuck, you love this psycho and all his crazy," he breathes. I bite my lower lip, nodding imperceptibly.

Zach prowls around the sofa like a predator and repeats, "I wasn't done with her, but that's okay. Little Thief can take two cocks just as well as she can take one." I brace myself when I feel his chest against my shoulder blade, expecting him back in my ass.

Instead, the blunt head of his now condom-free dick presses against my slit, right where V and I are joined. "Fuck, man," V swears. "I'm not crossing swords with you. Take her ass if you want, but you're not getting in here. Her pussy's mine."

The knife reappears against V's throat. "Why?" Zach taunts, not stopping his forward motion inside me. "Are you scared, Viraj? Let me tell you one thing. Olivia will be sore tonight. She'll lie in bed, and her weeping pussy will remind her of how thoroughly fucked she was. When she thinks about the stretch, do you want her to remember Max's massive dick or the two of us shoving her over the edge so spectacularly, it'll be our names on her lips in her dreams?"

V doesn't move, doesn't even breathe for a moment before he locks eyes with Zach over my shoulder and nods his head. Zach's hips start moving, and he pushes inside slowly, dragging my pleasure along for the ride as he makes it work. V grinds his teeth at the pressure of them both fitting inside me.

It's even more intense than before. I can feel them both rubbing inside, pushing my walls to the limit. I've never felt anything like this, it's too much, and I want them to stop. I also want them to stay like this forever.

I'm not in control of my body anymore. Dizziness overtakes my senses, overwhelmed by the pleasure and blazing heat that radiates from their cocks and through me. My breaths are loud, and my pulse, deafening.

For a minute, V seems indecisive, and Zach uses us both for his own pleasure, thrusting inside me.

Then Viraj nods and starts moving, too.

All my senses are overloaded with pleasure. Zach is right; this will be a bitch when the endorphins fade. My pussy's never been so full, stuffed to the limit of explosion.

Shouts, pleas, and moans escape my lips, but I'm too far gone to articulate conscious thoughts. "Yes, Doc, V, shit... fuck, ahhh!"

My orgasm rises like a tidal wave, and I know it'll destroy everything in its path. I kiss Viraj, desperately seeking his strength, his power, as I brace for the pleasure about to wreak havoc on my body.

"Yes, Little Thief, take us. Take all of us," Zach whispers in my ear. Then he bites my neck, right next to where Viraj marked me.

I climax so hard I see stars and rake my nails along Viraj's muscled back. This time, both V and Zach detonate with me, filling me with their cum. V presses his mouth against mine as if he never wants to let me go. Warmth suffuses my body because I don't want him to go either.

When Zach pulls out of me for the second time tonight, I collapse on V's chest. We stay like this a moment, him caressing my hair as I relearn how to breathe.

Max appears behind me. "Come on, Liv, let's get you in bed." He cleans me up with a tissue then carries me to the alcove. He lays us down, spooning from behind and peppering my shoulder with kisses.

I want to sleep. I should sleep. We have loads to do tomorrow and a heist to pull off the day after.

Except I've wanted to be with these four guys for as long as I can remember, and the hard dick of the only one I haven't fucked tonight is resting between my ass cheeks.

"Max?" I purr.

"Yes, love?" My chest fills with warmth at his words. He's called me "love" a million times before, but this time feels different. He just watched me get railed by three guys that aren't him and his tone has never been more loving.

"Fuck me. Please."

Without a word, he angles his hips so his gigantic cock breaches my entrance. His arms are wrapped around me, cocooning me, protecting me with his big body.

The other three are fighting for a turn in the bathroom from the noises I can hear, but my head position blocks us off from seeing them. That means it's just him and me now.

Max's dick is big, even if my pussy's been stretched like never before. The width is okay; I can take it without any issues. The problem is the length. When he pushes fully inside, I can feel him bump into my cervix and electricity sparks into my core.

He's going slow but deep, as I just rest on my side and enjoy it. The combined sensations of the long strokes against my G-spot and pressure against my cervix quickly bring me back to the brink of an orgasm.

I arch against him, seeking more contact and grab his neck, needing something to hold on to. "Max," I moan.

"Yes, love, I got you." His left hand wraps around my breast while the other plays with my clit, and I claw at his leg as my last orgasm of the evening takes me.

I cry out as Max spills inside me, ending the night in fireworks.

"I love you, Olivia Wraith," he whispers. "And this time, I'm not letting you go."

I freeze. I'm elated, and the well of emotion threatens to overwhelm me. Before I look him in the eye and return the sentiment, the bathroom door bangs open and our moment breaks.

"Come with me to the terrace?" I offer.

"I'll go anywhere with you," he says, sending my heart tripping over itself. I wiggle to face him, making his softening dick slip out of me, and he's looking at me with a gentle smile. He's not mad at me for not saying it back in the moment, even though I'm kicking myself over it.

I quickly put on the clothes I find closest to me. Max's shirt hangs like a dress on me, and I only bother doing up two of the buttons to keep it closed in the night breeze. We head up to the terrace, fingers woven together as he leads the way.

Before I can say anything, he starts, "I don't want you to choose between us. I watched it all tonight, and I'm okay with what happened. More than okay. I wasn't able to think of you being with anyone else all those years ago, but I grew up, it seems." His smile stirs again. "Fortunately. So all I'm saying is that I love you, Olivia, and I don't expect anything from you in return. I just want to be a part of your life. You don't even have to say it back."

I meet his eyes unflinchingly. "I love you, too. I always have." Finally, his smile reaches his eyes, and he kisses me softly. Tears prickle behind my eyes, and I let my lids drift shut, soaking in this moment with Max. He wraps his arm around my shoulders and pulls me against him, cocooning me in his warmth. His chin rests on the top of my head, and for a perfect moment, we stay like this, basking in each other's love.

"And you love them too, don't you?" he asks after leaning back and raising a hand so his index finger pushes up my chin.

I nod. "But I'll fuck my disco dildo hard drive before I say it first." Vulnerability is new to me, but I think I'm willing to give it a shot. And if needed, I'll get my fancy hard drive back from Rory to follow through on my promise.

"I'm going to pray they take their sweet time, then." And he kisses me again, deeper this time. Our tongues caress and dance together, and I melt into his arms.

Zach, Rory, and V find us still caught up in our embrace. I break our kiss and turn to look at the view, leaning on the railing without letting go of Max's hand.

"Are we going to talk about what just happened?" Rory asks. For a moment, I think he heard our conversation and is mad at this new development. Then I remember the massive orgy. Oops, it had slipped my mind. "In two days, this job will be over," he adds.

Max starts drawing soothing patterns on the back of my hand. "What are you saying, exactly?"

"I don't know." He stays silent for a moment. "This was nice."

"Hey, Roar." I palm his cheek. "It doesn't have to be over." My heart is beating so hard in my chest I feel like it might destroy my rib cage. Twelve years ago, a very similar conversation ended very badly. Have we all changed enough for the outcome to be different?

"What are you saying?" my Irishman questions. "That we could all keep doing jobs together and move in with you permanently? That'd never work."

"Why not?" I challenge, staring into his blue eyes. "Were these past weeks so bad? It worked, didn't it? We cohabitated, nobody died, nobody got killed"—Zach coughs loudly—"nobody important got killed. I think this could work long term, don't you?" There's a battle of wills going on in his head. He wants to say yes, but the fear of the unknown is too strong. He needs a push.

I kiss Roark with everything I've got. His hands roam my body, even sneaking under my borrowed shirt to grab my ass.

Panting, he takes a deep breath. "Okay."

"Really?"

"Yes. You're right; it wasn't so bad. Plus, everyone here has tons of obligations, so it's not like we'll always be together." Rory shrugs and the man has a point... for now.

I'll let him underestimate me for the time being because it serves my plan, but I fully intend on having us all together as much as possible.

"Zach?" Max asks.

"The only reason I'm not living with her is 'cause you idiots wouldn't have tolerated it. Little Thief knows I'll do whatever makes her happy."

I then turn towards the one whose answer I fear most as my heart beats erratically in my chest. "V?" A sliver of terror snakes down my spine.

He comes closer and cradles my face in his hands, expression tender and sweet.

This is bad. This is very bad. Viraj's love language is snarking and throwing out insults and taunts. Him, tender? That's bad news.

I lean into his touch, enjoying every second of contact since it might not last.

"I'm sorry, Ollie," he starts. "But I won't move back to England. I can't. I have a life in the States, and I like it. You said you needed me for this job, so I came to help, but this cannot be long term." My heart breaks. Right there in my chest, it splinters into a thousand pieces, but knowing the others are willing to give this a shot with me keeps me upright instead of in a heap on the floor. Even if I expected his refusal, part of me still hoped he would agree. "I won't stop you from being with the others, though. I'm sure you'll be very happy together."

Shit. Three out of four said yes, but the last one has broken my heart, and there's nothing I can do to stem the maelstrom in my chest. I went all in this time, sure it'd work out.

Viraj leans down as if to kiss me, and this would be goodbye, I'm sure. I can't have that. It'd end me. My eyes widen, and my heart races as I lean back, trying to escape V's hands even as my eyes plead with him to reconsider. It's futile, I know, but fuck if I don't convey everything in my soul through my gaze.

Suddenly, Viraj is wrestled away from me, and Zach wraps me under his arm. I lean into his warmth, nuzzling his chest, before realising that he's pointing the knife from earlier in V's direction. "You stay away from her, or I'll use the scratch I gave you earlier for target practice. The trachea is a fascinating organ; I'd love to see yours out of your body."

We need to de-escalate this and fast. "Zach, it's okay. Let's just go to bed; I'm tired." I don't want V to die at Zach's hands. At anyone's hands, really. He's made his choice, and for all my scheming and planning, it's not the one I had hoped for. There's really nothing left to do if I'm to respect his choice the same way I would expect him to respect mine.

Zach carries me down the stairs and helps me navigate the room as if worried that I'll break if I bump into anything at all.

I shower and get ready for sleep, then lie down in the bed, and curl into a ball in the crook of Zach's arm.

Roark switches off the lights, and shortly after, I feel a weight dipping the bed behind my back. "It's me, Liv," Max whispers in my ear. "I love you."

I feel a little better knowing that he's here with me. As soon as I'm back home, I'm buying a giant bed, because I need Roark with us.

Even though I've been filled in multiple ways tonight, I'm feeling desperately empty with a Viraj-shaped void in my chest.

Chapter Twenty-Seven

Olivia
Year Thirteen
April

The school is all abuzz over the end of the year. Exams are in three weeks, but before that, we have prom. Somehow, over the last ten years, the American high school rite of passage sailed its way across the pond and has taken up importance in our secondary schools. St Stephen's Boarding School is no exception to the phenomenon.

The notices tacked up along the corridors promise a "night to remember," and after putting things into motion for the last month, that's going to prove truthful in more than one way.

I've just finished a marathon study session with Rory, who kept opening and closing his mouth like he had something to say, but never did, no matter how many times I asked. We finally finished, and I'm desperate for a break, but Rory said he wanted to keep going another hour. Alas, a break doesn't seem to be in the cards for either of us.

Max and Viraj are standing outside my door, whispering furiously. I slow my steps and watch as the two of them square off in their school blazers—each so different and yet eerily similar in so many ways. My heart pitter-patters in my chest when I look at them standing there, apparently waiting for me.

They haven't noticed me yet, and I take the time to admire them. I've been with Zach more times than I can count by now, and while he thrills me and we learn what kinds of things we're into, one thing is certain: I want more.

Zach and I have sex. I have no doubt he likes me, because otherwise, I'd be dead. But I'd also like to feel how sweet it can be to fall in love. I have feelings for Zach; I'm not sure what they are, but I know they'll never be reciprocated. Or he will lie to live up to my expectations, and that's not something I want either.

Call me greedy, call me what you like, but I don't think what I have with Zach is enough for me long term. My first sexual experience was in a forbidden room with a guy who scared the hell out of me. Zach doesn't do patient or tender. But I bet Max does. V's demeanour screams passion. And Rory, my sweet Rory, I wonder what it would be like to gaze into his eyes as he pumps into me and holds my body over a precipice before diving over the edge with me.

Fucking teenage hormones.

A door next to me opens, drawing the attention of Max and V. They spin towards me, each staring intently. I hear a noise behind me and find Roark coming up the stairs, his footsteps louder and more pronounced than usual, like a man on a mission.

He falters at the sight of the other two at my door but corrects his steps and continues towards me.

"Liv, could I speak with you?" Max asks.

V whacks him on the arm. "That's what I'm here for too."

Rory clears his throat when he catches up. "Me three."

"And you all need to speak to me right now?" I ask, knowing where this is going, and realising there is only one solution.

"Yes," they answer in unison, eyeing the others warily.

I shrug and open the door. "Then in you go. I have to take a nap after what Rory just put me through. I'm wiped."

Max and V whirl on Rory, who lifts his hands, palms outward-facing. "We were studying, Via. Feck, you're going to get me killed."

I cackle and close the door when they're all inside. "So, what's up?" I ask, eager to see how this plays out.

They all decide to start speaking at the same time.

"We've been spending a lot of time together," Max begins.

"Prom is coming up," Viraj says.

"I was wondering..." Roark hedges.

All three of them stop speaking at once, glaring at the others. It's like some kind of weird standoff, and I'm the witness.

I drop down onto my bed, crossing my legs as the three of them shift from foot to foot, obviously not having expected to compete for me as a date to prom.

Before I can explain that I can't pick one of them to go to the dance with, they all speak in unison, "Will you go to prom with me?"

I knew they could work well together if they just coordinated. I just wish it was on something other than setting us all up for disappointment. What guy wants to share his prom date with two others?

"You all want me to go to prom with you?" I ask and watch their heads nod in unison. I consider it, desperate to find a way to make it work, despite knowing the outcome. If I pick one of them, the others will be upset. I'd be sure to lose one if not all of them if I opted for any of the three amazing guys in front of me. I fucking hate this predicament, and no matter how often Ellie makes jokes about my harem of boys, that's not how reality works.

Reality means people get hurt, crushed, and stomped on when their feelings aren't reciprocated. The only thing is, my feelings for all of them are there. Daily, hourly, every damned moment of every day, they're aching and clawing from within my chest, begging me to set them free. The only issue is, with their rivalry, general condescension regarding Roark, and wary unease about Zach, none of them would be open to anything unconventional. And no way can I pick just one of them.

But is it worth a shot?

"Can I go with all of you?"

"No," Max and Viraj state together. Roark keeps quiet though, and his face is crestfallen.

"Then no."

They all audibly swallow as they keep their eyes on me, refusing to look at each other in the face of my rejection. I wish I could scoop it out of the air between us and shove it back inside.

"I'm sorry. Liv, who are you saying no to?" Max asks as the first to gain control of his tongue again. Roark looks dejected, and Viraj looks angry.

"All of you." I toe off my shoes and start kicking my legs back and forth in front of me. "If I pick one of you, the others will be pissed. So I choose none of you. Or all of you, but your egos won't let that happen."

"Damn right." V seethes.

"See?" I say, waving a hand at our angry friend. Rory doesn't look opposed to the idea of me going with all of them, but it's either all of them or none of them. I won't compromise when they each hold a piece of me without even realising it.

"I will be at prom, and so will you. I'm happy to spend time with all of you there, but I won't be a point of contention when we have bigger things to worry about. Like the downfall of a certain headmaster in a very public manner."

Rory smiles softly and nods, seemingly understanding my position on this. Viraj and Max, however, react differently. Max exhales deeply, and Viraj moves for the door, throwing it open and leaving in a huff.

After saying he gets it but doesn't like it, Max follows, and then Rory leaves after, telling me it's okay and to save him a dance.

It could have gone a lot worse. Nobody got punched, for starters.

I grab my mobile and text Zach. Most of the time, our exchanges are times and locations of where to burn off our sexual energy, but this time it's different.

Me: You're going to prom.
Zach: Fine.

The beauty with Zach is that he doesn't assert some kind of claim over me because we're fucking. He doesn't care about my crushes. He only cares that he gets to have me. Everything else I do is entirely up to me.

THE BALLROOM OF THE MERRICK HOTEL IS DECKED OUT IN streamers, balloons, and fancy table settings. I was here this afternoon with the rest of the party committee, but we all left about an hour ago to get ready. The benefit of this swanky school is that they provide dinner along with dancing, so Zach and I finished getting ready in our respective rooms, then took a black cab here. Others opted for limos or rented cars, but between the two of us, we didn't see the appeal and figured we could split the cab fare.

Zach looks dashing in his tux, with his chestnut hair swept back, and shiny shoes. My breath hitches in my chest when I see him, envisioning the two of us ripping our clothes off later for a roll in the psychologist's office again.

I opted for a deep blue wrap dress that flutters around my calves. My hair is up in a simple half up-do as the rest trails down my back. I look exactly like every other student in attendance, as planned, but my bag has something very important inside. No, it's not a bottle of booze. That's in the little flask around my thigh.

We find Max, V, and Rory at the table I arranged for us, thanks to my party committee role. The three of them are all looking around with varying degrees of annoyance on their faces, but they knew we would be working tonight. Roark is the first to spot me and sends a wide grin my way. Butterflies erupt in my stomach when I take in the three of them. They're all in tuxedos, and I know they're going to continue to all grow into handsome and devilish men. Even though Rory is more of a rule follower than a rule breaker, between the hacking he already knows and the shit he's currently learning, I bet he'll soon be just as devious as the others.

Max and V catch on quickly, and suddenly they're all standing as I join them at the table. Zach pulls my chair out for me, and I sit down.

"You look beautiful, Olivia," Max says, oozing that charm he's known for.

Not to be outdone, V tosses a similar comment, and Roark agrees.

It gives me a thrill deep in my belly that no one opted to bring a date after I said no to their requests. It would have been easy for them to find someone else, but with the plan we've been working on, being as unencumbered as possible is a good move.

Plus, I want them all to myself.

I check my mobile, finding it's twenty minutes until showtime. A waiter comes by with dishes of the entree and the five of us tuck in. Ellie is at a table on the other side of the room with her date, one of the guys from her chemistry class. I'm not a huge fan, but who am I to judge? Max and V keep waving off girls who pluck up the courage to ask them to join their tables or save them a dance later.

Zach is silent next to me, only running his hand up my thigh under the table and spinning his steak knife between his fingers after he finishes his food. The lights begin to dim.

A few of the school benefactors are stationed throughout the room, no doubt checking on their investments. Teachers are milling about, acting as chaperones. And I dropped a couple of anonymous tips to newspapers that something monumental was going to happen here tonight, thus explaining the members of the press watching from the wings.

The Cleanup

I instructed them to get permission from the headmaster by saying they wanted to write an article about how well-behaved the students of St Stephen's are and the strides they are making academically while still finding enough balance to enjoy their adolescence.

More students mean more money. What school doesn't want that? The caveat to their presence was that they could only be here during the dinner portion of the evening, thus leaving the students to dance in peace. Fine by me.

Headmaster Barkley climbs the small stairs to the stage at the front of the room, and the band quiets down, playing a simple and calm tune for ambience.

I look at my phone. Right on schedule.

"Saint Stephen's Boarding School is proud to host our tenth prom night for our students. Academically, these are the best and brightest among their peers. They will go on to do great things with their lives. We push our students, but we also give them so much in return." His speech reads like a newspaper article, and I bet he's counting on that as the press hold up their recording devices.

The lights cut out, and the projector above the dance floor flares to life when I push the remote in my purse and play the video on my phone over the Bluetooth connection I set up earlier. A shadowed figure appears on the wall as our display takes place.

A distorted voice rings out in the ballroom and the students and adults have all swivelled their heads towards the projection. "Headmaster Barkley spent three years hosting an independent study course for me. Little did I know, he was grooming me for Lord Canton, one of the school benefactors."

When the garbled voice pauses, there's a collective gasp around the room at the information. The press are holding devices in one hand and scribbling notes with the other, using any flat surface for their notepads or tablets.

Unfortunately, Lord Canton isn't in attendance, but this will be enough for the police to investigate his wrongdoings.

"It started with small comments about my appearance or how I dressed. Not often, and not during every independent study meeting, but enough that it resonated. Eventually, the comments moved on to other topics. Ones that no school administrator should bring up with a student." The voice pauses. "Eventually, the touching began."

Students are glaring at the headmaster as he sputters his refusal of the account. Teachers have their hands over their mouths in shock, and the benefactors are standing there, jaws hanging open at what goes on in the school they help to fund.

"I tried to go to the school therapist about it, and she said I was reading into things that weren't there. That I was making it all up." Dr Forsyth—who is in attendance because Zach asked her to be here during his last session, feigning needing emotional support—has tears running down her face. Not ones of sadness, no. That's guilt. According to the secretary's phone I swiped, she and Headmaster Barkley have been sleeping together for years.

Headmaster Barkley is shouting for someone to turn it off, but it's too high for anyone to reach, and I very conveniently stashed the remote in my purse. Whoops.

The voice continues. "I met Lord Canton at a student mixer over Christmas two years ago. He spoke to me inappropriately and mentioned that Headmaster Barkley was doing a good job with me. Lord Canton paid Headmaster Barkley handsomely to find students who could be moulded and coerced. Canton used a man in power to find young students and prepare them for life after school with a predator. I finally told my parents what was happening and got out. Payments to Headmaster Barkley stopped the month I dropped out of St Stephen's Boarding School. Documentation can be found in all school administrator's inboxes, along with the copies I have forwarded to the authorities."

The room is awash with silent rage. The students are staring at the administrator who was supposed to help guide them. Not throw them under the metaphorical bus and sell them into modern-day sex slavery.

"Members of the press, publishing this story could make a differ-

The Cleanup

ence to other young girls and stop them from becoming victims, knowing that justice can prevail if they speak up rather than staying silent. I encourage you to look at who you're putting in positions of authority over children and young adults. You could be the difference between someone's son or daughter going through the same thing."

The feed cuts out, and the room bursts into an uproar. Headmaster Barkley has no chance of slipping away as the eyes of the entire room land on him. Mr Hall has a phone to his ear, calling for the police to come and investigate what's happened, though the flashing lights outside tell us they've already arrived.

I sit back in my chair and look around the table.

"The girl in the video had a pen behind her ear," Roark says. Ever astute, my Roark. It's not like I could ask Rachel to dish her entire story again on a video for her peers. But she did agree to testify and fully cooperate with the investigation.

I grab my doctored pen, the one that had awful balance without its cap but now spins beautifully because the guys fixed it up for me, and start twirling it in my hand.

"You mean this pen?" I ask.

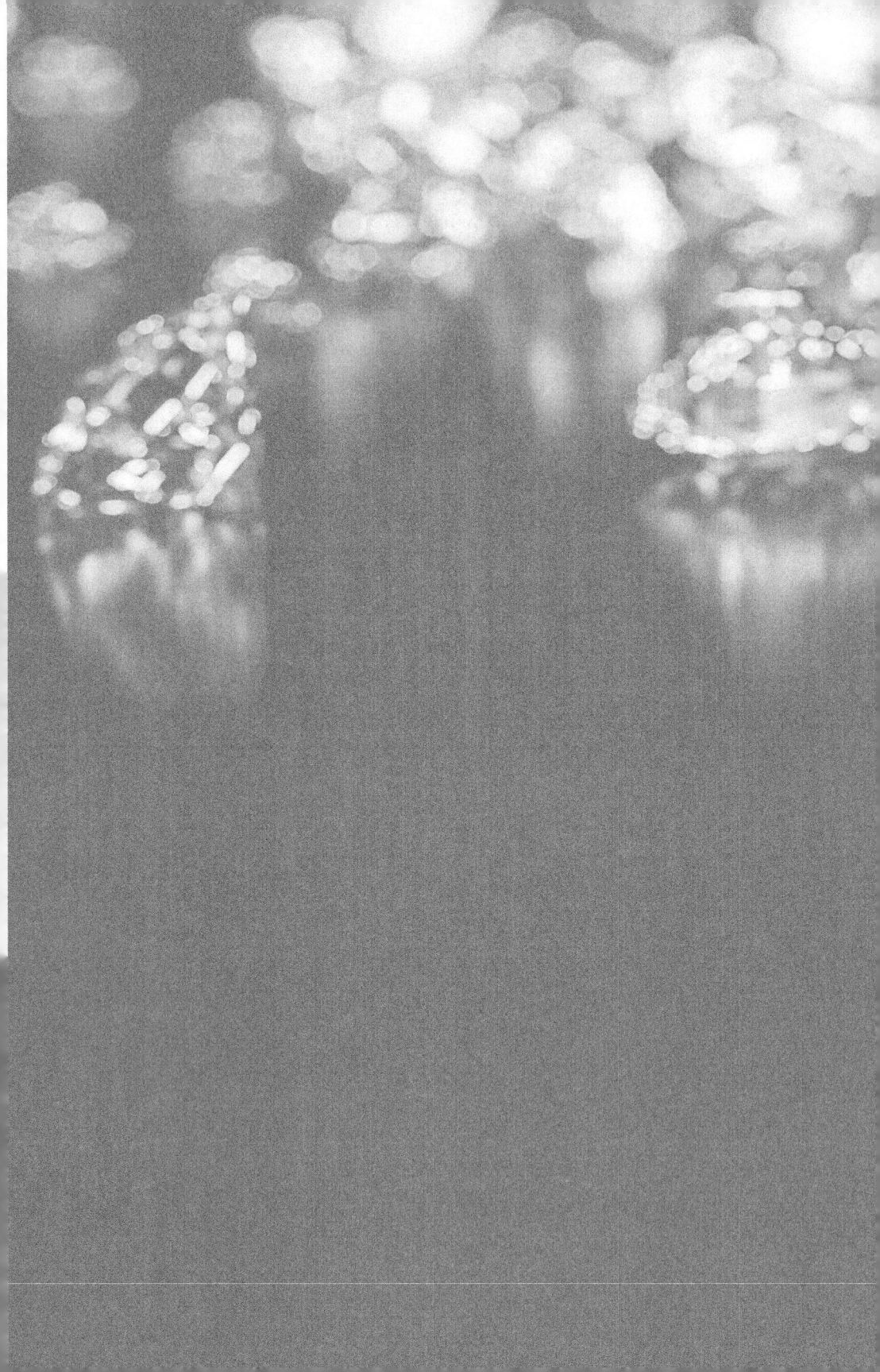

Chapter Twenty-Eight

Max
Present Day

Today is heist day.

After the group fun on Friday night following the party and the subsequent discussion, everyone went to bed in a mood, but Olivia woke up determined as fuck. We spent yesterday reworking plans and changing tactics.

After cancelling plans A through F, we finally have a way forward with good old plan G. I just hope like hell this works.

All damned day, we could hear the sound of revving engines through the city as the Alpine Race, Formula 1 practice session, the qualifying session, and the Formula 2 race ran from ten in the morning until half past six. My mind buzzed all night with the whirr of engines, and the anticipation for today kept me up far later than I should have been.

It's why I dabbed on concealer this morning. I have to look good because, yet again, I am the bait.

Today's races started at ten a.m. again, and we watched the people file in from all over the city towards the centre. Traffic has been a nightmare, so we've decided to go later in the day. The driver's presentation happened at one o'clock, and it's currently two. We would arrive for the national anthem and watch the entire two-hour race. It would have been suspicious if I missed the bulk of the event, even though I had absolutely no interest in repeatedly watching cars go vroom vroom around a track.

After our rendezvous at the Monte Carlo Casino party, I had a feeling I'd be keeping Natasha at arm's length as much as possible. I also don't want to spend much time with her if she shows up for the entire race. Her part only comes at the end for the trophy presentation with the royal family.

The alarm on Roark's phone rings in his pocket, shocking me out of my musings.

Time to go.

Olivia pulls us all into a huddle in our tiny flat. We moved the essentials to our planned getaway car yesterday, and now the place looks shockingly empty. Despite the tension in the air, we all know this is the moment we've been working towards. Olivia called us from our corners of the globe for this, all to help her friend. We couldn't let her down now, not after everything.

Eleanor may not be vital to any of us, but she's Olivia's ride or die. What man wouldn't step up to help? Sure, the sex incentive might have hooked us at first, but now? Fuck. I would do anything for the woman in front of me.

"You guys ready?"

"Yes, Little Thief." Zach's confidence has never wavered, and I hate to admit I'm envious of that.

"The boat crew?" Olivia asks me.

"Have been set up in a hotel in Nice since yesterday for paid holidays and are spending their day at the races. I got tickets for the start/finish rooftop viewing location, and they should already be there," I say, checking my watch.

Roark pulls his phone from his pocket, flipping through the camera angles on the boat. He confirms, "They left two days ago for Nice and there's been no one on the boat since. I remotely locked it and have the cameras on my feed, so no one is getting back on."

I grimace at what's waiting for my beloved boat and Olivia nods. "Zach, you're with V in the general admission area. Rory, you ready to play bodyguard?"

Roark stands with his feet shoulder-width apart, and with his sombre black suit at odds with my spring attire, the sheer change from school is startling. He's posing as my security for today's plan, and he stepped into character rather easily.

"You know your role?" Liv asks him.

"Yep. Keep Max from getting into trouble so he can do his part."

We split up as we leave the flat. Olivia goes first, followed by V and Zach, and finally Roark and me. As we make our way to the racetrack and the premier seating, the press of tourists around us has me feeling grateful Roark is blocking people as my buffer. He's giving off this menacing energy with his stance, and people are clearing a route for us.

There are far too many bodies milling about; the city's central area has been blocked off from cars during the race, but the place is laden with people who came to watch but couldn't get a ticket to the actual seating, which is where V and Zach will be blending in.

As we approach the track, I feel like I'm about to suffocate from the onslaught. We find the path carved out for pass holders. I gratefully follow the carpeted pathway, and when I reach the security guards blocking the entrance, I hand over my premier ticket. Roark's weapons are catalogued before he's directed to stand with the other bodyguards at the back of the space.

I climb the steps to the open-air tent. It looks like a wedding reception with adorned tables, plush chairs, and gauzy fabric stretched from the centre of the domed ceiling to the corners. The red carpet below our feet is springy, and I feel bad for Zach and V as they're positioned outside in the throng of people, not to mention Olivia who's out working in the late-spring sun.

I have my comms device in the depths of my pocket for now, but will put it in when necessary. Roark already has his in as my security guard, and it looks natural with all the other bodyguards connected to their teams via the same systems.

I make a pit stop—ha—at the bar towards the back of the tent to grab a club soda with lime, and find my seat. I'm perfectly positioned to watch the starting line, and when a waiter comes by with appetisers, I unburden him of the tray, gently placing it in the centre of my small table. With all five of us sharing the small space and a tiny refrigerator in the flat, food has been a little scarce because no one wants to do the shopping. I scan the seating area and note that there's no sign of Natasha yet, but we factored that possibility into our plan.

As the excitement builds around me, rising like a wave before cresting, the rev of the engines becomes deafening. The spectators all stand, and the other attendees in the premier tent join in. Roark is just behind me and I see him assessing the tent, quiet the whole time, but vigilant. He talked about some video game that required this kind of attention and reconnaissance, and honestly, it sounds pretty fun.

The race begins at three o'clock on the dot, and when the signal lights go out, the cars tear away at a blinding speed. I sit back in my seat, knowing this thing goes for two hours or seventy-eight laps, whichever comes first.

"Well, this is dreadfully dull," a voice says to my right. I see movement to my left and turn to find an old friend from uni.

"Unfortunately correct," I agree as I extend a hand in greeting. He clasps mine, giving it a shake before dropping into the chair next to me. "How are you, Donaldson? It's been ages since Imperial." There is chatter around us as the other guests mingle between laps and watch the screens in the corners of the open-air premier box. The line for the bar is forming despite the waiters moving through the room with champagne. "This is nothing like a horse race," I grumble.

"You're still doing that?" Donaldson asks as he turns to face me. His features are the same as they always were, slightly pinched, ever annoyed. But right now, he's the only one I know here aside from Roark and this looks like it's going to be a dull afternoon.

"Well, yeah." I shrug. "It's entirely different from this. You can see the whole track, watch as the horses and the jockeys give it their all, flying down the straights and rounding the corners with perfect synchronicity. That last home stretch is where the magic happens."

I miss John Henry. He may not be a racehorse, but he's incredible in dressage. I can't wait for Olivia to meet him in real life.

Donaldson just hums in mock agreement and snags an hors d'oeuvre from the plate in front of us. While he's eating and yammering about the latest dip in the stock market, I pull the comms piece from my pocket and pop it into my ear where Donaldson can't see. Now that I'm past security, it's easier to wear them unnoticed.

"And everything's good with you?" I ask loudly to interrupt Donaldson and check in on my team.

Olivia groans about volume reduction while my old acquaintance takes up the thread of conversation and begins recounting his last ten years or so. "All good," Olivia assures me. Roark echoes the sentiment from behind me.

"No sign of Natasha yet," Roark says.

"Give it time. She likes to make an entrance." Olivia is right. I've seen the articles, and they always mention her sauntering in late.

Lord Winchester, a peer of my father's, waves his hand at me from across the box. Ah, fuck. More mingling. I stretch my mouth into a smile that hopefully passes as pleasant and rise from my seat, gratefully slipping away from Donaldson in the process.

I'm hauled from group to group, introduced to dignitaries and celebrities, while conversation pauses when the roar of an engine passes by on yet another lap. The staccato nature is frustrating and keeps tearing my focus from where it should be.

My head is swimming with the chatter and one-upping stories everyone feels inclined to share. Drinks are consumed over backroom deals, insider trading tips passed from lips to ears, and more money changes hands in bets than some nations' gross domestic product.

I was in the middle of a particularly tedious conversation on the British monarchy when static crackled in my ear. Liv's voice came through moments later. "In position. Natasha has arrived."

Roark, who had stayed posted on the back wall with the other guards, nods his head, and V answers, "Showtime."

I straighten my spine and excuse myself from the conversation, heading to the bar. Roark will let me know when she approaches.

Two cars race by again, and I order a drink. I wait patiently at the bar, keeping my back turned when Roark's voice whispers, "Three, two..."

"Max," Natasha purrs into my ear as she leans in close.

I smile, pretending she's Olivia, and suddenly the forced grin becomes much more natural as I turn towards her. "Hello, Natasha." I take her hand in mine and brush my lips over her knuckles.

She inhales sharply, and I peek up, winking at her before slowly running my tongue between two of her fingers, mimicking a tongue over another slit. "Mmm, delicious as always."

Natasha lifts her free hand and tucks her blonde hair behind her ear. Today she's wearing a cream coloured dress, perfectly tailored with a high neckline, cap-sleeves, and a hem that reaches her knees. Her glitter rose gold heels match the hardware on her clutch, as she dresses the part of the award presenter superbly.

Her hand is warm in my grip, and I pull her closer. "I missed you yesterday," I whisper conspiratorially.

Suddenly, Liv's voice booms in my ear "This is a fucked-up plan. I hate it. Let's just kidnap Natasha and give her to Zach."

Roark lets out a snort from the wall of bodyguards and tries to turn it into a cough. It is entirely unconvincing. I hear Zach's voice in my ear. "Like I'd want her when I can have you. Max thinks the same, Little Thief."

Olivia huffs, and I keep my attention on Natasha. "You look ravishing, *zolotse*," I purr, pulling a Russian term of endearment from the short bank of words Liv taught me.

I keep her hand in mine and pull her to the barstool beside me. "Thank you." A blush colours her pale cheeks, and her eyes flash at the bartender as he interrupts us, placing my drink before me.

"For you, *Madame*?" he asks politely.

"Champagne," she says, and he turns away to pour her a flute. I direct her face back towards me. "What are you having? Not scotch like the other night," she notes.

The waiter places the flute on the bar top before her and turns to focus on another patron. "Variety is the spice of life, Natasha," I answer. "It doesn't matter, anyway. I plan to replace the taste of the drink with the taste of you just as soon as I can drag you out of here."

A shiver wracks her body, and her eyes become hooded. "Cocky, are we?"

"You have no idea. Well, maybe some idea after the other night," I answer before taking a sip of my drink. Her eyes light up, and she drags her bottom lip through her teeth.

"How much longer is the race?" she asks impatiently, looking up at the screen.

I check and see the pack leader only has eight more laps and will finish well before the two-hour time limit is up. "About ten minutes if De Rossi keeps his pace, and he'd better. I have money on him."

"I'm sure you can afford to lose a bit." Natasha eyes my designer clothes and my impeccable footwear.

I laugh. "Doesn't mean I want to, *zolotse*."

She blushes at my endearment in her native tongue and leans in closer, her breasts brushing against my elbow. "What do you say we make our own bet?"

Arching a brow, I ask, "What did you have in mind?"

She takes a sip of her champagne, and I swirl my drink as I keep my eyes on her. Her scarlet-tipped fingernails drag on the back of my hand, her teeth biting my earlobe. "If your guy wins, as soon as the award ceremony is done, you take me back to my suite and fuck me raw."

I hum from deep in my chest. "And if your pick wins?"

"The same stakes apply."

"Win-win." I nod in agreement, and her tongue trails along my jawline. I pull away, and the driver completes another lap. "Tsk," I reprimand Natasha. "Not yet. We've got a few laps left."

She pulls back with a pout, and I grasp her jaw, ensnaring her eyes and keeping her focus on me. "Impatient, are we?"

Natasha slides forward on her stool, my grip keeping her far enough away to stop her advance. She's a gorgeous woman, truthfully. If I wasn't in love with Olivia and Natasha weren't the leader of an international crime syndicate, I would have given this a go. She is intelligent, responsive to touch, and looking for a good time after her late husband. All things I would have praised her for if we had met in another life.

Right now, though, she's standing between my girl's best friend and her job.

The cars zoom by again, my pick still in the lead as they round the bend. I give Natasha a stern look, and she drops her eyes in submission. *Good girl*, I think.

Natasha idly drinks her champagne and both of us are now turned towards the racetrack as the final laps begin. The surrounding air is charged as the other attendees in our tent pause their dealings and chit chat to watch the conclusion. De Rossi is still in the lead by a few car lengths, but Bordeaux is right behind him. Either way, it doesn't matter. The only reason I'd pretend to cash in on Natasha's bet is if our plan fails on the first attempt. But I really don't want to go back to her room.

I sip my drink, holding the liquid on my tongue and feeling the burn. One more lap to go.

The cheering intensifies thirty seconds later as the roar of the engines come down the home stretch. The cars are barreling towards us and Natasha has a death grip on my arm as we watch them careen along the track.

I see Roark against the wall, ignoring everyone and everything. "Stop staring at me," he says in my ear. I barely catch my laugh at his disgruntled voice. I stifle it with another sip of my drink and hear Olivia next. "Ready to go."

De Rossi comes racing towards the finish line, the driver behind him doing his best to inch forward, but there's no use. My pick crosses the line, and a wave of cheers and groans go up around us.

I put my glass on the bar top and turn towards Natasha, taking her face in my hands. My lips crash into hers with a bruising kiss, my tongue slipping inside and encouraging hers to join in the dance. She moans into my mouth, and in moments we're making out like two horny teenagers who are sharing their first kiss. I push saliva and the remnants of my drink into her mouth, but she doesn't seem to notice or care as she grips the lapels of my jacket, hauling me closer.

The lip lock goes on as champagne is poured and money changes hands around us. More cars are crossing the finishing line, and I pull back, leaving a gentle kiss on Natasha's lips. She chases my lips with hers as her eyes flutter open. "Wow," she breathes.

Natasha's face scrunches up, and she raises her fingertips to her lips. "They're tingling," she confesses. I smile down at her, then look up and see Roark watching us from the wall, giving me a death glare.

Good.

"Mine, too. You are exquisite." She blushes at my compliment, but it doesn't erase the concern from her face.

"No, I mean, they're *actually* tingling. What were you drinking?"

"Vodka and club soda," I answer.

Her eyes widen slightly as she gasps for air. "Potato allergy. Fuck."

"Oh my god, I'd completely forgotten," I lie. "You said it wasn't life-threatening, right?" I ask. Before she answers, I raise my voice and call out, "Does anyone have any allergy medication?"

Roark steps forward, along with five other attendees who heard me shout, each offering one version or another of an antihistamine.

Roark

Present Day

I have to admit; Max played that beautifully.

Max calls for help across the loud seating area, and I dig my hand into my pocket, pulling out my wallet in the process, and rushing over.

"Sir, are you okay?" I ask as I arrive next to them.

"Natasha, this is my personal security. My father insists I never go anywhere without him. He has seasonal allergies," Max explains as I drag out a packet of antihistamine.

I'm suddenly shoved from the side when her own security team arrives, and Natasha, Max, and I are hustled to the side away from the bar area and into a blessedly quiet corner. The three of them start speaking in rapid-fire Russian and Olivia translates over comms.

"They're asking if she's okay, if she's been attacked, and what she needs. Oh, and offering to kill Max," she says.

The man in question gulps and rips the packet of medicine from my hand.

"I'm so sorry, Natasha. I forgot entirely. Here," he offers her the medicine, but one of her guards swats it away. Instead, he reaches into his pocket and procures his own pills.

Max turns to me in explanation, as if we didn't spend the bulk of yesterday planning this. "She has a potato allergy, and I kissed her after having some vodka." He looks genuinely concerned, his hands gently palming her shoulders in reassurance.

"How serious is your allergy?" I ask.

"Not very. Annoying more than anything else." She takes the proffered medicine from her guards and asks them to back up. They follow her instructions immediately, but one keeps her within arm's reach.

"Your lips are swelling, Natasha," Max says. He looks genuinely concerned, like this is going to kill her.

She opens her mouth, testing her new engorged lips. She lets out a curse and wiggles her tongue in her open mouth. I see her tongue is swelling, and the tongue bar is stretching its limits, keeping the centre pressed down while the rest inflames.

"Natasha. Your lips and tongue are swollen," Max says. "You need to remove the piercing before the flesh of the tongue swallows the stopper on the top and bottom. That would need surgery to fix. Something similar happened to my cousin a few years ago."

Her watery blue eyes flare in panic. "Fuck, I'll just pop into the bathroom to remove it. I'll be fine."

"Natasha, I'm so sorry," Max keeps saying over and over again, really selling his regret. If he lies this smoothly, I'll have to make sure he never does the same to Olivia.

She grasps the medicine and Max is still apologising, but she reassures him with a kiss on his lips. "You trying to make it worse?" I ask, and she giggles.

"Can't seem to help it," she says to me with a wink, then turns to Max. "You'll be here? I have to do the awards ceremony."

"It's not like I'm going to go rushing off when there's a bet to collect." He winks, and I swear I see her swoon.

Her guards fall into step with her, leading her to the toilets just behind the bar. She tosses her hands in the air when she sees the sign over the front saying they're out of order. There are directions to use the ones just behind the platform we're all standing on, so they make their way down the stairs and towards the bathrooms.

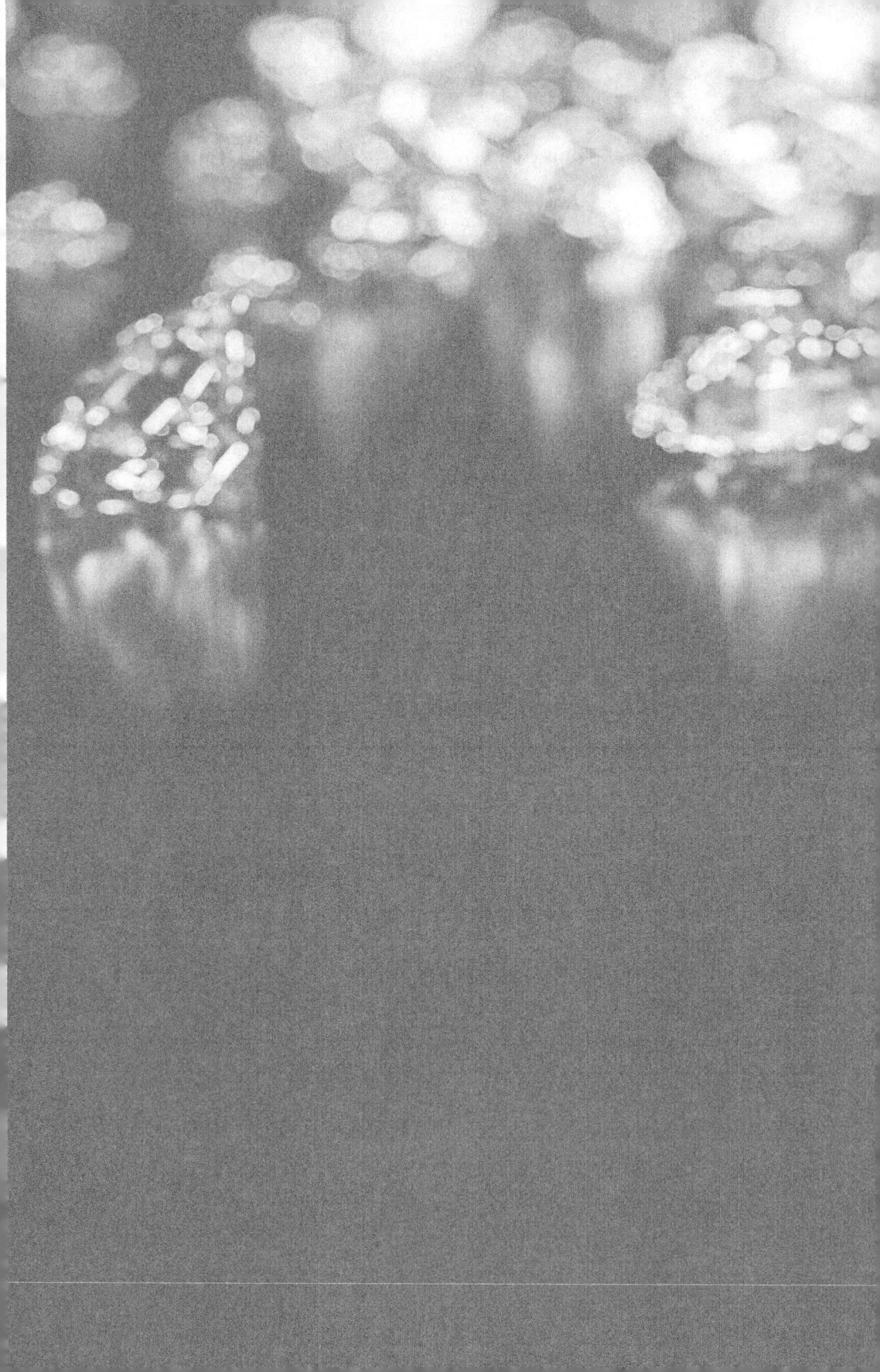

Chapter Twenty-Nine

Olivia
Present Day

Listening to someone make out with the guy who recently professed his love to you is a little jarring, not gonna lie.

The exchange between Natasha, Max, and Roark plays through my earpiece, and I know my part of the plan is up next. I position my cart just inside the women's bathroom and stick a sign out front saying that the floors are wet. I'm delighted Max stuck to the timeline. The last laps mean everyone is watching the track and not milling around.

The door pushes open, and Natasha enters with a huff. I keep my eyes downcast as I wipe up the countertops, keeping to the left side of the sinks as she stops in front of the big mirror.

"*Pizda*," she spits with a lisp as she looks at her tongue in the mirror. Calling her tongue a cunt was unexpected from the refined Natasha, but I get it. Kissing Max is pretty great. I'd be pissed if I were interrupted as well.

She wholly ignores me as she washes her hands at the sink.

Natasha stares into the mirror, and her swollen lips look like they're one lousy filler job away from exploding. The skin is stretched tight, and it must be really uncomfortable. I move one step to the right, cleaning the faucet of one sink and slowly inching closer to my target.

"Are you okay?" I ask, feigning a French accent and making eye contact through the mirror. A protective mask is stretched across the bottom of my face to keep the cleaning fumes from being inhaled, and my dark brown wig and brown contacts make me look relatively unremarkable. Just the way I like it.

"Allergies," she grunts out around the giant balloon lips. "I'll be fine soon." She points to the individual packet of loratadine she dropped on the counter.

"Oh my gosh, do you need anything?" I ask, letting some panic bleed into my eyes and tone.

"No, thank you. I just need to get this fucking piercing out." It's hard to understand her, but knowing what's going on certainly gives me the context to figure it out.

I nod my head and continue my task, keeping her in my peripherals the entire time. I'm not missing a damned thing.

She dries her hands with the paper towels and sticks her tongue out. I peek up from under my lashes and see her swollen flesh. I feel a little bad for a second, but we would have figured out another way if this was a life-threatening allergy. Probably. No, definitely. We would have tried something else.

She grips the bottom of her tongue ring and begins twisting.

Come on, baby. Come on. Come on!

Natasha winces as she disentangles the metal bar and groans in relief as she twists, giving her poor tongue more space to swell.

The Cleanup

I move one sink closer, keeping up my work on the countertops. No one pays much attention to a cleaner, and after our initial words, she went right back to ignoring me. I smile to myself, knowing my cover is fucking perfect.

Natasha places the metal bar on the marble and tilts her head down with her palm cupped in front of her lips. She moves her mouth and pulls away with the one-carat diamond sitting in her palm.

Fucking jackpot!

My inner self is doing the Macarena, then waving our hands in the air like we just don't care. My outer self, however, keeps a straight face and an eagle eye on the task at hand.

"Actually, do you have a cup or something?" she asks, picking up the medication packet from where she dropped it. "I can't go out there looking like a fish." She laughs at her reflection, and yeah, if circumstances were different, I think we could actually be friends. She actually seems pretty chill. There's just the slight fact that she made out with Max. Yes, it was my plan—again—but it feels unforgivable to our hypothetical friendship.

"*Oui*, one second." I rush over to my cart and pull out a plastic-wrapped package of small cups. Why would a cleaning lady have these? Who the hell knows, and Natasha doesn't question it—just gratefully takes one from the pack after I open it.

She puts the diamond next to the metal bar to open the loratadine packet with both hands. I would stuff the damned thing in my bra if it were that valuable, but her dress is high-necked and moulded to her body. I doubt she could fit her hand through the openings if she tried.

I move closer, working on the counter again as she fills up her cup with water, and holds the tiny pill in the other hand. She deposits the medication in her mouth and lifts the cup to chase it down.

Pulling a tongue ring I bought at some cheap tourist shop yesterday from my pocket, I put it between my fingers while Natasha is busy drinking. The only problem with it is that the metal is a bright silver while the one she removed is more of a gunmetal grey. It's not like I could check the bar before she removed it, what with it being stuck through her tongue. Fuck, it means she could notice it faster, but I have no other option. It has to go down the drain.

I let the rag fly a bit wildly, watching the edge curl around the diamond and the tongue stud, and send the spares towards the sink, while the originals fly towards my waiting hand at the lip of the counter. Natasha and I watch in horror as both the cheap metal bar and the fake diamond drop into the sink. They circle the basin, both pieces going at different speeds due to weight, and her hands chase the diamond before it goes *plunk*.

"No!" she shouts, scrambling with the removable drain cover as I place the coveted diamond and the metal bar in my pocket and drop the rag in the other sink. The plan was to knock it to the floor, but I made an executive decision when I saw the colour of the metal.

The mafia queen whirls towards me, fire brimming in her eyes and her lips stretch into what must be an uncomfortable grimace. "You! What the fuck?!"

"I'm—I'm so sorry!" I pitch my voice low and remorseful. "The rag slipped on a soap spill. It'll be okay. Don't run the water. I can get maintenance."

She glares at me, enunciating each word clearly so there's no way I can misinterpret it with her slurred speech. "That better not be gone. That diamond is worth more than your life."

Natasha bends down and starts rummaging below the sink, checking out the U-bend, no doubt.

"Okay," she says. "It looks like you'll survive today after all."

Her voice has been stripped of the irritating blonde bimbo cheer she has shown until now. It's now plainly stating that she won't kill me for what I did.

Am I in over my head here?

Nah, I lost my virginity to a serial killer. I'll be fine. She can't be more dangerous than Zach.

Then, she turns around to face me, and I instantly change my mind. The look in her eyes is one I know all too well. It's cold, calculating. Shit. She looks at me just like Zach looks at cats. Like I'm a pest, and she'll crush me under her heel.

"Do you have gloves and a wrench?" she says with the exact same tone as before.

Will hypnosis even work on her? If her brain is wired the same way as Zach's, she will have a natural resistance to it. I practised on my psycho, but still, I did not expect to come face to face with another one. What were the odds of that happening?

What does that say about me?

In hindsight, since she offed her husband, we probably should have given it more consideration. Then again, how many of the women who kill their husbands do it in self-defence? It's not too hard to imagine a Bratva leader as a less-than-ideal husband. The reason my hypnosis training with Zach is so tough is because he's expecting it. He's ready to try and shut down my efforts. How many cleaning ladies do you know that are suddenly going to hypnotise you? It's absurd.

Focus, Olivia, otherwise the diamond will be the least of your worries.

Fortunately for me, two types of hypnosis techniques exist; the slow, quiet, relaxing one and rapid induction, essentially relying on surprise. Guess which one I'm picking now?

I tell her maintenance will have a wrench, and I'll call them to come immediately as I start rummaging in my cart, looking for the gloves as she requested. When I finally find them, I rapidly flick them in front of her face and snap my finger with all the determination in the world.

It creates the element of surprise I need for the hypnosis to work. I grab the back of her neck and press on her sternum with my other hand, raising my voice as I say, "And now *sleep.*"

She slumps down.

I know, I wish our final showdown was more impressive than that, too. But holy fucking shit, it worked! I only got this to work on

Zach twice in my life, and even then, he snapped out of it within minutes. I have to fucking move.

Her breathing has evened out. "Good job, Natasha." I pat her condescendingly on the cheek. She doesn't move an inch. "Now, I'm going to slip out the door, and you will lock it after me, so no one comes in. We don't want anyone going near that sink." She straightens up and nods at my words, completely missing the fact I used her name without her having given it. "Good. You'll wait for me to get the wrench, then we'll get your jewellery out of there, okay?"

"Okay. Okay. But if we don't—" She trails off, and I know Natasha will be quick to shake off my hypnosis, the desperation to get the diamond back is both working in my favour and against me. Her mind knows it's necessary and I'm feeding her the information she wants to get it back in her hands. The problem is, she's just like Zach —strong-willed and strong-minded.

Be sceptical of hypnosis all you like, but there's a reason there have been street performers luring in customers with it for decades. It's not perfect, and it's not the easiest thing to do, but in this case, it's giving me time. And that's all I need. A few minutes to get the fuck out of the bathroom.

"We're at the meeting point," V says in my ear. *Good. One less thing to worry about.*

"Listen." I keep my voice calm and even, despite my galloping heart rate, and play up the retrieval as an incentive to follow my instructions. "You will get it back. Do not open this door for anyone. No one else will come in here after you lock it. Your jewellery is safe, and that's the only thing that matters."

She nods, keeping her eyes closed.

"Okay, I'm going now. You will stay here and not open the door for anyone. Do you understand?"

"Yes," she whispers.

Her breathing has slowed, and she is in a relaxed state—but who knows for how long? Time to fucking book it.

"Come lock the door." She slowly opens her glazed-over eyes and follows me like a zombie, a slight hitch in her breathing. I leave the cart where it is and pull the door open. Her guards peer in, and I seethe. "Don't look into the ladies' toilets! What would your mothers say?" They immediately pull back when they see Natasha standing just inside, fine and unharmed.

I am two steps away from the door when I hear the lock click into place.

Hypnosis is awesome, but can be unreliable, and in this case, the odds are stacked against me.

Emerging from the small hallway, the sounds of the race assault my ears. I have to get to the meeting point. Putting the tongue bar and diamond in a special pocket I sewed in my sports bra, I strip off my cleaning overshirt, rip the wig from my head, and unhook my cleaning mask from around my ears as soon as I'm distant enough. I pinch the contacts from my eyes and stuff everything into a garbage bin and pick up my pace.

Darting through the gathered people, I find Zach and V standing at our meeting point and searching for me in the crowd. Viraj is the first to spot me, and a smile breaks out over his face when he sees the victory etched on mine.

I run closer, jumping over litter strewn on the floor, and he catches me with an arm around my hips as I wrap my legs around him. "I got it. Let's get the fuck out of here."

Zach turns towards me. Assessing eyes run over my body as he checks me up and down for any injury. "I'm fine! Let's go!"

Roark's voice crackles in over the comms. "Natasha just came back to the tent with two of her security guards in tow. They're causing a ruckus. Natasha is demanding a wrench, but refuses to let maintenance handle her problem."

"Fuck," V spits.

"The hypnosis wore off faster than I thought it would. But fucking hell, it worked when I needed it to. Hopefully the event security resents the idea of handing sketchy looking guys a wrench as much as I would and delays them a bit longer. Is the boat ready? Get it moving, Rory."

"On it."

Over the comms, I hear Natasha speaking to her guards in Russian. She doesn't say anything about losing time, but she does mention her piercing going down the drain, and threatens to murder everyone if she doesn't get it back.

A bit dramatic to my tastes. Then again, who am I to judge?

"I want my motherfucking diamond back," she insists in that ice-cold tone she hides so well.

Roark's voice comes through the device again. "You have to move. Head for the cliffs. We'll catch up."

Do her bodyguards even know she had a diamond containing the world's most dangerous secrets? Or did she tell them it was just a diamond? How will a billionaire explain the need to recover a one-carat diamond when the champagne she was drinking earlier costs the same by the glass? Her guards must know, otherwise, why would they obey her? Then I remember the look that stole over her features when she threatened my life. That lifeless void she withdrew into was scary as shit.

Yeah, maybe she doesn't need to mention life-changing data for her underlings to be fearful of her. I snake a finger inside my bra and let out a breath. The diamond is still safe where I tucked it.

No, I was not touching my breast in the middle of a crowd just because it feels nice. Even though it does feel nice.

V smiles wide because he knows what comes next. "Oh, hell yes," he says. "This is going to be awesome."

"I can't fucking believe this is happening," Max grumbles over the comms.

As we're traversing the steep streets towards the hiking trail at the base of the cliffs, I turn around to watch as *Unsinkable II* pulls away from the harbour. Max starts shouting about how his boat is moving when it shouldn't be and that someone must be stealing it. Roark is remotely controlling it, and it slips free from the loose knots we tied at the dock early this morning under the cover of darkness.

The boat picks up speed as it clears the slow zone—which we took as a suggestion rather than a requirement—and police are clambering into two boats to give chase. Fuck, they take their security seriously here.

"What the fuck is that? Someone is stealing my boat!" Max shouts, cutting through the cacophony of sound around us. He's pulling attention in the opposite direction of us. "Help! Somebody help! Officers," he says in relief as if he's just found the salvation he was looking for, "someone stop that boat! It's not supposed to be going anywhere until I leave, and the crew is here in the city."

The premier box has a view of Hercule Harbour, so Max will get to watch the show with front row seating. Zach, V, and I continue our run-walk towards the trail, trying not to look conspicuous amidst all the people looking and moving in the opposite direction towards the race track.

We have to make careful progress because, at this point, we're heading towards escape plan H. Do you know how hard it is to come up with *one* plan out of Monaco when they go into lockdown? Let alone fucking *eight*? If this doesn't work, we'll be trapped like rats.

Over the loudspeakers, I hear the announcers describing and summing up the race, meaning Natasha is due to present the trophies with the royal family soon, and for appearance's sake, I hedge my bets that she'll be in attendance even if her guards aren't all present. Despite what we have planned for Max's boat, they can't stop all the festivities; there's too much money coming in from this event.

The crowd surges forward towards the track, allowing us to slip by. We haul ass towards the base of the hills and the cliffs, using lateral roads and crossing through gardens as all heads are turned towards the harbour.

I feel the shock before I hear it. That eerie absence of sound rocks me to my core, and my body jerks as I turn around. BOOM!

The street we're currently in allows for an uninterrupted view of the bay and the glistening water of the Mediterranean.

Unsinkable II is a ball of flames on the mirror-like surface of the sea, burning like an inferno as the various accelerants catch and create minor booms as it lists to one side. I can't watch for long because I'm yanked forward by Zach.

The city goes quiet in the aftermath as jaws hang open. Max shouts at the destruction of his yacht, demanding to speak to the police chief and swearing the Monegasque police have just made a very powerful enemy.

I hear an officer speak with him, insisting he tell them everything he can about the boat and why they chose that particular one to flee on. Max, on the other hand, reams the officer for lax security at the harbour, that it's inadmissible his boat would be stolen in the middle of such a reputable port, incompetent and shoddy police work, and promises to bring this to the British Monarchy.

"That was way more fun than in video games," Roark says through the comms. His voice turns muffled as he speaks to us directly, probably shielding his mouth in the process. "We'll meet you at the bottom of the cliffs as soon as we can."

Viraj lets out a manic laugh as he grabs my other hand. He and Zach are pulling me along as we head towards our escape.

"I'll buy you *Unsinkable III*," I assure Max over the earpiece, even as he's interrogated by the police and Roark stands guard, keeping his distance, but I know he's got Max's back in this.

He grumbles something about the things he does for love, and I can't help the grin that stretches across my face.

Max answers questions, acting haughty and distraught all at the same time as V, Zach, and I hustle towards the meeting point. Rory butts into the questioning, demanding he get his boss to his hotel and out of the way in case this is a personal attack on him.

The point of all this? Clearing Max of suspicion. He couldn't exactly escape from a very public event right as an invaluable diamond was stolen; it'd paint him as a prime suspect. Now, when

The Cleanup

Natasha comes back from the bathroom and asks where he's gone, people will tell her his boat was stolen, blown up, and he had to head to his hotel.

If we're lucky, she'll even think the theft of the diamond and the theft of the boat were related, and she'll lose precious time sending goons to check the wreck.

As they talk to the police, Roark's voice is commanding and intense—a tone I've never heard from him before—telling the officers they can question Lord Arondale when he is safe in his hotel and has his lawyer present. The premier box is exposed and they have to take his safety into account. Max groans about having to call his father and explain, not to mention the lawyers, insurance company, and his private investigators due to the incompetence of the Monegasque harbour patrol.

Since Max is accounted for, was nowhere near the boat, and the threat to his safety is a concern with the whole yacht explosion, they agree to come to his hotel for more questions later. Rory rattles off the name of a hotel on the north side of the city and gives the officer a fake contact number to set up a time for questioning. The two of them are hustled out of the premier tent as the officers around them talk about locking down the city.

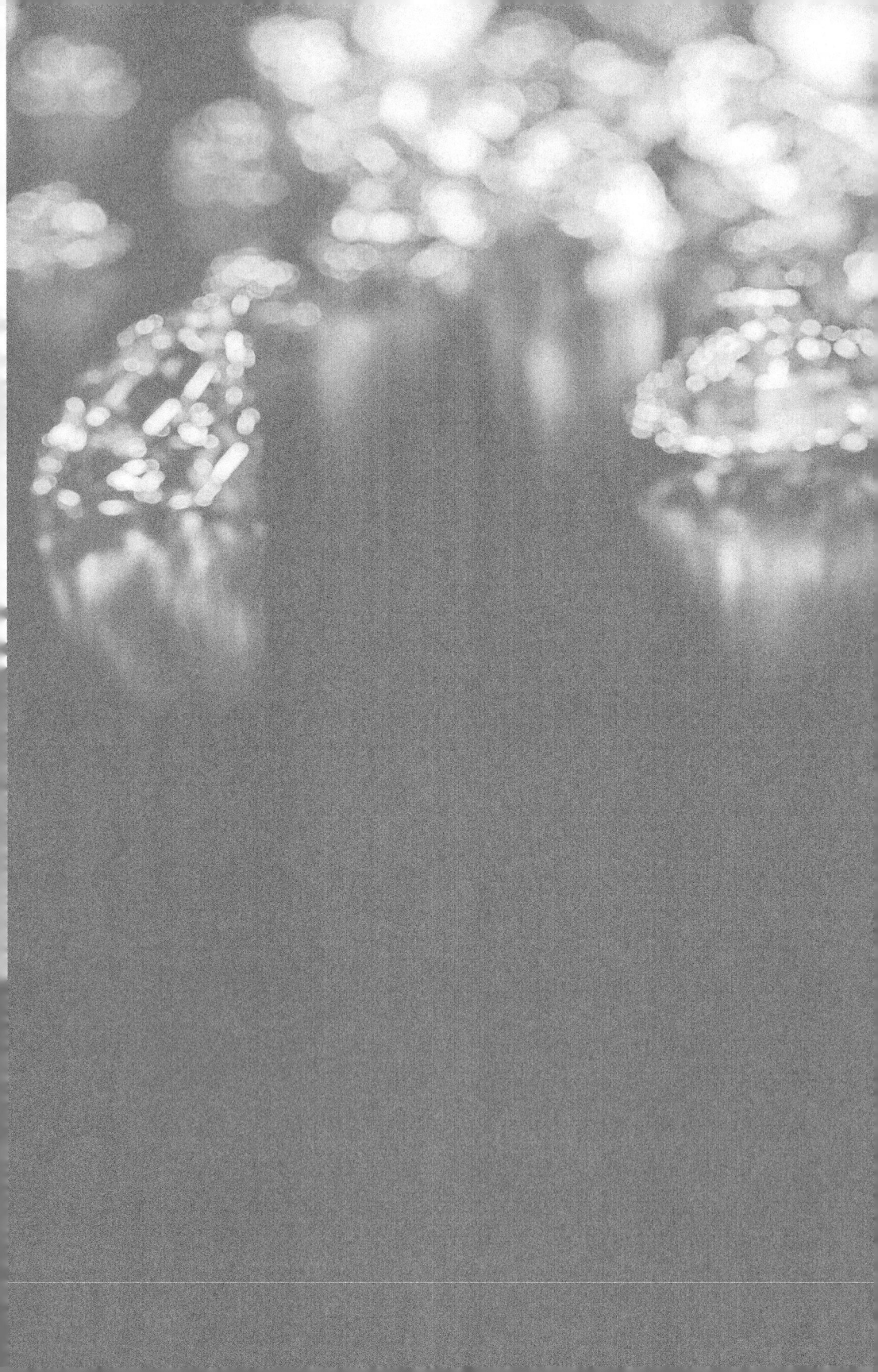

Chapter Thirty

Olivia
Present Day

The cliffs are farther than they seem, especially on foot. I've studied Monaco's lockdown protocol, and they heavily monitor the roads, which is why all our plans involve our car waiting for us outside the city borders so we could get to the rendezvous point with Interpol. Now, we just have to reach it.

Natasha was smart in hiding the diamond in her tongue piercing, but it'll be a disadvantage now that a multimillion dollar yacht has exploded in the bay. Compared to *Unsinkable II*, a measly piercing is small potatoes—even if the low-quality, artificial stone on it is worth more than some people's paycheck. This means that the police will be focusing on the boat, and not on her problem, unless she wants to tell them she stole important data from Interpol. Our main obstacle will be her security team. But our escape plan is creative enough for me to be confident—they won't find us.

Monaco has gone into lockdown, but it's a pretty relaxed one on this side of the city, considering the focus is on the harbour at the moment. No search parties are organised on the trails that lead to the cliffs. No dogs are nipping at our heels. And it's a fucking relief because the uphill hike isn't so easy.

During the start of the trail, Max and Roark kept reassuring me they were on their way, but the police questioning took way too much time in my opinion, and I'm worried they might not make it.

Going through the first steps of our escape without them is excruciating, but we don't exactly have a choice here. They're on their way, and that has to be enough for right now.

We've practised the hike and climb during our month-long stay in Monaco. Alternating between diving and climbing, reconnoitring the area, and schmoozing with the elite at the Monte Carlo Casino's party two nights ago—and the subsequent orgy—it's been a whirlwind of activity.

I wouldn't change a damned thing.

But going on a hike without pressure and going on a hike after you've stolen a priceless diamond from a mafia queen are two *very* different things. Even if I'm used to high adrenaline situations, my heart is in my throat, and my pulse is beating faster by the time we arrive at the bottom of the cliffs.

It's a beautiful Sunday, and the view from here is gorgeous, so the place is crowded with those who didn't have tickets to the race or wanted to see the city from above. Which is exactly what we needed, since the numerous rock climbing groups will help us go unnoticed. Just as planned. Hiding in plain sight.

Zach rustles in some nearby hedges, pulling out the packs we stashed here yesterday. We quickly change behind the bushes so no one sees our naked asses out here and takes note of us. We've changed into versions of sports attire and we have a few small packs of supplies strapped to us.

Roark won't be able to ditch the gun along the way, and it would be smarter not to, so I talk to him over the comms and tell him to stick it into his pack when he arrives. At least that way, we have it if Natasha's guards catch up with us. None of us wants to use it, but the weapon is reassuring in this case.

V and I exchange a look, and despite the joy in his face at the climb, mine morphs into a grimace knowing the end is coming and we'll be splitting up again. He's barely broken a sweat on the walk, but the exhilaration of moving his body seems to be getting to him. The smile on his face exposes his perfect teeth, and his dark curls are brushed back by the marine wind. As we enter his element, his back progressively straightens, and the way he's carrying himself now enhances his natural sex appeal.

After his admission two days ago that he'll go back to the States after this as if nothing ever happened, hurts. I don't want him to go.

It's in that moment, that acceptance washes over me. I may not want him to take off after all this is over, but whatever he does, I wish him happiness, whether it's with me—with us—or someone else. Viraj has hardened over the years. We all have, I think. The experiences of our past have shaped us into who we are, and I can't stand in the way of that if his mind and heart are pulling him elsewhere.

I walk up to him, pull his face down to mine, and kiss him with soft lips and a bleeding heart. He will be okay. *We* will be okay. No matter the outcome, no matter if we're together or apart. Maybe I'm selfish to want them all to myself. I'm a thief. Greed is my middle name, but in this case, for all of our sanity, maybe that needs to change.

I pull back from the kiss, finding his eyes still closed, and my heart breaks for what's to come. "Adrenaline God," I tease without real humour in my voice, "it's your time to shine."

He gives me a nod, despite the concern etched into his features, and quickly puts on his harness as we imitate him. V taught us everything we needed to know in the event of this plan being necessary, so it takes us less than two minutes.

I feel the shift into job mode. Emotions get you caught, killed even. The thief in my head is calling the shots right now. Fortunately. Because if it wasn't, I might notice how hot my men's asses look strapped in their equipment and drool all over the place.

V stashed everything we would need at the bottom of the cliff, and as he pulls all our stuff out of the hiding spot, I look up at the monolith before us. It's divided into three parts, meaning we'll have to do two pauses to regroup before attacking the next part.

"As I told you during our trial runs," V says, "I'll go first to set the ropes in the anchors, but this route doesn't present any real difficulties—not for me, anyway—so everything will be fine. I'll install ladders and extra holds whenever I can to make it quicker for you guys. When he arrives, let Roark know to recover it all so our pursuit is harder.

"Pace yourselves; focus. We have a rather long climb ahead. I have the necessary gear to haul you up if I have to, but I'd rather not, so be careful and wear your helmets."

Zach and I nod. We rope ourselves to each other and to V, and he meticulously checks our knots, giving them a sharp tug that has us stumbling forward.

I'm deranged because feeling his strong hand pulling my harness forward has my panties wet. Shit. I shake my head, trying to keep my focused mentality instead of imagining him fucking me after tying me up in expert knots.

"Ready?" Viraj asks.

"Ready," I confirm. And my own internal thoughts add *for you to tie me up*. See? Deranged.

With the grace of a dancer and the softness of someone touching a lover, V lays his hands on the rocky surface. He immediately leans back and finds holds for his feet. In a few seconds, he's already reaching the first anchor point, movements as fluid as if he were on solid ground. Viraj doesn't hurry but doesn't hesitate either, and he

The Cleanup

elevates himself much faster than I thought he would, fastening all the equipment to the rock face that will facilitate our climb as he goes.

Soon, he reaches the first belay stance and hollers, "Off belay."

Now's the time. Max and Roark should be here any minute, and if they aren't, we're screwed.

I hear a bristling noise coming from the bushes behind us and let out a screech of joy when I see my favourite hacker and aristocrat have made it. If I wasn't roped to a cliff, I'd jump to their necks right now.

A rope falls from the top of the cliffs where V threw it and accompanied by an excited yell. "Maxi Pad!" V shouts.

And that's it. Nothing else. The wind muffles his words and makes it hard to understand him.

Max and Roark have already stripped out of their suits, revealing their athletic clothing they had hidden beneath, and quickly get ready to climb. Max ties himself to the rope V just dropped while Roark uses the one lying on the ground since he'll climb with Zach. Reminding Roark to gather supplies as he climbs, he nods his head and we turn towards the rock face.

I remove the device I used to belay V from the rope as he starts to pull mine and Max's rope up. As soon as both strands are taut, we adjust our climbing shoes—these things hurt like a motherfucker; I'm not murdering my feet before I absolutely have to—and start going up.

I always have to sneak in and out of places, so I'm a lot better at this than Max is, and since we're climbing side by side, I leave him the best holds and easiest route.

We reach the first belay stance without issues, and I take a look back to the port, seeing that *Unsinkable II* has finished burning.

Max reproduces the same movements Viraj did to switch from climber to belayer and starts guiding Zach and Roark from above as I do the same for V from below, each of us paying close attention to the ropes in our hands in case someone slips.

Everything is going well until I hear a commotion coming from the bottom of the hiking trail. I take my eyes off Viraj for one second to look down, and, sure enough, Natasha's men have found us. How the fuck did that happen?

More importantly, how do we make sure it doesn't happen again? Fucking think, Olivia. A look to the side confirms the roads to the city are blocked, so at least they can't wait for us at the top of the climb unless they have people outside Monaco, too. But with Natasha being front and centre for the awards ceremony, it's unlikely. Still, this isn't good.

I have to figure out what we did wrong that allowed them to find us so fucking fast. We still have time before they become a real problem; they have to take the hike to the area below us before anything happens. Max starts pulling harder on the guys' ropes, helping them as much as he can so they'll go faster.

My eyes anxiously observe V's progression, which is still as calm and graceful as ever.

He shouts, "Off belay!" again, and the time he takes to pull up the rope feels like an eternity. We're observing the Bratva men getting closer, and there's nothing we can do about it from way up here.

As soon as V is safely tied to the rock and doesn't need me to belay him, I focus completely on figuring out how they found us. I wish I could twirl a pen right now. Then again, pen spinning while people you care about climb below you is probably not a good idea. It'd be a shame if one of them got impaled because I dropped it.

What would I do if I were Natasha and had to protect a diamond at all costs? I facepalm when the solution dawns on me. "There's a tracker in the piercing," I say.

"Huh?" Max answers.

"That's the only possibility! The bar must have an embedded tracker, and that's how they found us." I paw through my clothing as I speak and find the offending piece of jewellery. The diamond goes back in my hidden pocket while I hold the bar between my index finger and thumb, looking at it from up close as if I expect it to talk to me and confess all its secrets.

Spoiler alert; it doesn't.

I grab a big rock that is starting to detach from the cliff and find a fracture in it where I stick the metal bar of the piercing. Now that the revelation has passed, I'm beating myself up for not thinking of it, but hey, it's my first time stealing something like this.

Roark and Zach reach us, the former bringing up the ladders and other gear V left for us to delay the men below. It's all hanging from Rory's harness, making clanging noises when he moves.

"Here," I say, handing him the stone with the tracker in it. "Show us those axe-throwing skills of yours."

He looks at me like I'm deranged. "This is a stone, Via."

"I know it's a fucking stone. It's got a tracker in it that was attached to the diamond. Throw it as far as you can."

I know they already found us, but maybe more of them are coming and following the signal. The more of them we can lose, the safer we are.

When what I'm telling him finally registers, Roark rips the big stone from my hands and throws it as far as he can. We're so high it almost looks like it'll fall into the sea. Instead, we see it go through the bushes and start rolling down the hill. "Good riddance," Zach says. "Are you sure this was the only one?"

"I have no way to be sure, but the other side of the piercing was only the diamond with a little metal around it. They might still tail us or find us through security cameras, but I don't think we will be tracked again." Roark looks impressed at the ingenuity of the little bar as a tracker, but it isn't the freaking time.

After that, Max and I start climbing again as quickly as we can. The first rest stop was relatively hidden from the bottom of the cliff, but as we get higher, we'll be sitting ducks. I try to monitor everything as Max and I move up: the men's approach, if V can take cover, if Roark and Zach are hidden, if Max isn't having difficulties... Nothing escapes me. Adrenaline floods my veins. I've never been in a situation this precarious before.

We arrive at an overhang section of our route, and Max reaches for the rope ladder V has left for him. The holds are big on my side, so I don't wait for him to be done with the ladder to climb, still looking everywhere as I do.

One of the men in black reaches the bottom of the cliff, and I see him take a gun out of his pocket. Time freezes as I watch him aim at Max, who's dangling like a ham leg from his rope ladder.

"No," I mutter.

My body decides before I do. Knowing the rope will catch me, I jump off the rockface, pushing myself in Max's direction. I hear the gunshot resonate against the stone just as I reach him. We collide in the air, and I grab him, pushing him out of the bullet's trajectory just as searing, white-hot pain tears through my leg.

"Fuck," I shout, the agony roaring through my thigh and overpowering everything else. I've never felt anything like this.

Dangling as we are, Max can't see what happened.

"Olivia, what happened? Are you okay?"

"I'm fine! Climb! We have to take cover, and as soon as we're done with this overhang, we'll have it. Hurry!"

I'm not fine. Blood is gushing through the hole in my leg, but we have to move, or we'll be turned into swiss cheese soon.

Fortunately, the gunshot noise alerted Roark and Zach, and the former seems to have handed the gun to the latter. Zach is firing back, but with the angle, it's hard to get a good shot. Roark is heaving rocks over the side, aiming for the pursuers. It's not very efficient as far as taking them out is concerned, but now they have to stand farther away and look for cover, so it's harder to aim.

"Max, when you get to the next level, tell V to haul me up if he can. My leg is hurt."

"Liv..." Max tries to look at me from his position on the ladder.

"Climb, Max. There's nothing you can do now," I snap. The longer we're sitting here, the more bullets we'll have to contend with.

The Cleanup

I hear a clicking sound and despair fills my chest that Zach is out of ammo.

I take off my shirt and tie it around the wound as best as I can, my harness getting in the way. Fuck, that hurts.

Faint cries echo from the bottom of the cliff—no doubt because of the men shooting at us. They're muffled by the wind and the distance, but definitely there. Fortunately, V picked a route that keeps us away from the other groups.

Max is done with the ladder, though, which means I can use it. Ignoring my pain as the bullets fly around me, I use my arms and good leg to pull myself up, then wait for V to pull the rope tight and repeat the motions.

It's exhausting, my leg is completely dead weight, but I make it to the end of the ladder and above the overhang. At least I'm not at risk of getting shot anymore, but Zach and Roark are. I pause to catch my breath and adjust my makeshift bandage.

The wound is bleeding way too much, the bandage already soaked, and I'm starting to feel dizzy. Shit, if I pass out now, we're screwed.

As this thought crosses my mind, the rope connecting me to V starts pulling me up at an impressive speed. The two of them are hauling me up, no doubt.

Horrified expressions appear on their faces when they take in the state of my leg. V's eyes are wide open, and Max looks like only rage is keeping his tears away.

"The overhang section is too exposed," I say. "The plan has to change."

"And you got shot," V adds. He pauses a second to think. "Okay. Max, you need to staunch the bleeding. I'll belay Roark and Zach up. I'm not eager to have a psychopath lose his shit right next to me, but our psychopath also happens to be a medic with supplies in his pack, and we need him here."

The fact that he said "our" psychopath warms my aching body right up. Funny what our mind clings to when life is leaving us.

Max immediately moves, kneeling by my side as much as possible with his harness securing him to the rock. He takes a pen from my pack—because of course I have one—and slips it through the knot, tightening the tourniquet with each twist of the pen.

I hiss in pain as the material constricts my burning leg. Fuck, that shit hurts. I refuse to look down. If I see the injury and the blood I can feel running down my leg, it'll make it real, and I don't need that right now. The expression on Max's face is already enough to tell me it's bad.

"I'll be okay," I reassure him. "I survived being friends with Zachary Bennett for over a decade. A measly bullet won't take me down."

A tiny smile stirs his lips. Fuck, he's handsome. I can't die now, not when I'll finally have three of them all to myself. That'd be an awful end to our story. We should have always been embedded in each others' lives.

"I think I've got the bleeding under control," Max says.

"Then grab some stones." V orders. "You gotta distract the shooters below while Roark and Zach are going through the overhang section."

"Give me some too. I can help," I say, ignoring the shaky quality of my voice.

They both glare at me, but I don't back down. Our situation is more than precarious. If Zach or Roark get shot, we're toast. They seem to understand my silent message because Max hands me a stone without a word.

Max and I start dropping our cargo, making sure Natasha's men risk their heads being crushed if they aim at our friends.

This is why you always need a helmet when going to a climbing site. You never know what idiots are going to throw at you.

After unending minutes, Zach and Roark's heads finally pop over the side of the ledge. They both take in the three of us and immediately know something's wrong. Viraj should already be gone on the next portion of the climb, yet he's still here. This far up, the wind is deafening, so we couldn't shout anything and let them know what the fuck was going on. V fills them in on the whole shot-in-the-leg thing.

Then their eyes narrow in on my leg, and Zach's voice is pure threat. "Little Thief, you're hurt. Did they do this to you?" He tilts his head in the direction of the men below. I nod. That's definitely where the bullet came from. "They're dead. All of them. It might take some time, but from now on, they're living corpses."

Despite the pain, a shiver runs up my spine. Or maybe it's because of the pain.

Both Roark and Zach do the necessary security checks, then Doc comes to my side. "Not bad," he says as he takes in the tourniquet around my leg. "I think your pretty boy managed to get the bleeding under control. Do you know if the bullet is still inside?"

"There's no exit wound," Max chimes in.

"Okay, I'm not going to touch anything then. The bullet could be what's keeping you from bleeding out. But we need to get you to surgery, Little Thief." Zach turns to face Viraj. "What's the plan now?"

"The fastest way out is tying her to my back, and I'll carry her to the top. Then I'll belay the three of you up."

"That's too dangerous," Roark says. "With her on your back, she'll be acting as a shield for you, and the mass is bigger, making her a prime target. Then there's the added question: what if you guys fall?"

"I won't," V answers, his voice like steel, the set of his shoulders unflinching. "The last part of our route is the easiest, and the angle should be harder for them to take aim at us. Plus, staying here is worse."

"The two of you should go," Max says. "Get her to a hospital, then come back for us."

"No," I protest feebly. "Natasha's men will start climbing soon. We go together. Viraj's idea is the best." I move to stand, effectively ending the conversation. I'm already loopy from the blood I lost, which is concerning.

I bite the inside of my cheek to muffle a shout of pain when they secure me to V's back like an overgrown backpack. As Viraj dips his hands in his chalk bag and claps together to remove the excess, Zach bends over and whispers in my ear, his hand palming my cheek, "Hang in there, Little Thief. I've been told my feelings for you are dependence and obsession, not love, but the difference is irrelevant. Natasha's men will not survive my mania if you do not live. I will bathe in their blood, burn them alive on a pyre to your memory, then join them amidst the flames.

"Wherever you are, I'll come for you. Death separates people who love each other, but nothing will prevent my obsessed soul from finding yours in the afterlife. And punishing you for dying and making me suffer."

He wraps his hand around my wounded thigh and pushes his thumb inside the gaping hole, through the T-shirt.

Pain shoots through my body, quickly followed by arousal so intense it's embarrassing. Zach welds his lips to mine as if trying to devour me and spears his finger in harder, as if trying to bury under my skin. A moan is ripped from my throat, and I can't tell if it's of pain or pleasure.

I'm hurting, but my panties are so damp V can probably feel it through his T-shirt. "Fuck, you guys are sick," I hear him mutter.

Zach breaks the kiss, ignoring him. "Is the pain better, Little Thief?"

Again, this is fucked up. And again, I don't care. "A little."

My doc levels Viraj with a challenging look. "I'll do whatever it takes to get her to safety. Will you?"

Without a word, Viraj starts climbing.

I'm jostled left and right, and it's fucking agony, but I can't complain. Despite my added weight, Viraj is climbing fast, his movements as fluid as ever. Since we're higher and protected by the rock, fewer bullets reach us.

"You're amazing at this," I observe.

"Did you ever doubt me?"

The Cleanup

Not once. V is a cocky asshole, but only because he has the skills to put his money where his mouth is. It's fucking hot if you ask me.

He focuses as we go through a more complex portion, and suddenly we've reached the top.

Viraj unties me so I can sit down on the ledge, both of us safely tied to the rock. Looking around, I take in the sea, Monaco below, and angle my face so the setting sun will warm me. Dizziness is slowly taking over my body, and I'm fighting to remain conscious, but if these moments are my last, they're pretty fucking perfect.

The view is incredible, yet my eyes close to focus on the sensations of the wind on my face and sunlight on my skin.

When I open them again, V is looking at me intently. "Stay with me, Ollie. Zach isn't the only one who'll do whatever it takes." His eyes land on my lips, and for a moment, I think he's going to kiss me. That would only make my last moments all the more sweet.

Instead, he shakes his head and turns back to his anchor, preparing the devices and ropes to belay the guys.

They climb so fast it feels like they have a fire lit under their asses. Viraj pulls on the ropes at break-neck speed, sometimes looking like he's struggling to keep up with them.

Soon, we're all on top of the cliff, and I beg V to stop for just a second. All of the jostling has sent white-hot pain searing through my body, and I need a fucking breather.

Viraj watches me in silence, and I pat the diamond on my chest with a small smile, knowing we fucking got it; just like we got our headmaster all those years ago. He carries me bridal-style to our parked getaway car and as soon as my ass touches the expensive leather, I pass right the fuck out.

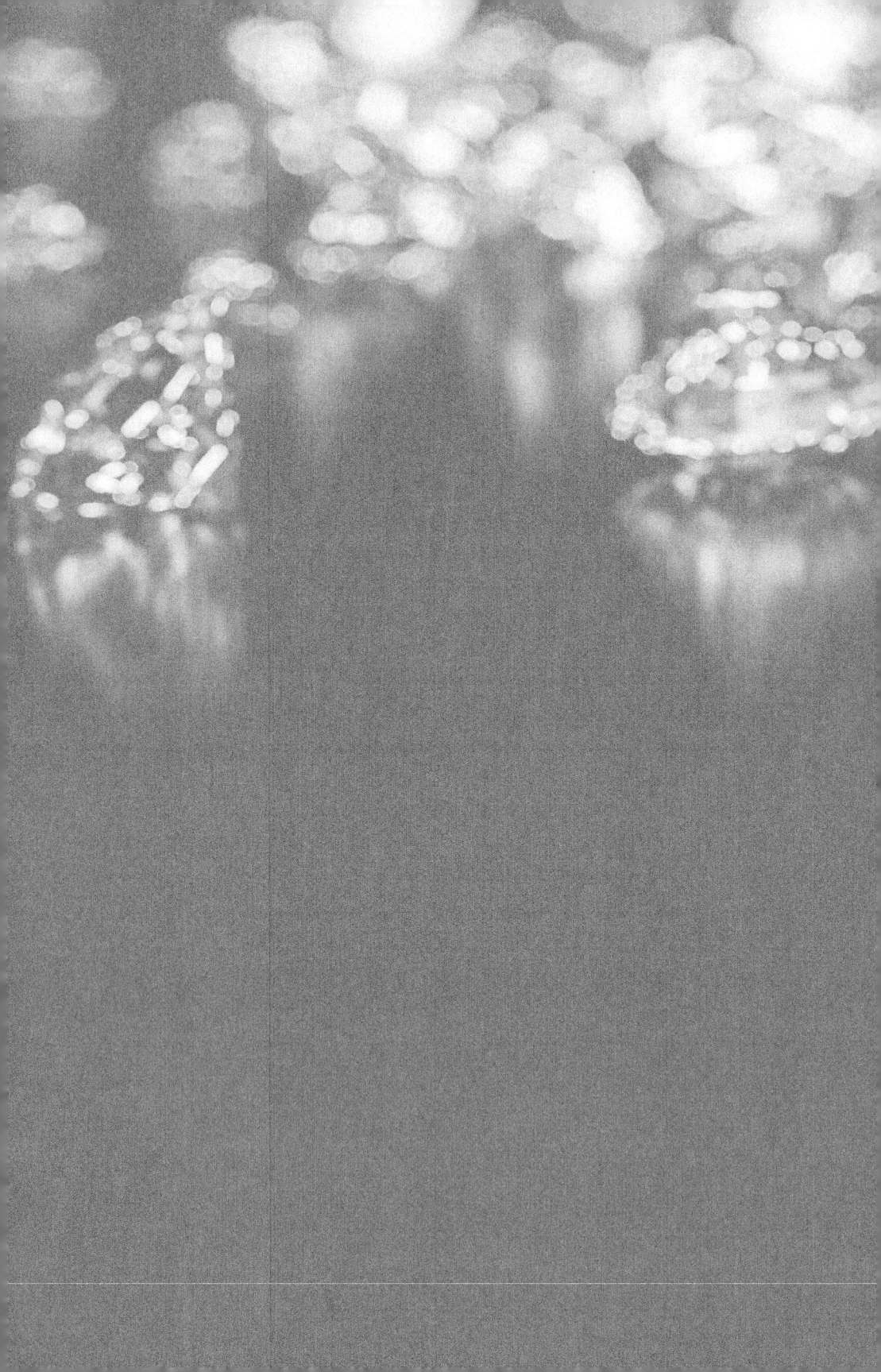

Chapter Thirty-One

Olivia
Year Thirteen
June

I feel oddly lost during the weeks following our headmaster's demise. It's like I had this big goal, this objective to work towards, and now my life is empty, devoid of purpose. I've been accepted to a bunch of great universities that I could begin in September—provided my A-level grades are good enough, of course—but now it doesn't feel as exciting as playing with secrets the way we did at prom.

I'm bored and lost, and I hate it.

So I do what feels right, which is to lose myself in coursework. Going to a top university doesn't sound like the dream it once was, but I still want to have options at the end of it. More than ever, I am convinced an office job and a picket fence with two point five kids isn't the future I want. Instead, I'll take what I learn and apply it to make my life exactly what I've always envisioned. One of travel and luxury, perhaps with some thieving and manipulation on the side. They say your school days are when you learn what you want to be when you grow up, and for me, apparently, that involves working in the shadows.

Rory, Ellie, and I spend the last two weeks before our exams studying like our lives depend on it. I also take more breaks than I care to admit where Zach fucks my brains out and I return to my rooms relaxed and deliciously loopy. He sometimes even walks me there.

For once, the guys' plans are better defined than mine. Roark is hellbent on studying Computer Science at Oxford, and Lord Arondale promised he'd get him a scholarship, which made Max seethe. Surprisingly enough, Zach wants to go to med school. When I asked him about it, he said it was the only career where he could get paid for cutting people open without going to jail. Obviously, I left it at that.

Viraj was accepted at Columbia in New York, and will be moving during the summer. Selling the idea to his parents was hard, but he somehow managed, promising them that graduating in international law would be an asset to their business. He isn't wrong.

And just like the rest of his family, Max will study business at the Imperial College of London. We'll all go our own ways, and that's definitely adding to my morose mood.

"You know," Ellie said one night when we were discussing my concerns in our room. "You could come with me next year, instead of going straight to uni." She's taking a gap year. She's planning on travelling the world, doing odd jobs and woofing—helping with harvests in exchange for food and board—to support herself. I think it's completely out of character for her and insane, but then again, when has that ever been an issue for me?

The Cleanup

My real issue with making plans is that no matter what, I'm afraid it'll feel like I'm losing more than I'm gaining.

Why do things have to change?

The day before our last exam, Rory, Ellie, and I are still studying after dinner when she declares she's beat and is leaving to go crash in our room. There is still an exercise that's resisting me, and I want to get it, so I stay at our table at the library instead.

"Did you understand the solution for exercise ninety-eight of chapter twelve?" I ask Roark. I'm a good student, but he kicks my ass in calculus.

"Why are you even studying that?" he questions, a brow raised. "They're additional, super challenging ones, you know that. The chance of anything remotely similar being in the exam is absurdly low."

"I want to be thorough, is all." It's a lie. I don't want to go to bed. Because if I sleep, time will fly, then it'll be tomorrow night already and the year will be over.

Taking my textbook in my hands, I round the table and sit next to Rory. "I don't understand how they know what x is, here," I prompt.

He explains multiple times, repeating it in different ways until I finally understand. "Oh, I get it now!" I exclaim. "I can't believe I didn't see this before. Sorry for disturbing you, that was a dumb question."

Rory lays a shy, soft hand on my forearm, and our eyes meet. "Your questions are never dumb. This was difficult." He takes a deep breath then says, staring at the table in front of us, "In fact, I think you're the smartest person I know." He's too serious for me to toss a smartass answer back at him, so I stay silent, sensing there's more to it. "I really like it." His eyes snap back to mine. "I really like you."

He's frowning a little, and bracing himself, as if preparing for rejection. We're alone in this corner of the library, so I answer his confession the best way I know how.

I palm his cheek and kiss him softly, my lips caressing his in the most tender contact. He doesn't move at first, then starts tracing designs on my forearm with his thumb, in an unsure, encouraging caress. I press our lips harder together, hoping he'll part his for me.

Suddenly, I hear footsteps behind us and a voice I know all too well whisper-shouts, "Are you fucking serious?" Max. Shit.

I break our kiss. The moment has passed. "What are you doing here?" I ask, voice colder than intended.

Max recoils as if I'd hit him. "I came to ask you if the rumours I'd heard were true about you and Zach. I couldn't believe it, but now, I guess it's fitting. The psycho and the penniless geek. I guess you must really like losers."

I'm halfway between tears and rage. "What are you talking about?" Rory asks.

"Apparently, your little *girlfriend* has been fucking Zach for months!" Max exclaims. "All this time, they've been doing freaky shit while she flirted with the rest of us so we'd help her with her crazy-ass plans!" He throws his arms in the air.

"Max, no," I protest. "It was never like that."

"Why didn't you tell us, then? That you two were together?"

"Because we're not. Again, it's not like that." It's not like anyone could ever date Zach. He once mentioned that the construct makes no sense to him. Why test out a variety of people when he's already found his obsession? But with his attention come threats of pleasure and pain, and I'm helpless to resist. Our plan of flying under the radar lasted a whole school year, but apparently, someone recently found out and started the rumours that led to Max cornering me here.

Roark grabs my hand, making me look at him. "Via, is this true or not? Are you and Zach sleeping together?" A world of hurt flashes in his blue-grey eyes, and I hate the words that will leave my mouth before I even say them.

"Yes, it is true. Rory, I promise I wasn't keeping it to myself to manipulate you."

"Why, then?"

"It just felt private." And it's the truth. The honest, simple truth. Roark looks away, and my heart breaks a little. "Rory—"

The Cleanup

"Don't, Olivia," he cuts me off. "It's okay, you don't owe me anything anyway. I just believed... but it was stupid. That's on me. I'm going to bed now."

"Rory," I call again, but he ignores me, gathering his stuff and heading out of the library.

I start gathering my stuff, too, ignoring Max because I do not want to see his face right now.

"And to think I asked you to prom," he says. The disgust is audible in his voice. "I fought over you, when all this time you were just manipulating us like everyone else and fucking that psychopath."

"Don't call him that!" I turn to face Max, fists clenched. It's an accurate description, but still, the word sounds gross in his mouth. "And I told you when you all asked me to prom that I couldn't decide between you all without someone getting hurt. And I didn't. I respected your stance and let it be. Instead, I picked myself, and I'll never regret that. Zach and I have something, yes. And I won't apologise for that. And I also won't stand for you tearing him down."

"Why? That's what he is, you know! Why are you defending him? Are you in love with him?!"

I open my mouth to protest and realise I don't want to lie. And saying I don't love Zach would be a lie. I do love him, in a weird, twisted way that makes the dark part of my soul happy. But at the same time, I love all of them. Zach, Roark, Viraj, and Max all hold a part of my soul that has somehow become theirs over the course of the last two years.

"This is disgusting," he says. "I can't believe I fell for it."

I see red. Because it wasn't like that, and he's twisting everything. Contorting everything into so many knots because in no universe would the four of them be receptive to the fact that it's possible to love more than one person. I wanted to go to prom with all of them, but he clearly saw that as selfish on my part. Maybe it was. But it doesn't change the fact that I want them all, and each for a genuine reason.

"You know what, Max?" I stand from my chair and crowd his

space, poking at his chest. "Maybe the reason why you didn't see me treating you, V, or Roark any differently than I treat Zach is because it was real, all of it. Maybe I flirted with you all because somehow I fell in love with all of you. Maybe that's why I wanted you close."

"So that's your explanation. That you're in love with four guys? This is sick."

I'm done with this conversation. "Max, just because your father has a limited amount of love to give doesn't mean the same thing applies for everyone else."

My stuff is already mostly in my bag, so I swing it over my shoulder and head to the library exit, shoulder checking Max on the way out.

He doesn't move to follow me, and I can't decide if I even want him to. Halfway to our dorm, a stray tear escapes from my eye. Once that first one is rolling down my cheek, I can't hold in the others.

Not unlike the day of our first time together, an arm snaps out of a dark corner of the hallway and grabs me, sending me crashing against a rock-hard chest. I breathe in his unmistakable scent of copper and peppermint and instantly relax.

"What happened, Little Thief?" Zach whispers in my ear. "Who hurt you?" Releasing my waist, he cradles my face in his hands, drying my tears with his thumb. "Point me in their direction, and I will skin them alive."

A snort-laugh escapes me. "Please don't. It was stupid."

"Who was it?" he asks again, making me look at him. His caramel eyes are full of concern and barely controlled rage.

"No one. It's okay, I'll be fine." I inject steel into my voice, hoping he will buy it. "I'm stressed, that's all."

"Fucking Roark, Max, and Viraj," he grunts.

"No! Wait, how do you know? And Viraj didn't do anything."

"They're the only people you would protect this way." He kisses my forehead.

"Please don't hurt them."

He looks at me like I'm exasperating. He sighs, even as his

muscles remain tense and his fist clenches at his side. "Fine. I won't hurt them this time. But only because it would hurt you, Little Thief."

I let out a big breath, my tears almost dry now.

Scrunching his nose like this is physically costing him, he asks, "Do you want to talk about it?"

The laugh that escapes my lips is real this time. Zach's therapist is rubbing off on him.

"No. Definitely not. But thank you for asking." Hey, if he wants to become more human, you bet your ass I'm going to encourage him. "Zach?" I ask as we start to walk in the direction of my room.

"Yes, Little Thief?"

"I think I'm going to need some space."

Zach stops dead in his tracks and grabs my hand, pulling me into him. His right hand grabs my hair and wraps it around his palm, controlling my head. Bending my head backwards to the limit of pain, he makes me look at him. "Never apologise for listening to your own needs, Little Thief. Nobody else will do it for you." Zach brings our faces closer together and whispers against my lips, "I will give you the time and space you need, but remember, I'm yours. It means someday, I will hunt you down. I will find you, and we'll have months of separation to catch up on. Are you sure you're ready for this?"

I nod as much as his tight grip around my hair allows me.

"Very good. I will wait then. For a bit."

He abruptly lets go of my hair, and we head back to my room in silence. Ellie is already asleep when we arrive, so I sneak inside without a noise and go directly to bed.

THE CALCULUS EXAM I WAS STUDYING FOR LAST NIGHT WENT well. I poured all the rage and injustice I felt yesterday into the solving of the equations, and the bitches yielded before my might.

Or something like that.

This morning, Roark and Max avoided me, which hurt more than their words from last night. I thought we had built more than this, and we should be able to talk things through. Zach has followed me everywhere like a second shadow though, and it warmed my broken heart a little.

Right after lunch, Viraj corners me as Ellie and I go back to our room. "Can I talk to you for a minute?" he asks, blocking my way.

Has Max spoken to him? Roark? After answering the litany of questions for the exam, the least I can do is have the civil discussion I was hoping for with the others. Remembering that he's done nothing wrong, I nod.

He pulls me inside an empty classroom as I gesture to Zach that everything will be okay so he doesn't murder our innocent Indian friend on the spot.

"I heard about what happened yesterday in the library," he starts, getting straight to the point. Fuck.

"And?" I prompt.

"Well, I guess I thought that Max's loss might be my gain." What exactly has he heard? I guess we were being pretty loud, so it's not too surprising that the rumours have started, but how distorted is his information? "So I thought I'd ask you if you wanted to move to New York with me."

I blink. Several times. What the... What? "It would be fun," he continues. "It'd be a change of scenery. I bet you could get into an incredible university there too. And in a city that big, we could definitely get up to no good." He flashes me a tentative smile.

Fuck. The thought isn't appealing at all. Living with V would remind me every single minute that passes the others aren't there. This feels like slowly dying and not like the fresh start it appears I need.

"No," I say. "I can't, V."

"Why?" He frowns. "Is it because it's true, and you're in love with Zach?"

Ah, shit. The anger from yesterday is starting to resurface. "No, it's just... I can't just move to the States, V. My family doesn't have the kind of money yours has. It wouldn't work."

V grabs both my hands in his. "I could help you if you need it. Money doesn't have to be an issue."

My next words are harsh, but he's not listening, nor is he showing any signs of talking this through logically. Rather, it's like slapping a bandage over a bleeding artery and hoping for the best. "No, V. I don't want to move to New York with you. That's why I won't do it." I remove my hands from his, and when I look up, the expression on his face is of pure shock. "I'm sorry, I didn't mean—"

"I know exactly what you meant."

And he leaves the room. Fuck. What do I do? Do I run after him and explain? But also, fuck him. Fuck them all. It's not as if I'd promised I wasn't sleeping with anyone. It's not as if I was questioning who they were fucking. Why do they think it was okay to judge me for my sex life? We're teenagers, for Christ's sake. We're learning this shit as we go.

If adults can't get their shit together enough to communicate, how are five hormone-fuelled adolescents supposed to? The whole year, I was a single, pretty good-looking eighteen-year-old, and I decided to fool around with my friend. There was nothing wrong with that.

I straighten my back, lift my chin, and head back to my room, staring the whispering students dead in the eyes as I pass. Every single one of them averts their gazes.

When I get to our shared room with Ellie—calculating the small nest egg I've been hoarding and factoring in work to pay for room and board—I barge in, announcing, "I'm in for the world tour! When do we leave?"

"FUCKING HELL, O! FORGET YOUR FREAKING PEN, WE'LL MISS the plane if you keep looking."

I could have sworn I had taken it with me. It was in my suitcase when we left St Stephen's, and it should be here somewhere.

Yesterday, my parents came to pick me up the day after our last exam, and so did Eleanor's. The six of us went out for dinner at a pub near the hotel and are staying near St Stephen's before the two of us jet off. We discussed our world travel plans for the gap year over fish and chips, and our parents exchanged information to keep each other in the loop during our trip.

It's the morning after the info-dump dinner, and her family is driving both of us to the airport, and not finding my pen—the one with the perfect balance, the one the guys came together to steal for me—is driving me batshit crazy.

"Olivia, let's *go*," Ellie whines. "I promise I'll buy you one at the airport."

I want to scold her for being insensitive, but I can't. She doesn't know all the events that happened and made this pen so important to me.

She doesn't know admitting that I lost it would feel a lot like a definitive goodbye.

Like admitting I had lost something else.

Someone else.

Or several someones, as it happens.

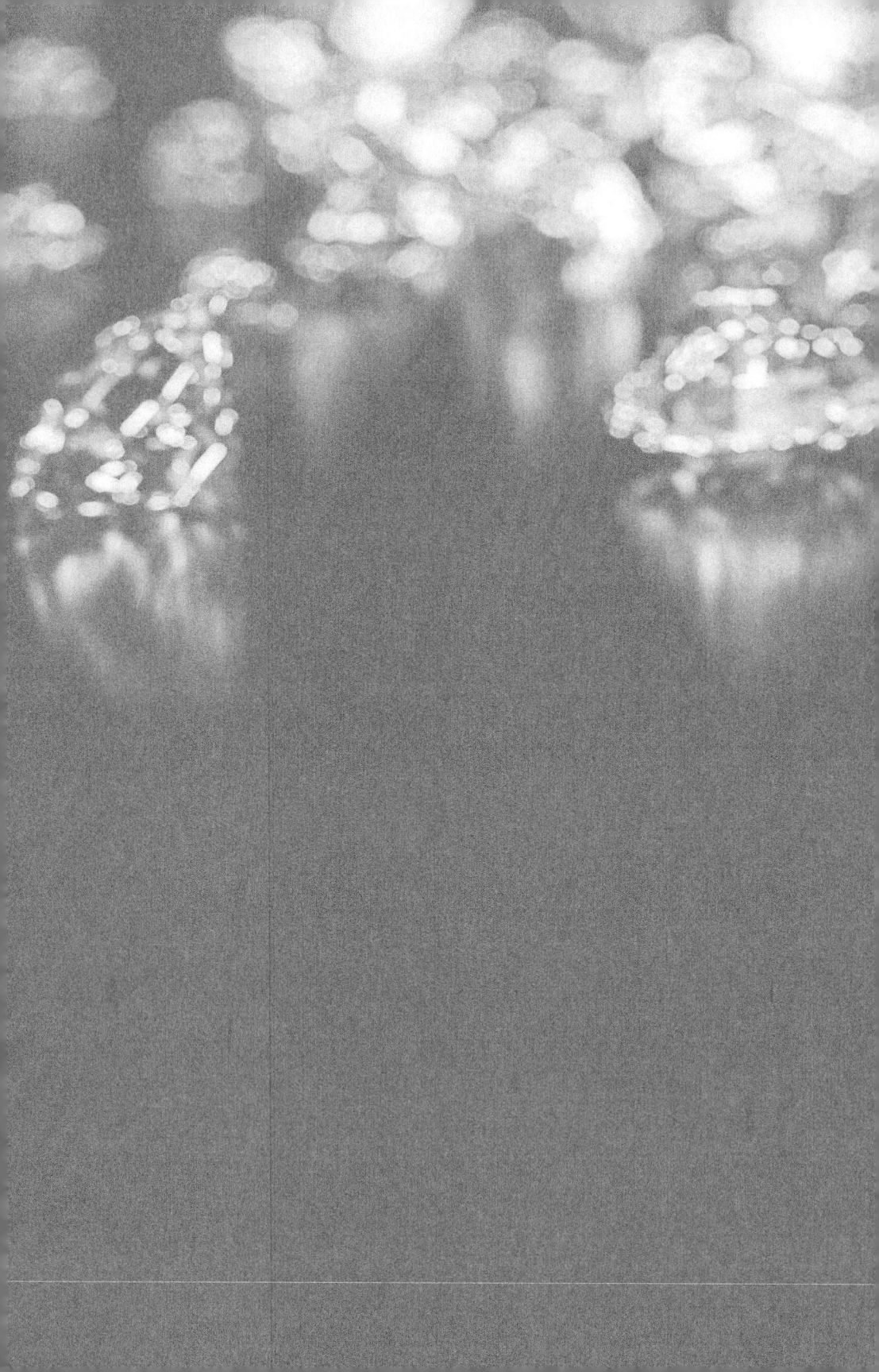

Chapter Thirty-Two

Viraj
Present Day

"We need to get her to a hospital," Max says as we get inside the car.

Zach and I answer in perfect synchronicity, "No." We turn to face each other, disbelieving. I don't think we've ever agreed on anything before.

"The Bratva is still looking for us." I get situated in the driver's seat. "There aren't enough hospitals in the region for us to hide. Especially since they know she's been hit."

Zach pulls Ollie's leg onto his lap so he can see her injury. Roark's beside me in the passenger seat, but his eyes keep going back to our girl. Max cradles Olivia's head on his lap.

"Also," Zach starts, "French doctors barely have any education on gunshot wounds unless they're in a metro area. And this type of injury is so unusual here that they have time to forget what little they learned in med school. I'm not letting any of them touch her."

"But you have the necessary skills to save her?" Max questions. "The UK isn't particularly famous for its shootings either."

"I'm self-taught." A devious smile stretches Zach's lips, the psychopath no doubt remembering the guinea pigs he practised on. Max seems to understand leaving it at that is the better option, and I sigh in relief. I don't want to know what Zach did to make him confident around gunshot wounds.

"Interpol is our best bet. The plan remains the same," I say.

"Agreed." Zach nods in approval.

"I texted Ellie to tell her we're coming. They're at the rendezvous point already." I look to the side, and sure enough, Roark is holding Ollie's phone in his hand.

"You have her password?" I'm incredulous. All this time, he could have stopped the unbearable music and didn't?

Roark just shrugs.

Okay, time to gun it.

We put the things we couldn't live without in the trunk yesterday, so the car is heavier than the other times I've driven it. It's still a technological marvel, though, and the engine starts without a noise. Before entering the car, I also recovered the diamond from Ollie's sports bra.

When he finished the climb, Roark explained how we'd been found because of a tracking device, and that they'd thrown it off the cliff. Fuck it, so long as we got what we came for and Natasha's guards can't follow us from here, we should be fine. We just have to get Ollie some help.

Calmly driving the car, I head in the direction of the mountains. Just like our test drives, I follow the speed limit until we reach the side roads, then I push the Porsche to its maximum, pressing the pedal to the floor.

Cold sweat runs down my spine every time I hear Ollie whimper in the back seat. Her state is audibly worsening. Zach's face is carefully devoid of expression, but his knee is taken with nervous tremors. Max looks like he's going to puke.

Seeing me watch him, he explains, "The bullet was meant for me. She jumped in front of it."

"It's not your fault," Roark says.

"Yes, it is. I could have climbed quicker and been more careful. If I had, she'd be fine now."

We all fall silent after that. What is there to say? Olivia dying would destroy us. I could bear living without her knowing she's alive and well, but will life still have its flavour if Olivia Wraith is not here to witness it? What will be the point of winning medals if I know she's not stalking me and hacking into the cameras of the award ceremonies? My wins aren't wins at all if she isn't alive to see them.

Maybe I'd join Zach on that pyre.

My emotions are pure turmoil in my chest as I drive faster than I've ever driven before.

A nondescript black SUV starts closing in on us about halfway to the meeting point.

"Oh, fuck no, you don't," I mutter. How the hell did they get up the mountain and into a car? They must have had people outside the borders of the city.

I saw a bunch of sketchy looking people eyeing us as I drove, but I assumed it was because of the beauty of the car—most of them probably were just admiring the engineering. But if I were Natasha, I'd have set eyes on the roads to spot us if we ended up surviving the climb. That must be what happened.

Or we were somehow tracked again, and I have no clue how, so we're screwed.

"Are our phones traceable?" I ask Roark.

Despite the direness of the situation, he snorts. "Of course not."

I open my mouth, but he beats me to it. "Trust me, V, they're not.

Neither is this car, our computers, or even Via's dildo hard drive. If you lose them, we're clear."

Their car is expensive, and they're driving at about twice the speed limit to catch up to us. That can only be Natasha's men on a mission to kill us and recover the diamond.

Not going to happen.

I take an abrupt right and enter a side road, passing through villages and across rivers using the mountain roads as a race track. As soon as the SUV isn't in our line of sight, I switch off the head and tail lamps to take advantage of the mountain dusk light to hide.

At this point, I have done enough recon on these roads to drive with my eyes closed, so the lack of headlight is just a formality.

A pained moan escapes Olivia's lips.

"She's getting worse," Zach says, panicked. "We have to get there soon."

"She won't make it through the hike." My mind is going as fast as the car I'm currently driving. What was Interpol thinking, giving us a meeting point that remote? I know, discretion. But fuck discretion, Olivia is d—No! Olivia cannot die.

Fuelled by rage, I drive, trusting my honed reflexes and memory not to send us over a precipice.

After what feels like an eternity, we arrive at the trail's starting point leading to our rendezvous. I stop the car and look in the rearview mirror. Ollie's shivering now, and I can't bear to look at her.

"Can't we attempt a blood transfusion?" Max asks.

"Her survival chances are still better if we walk," Zach says. "This isn't Hollywood. I can't do a blood transfusion with a pencil and a knife."

"We can take turns carrying her," Roark offers.

"It's still a two-hour hike through the forest. It would be fine if we stashed the car and all of us could walk it, but that's not really an option anymore." My knuckles turn white on the steering wheel. "But I have an idea. Roark, unlock her phone and get me Ellie."

THE CLEANUP

She picks up on the first ring, her voice loud over speakerphone. "O, is everything okay?"

"Eleanor," I say. Only one word and she knows something's wrong. I said her name like a warning and a threat, all at once.

"Viraj. What happened?" she answers in a similar tone.

"Ollie's down. She was shot in the leg, and it's bad. Natasha's men were tailing us, but I lost them. We're at the beginning of the trail, and we have the diamond, but there's no way Olivia will make it through the hike. You have to get us that chopper here now."

"Give me a minute." She mutes the phone, no doubt to talk to the pilot. "Viraj," she says, and her voice is pleading. Fuck. "He said no. He can't take the risk to meet you so close to a public area." I punch the steering wheel, making a brief honk erupt from the car.

"She's going to die. She's in this because of you, and she's going to die."

"Don't you think I fucking know that?! I can't fly a chopper, asshole, or I would come and get her myself." It sounds like she's seconds from crying.

"Eleanor," I say, my voice calm, bland, cold. "Hand the pilot your phone, please." I connect the call to the car's loudspeakers and nod in Roark's direction. His laptop is on his knees—thank fuck he'd stashed it in the car before everything went down along with Ollie's dildo hard drive—and the voice recognition software he developed a few years ago is already running. When he mentioned it during our first week together in London, Olivia went goo-goo over it and they've been testing it non-stop on the rest of us.

"Hello," a male voice resonates in the enclosed space of the car.

"Good evening, Agent..." I pause; maybe he'll be dumb and give me his name.

"'Sir' is enough," he says instead. It was worth a shot. But the software is already running, so it doesn't matter if he'd rather keep his identity to himself. It won't happen.

"So, sir, it is my understanding that you won't fly the chopper to meet us."

"That's correct. I have orders." His voice is rough, as if he doesn't use it very often.

"Well, let me tell you something, sir." My tone becomes threatening. "If I were you, I would. Orders be damned. Because you've got a group of very dangerous men gathered together in a car, and the love of their lives is bleeding out on top of them." Yes, I said the 'L' word. I don't care. "Let me introduce my colleagues so you'll know exactly how much trouble you and your hierarchy are in.

"My name is Viraj Goenka. My parents own one of India's conglomerates. I'm filthy rich, and that alone should be enough for you to think twice before making an enemy out of me. But I'm also a partner in one of the most prominent law firms in New York City, and if this woman dies, I promise you Interpol will face the biggest scandal it's ever seen. I will sue the fuck out of your entire organisation until you have no tears left to cry. I will broadcast everything I know on every media outlet that will listen to me, and I guarantee there will be a metric tonne of them. And whoever says no, I will bribe them to high heaven to run the story. I'm sure Fox News would love the scoop on a diamond full of state secrets ending up in the hands of the Russian Bratva.

"So this is your first warning, sir. Save this woman, or you'll have World War III on your hands. I will personally make sure of it."

"Do it, then," the man challenges. "You have no proof."

Right that second, Roark confirms with a nod that we have him. "I'm glad you mentioned this, sir, because see, I'm not the only occupant of this car. Right next to me is Roark O'Sullivan. You probably don't know his name, but I can guarantee he's designed at least one of the apps on your phone." Roark angles the computer so I can see the man's file he found, all because of that man's voice. "By the way, how is your aunt Susie? Is the leak in her plumbing fixed, or should we go there and help her?"

The Interpol agent starts breathing harder, and I continue. "Now, the third occupant of this car—who's currently staunching the bleeding gunshot wound of his soulmate—is Maximillian Arondale

IV. I will let the industry and press loose on your ass if Olivia doesn't make it safe and sound, but he will pit the aristocracy against you. You know these old families have more connections than a tree has branches, right? Well, he's the heir to one of them. And he'll destroy you.

"But even before you get worried about your reputation and career, I think you should be scared for your life. Please Google these exact words, 'Crawford Prep 2007.'" I exaggeratedly articulate the words, making my threat clear. "There was a scandal that year; you'll find it easily. Cats were massacred, blood everywhere, and a teacher disappeared. Shortly after, a student was expelled, and the only school that would take him in was Saint Stephen's. Can you find his name for me?" Zach preens when I mention his exploits.

I hear the agent swallow, then he says, "Zachary Bennett."

"Hello, sir. Although, I go by Doctor Zachary Bennett now. Very nice to meet you. I really hope your aunt's issue is fixed. Plumbing can be such a chore. And just so you know, that teacher got what he deserved." Zach's voice is cold, terrifying. If the chopper smells like excrement when it arrives, we'll know the agent shat himself, and I wouldn't blame him.

Still, I continue. "That same student made it on to the national news once, and that was fifteen years ago. His therapist attributed his improved behaviour to the methods of St Stephen's. But the reason he never went on a rampage again wasn't a method. It was a person, and she's currently bleeding out in his lap.

"As I said, if I were you, sir, I'd make sure she lives."

I'm panting as I finish my speech. I've done everything I could to get him to cooperate and give Olivia a fucking chance at surviving this. There's no alternative. I may have just shot us all in the foot by threatening his life, but if Interpol wants this diamond that badly, they need to fucking move their asses.

All the rhetoric I learned while practising law went into my discourse. If that doesn't make him fly here, I'll carry her up to the rendezvous point, but Olivia's chances of survival are much better if the chopper comes to us.

I mentally go through my words, and a sort of eureka moment happens in my mind. It's never made sense why Olivia wanted us all. But now that I've had to detail all the ways we'll destroy him if she doesn't make it to a stranger, I get it. We're powerful, smart, dangerous men and utterly devoted to her—even me, who refuses to admit it.

And she's never been one to shy away from her emotions or needs, so the moment she saw a possibility to have us all, she started scheming to make it happen, playing the long game.

It's irrefutable now; she won. Because if she makes it, I'm never leaving her side again.

It took her almost fifteen years, but Olivia Wraith finally made me see the truth.

I can't live without her.

And I don't want to.

Even if that means I'm living with the others too.

I lift my eyes and look at the others in the rearview mirror. They all wear a mix of emotions on their faces—anxiety, fear, sadness, but also pride and determination. My eyes then lock on to Zach's. The nod he addresses me with is almost respectful.

The phone clicks. "We'll be down in ten minutes," the agent says before hanging up, and a relieved sigh leaves my chest. She will be okay. I refuse to consider the alternative.

"Can someone put some music on?" Olivia suddenly slurs, voice raw with pain. "I loved the speech, V-card, but if these are my last moments on this planet, I deserve at least one good song."

Do I let her pick the tune? No doubt she'll use this as an opportunity to torture us.

I sigh. The woman is fucking dying. "Song?" I relent.

"'The Bad Touch' by Bloodhound Gang," she manages to articulate.

"Come on!" Max protests. "Liv, no!" The music starts playing anyway.

"I love you all. Not like someone loves their friends. Love, love. I'm in love with the four of you." Before we have time to say anything, she passes out again.

A stunned silence invades the car when the music ends.

She can't die. I look at Zach in the rearview mirror, and he shakes his head. His index and middle fingers are at the base of her thumb, measuring her pulse.

"We have to keep her awake," I say.

Getting out of the car, I angrily open the door right by her head and kneel in the dirt so I can whisper in her ear. "Ollie. Ollie, wake up." I gently slap her cheek, hoping to jolt her awake. "Ollie, you're stronger than this." I'm losing my shit, and it's turning me into a mushy sap. "You're fucking unbeatable, okay? A bullet isn't stronger than you." Her eyes open, feebly, just enough for me to see a bit of blue and the brown spot staining her left eye. It's never looked so beautiful.

Her hand lifts almost imperceptibly before falling back down again. "V," she mumbles.

"I'm here, love. I'm not going anywhere. You have to hang on; the chopper will be here any minute now. You did it. You stole a diamond from an impregnable city. You can't give up now."

"It hurts."

"I know." Shit, tears are running down my cheeks now. I caress her long hair, whispering soothing words and completely freaking out. Despite all my posturing, today has exhausted me. Adrenaline and rage are fading, and all I want to do now is stay with her. And for her to stay with me. "Ollie, keep your eyes open, and I'll tell you a secret."

The blue orbs flash open, and a pained chuckle escapes my throat. She never could resist a good secret. "Just a little bit longer, love. As soon as we hear the helicopter, I'll tell you." My hands tangle soothingly in the golden strands of her hair. There's a threat in the depth of her eyes now. Good. If she's plotting ways of ripping my balls off, then it means she's alive. "I promise it's a secret you'll want to hear. I even have a present for you."

I'm basically lying down in Max's lap to reach Olivia, but I don't fucking care. I want to be with her, and even having a monster dick way too close to my face won't deter me. It's trapped in his pants anyway.

I keep murmuring sweet nothings until we hear a rumble in the distance, and I whisper my secret in Olivia's ear.

Her eyebrows scrunch, and a flash of rage sparks in her eyes. Then she murmurs, "You stole it? And kept it?" and it seems like wetness is gathering at her lower lash line.

"I love you. I've always loved you," I whisper as my only answer, immediately standing up so I can't see the expression on her face.

The helicopter approaches as I stand in the middle of the field where it'll land, my hair slapping my face and clothes flying around my body.

If I never get to speak to her again, at least I'll have no regrets.

Our twelve years apart excepted.

Chapter Thirty-Three

Olivia
Present Day

My eyes blink open slowly, as if something heavy was weighing down my eyelids. My thigh hurts, a distant sort of pain, and I guess it'll flash back to life as soon as the anaesthesia wears off. An IV line is connected to my left hand, and the regular beep of the machines connected to me tells me my pulse is stable.

I open my eyes again, more decidedly this time. *Olivia Wraith is back in the land of the living, bitches!*

My pulse accelerates, and immediately, steps can be heard in the corridor. I look around. Viraj and Max are seated on chairs at my side, and Roark, Zach, and Ellie appear as soon as my heartbeat tells them I'm awake.

My eyes narrow in on V. "You. Give back my pen."

That's what he whispered to me as I was dying in the car. The ridiculous secret that made me hang on to his voice like a lifeline.

He stole my favourite pen from our school days and held on to it ever since. The motherfucking asshole.

It's also weirdly sweet.

He tilts his head in the direction of the bedside table, where my baby's waiting for me. It's gorgeous, all worn out, the messages the guys wrote me thirteen years ago still wrapped around it. I extend my free arm to grab it, and sure enough, it still has the perfect balance that made me fall in love with it all those years ago.

I twirl the pen around my fingers, staring at it in awe, making it jump over my third knuckle just like Zach taught me when we first met.

And then, just when I think it can't get any better, Viraj pulls the cap out of his pocket. "When Max and I crash-landed on Mr Hall's desk, it went skittering across the room. I found it wedged under one of the desk's feet a week later. By then, we'd already fixed this one's balance and I just couldn't bring myself to hand this back to you or pitch it in the trash."

My eyes water hearing that. The whole fucking time, he had it.

"I'm sorry to interrupt this touching reunion," Ellie says. "But how are you feeling?"

"Better now that my baby's back." I hug the pen and cap to my chest for a moment before returning to the spinning.

Ellie rolls her eyes. It's okay, she never quite understood my obsession.

"O," she insists, grabbing my hand, preventing the pen from moving. I hate it when people do that. "Really. You almost bled out. Are you okay now?"

"I would be better if a certain someone hadn't stolen my favourite object from me." I pout.

Viraj scoffs. "You love that I kept it."

I glare at him, but he isn't wrong. I also remember his words from the car. Every single one of them. He said he's never leaving me again. Did he mean it?

Reading the turmoil on my face, Zach immediately reaches for my other hand as I stare into V's eyes. "I meant it," he confirms. "All of it. I already called the office to let them know I'll be working from home for some time."

"We all did," Max adds.

"You did?" I ask. He nods. "And how is John Henry going to survive without his daddy?" Everybody chuckles as Max frowns.

My teasing seems to finally convince them I'm okay. "Where are we?" I ask, suddenly noticing the fact that there are no windows anywhere.

"Interpol safehouse in Sanremo, Italy. I've been stationed here while you were working in Monaco," Ellie answers. "You had Natasha's men tailing you when we found you, so we had to fly fast and far to hide you somewhere safe and get you the surgery you needed. They had just reached the car as we were flying over the border."

"Surgery?"

"Yes, to remove the bullet, and do a blood transfusion. An Interpol medical team was prepared to do it, but Zach started growling at them, so they only stayed as backup while he operated."

I tenderly squeeze his hand, not-so-secretly loving his protectiveness.

"And now you have a scar that I didn't give you, but at least I had a hand in repairing, Little Thief. No one will ever touch this body again." His amber eyes dive into mine, as if trying to decipher the secrets of my soul.

Max clears his throat loudly.

"Fine, no one but the four of us," Zach amends.

Not breaking our eye contact, I say, "Thank you for saving my life, Doc." Looking around, I continue, "And thank you all for taking me to safety and helping me on this job. I could never have done it without you."

There's a pause, a heavy moment of silence.

"About that," Ellie says. "You guys aren't safe yet. We'll exfiltrate you and help you lie low, but Natasha has put a price on your head. You'll need a place to stay."

I raise my hand as if in school and looking for the teacher's attention, then wince when I'm reminded of the IV by a sharp, pulling pain. No regrets, my other hand was busy holding Zach's.

"Yes, O, what is it?"

"I have a plan for that."

A chorus of sighs, snorts, and chuckles answers me. Viraj pinches his nose between his thumb and index finger. "Of fucking course she has a plan."

"Excuse you," I protest. "I have a dangerous job and always knew I would make powerful enemies. Of course I have a place to lie low. Ellie, do you still have the dinosaur?"

"The dinosaur? What fucking dinosaur?" Her brows shoot up as she understands. "The onesie?"

"Yes, do you have it?"

She suddenly looks sheepish. "I do. It's comfortable. The guys always set the safehouse's AC way too cold, so having a comfy outfit to read books in when I'm alone is a must."

I blow her a kiss. "I knew you loved me."

"What the fuck are you guys talking about?" V throws his arm up in the air. "How the hell is a fucking dinosaur onesie going to help us?"

I ignore him. "Could you fetch it, Ellie, please?" I then turn to the incredulous lawyer. "Calm down, V-Card. Dinosaur onesies make everything better, everyone knows that."

The three others chuckle quietly, knowing full well my antics often hide carefully thought-out schemes. And V's anger, well, it's foreplay at this stage.

Ellie returns moments later, the spikey tail of the costume bouncing gaily as she power walks into the room.

She hands me the soft ball of fluff, and I turn it around to find the hidden zipper in the tail. It makes a funny noise as I slide it open, and I pull out five fake passports, a set of credit cards with all our new fake names on them, keys, and a phone that controls all the locks to my personal safe house and pet project.

"Are you kidding me?" Ellie asks, faking indignation. "Did I smuggle all this through customs for you?"

Roark laughs from the corner, noting the exasperation on Ellie's face and the ridiculousness of the whole situation. At least the grave look has been wiped away. His nose ring glints in the light, and I drag my eyes away from him to focus on Ellie.

"Yup. But I got your diamond back, so now we're even. And what they say is wrong. You should always look a gift dinosaur in the mouth. Or in the tail, in this case." I pause, frowning. "I'm sure there's a dirty joke in there somewhere."

"So, where are we going?" V asks.

I dive into his dark eyes with a smirk on my lips. "We?"

"We."

"The Maldives. I don't know about you guys, but I'm feeling tropical waters and lack of extradition laws. Plus, I might have built a small safe house there."

"How small?" Max immediately questions. "I've slept in enough bunk beds for an entire lifetime."

"Don't worry, Your Highness, you'll be fine. We'll let you on the top one. We all know you loved it in London." I'm just fucking with him. This house has been a project of mine—a hope, really—for years, and it's bigger than my London one. We'll be more than comfortable.

"You should leave as soon as possible," Ellie says in a strangled voice. "According to our intel, Natasha doesn't know you're here, but chances are, my former partner isn't the only one from our organisation she has working for her. If any information gets passed on, you have to be far, far away."

"Don't worry about us, Ellie. When she finds me, I'll win her over with my irresistible personality. Or I'll offer to steal shit for her so she'll forgive me. It'll be fine."

"Oddly enough," my bestie says. "I believe that. Just please don't steal anything from Interpol."

I wiggle my eyebrows. "Make sure your security protocols are on point, then." Letting go of Zach's hand, I shift carefully, mindful of my healing leg, and extend my arms to give her a hug. "I'm going to miss you."

"Be safe, O. And call me if there's a wedding. A vacation on the beach sounds pretty awesome now that I'm thinking about it. I'm happy for the five of you, even if we all knew it was just a matter of time."

My smile is wide when she breaks our hug.

Roark

Present Day

To Max's horror, we couldn't use the Arondale jet to fly to the Maldives. We had to fly commercial since Natasha knows who he is, and he can't be noticed at any cost, meaning economy class all the way, baby.

He complained the whole time, across multiple flights, and for a good two hours after we landed in Male. Olivia guided us to the taxi stop, and he finally shut up when we arrived at the harbour and Via gestured towards a gorgeous white yacht.

"*Floatable I*," Max reads.

Olivia shrugs. "I wanted to continue the line, but I didn't know how many Unsinkables would lie at the bottom of the ocean by the time we needed this one." Her cool-as-fuck expression as she says these words combined with Max's frown makes it hard for Viraj and me to contain our laughter. As usual, Zach's expression is unreadable.

The Cleanup

We embark, and the crew is almost immediately ready for our departure. Back in his usual level of luxury, Max finally shuts up, and we enjoy the sun and sea breeze in silence. This version doesn't have the same calibre of submersible as *Unsinkable II* had—may it rest in peace—but there's a two-seater down below for any maritime adventures Max wants to have in the future.

Olivia clammed up about our destination when we left the plane. We've tried questioning her about the house but couldn't get anything out of her. She seems almost nervous, and this intrigues me more than anything. Because of her leg, she walks everywhere using crutches, and that also makes her supremely grumpy, so we don't insist too much.

A small island appears in the distance. If I didn't know better, I'd say it was uninhabited. Dense vegetation crowds its middle, surrounded by white sand and turquoise water. I don't think I've ever seen a more beautiful place.

Olivia pulls the phone she got from the dinosaur's tail out of her pocket and starts typing lines of code as I watch her with interest. "Nobody gets on the island without this. It's probably the most secure place on the planet. Not even I can touch the sand if it's in lockdown mode."

"Did you try?"

"Of course I did. Right after I finished designing the security system."

"Do you—" I start before trailing off.

"—own the entire island? You bet your ass I do. I bought it after I completed my first big job."

"Does it have a name?"

"Yes." Her code finished, she lifts her eyes from the phone. "Welcome to Ekuverikan, Roark."

Before I have time to ask her if it means anything, she crutches herself over to the side of the main deck where we're getting close to a small pier.

The five of us walk down the gangway one after the other, Olivia fiercely watched by Zach and V as she's sandwiched between them. We have to cross the sandy beach, meaning V scoops Olivia into his arms and trudges forward while Max picks up the discarded crutches. Only once we're under the tree cover, do we see the gorgeous house Olivia built.

It's not small. Not by any means.

There are two floors, and the only reason why we couldn't see the roof tipping through the canopy is because it's precisely the same colour as the vegetation around it. Taking a closer look at the construction, I see that the house has been built around the trees, leaving the treeline intact.

Huge windows occupy an entire side of the building, offering an uninterrupted view of the sea, no doubt.

Olivia dials more code on her phone, and one of the glass doors slides open. "Welcome home," she says as the chorus of "Oops... I did it again" by Britney Spears erupts from hidden speakers.

A show of grunts, growls, and eyerolls erupts from our side. The reason I never changed Olivia's music choices even though I had access to her phone was that I realised why these songs were important to her. Sure some—like the one currently blasting—are a bit older, but the majority of them were popular when we were all in school together. I don't know if she held on to them because they reminded her of when we all got along, or if it's just because mid 00s bangers are her favourite, but the more we listened to her insanity, the more I enjoyed it.

We spend at least a good half hour exploring the palace Via built with us in mind. There's absolutely no doubt about that fact.

The house has six bedrooms, each decorated perfectly to the tastes of the guys and Ellie. Or that's what I assume, seeing the expression on their faces when they discover their space in this paradise.

Mine has a complete gaming setup that must have cost a fortune to import. The room is dark and cosy, perfect for spending hours in front of a computer.

The Cleanup

Via filled Max's closet with designer clothes, and all the fabrics are soft and luxurious. There's even a photo of John Henry above his dresser.

Zach and Viraj's rooms are pretty standard, but as we make our way through the house, Via comments, "There's a climbing wall out back, plus some bikes, scuba diving equipment, and I also bought kite surfing stuff that must be somewhere. And Doc, I set up a basement for the two of us."

Zach's eyes twinkle deviously at her words, but he doesn't respond.

The rooms surround an inside garden where Via also had a pool built, and this place is everything I never knew I wanted.

Groceries are delivered to the pier, and as we eat that night, Viraj finally asks the question that's been burning in my mind, "Did you always plan to bring us here?"

Olivia puts down her knife and stares at her plate, carefully wording her answer. "It wasn't a plan, not exactly. More like a dream, a hope, wishful thinking, even. I couldn't bear the idea of us never being together again, so I built this as a symbol that our reunion was possible. If we ever had the chance to be us again, I didn't want real estate to be an issue, I guess."

"When did you start working on this?"

She meets his eyes. "As soon as we finished school. It took me five years to save enough to buy the island. Then about two more to get the money for the construction. The work lasted for about two years, then the decoration and importation of everything we'd possibly need, another ten months. The house has been ready for us to move in for about a year."

For a minute, it looks like Viraj will get up and leave. Despite knowing Via so well, the man loves to believe he's in control. This house is just giant proof that he isn't—and never was.

Then, he stands up and kisses the shit out of her instead.

She protests because—if I understand the situation correctly—her mouth is full of fish. She manages to swallow and relaxes as he cradles her face in his hands.

Max clears his throat—that annoying sound he makes when he doesn't have the attention he thinks he deserves—preventing the situation from escalating.

Via looks at Viraj sitting back down as if her dessert has just been stolen from her. Out of the corner of my eye, I see Zach discreetly readjusting himself in his beach shorts.

This is fucking paradise, but I still have one thing left to do. One thing all the other guys have done, but I haven't.

"Via, would you like to take a walk with me?" Despite looking like a nearly two-hundred-pound Viking, I still behave like the scrawny nerd I was when we were in school sometimes.

"Sure, wanna go now? I'm full."

Fuck, I wanted more time. I nod. "Let's go."

Via grabs her crutches and tilts her head, signalling me to follow her in the direction of the beach. The night is pitch black, and we can barely see the waves, the noise they make is our only actual clue as to where they are.

Wrapping an arm around her back and swooping another under her knees, I carry her onwards and into the night. For a few minutes, I silently walk with Via in my arms until we reach the small pier where we arrived this morning.

I help her down and gesture for her to sit. Her hair is windblown around her face, and she looks happy. Genuinely and positively happy. I take a deep breath, inhaling the scents of the island and that cherry blossom perfume Via never stopped wearing. Five little words have been trapped in my chest for a lifetime. Five simple, easy words, but I haven't been able to let them out.

I've hacked nations, developed some of the most sophisticated apps and software in the world, but those five words, these twenty-six characters... They've resisted me.

Tonight, I'm going to set them free.

"I love you, Olivia Wraith."

Chapter Thirty-Four

Olivia
One year after graduation

My hands shake as I head to the cafe. Max and I are meeting for the first time since we fought.

We texted a few times while I was travelling the world with Ellie, and our brief exchanges have been, well, a whole host of things.

His first text sent me spiralling into a fit of rage and despair. It said, "I miss you," and after the words that came out of his mouth the last time we'd spoken, I couldn't handle it.

Ellie and I were staying at this hostel in Thailand, and after the message appeared, I got stupid drunk at a beach party then fucked a hot Australian under the cover of the trees while mosquitos went to town on my ass. It was my first time with anyone other than Zach, and I'm not ashamed to say it was boring as fuck.

Very mature, I know.

I still answered, "I miss you, too." Because even though we'd been asses to each other, it was true.

I missed Max's swagger and his never-ending confidence. I missed his irresistible charm and polished manners.

But most of all, I missed how his clever eyes took in people and instantly knew everything about them. How he could light up my day with a charming smile or a clever word.

After that, he sent more messages, and I always answered, but we never spoke about what happened. Our conversations were very basic, never going into details.

How are you?

How's the trip?

How's university?

Rory, V, and I had our own back and forth of texts as well, and I planned to meet with them, too. Even if I was pissed at them and hurt when school ended, the time away has helped me figure out that I still want them in my life, and I should have been more honest—or at least forthcoming—back then. I had lied by omission, and fuck, it was a bitter pill to swallow when I finally faced it.

Now that I'm back in London, I've decided to start with the hardest conversation, rip the Band-Aid off once and for all.

"Hello, Max," I say as I take a seat across from him. The menus haven't been delivered yet, so he hasn't been here for long. He chose a cute little cafe near the tube station, as if the proximity to an escape was part of his plan. I don't blame him.

"Hello, Olivia," he says, his dark eyes moving up to meet mine.

He's wearing a beige wool coat over a brown sweater and dark wash jeans. His short beard and hair are impeccably trimmed, and his nails neatly cut.

The scent of his cologne floats in the air, and it hits me hard as if I was time-travelling. Suddenly, I'm the Olivia I was a year ago, hiding and heartbroken in the corridors of St Stephen's after everything that occurred in the library.

We sit in silence for a moment, taking the other in. The waiter comes to take our order, then brings back our drinks: a coffee for me and an Earl Grey for him. He takes a sip of it and hums at the taste.

Max takes a deep breath, looking into the depths of his tea like he wants to drown in it, and I drag up the words from deep within my soul, ready to face the consequences of my actions. "I'm sorry," we say at the same time.

When our eyes meet again, we've got matching smiles on our faces.

"Ladies first," he says with an inviting gesture.

"You're much more ladylike than I am," I tease, taking a risk that jokes are okay despite the serious topics we're circling around.

The corner of his mouth tilts higher up. "Touché." He shrugs. "I'm sorry I was a dick to you. It was without a doubt the stupidest thing I've ever done. I was hotheaded and yelled when we should have had an honest, open conversation. I acted like an entitled asshole and expected you to become my girlfriend because I was nice to you—which isn't fair. I see that now. You had every right to sleep with Zach, and I regret what I said."

I'm trying really hard not to show how deeply his words touch me. My eyes shine with unshed tears, but I won't let them fall. "Your turn now," he prompts.

I let out an uneasy chuckle. "I'm sorry I was selfish and naive. I'm sorry I never told you guys about Zach. I did manipulate you all a little, but it was never intended to hurt you. It was because I liked you and needed you, and I'm a bossy-ass bitch sometimes. I'm sorry I made you angry and caused you to doubt me. I was a clumsy, greedy teenager, convinced her dreams would come true if she worked hard enough."

"So your dream was to have all of us?" he asks with a raised brow.

I pull out the shitty pen I had in my hair, making it cascade down my shoulders in a golden waterfall. "Yes," I say simply. I start playing with the pen between my fingers, and I can't help but compare it to the one I've lost. The one that reminds me of *them*. "And I accept your apology. What about you? Are we good?" Something tightens in my chest.

"I think I forgave you a long time ago. My temper got the better of me, but deep down, I knew you truly liked us; there was no way you were faking that kind of interest."

I bite my lower lip, repressing the huge-ass smile that wants to stretch out. The silence that ensues is a comfortable one. Max drinks his tea while I gulp down my coffee. I've been busy the past few days, and I need all the caffeine I can get.

"Have you been in touch with V and Rory?" I ask.

"Not really. My dad can't shut up about how well Roark is doing at Oxford, but that's all I know. And V is an athlete now, according to his social media. Though, are you and Zach still together?"

"Not really. Things aren't over, but he's been giving me space. He'll find me when he thinks it's time." As per our agreement from a year ago. He hasn't texted or called, but Zachary Bennett isn't the kind of lover who'll show his affection that way. If he even feels affection at all.

It's Max's turn to nod.

"Are you planning to talk to Roark and Viraj?"

"They're on my to-do list."

"So you're putting the gang back together, huh?"

Shaking my head, I explain, "No, not really. I just missed my friends and hope everything isn't ruined between us."

"Awesome. I can't say I've missed Viraj's arrogant ass. Imagine how much bigger his head must be now that he's won a bunch of competitions?"

I laugh; he's not wrong. "It'll be a miracle if he can step through doors at all." Max laughs with me, exposing his straight white teeth. If I look hard enough, I think I can see him missing his old rival nearly as much as I do. Maybe the verbal sparring partners at Imperial aren't of the same calibre. "And how have you been?"

"I'm good. I'm enjoying university life to the fullest and probably destroying my liver a little in the process, but things are great. My grades are even okay, so I got my dad off my back." He looks down at his tea again. "I also have a girlfriend."

"Really?" I exclaim. I start babbling as I brainwash myself into thinking it's not a big deal. "Who is she? How did you guys meet? Can I see pictures?"

"Her name is Laurie. She's really nice, you'd like her. And it's a boring story, really. We met at a party, hooked up, and now we're doing our thing. And there you go." I look at the picture he pulled up on his phone. She's pretty, with blonde hair a little lighter than mine and big blue eyes with no splotch of brown to stain them. A flicker of hope I had no idea still existed inside of me dies as I look at the screen.

"Is it serious?" I inquire.

"It's a little early to say. I like her, but only time will tell." And *ping*, the hope lightbulb is back on. "And what about you, what are your plans for the future?"

"What makes you think I have plans?" He just looks at me like I'm intentionally being dense. And I am, so I chuckle before explaining, "I'm going to do a combined bachelor's and entrepreneurship master's degree, and I'm creating a company at the same time. It's a lot of work so far, but I love it, so it's okay."

His brows furrow. "This all seems very... normal. What will this company be doing?"

"Cleaning offices, for the most part. There seems to be demand without enough supply in that sector." I meet his eyes, plastering the most innocent look on my face I can conjure.

"And will you need investors? This type of endeavour takes a lot of money."

"Nope," I say, popping the p. "I'm good."

"Liv, are you doing something illegal?"

I sigh. "Don't make me lie to you, Max. I want us to start over and not be connected by jobs or favours."

He looks at me with puppy dog eyes, and I know I'll tell him soon if he keeps insisting. Not today, though. Today we'll just be friends having a drink and reminiscing about old times.

Understanding my silence over this topic, Max changes the subject. "What will the name of this mysterious business be, then?"

"I'm thinking of calling it The Cleanup."

Epilogue

Olivia
Present Day

TODAY'S THE DAY I CAN OFFICIALLY DO STUFF ON MY OWN again.

It's been almost eight weeks since I got shot, and Zach insisted I take this time to just rest, meaning he growls at anyone who suggests any sort of strenuous activity.

You know, like stand up, reach for the remote control, brush my teeth. Anything, really, he insists on doing it for me.

I set the limit at teeth-brushing. No way am I not doing that on my own. I had to explain that it was my leg that got hurt, not my arm, but still, it was a negotiation.

I think my near-death experience scared Zach a little. It scared all of us, really.

When I got shot, we were too high up the cliff for anyone to recognise us, especially with our helmets and the rest of our gear on, so I'm not worried about Max being under any real scrutiny.

Still, like a true gentleman, he texted Natasha the week following the event, complimenting her speech as she gave his prize to the winner of the Grand Prix, and apologising for his abrupt departure. He even added he hoped to see her soon, but alas urgent business required his presence in India. I helped him draft the messages and had to refrain from puking all over his feet.

Because of the meds I was taking, of course.

Natasha answered that she understood, and she hoped nothing bad had happened. Snort.

To finish covering his tracks, I made sure someone looking suspiciously like Max got caught by The Sun having fun at one of Max's peers' bachelor parties. The pictures show the doppelganger with his face between a stripper's boobs—the perfect camouflage, if you ask me.

Nobody came for Max's body double, so he's off the hook. And before you ask, yes, I risked the life of an innocent actor to make sure my man was safe. Zach and I have more in common than most think.

Since my doctor insisted on complete bed rest, I had time to plot and plan things—after we established that typing on my computer wasn't life-threatening, of course.

I organised surprises. Four of them, to be exact, and now that it's almost time to reveal them, I'm freaking out a little. I have to ask them a very important question, and I don't like it. Everything's much easier when you just boss people around.

Letting people make their own choices is exhausting.

Still, I want that for us.

I've also spent a lot of time chatting with Ellie and scolding her in all caps because she does not immediately answer. Who knew working for Interpol kept her that busy? She's monitoring the Natasha situation. Apparently, the Russian psycho went on a rampage and is now trying to get the diamond back whatever the cost; hence, trying to find us—me.

But it's okay. She'll never find us on Ekuverikan, and the defence system I built on the island will protect us if it ever comes to that. The irony isn't lost on me that the name means friendship in Dhivehi. Like so many times before, friendship will protect us.

"Zach," I whine as he cleans up my scar to check everything is okay. "I promise I'm healed." I only have pink skin where the gaping wound used to be, but he still insists on disinfecting it.

Letting him do it is easier than arguing, so these days, I wait it out.

Plus, I kind of like being pampered.

Once he's satisfied I'm not dying from my scar, he palms my calf and says, "All good, Little Thief. You can stand now." I resist the urge to roll my eyes. I have been walking around a little when he's not looking, and I know my thigh is fully functional.

I mean, I wouldn't run a marathon, but going to the bathroom by myself is totally manageable.

Zach watches me with unblinking eyes as I slowly stand, searching for winces or signs that I'm not fully comfortable taking my first steps. He won't find any because I am completely at ease, aside from the intensity of his stare on my skin.

He's standing right next to the bed, and I take two steps to get close to him. He stiffens when my arms wrap around his middle. We've never been into PDA, he and I, but I want to change that. It's out of his comfort zone, but I always did like pushing his boundaries. If something truly upset him, he would have no reservations in telling me. Or showing me. Probably with a sharp object.

Snuggling against his chest, I whisper, "Thank you for taking care of me." His peppermint and copper scent envelops me, making me feel safe.

To my surprise, he tenderly strokes my hair with his hand and answers, "Always, Little Thief. Always." Then he kisses my forehead. "Go tell your men the doctor officially cleared you."

I steal a kiss before heading to the living room, pretending my tentative steps are a lot more assured than they truly are. After two months of lying down, my sense of balance is a little wonky, and my knees are slightly weak. I'm determined to not fall on my ass though, so I just focus on putting one foot in front of the other until I get to the living room.

Who's the idiot who built a house this big?

Oh, wait.

Roark, Max, and V are chatting, sitting on the massive sectional sofa as I approach. When they hear my steps, they turn towards me and watch me amble up to them with expectant eyes. I'm grateful nobody stands to help me because I can do it on my own. I need to after all the coddling lately.

Well, that, and Zach is probably walking a foot behind me to catch me if I fall.

I sit down on one side of the sofa, gathering my strength to say what I need to. Of course, we talked during my convalescence, but I was keeping the big talks for when I was declared fully functional again. They were so focused on getting me healed and managing things at home from abroad that adding to the stressors felt wrong.

I take a deep breath as they wait in silence, sensing that what I have to say is important. I grabbed my pen when I left my bed, and I start twirling it in my hand, the familiar weight in my hand comforting me.

"So," I start, "I wanted to say thank you. You came to Ellie's rescue, and I am forever grateful."

"Does that mean you owe us one?" Max teases. "Because I can think of ways for you to repay me."

I chuckle and relax a little at his joke. "Yes, it does." Now comes the hard part. "Speaking of, I wanted to tell you that you don't have to stay stuck on this island. If you want me to, I will arrange for you to go back to your normal lives. Natasha's hunt for the diamond can only go on for so much longer, and none of you were identified as far as we know, but I'm having Ellie check what she can from within Interpol. I'll come out as an international thief and take full responsibility for what went down in Monaco if I need to. I'll be on the run, but I'll gladly do it to protect you." I lift my gaze from my pen, looking each of my guys in the eye.

Rory looks a little lost, Max is exasperated, and V is amused. Zach is standing behind where I'm sitting on the sofa, so I can't see his expression, but he gently squeezes my shoulder.

V smothers a laugh with his arm and says, "Before I tell you my answer, there's something I need to know... Who are you and what did you do to Olivia?" We all laugh. I know, I'm usually the bossy type. He tenderly smiles at me, and I go all mushy inside. "Ollie, none of us are going anywhere. It might have taken you getting seriously hurt for us to figure it out, but we're family. We belong with you."

I meet the eyes of the others, and they nod silently. A cocky smile stretches on my lips. "Okay, then I have surprises for you guys. Gentlemen, prepare yourselves because we're going on dates."

Should I be insulted that they suddenly look worried?

We chat in the living room for a couple of hours, and I spend the time dodging questions about the dates and enjoying my newfound freedom. Around four, I tilt my head in Roark's direction. "Can I talk to you for a second?" He furrows his brow but stands up and follows me into the hallway.

A sheepish smile stretches on my lips, and I feel oddly shy. "I wanted to ask you something... Will you go out with me?" His entire face lights up, and I wonder why it took me fourteen fucking years to ask him that. Roark deserves all the love in the world and more. "I organised something for us tonight. Is that okay?"

"Of course, Via, what is it?"

"A surprise. I also got you an outfit, but you don't have to wear it if you don't want to." He looks at me like I just grew a second head.

Yeah, I know, I'm not used to giving people choices either. "Move along, then," I order as he stares at me. "We're already late!"

I power walk to my room—because Zach will skin me alive if he sees me run with excitement—and start getting ready.

For tonight, I picked a dark red silk dress with spaghetti straps. It demurely falls down to my knees, but flows around my body in a sinful way. I paint my lips with matching red lipstick and voila... I'm ready to go.

I got Roark a simple short-sleeved shirt to show off his tattoos and fitted black jeans, but still, he is a vision. His long blonde hair is loose and silky over his shoulders, and his piercings glimmer in the dim light of the corridor.

This man is fucking brilliant and gorgeous, and I plan to repeat it to him every day for the rest of our lives. "How do I look?" he asks, pointing at his body.

I make a show of giving him a once-over. "Edible. Let's go."

Wrapping my arm around his, I guide him out of the house. As we pass the other guys in the living room, they whistle and holler as I throw winks around. "What do I have to do to get the same treatment?" Max asks.

"Behave and be patient," I scold. "Your turn's tomorrow."

I decided to start with Roark because I know his insecurities run deep, and I didn't want him to think he wasn't my first choice. My problem is that I have four first choices, but the three others won't be hurt if they wait a little.

We head to the pier, where *Floatable I* is waiting for us. Once aboard, I lead Roark to the upper deck where a table is set with champagne and cheese and ham platters. "Via," Roark asks. "What is all this?"

"Our first date."

He smiles sweetly at me and deposits an oh-so-careful kiss on my lips. For a moment, I wonder why he isn't being more passionate. Then I remember the lipstick.

I know the crew is already on board, so I'm not surprised when the boat departs as soon as we sit.

I pop open the champagne, and we toast, taking in the beauty of the ocean all around us. When we arrive at an apparently random spot, the captain cuts off the engine and silence returns.

We drink our champagne without a word as the sun starts to set. Since we're so close to the equator, the night starts early, and soon, the ocean will be draped with the most gorgeous colours.

For now, we're waiting for something I want Roark to see. If we're lucky, we shouldn't have to wait too long.

About ten minutes after we arrive, it starts. The first humpback whale erupts from the water and falls back down in an explosion of spray, quickly followed by two others. They're far enough for us not to bother them, or them us, and we watch the sunset over the dance of the giant mammals.

"This is incredible," Roark whispers, eyes focused on the show.

"Rory, I wanted to ask you something," I say. If I don't do it now, there will never be a more perfect moment.

He wraps his arm around my shoulders and pulls me against him on the bench. "Of course, Via, what is it?"

I look him straight in the eyes, their colour eerily similar to the ocean around us. "Will you be one of my four boyfriends?"

The laughter that erupts from his chest is loud and carefree. "I would have thought we were already past that point."

"Are we?"

He focuses back on me. "I think we are. You took a bullet for Max, and I don't doubt you would do the same for me, V, or Zach. I would be honoured to be one of your four boyfriends."

"I love you, Rory."

"And I love you, Via."

As the night falls, the air becomes colder, and I snuggle into his larger frame, drinking champagne and watching the ocean.

"WE HAVE VERY DIFFERENT IDEAS OF WHAT CONSTITUTES AN ideal date, Liv," Max complains as we traipse through the bushes towards our final destination. He's been complaining ever since we left the house, saying that the branches are getting tangled in his hair, that there could be snakes—there aren't—and that he never agreed to this. He wanted the red dress and the boat ride, but I persuaded him that this was better.

The insects have to let up, though, or he'll hightail it out of here.

My surprise for Max is the most ambitious of the four, and it's not fully finished yet. For instance, the path from the house to the stable I had built isn't fully paved.

There will be a clear path, but with only two months to work and being bedridden, there was a limit to what I could accomplish.

It turns out importing two horses to the Maldives is harder than stealing a diamond from Monaco. Who would have thought?

The pile of paperwork I had to do almost drove me to insanity. John Henry and Marie Suzette had to get vaccinated, tested, and quarantined. I'll take the exact details of the process to my grave because I don't want to witness the meltdown Max will have if he learns about what his horse went through.

The foliage finally becomes thinner, and Max lays his eyes on the stable I built for him.

Incredulity colours every single one of his features. "Did you build me a stable?" he asks.

"I did."

"It's incredible. John Henry can live here too now." A knowing smirk stretches on my lips. "No," he says. "You didn't."

"Sure did." I wink. "We're going on a ride today. Now tell me this isn't the best date of your entire existence."

He beams and runs to the building instead of answering me.

I picked this location because right next to it is a wide clearing in the trees, which will be perfect for the horses to live. It's a little far from the house, but once the path is built, it shouldn't take more than ten minutes on foot to arrive.

I follow Max inside to find him hugging his stallion, and I head towards the smaller white mare in the stall next to him. I gently start

The Cleanup

petting her muzzle, whispering in Marie Suzette's ear, "I'm going to give them a little privacy so they can catch up."

Max is behaving like he just found a long-lost friend, asking loads of questions and behaving as if the horse will answer them all.

Part of me thinks it's ridiculous. Another part of me thinks it's adorable. I'm still on the fence about which one is winning the battle.

"Liv," Max suddenly calls. "Do you want to meet him?"

"Of course." I swear I'm being sincere. John Henry is even more important to Max than his goddamn boat—boats. Henceforth, the horse is important to me.

We'll just forget about the little episode when I blew up his yacht. John Henry should be safe.

"John Henry," Max says. "This is Olivia. She's your new mummy." Oh, what the fuck? I extend a tentative hand and caress the stallion's muzzle. He presses himself against my palm, as if to say he wants more. "He likes you," Max observes, beaming.

"He's gorgeous. Wanna go for a ride?"

"Are they well enough to go? The trip must have stressed them out."

I had a vet confirm that they were safe and sound, but I understand Max's concern. "We can walk beside them if you want, but I think it'd be good to take them out a little." Max nods.

We spend the afternoon walking around the clearing, guiding the horses with lead ropes to get them used to their new environment. Max seems ecstatic, his smile so wide he looks like the joker, and on a normal day, I'd be concerned.

As the sun starts to set, we get the horses back inside and settled for the night. "Who's been taking care of them?" Max asks. "You were resting."

"I hired stable hands to help us. They come in the morning and go back home at night. We also have an on-call vet, and if you think we need anyone—or anything—else, just let me know."

Max being seemingly satisfied with the living conditions of his stallion, we head back to the house. As we exit the stable, I stop him and finally ask, "Max, will you be one of my four boyfriends?"

"Of course." He flashes me a shit-eating grin. "I told John Henry you were his mummy, so you have to be my girlfriend now. And I love you, Liv."

"More than John Henry?"

"Come on, don't make me choose between you and my baby."

I press a soft kiss on his lips. "I love you, Max. Quirks and all."

TODAY'S THE DAY OF ZACH'S SURPRISE, AND NOSTALGIA ALMOST overcomes me as I prepare it.

I'm setting everything up in the office I created for him, on a counter planned exactly for this type of activity.

Dissections, I mean.

To make the island horse-safe, we had to remove the few Indian wolf snakes that lived here. They're not venomous, but like to bite. And I'm not ready for Max's meltdown if John Henry gets bitten by a snake.

So, I killed two birds with one stone and kept a few of the snakes for today's activity. Knowing Zach, he should like the attention.

I thought of finding Bellatrix's body—the cat from St Stephen's—and giving it to him as a present instead, but even I have limits. It was too gross, even if it would have made him happier than snakes.

And I was definitely not getting a cat just to dissect it. Someone would have eventually named it, then it would have been harder to go through with the plan.

I told Zach to meet me at ten a.m., and as soon as the clock marks the hour, he stomps inside the room, grabbing me by the throat and slamming my back against the wall.

This shouldn't make me wet but, fuck, his anger is hot.

Face a breath away from mine, he growls, "Don't even *think* of asking me to be your boyfriend. I will never, *ever* be that."

The Cleanup

He probably followed me yesterday and heard my conversation with Max. "Okay?" I say tentatively.

"You're my life," he continues, his anger and aggression barely contained. "My obsession. The drug I can't live without. The venom slowly killing me. You're my addiction and my redemption, and I will not insult all of that by calling you *girlfriend*." He bares his teeth, and I take advantage of our proximity to bite his lower lip.

An animalistic grunt escapes his mouth, and his hand tightens around my neck.

The only thing I can do is bite harder. I push my hips forward to bring our bodies flush, and when his hard cock presses against my stomach, he relaxes and starts kissing me.

His lips are as aggressive as his words, and I meet him stroke for stroke, relentlessly.

I guess I'll have three boyfriends and a psychopath, then. Perfect.

He releases my mouth and throat at the same time, and I gulp down air greedily.

My breathing calms, and I meet his eyes, a brow raised. "So, since we've cleared that up, wanna dissect snakes? Also, I love you."

I DON'T THINK I'VE EVER FELT THIS INSECURE. THIS FEELS terrible. For V, I planned something super sexy and romantic, Valentine's Day style. It isn't Valentine's Day, but fuck that.

We've never had a moment like that, or at least not one when I thought there would be more after that. Whenever we fucked in Monaco, there was taunting and snarking involved, unresolved conflict in the air and anger warming my blood.

Don't get me wrong, hate sex gets me going like nothing else. But shouldn't we at least check if we're capable of having loving sex, too? Or even friendly sex?

Also, we've never fucked just the two of us, and I want to rectify that. I've also only had threesomes or orgies with Max, but we've been friends for longer, so I'm less worried.

That's why I invited V to come to my room tonight. I'm sprawled across my bed, wearing my sexiest red lingerie and skyscraper high heels.

The house has six rooms, and the sleeping arrangements vary from night to night. My bed is big enough for three of us to comfortably sleep together, but it's not always full. I like to sleep alone from time to time, and having a couple's night with one of my guys is nice, too.

We're making it up as we go, but it seems to be working so far.

I only had to deliver a threat to hypnotise them and make them do ridiculous shit before posting it on TikTok if they didn't behave.

Viraj knocks on my door, and I stiffen. What if, without the anger, we have no chemistry at all?

"Come in!"

He pushes open the door and stops dead in his tracks when he sees me. I'm trying really hard to pose like the sexy badass I am, but his immobility is making me question if this was a good idea.

"V? Are you okay?"

He shakes his head. "No. I mean, yes. What is this?"

Deep breath, Olivia, he's not outright rejecting you. "I wondered if... maybe you would like to spend the night?"

"What? Of course, I would!"

"Then maybe you should come in and close the door?" Otherwise one of the other three will see me dressed like this, and there's no way we'll make them leave after that.

"Huh? Oh, yes, sure!" He does as I said—good boy—but stays frozen with his back almost touching the door.

He did say he was into it, though, so that means I can play a little, doesn't it?

I roll off the bed like a sexy cat—or at least that's the intended effect—and stand next to it. Sashaying my hips, I walk to him and push my hand under his T-shirt. Fingers running over his chiselled abs, I pepper soft kisses on the side of his neck.

When my hands get high enough for his T-shirt to be in the way, he helps me pull the offending garment over his head with one arm. Licking my lips, I watch him do it, panties already wet with anticipation.

"So? Where has all that cocky swagger gone, Adrenaline God?" I whisper against his neck. "You made me a promise, not so long ago. You said you would make me forget anyone that wasn't you and turn me to putty in your arms. Was that just talk?"

His dark eyes light up at the challenge. He picks me up and throws me on the massive bed like I weigh nothing before freeing himself of his jeans and underwear. I land on my ass and watch him prowl naked on my soft sheets.

This isn't starting out as cute or soft, but I'm more and more convinced I don't need that.

V fucking me into oblivion, on the other hand...

"I never make empty promises, Ollie. I'm going to fuck you so hard your legs will still be wobbly tomorrow." Are we starting a contest of who can make me come harder? Yes, please!

"Stop talking then, and start fucking."

"I'll do it on one condition." I raise a brow. "You swallow me first. I want to feel you gag around my cock while you're dressed like this." Yup, not cute. Not cute at all. But my panties are still flooded.

V lies down beside me, and I don't wait a second. His words have made my mouth crave his cock like my lungs need oxygen.

Without using my hands, I catch his tip between my lips and circle my tongue around his head. Barely letting him in, I tease him with my mouth until he starts twitching and losing control of his movements. Nothing I'm doing is enough to get him off, and I know it. It's a sweet torture he loves going through.

He whimpers when I touch his sensitive tip with my teeth.

"Ollie," he begs, eyes rolling back in his skull.

I obey his silent order, grabbing his balls in my hand and caressing them at the same time.

When his cock hits the back of my throat, I push through feeling the pressure and avoid gagging as his hips lift up of their own accord. Suddenly, my lips are flush with his pelvis, and he lets out a long moan. "Oh, yes, Ollie. That's so good."

I move my head back up and start bobbing up and down as his hand tangles in my hair. He pushes it away from my face, intently watching my every move. I moan and hum in encouragement, determined to make him lose it and fuck my throat.

I watch his dick become shiny with saliva as I move along his length, and finally, he weaves his fingers through my hair and starts pushing me down more. His hips rise up as he forces me to swallow his dick, and it all becomes so intense I'm nearly coming without him touching me at all.

Then, he pulls me off of him with a desperate grunt and sits up for our lips to meet. Suddenly, he flips us around so I'm on my back under him. He's kneeling over me, and for a moment, he just watches me intently. "Fuck, you look gorgeous in these." He drags his fingertips under the lace of my thong.

Without further warning, he shoves it aside and slams his dick inside me.

The red lace rubs my pussy in all kinds of ways, but his cock feels so fucking good inside me that I don't want to stop to take it off, even if it's making me ache. He starts pumping, and I hold on to the headboard for dear life.

Changing positions, V sits back on his heels and pushes my hips up over his knees, securing my ankles on his shoulders.

This new angle is *deep*. I can feel him *everywhere*.

Thank fuck he's not as long as Max or my cervix would be destroyed by now.

Instead, he keeps hitting my G-spot, and I know the building orgasm will destroy me.

The sound of his hips slapping against my ass is obscene, and it becomes devious when he punctuates each of his thrusts by grunted words. "I. Fucking. Love. You."

I shove my hands in my panties to make myself come because this moment is too perfect to not see fireworks. Rubbing on my clit, I answer between pants, "I love you too!"

He loses control right when I do, and we both climax together, watching emotions flash in the other's eyes as it happens.

I've never really noticed before, but V's got a weird orgasm face, and I swear an oath then and there to give him shit about it the first chance I get.

I untangle my legs from his shoulders, and he collapses on my chest, breathing hard on top of me. As I caress his hair, I press gentle kisses on his forehead, holding him as we both come down from our high.

"Hey," I say. He groans to let me know he heard me. "You want to be one of my boyfriends?"

"Really, now?"

"Yeah, why not?"

He grunts in protest but still answers, "Yes, I'll be your boyfriend." I fist pump the air in victory, jiggling his head around between my boobs. Four out of four, I did it! Okay, technically, Zach said no, but we all know it wasn't a real no. "Fuck, why did I say yes, I'm already tired," V whines.

"Shut up. I'm amazing, and you know it." I reach to the nightstand and flick on the music. "It's Raining Men" by The Weather Girls comes blaring through right at the start of the chorus, and V groans. I continue my shimmy-dance under his body.

He pokes at my ribs, and his dick slips out of me when I start squirming around to escape his tickles, giggling like a madwoman. He grabs the remote and turns the music down, but it's still playing in the background.

"You're amazing, too!" I shout between fits of laughter, and his eyes light up at my words. He leans down, delivering a decadent kiss with his pillowy lips. We both sigh, relaxing into one another and basking in our very new, very real relationship.

See? I knew I'd be amazing at this girlfriend shit.

Later that night, after V and I clean up, we join the others in the living room, sprawled out over the furniture and enjoying a couple of beers. My phone pings on the small end table, making me instantly jump. My first thought is that it's something from Miranda, my manager for The Cleanup, but we spoke three days ago and she knows I'm on holiday.

But then, I realise it's the ringtone for one specific app. Via.

Does that mean we have a new job?

I debate ignoring the message. We're in hiding, and it wouldn't be wise to show our faces.

Then again, identities can be faked. And the Bratva doesn't have a foothold everywhere.

Reaching for my phone, I press on the notification, rapidly scanning the text and memorising the information. It's a job, and a fun one at that.

I lift my eyes, finding Rory, Zach, V, and Max looking at me expectantly.

"Gentlemen, anyone fancy another round?"

Afterword

Thank you so much for reading our book! We have loved writing this story so much. Every random text message and video call to discuss plot and diamond retrieval has been such a blast. Even the one where the diamond's hiding spot was still up in the air and one of us thought a butt plug was a good idea.

If you loved this book as much as we did, please leave a review on either Amazon or Goodreads, or both!

You can also hang out with other book finishers in The Cleanup Spoiler Room — our group on Facebook for all things The Cleanup.

Thank you for reading, and see you soon for more adventures...

Acknowledgments

Manu

This book was so freaking easy to write, yet these are the hardest acknowledgements I've ever written, so they might be a little shorter than my normal ones. And trust me on this, it's because shit has hit the fan, and some bad stuff happened.

So let's focus on the positive.

Mila, writing with you was incredible. Each book is a learning experience, but this one was so much more condensed than my first two. We never pressured ourselves into writing fast, yet somehow we wrote, edited—five rounds of edits, at least!—and published a pretty big book in two months and twenty days. This is something I never thought I was capable of, yet look! We did it. And I had fun while it happened, and I'm so proud of us. I really loved working with you, and I'm so grateful I got to do it in the first place.

To every single alpha, beta, ARC reader that supported us: thank you! Your enthusiasm is a big part of what kept us going, and I'm honestly loving to watch the fighting over Zach. Fortunately, he's ambidextrous and can do multiple things at once. Special thanks to Steph who helped us take care of all the holes in the Swiss cheese that was our plot.

To my friends outside the book community and family, I love you and I miss you. Thank you for always being proud of me!

Fer, I'm so fucking happy I get to see you two days after this book goes live. I love you, gato. Let's celebrate!

Z, we're thinking of you. So bad. And this is so freaking hard. Please come yell at me because this was too short of an acknowledgement. I love you, and I miss your crazy <3

Mila

First and foremost, a huge thank you to Manuela for being my partner in crime, my sounding board when my ideas went a little haywire, and for being my calm amidst this crazy ass train. You are an amazing writer, and an even better friend. This was the most fun I've ever had working on a project, and I know so, SO much of that comes down to you. I can't wait to actually hang out with you in two months!

I know Manu already thanked Steph, but I'll second it. You dove in as a dev editor and have been instrumental in finding tiny inconsistencies in the earliest stages and helped us make this book better than we could have imagined. You are an incredible reader and friend, and I am so glad our paths crossed all those months ago.

To our amazing alphas, betas, and arc readers: Thank you for putting in the time to help us get this book out so quickly. We appreciate you so much and we are honored to have you on our teams. We hope our book brought you as much joy to read as it brought us to write.

Alphas and Betas: Aidyn, Sullyn, Iris, Mary, Kim, Colbie, Steph, Tanya, Aisling, Leslie, Sam, Lori, Dee, Kerrie, Nicole, Marisa, Courtney, Oriane, Shawna, Skye, Jayne, Miranda, and SA. Thank you so, so so so much! We love you all and could not have done this book on such a tight deadline without you all. Thank you.

Zainab, we love you. This book was our personal Everest, but you made the editing a walk in the freaking park. We are thinking of you, and we love you so very much. Gimme more shouty caps, please.

To my family. My loves, Mr. Sin, and our little Toddler Sin. Most days you two drive me insane, but god, life would be so dull without you. I adore you both, and as soon as these acknowledgements are written, I'm gonna snuggle you two on the couch so freaking hard.

About Mila

Mila is a coffee addict, a bookworm, and an all around awkward woman with absolutely zero chill. She lives vicariously through book characters so she doesn't end up in prison. Her fan club is led by her husband, Mr. Sin, and the ever-charming Toddler Sin. When she's not imagining murder scenarios for her books, Mila teaches English as a second language and lives in a quaint town on the Croatian coast.

https://linktr.ee/milasin

Join Mila's newsletter here:
https://www.subscribepage.com/milasin

Also by Mila Sin

Maven of Mayhem Series

The Secrets We Keep—Book One
The Sacrifices We Make—Book Two
The Scars We Bare—Book Three

The Enchantment Series

The Howling Wind—Book One
The Raging Sea—Book Two
Title TBA—Book Three
Title TBA—Book Four

Standalones

The Cleanup

About Manuela

Manuela Rouget is a globe trotter and a polyglot who uses her experiences around the globe to build stories in her head.

She studied mechanical engineering and product design but has always been a bookworm and dreamt of writing her own stories.

In 2020, she fell in love with the reverse harem sub-genre and self-published her debut book in 2021, hopefully the first of many.

https://linktr.ee/manuelarouget

Also by Manuela Rouget

Flying High Duet
Aerial - Book One

Stellar - Book Two

Standalones

The Cleanup

Printed in Great Britain
by Amazon